Dan.

Dan.

MELANIE MARTINS

VAN DEN BOSCH SERIES

BOOK FOUR

Melanie Martins, LLC
www.melaniemartins.com

First published in the United States by Melanie Martins, LLC in 2023.

ISBSN ebook 979-8-9861626-5-2

ISBN Paperback 979-8-9861626-6-9

Printed and bound by CPI Group (UK) Ltd, Croydon, CR0 4YY

This is a 1st Edition.

DISCLAIMER

This novel is a work of fiction written in American-English and is intended for mature audiences. Names, characters, places and incidents are either the product of the author's imagination or used fictitiously. Any resemblance to actual persons, living or dead, is entirely coincidental. This novel contains strong and explicit language, graphic sexuality, and other sensitive content that may be disturbing for some readers.

To all my dear readers, thank you.

READING ORDER

While you don't need to have read the *Blossom in Winter* series to start this book, we recommend the following order to get the very best reading experience:

Blossom in Winter series (Petra & Alex's story)

1. Blossom in Winter
2. Lured into Love
3. Lured into Lies
4. Defying Eternity
5. Happily Ever After: Part 1, 2, 3, and 4

Van den Bosch series

1. Roxanne.
2. Andries.
3. Elise.
4. Dan. (You are here)
5. Julia.
6. Sebastian.
7. Hannah.
8. Johan.

CHAPTER 1

Dan

I had brought Andries into the study at the villa to talk, but now that we're here alone, nervous energy is consuming me. Pacing the length of the room, I open the windows facing the sea and let the fresh, briny air fill the space between us. All of a sudden everything feels so small, almost as if Andries and I are shut in some closet together with him breathing down my neck—not the open, spacious room before us.

Am I really going to do this? What choice do I have, anyway?

Andries breaks the silence first, shoving his hands in his pockets and looking at the ceiling. "Hey, man, I didn't mean to upset you. I only invited Johan because I felt bad that Elise had to be alone this entire trip. He was her first crush, and I figured that she'd love to see him again after all this time, you know?"

Finally I have to quit fidgeting with things and face him, crossing my arms, annoyed at his lame excuse. "Come on, Andries. Is that really why you invited him?"

He lowers his gaze back down to meet mine and raises his eyebrows. "Well, yeah, why wouldn't it be?"

"Enough." I sigh, scrubbing a hand over my face. "How long have you known about me and Elise?"

My friend opens his mouth as if to deny what I'm saying, but he looks at me and takes a second to absorb my stance and the look on my face. I know this is going to be a huge moment between Andries and me, and while I've tried to avoid him finding out the truth for so long, a part of me is relieved to just be done with it.

The two of us stand in silence, just observing each other, until Andries's shoulders fall and he pinches the bridge of his nose, letting out a long exhale.

"When we boarded the plane to Capri I had already heard a rumor that Elise had spent the night at your house. At first, I figured that rumors were probably nonsense—considering how cold the two of you were to each other on the plane—but then it occurred to me that you two weren't standoffish towards one another, and it confirmed to me that there was something going on between the two of you."

When he mentions Elise sleeping over the night before we left for Capri, I want to kick myself. I had been so reckless to let her stay, but in the moment, it'd have taken an act of God for me to make her leave my bed. "Where the hell did you get that information?"

"There is no way I'm going to tell you that," Andries scoffs, and this time it's him that paces off, staring out the window to avoid looking at me. He's pissed off, jaw clenched so tightly that it's obvious to me even from across the room.

I lower myself into one of the leather chairs in front of the desk, trying to think of who out of the people at the hookah party might have told Andries about Elise staying over. I can't think of anyone that would care enough to report such a thing, as most probably didn't even know who Elise was.

That at least makes the list shorter. Who had I invited that would recognize Elise by sight alone and would be aware enough of her that they would notice she spent the night? Whoever it was would have to know Andries, too, and have some sort of reason to want to get into his good graces.

When I consider all of that, it isn't hard to come to the only logical conclusion. "It was Tatiana."

Andries nearly jumps out of his skin when I speak so suddenly into the silence. "What?"

"Tatiana told you about Elise staying the night with me."

He narrows his eyes at me. "So you aren't even denying that she slept over?"

I lean forward in my seat, eyes fixed on his with just as much stubbornness. "And you aren't denying that it was Tatiana who was playing spy for you?"

"Don't you think *playing spy* is a little dramatic? Why can't it just be a friend looking out for a friend?"

I can't help the laugh that escapes my lips. "Maybe because Tatiana was in love with you for so long and still wants to be on good terms with you whenever possible?"

He turns pale, and then red. "Are you trying to say that I'm manipulating Tatiana? Using her, even?"

"More along the lines of Tatiana being so used to doing anything for you just for a scrap of your attention that it might be second nature to her now." I shrug, taking a pen off the desk and twirling it between my fingers. "Maybe a part of it was her being worried about Elise, but I think it had more to do with you than anything."

13

"Whatever, Dan," Andries snaps as if losing his patience. "Something tells me you're just trying to change the subject."

"Yeah, that makes sense," I say sarcastically. "I brought you in here to talk, remember?"

Andries drags a chair over and sits in it across from mine, leveling me with a stoic look. "So talk."

Well, it's now or never. After this moment, I can never take back Andries knowing that I not only broke my oath to him, but I'm actually in love with his sister. There is nothing else to be done though, and I just can't tolerate him bringing in some other past crush of hers right under my nose, especially not in the villa I paid for. He needs to know the extent of how I feel… Maybe if he knows it isn't just some one-time fling, he will feel differently about it?

I can only hope so.

I crack my knuckles, trying to dispel the nervous energy roiling around inside of me. "Look, you know that I value your friendship more than almost any other relationship in my life. I mean, I put together all of this," I motion around the room to indicate the villa at large, "just so you could have a brilliant pre-wedding experience, even with your family being jerks. I don't think you can deny that I've been a good friend to you."

His jaw still tight, Andries simply nods.

"I know we made that pact, or oath, or whatever when we were younger about me leaving your sister alone, and I honored that for a long time. But things change… and that's exactly what happened. Change. One day Elise stopped being just the annoying younger sister of my best friend and became this woman that I couldn't ignore no matter how hard I tried. And… I think she feels similarly about me. It wasn't like we sought each other out in the beginning, or did this just to get to you."

I lick my lips, closing my eyes, sucking in a deep, steadying breath before continuing. "Yeah, she slept over at my house—and we've been spending time alone here in Capri—but this isn't just some summer fling. I'm in love with your sister."

Rocketing up from his chair, Andries clenches and unclenches his fists a few times as he stands tall across the desk. "You fucker! You swore—"

I hold up a hand. "Let me finish. I'm in love with Elise, and at this point, I'm positive I was before we ever even had any physical contact. I love her so much, Andries, more than I've ever felt for any other woman. Hell, I don't think I even understood what love was before this thing between her and me. I want her in my life, and not just as your little sister—as my girlfriend."

With a sardonic laugh, Andries points a finger in my direction. "You are such a fool! After knowing for years I didn't want you to get involved with her here you are saying you love her, as if that should make me less pissed off about the whole thing. You are a fucking fool, Dan."

At first, I'm thrown by his vitriol. I hadn't exactly expected him to be happy about all of this, but I was so sure that with some heart-to-heart Andries and I could come to an understanding. Now, it feels like nothing I can say or do will change his mind.

"The world doesn't revolve around you, you know," I point out, acid in my tone. Andries just turns his back on me and starts pacing the room like the tormented man he pretends to be. "I'm not in love with Elise just to make you angry. In fact, you didn't factor into it at all, but here you are acting like this is some affront to you and not just two people falling for each other in less than perfect circumstances. This nonsense of trying to keep us apart isn't just cruel; it's selfish." I pause for a moment, observing the anger building up inside him. "Are you forgetting everything I've done for you? All the times I was there for you when no one else was? Now you can't even let me have this happiness because *you* don't like it."

There's a feeling of unbelievability to all of this, and I think Andries must feel the same. These ten days are supposed to be for him and Roxanne to celebrate the life they will be building together after the wedding. We're supposed to be making memories that will never be forgotten, but instead, here we are arguing about my relationship status with his sister, maybe angrier at each other than we ever have been before.

"It isn't just about me not liking it," he insists, his nostrils flaring as he speaks. "It's just wrong. And you made me a promise, so by seeing her you're also fucking up our friendship, too. I mean come on, Dan…"

"You forced me to make that promise, *remember*?" I snap back just as fast. Holding your rapier up to me—does that ring a bell?" At this point, I'm standing too, and while we're still across the room from one another, the angry tension between us is palpable.

"I didn't trust you to make it otherwise! You're such a fuckboy—"

Now it's my face that's flushing red. "She was FIFTEEN, Andries! What kind of person do you think I am?!"

"I saw the way you looked at her," he snarls, stepping closer. We're both so loud that I'm worried that they'll be able to hear us out on the terrace through the open windows, but it's too late to change that now.

"I thought she was beautiful, but I'd never—"

Andries scoffs, cutting me off. "As if I can believe you now."

I want to throttle him, maybe shake him until he sees sense, but I know that will get us nowhere. Plus, if I'm going to enact any violence, I'm going to save it for Johan and his stupid, royal face. Instead, I hold out my hands in front of me, trying to cut this argument off before it explodes into something neither of us can really handle.

"Listen, Andries. I'd treat her right, I swear," I tell him, my tone coming off more confident and hopeful than I thought. "When I say I love Elise, I mean it. I'd never hurt her. Isn't that what you want for your sister? Someone who has her best interests at heart, and who would do anything for her? I would move heaven and earth to make her happy."

Hesitation flickers across Andries's face, but he's so hard-headed that he doesn't give himself time to even consider my words before he launches into another diatribe about what a liar I am, until he's cut short when the door opens.

Shit, I thought I had locked it.

Elise, looking unsure and almost afraid, enters. "I could hear you two from the hallway."

Damn. That's what I'd been wanting to avoid. "Sorry. We were just—"

"Talking about how Dan betrayed my trust and broke an oath that he made to me," Andries blurts out in a failed attempt to humiliate me. "Can you leave so we can finish our little chat?"

Elise looks between the two of us before entering the room fully and shutting the door behind her. To my surprise, she comes to stand next to me. I'm not sure if it's a show of loyalty, or just where she's chosen to stand without there being any other motive behind it, but I like it either way. Too bad what I'm about to tell her is going to make her angry at me once more.

"Before you say anything," I tell her, looking down into her now-upturned face. "Andries knows the truth. About us."

She draws her brows together, a variety of emotions moving across her features. First there is anger, then fear, followed by relief, and then anger once more… at me.

"I thought we agreed to not tell anyone? And if we did, we were supposed to do it together. Now you just go off and tell Andries without even giving me a warning!"

I wish I could stroke a finger across her cheek, or take her hand in mine to reassure her, but there just isn't time for that now. Not right in front of her outraged brother. "Actually, I wasn't the first one to tell him. He found out because Tatiana told him about you sleeping over at my place."

Elise's mouth falls open. "Seriously? I can't believe her!"

I give all my attention to Elise, letting Andries continue to stew in his anger. "I clarified everything, but he's not happy."

"Stop talking about me like I'm not here," Andries grits out.

Now Elise whips around to her brother. "Let me guess, you've been here freaking out on Dan, even after all he's done for you?"

"…what?" he asks, clearly caught off guard by the rapid change in subject.

Elise approaches him and pokes one of her small fingers into his chest. "Dan has been the best friend you could ever ask for. Always. Just because he and I have a thing going on shouldn't change that. Honestly? It makes you look like a bad friend, not him."

"But you're my *sister*," he sputters, his frustration growing at each passing second.

"Yeah, I am, but right now you're being immature and childish, Andries. I'm a grown woman now and I can make my own decisions. I don't need you hovering over my shoulder all the time, telling me what I can and can't do." Since Elise is shorter than her brother, she has to tilt her head back to glare into his face, but she's pretty intimidating, nevertheless. "It's not like you ever take my advice, anyway, so why should I take yours?"

"Just because you're being stupid about this doesn't mean that Dan gets a free pass. This thing between you two is *not* happening." Andries rakes a hand through his hair, obviously uncomfortable arguing against two people now and not just one.

"It's already happening, and you have no say in it. Or anything else I do," Elise points out, crossing her arms.

Andries takes a deep breath like he has a lot more to say, but just then we all can hear Roxanne laughing at something on the terrace through the open windows. My friend shakes his head, his shoulders falling, and it's clear he's done with all of this for now. He wants to be with his fiancée, not argue with his sister and me, but I'm not so deluded that I believe that this is over.

"I feel like I don't even know the two of you anymore," he sighs. "I never thought you guys would collude against me like this, but here we are. Here's the thing; Johan *is* staying with us," he shifts his gaze to me. "You're the one who is in the wrong here, not me. He didn't do anything to make you be an asshole to him like that. If you want to try to salvage this friendship at all, then you need to at the very least behave while our guest is here."

He gently puts his hand on Elise's shoulder and moves her aside so he can leave. I know I should say something, insist that this is my villa and I'll behave however I see fit, but I don't want to continue this argument without having some time to gather my thoughts, so I just let him go. When he's in the doorway, he looks back over his shoulder at us.

"Oh, and Johan is also flying back to Amsterdam with us since he'll be attending the wedding."

With that, Andries disappears. Elise walks over and shuts the study door again, and leaning against it, she heaves a sigh of relief. "Well, I guess that went as well as can be expected, considering you're still alive."

"We'd never have been put in this position if Tatiana hadn't opened her big mouth," I grumble.

Elise hums in agreement. "Yes. She and I are going to have a talk once we're back in Amsterdam, that's for sure…"

She moves to the seat her brother was in and sinks into it, rubbing her temples. I follow suit, wishing that this was my own study back in Amsterdam so I could pull out my hidden bottle of whiskey. "I almost feel sorry for her," I hear myself saying as I picture Andries asking her to keep an eye on his sister. "Part of me thinks she didn't do it with any ill intent, but it still made things quite a bit worse."

"Speaking of making things worse… why were you so rude to Johan earlier? I get not loving someone else staying at the villa you paid for without being told, but people have been in and out the entire time we've been here."

I snort at this. She really isn't going to like what I have to say next. "Actually, I already knew who he was, so I hated him on principle. I saw the picture of you two all snuggled up when I was hiding from Andries in your study."

Elise rolls her eyes. "Of course you did."

"You can't blame me, considering that we'd just come back from our beach date to find your ex waiting for us," I point out, but Elise doesn't agree.

"That doesn't give you the right to be rude to him!" she rebukes, slamming her small hands down on the armrests of the chair.

Her annoyance is bleeding over to me, no matter how much I want to be calm. There is no denying that I'm pissed about Johan's presence, but Andries has backed me into a corner and there is nothing for me to do about it except ruin the entire trip by throwing Johan out on his ass. That doesn't mean I have to be a good host, though.

"I don't have to be nice to your ex, okay?" I seethe. "He isn't even supposed to be here!"

"But he is, so—"

"I can't believe what your brother did. Fuck!" I lower my head into my hands, at the edge of losing control. First there was admitting to Andries that I was in love with his sister, and now I have to face the reality that I'm no longer the only one here after her heart.

I've got my eyes clenched shut, so when I feel her soft touch on my shoulder as she lowers her body into my lap, my eyes jolt open. She's so close that I can smell the salt of the sea on her from our sojourn to the private cove and her own sweet scent. I stiffen, wanting to tell her to get off me, but she's too intoxicating, so instead my hands land on her legs where they are flung over the side of the chair. There are still grains of sand on her sun-warmed skin and I can feel them beneath my fingertips.

"Dan," she breathes, "It's been three years. I moved on from Johan a long time ago. I'm with you now, remember?"

Her hands stroke my face and the bare skin of my neck, making my body relax into her even as my thoughts are still racing. Then, while Elise is looking softly into my eyes, I can't help but ask, "What happened between the two of you? I see how he looks at you, and it isn't the look of a man that has totally moved on."

Her eyes drift away from mine, looking elsewhere while she nibbles her lip. "It was just normal teenage stuff…"

"You're lying, El."

She stiffens but gives me an answer. "I ghosted him, okay? I was really young and nervous, and since it was just a summer crush, it was way easier just to ghost him and be done with it."

"If it was a simple summer crush there wouldn't be a frame of the two of you hanging in your study. You still had feelings for that guy when you started college, didn't you?" I know she's bullshitting me, and the fear that there is some unfinished love story between Elise and Johan is growing bigger and bigger inside of me. They would be the perfect fit for one another, wouldn't they?

"It was just a good memory from camp," she insists, turning up the heat on the amount of attention she's heaping on me. I feel her lips graze the shell of my ear and suppress a shiver. "He means nothing to me now."

I have to get some space between her and me, or I'm going to be too distracted by her delicious weight in my lap and her lips on my neck. I take her by the shoulders and push her back a few inches, searching her face for subterfuge.

"Elise, is he the reason why you can't say…" I hesitate, the idea almost too painful to speak. "Is he the reason you can't say those three words?"

It takes her a second to figure out what I'm referencing, and once she does, her eyes go wide as saucers. "No! No… of course not. I just can't say that to someone so easily…" she trails off, her features betraying her just as fast.

"Did you tell Johan you loved him?" I press, and now Elise puts her hands on my wrists and tries to extricate herself from me. I hold her in place, though, desperate to know the answer. "Tell me."

"Why are you so fixated on this?" she huffs. "When you told me, you said you didn't mind if I wasn't ready to say it back. Now you're acting like it's a huge deal!"

I remove her carefully from my lap until she's the only one sitting in the chair and I'm heading for the door. I can hear my pulse pounding in my ears, my blood pressure rising.

"I was fifteen, okay!?" Elise blurts out from behind me, and I freeze. "I was young and stupid. I didn't know anything about love."

What she has just said is all I need to hear. Johan had gotten those three precious words from her, but I'm not worthy of them apparently. I pivot to face her, my heart stuck in my throat. "So let me get this straight… you meet a guy at summer camp and two months later you said you loved him? But after everything we've been through you can't figure out whether you love me or not?" The laugh that makes its way out of my mouth is bitter. "Maybe you still love him deep inside."

All I can hear in the study now is the sound of Elise's choked-up breathing, and as the seconds stretch out and she doesn't answer me, my stomach sinks. She's made it very, very clear where we stand.

"Figure your shit out, El," I bite out, fleeing before I fold and ask her why she doesn't love me.

Not knowing where else to go, I make my way back towards the group on the terrace as if on autopilot, figuring that I could at least get a drink and distract myself with some of the other guests. Unfortunately, as soon as I turn the corner and emerge into the outdoors, the first thing I see is Andries and Johan. The other man has his massive arm draped around my best friend's shoulder while Andries shows him something on his phone. Photos from the engagement party, no doubt. Another thing I had put together for Andries without wanting anything in return. Now he's out here with the closest thing I have to an enemy, laughing it up. All at once, I wonder if I've lost both Elise and Andries in one fell swoop, and the prospect is almost too much to swallow.

I turn on my heel, trying to decide where else I can find a moment alone without having Johan shoved in my face, eventually deciding on the villa gardens on the West side of the property. Compared to the terrace with its pool, hot tub, lounge chairs, dining table, and an unbeatable view, the garden is humble, but it's a perfect place for me to hide while I gather my thoughts.

Tropical flowers in shades of orange, yellow, and red gill the little hidden paradise, all pulled together by a fountain featuring a beautiful concrete woman pouring water from a pot, making it cascade down to the bottom of the fountain. There is a small stone bench under a draping palm tree, and I take a seat, content to smell the sweet floral scents and listen to the water flowing over the marble and stone fountain. I heave a sigh of relief, reveling in the quietness of the place.

Of course, my solitude is short-lived. Roxanne appears, her blonde, short hair is wet and slicked back and she is wearing a sheer amethyst tunic over her bathing suit. Silently she moves to sit next to me. I scoot over to allow her the room, figuring there is no reason to even try to get rid of her.

"Rough day?" she starts, hands folded in her lap as she looks ahead.

"That's an understatement," I grumble, crossing mine over my chest. "Listen, it's not too late to call off the wedding. Marrying into that family is a mistake, I'm sure of it now."

Roxanne's laugh is musical. "A little late for me, I think. Plus, something makes me think you wouldn't turn down a marriage proposal from a certain Van den Bosch daughter, either."

"I'll make sure to remember you saying this when we both attend her and Johan's wedding." I change positions, folding my hands behind my head, and look to the sky at the white clouds crawling along so slowly that they appear almost still.

"I didn't know you were as dramatic as your best friend," she quips. "Do you want to talk about it, though? The Johan thing?"

I shrug one shoulder. "What's there to talk about? Elise's royal ex is here and making eyes at her. That doesn't bode well for me."

"I take it that Andries knows everything about you and Elise, then," she offers, her eyes studying my face for an answer.

"If he knew, I know he told you too, so you don't have to pretend you're still in the dark, Roxie."

She nudges me with her shoulder, sliding me a glance. "I wasn't going to. So, why don't you fill me in on the rest so I know exactly what we're working with here?"

I look over at the small woman that has turned my best friend's life upside down. "I told Elise I love her."

Roxanne's eyes go wide and she blinks a few times. "Wow. That's... wow. Do you really love her?"

I nod. "Yeah. But it's become this whole charade because I swore an oath to Andries years ago that I would never have anything to do with her. Now here I am, head over heels for her, while my best friend is inviting her ex over to try and sabotage things."

Roxie winces and pats my knee in a show of comfort as if I'm a little kid. I won't stop her, though. I'll take whatever comfort I can get at this point, even if it makes me seem pathetic. "An oath? That's pretty serious. Why did you break it, though? Elise is one of the millions of girls that you could have."

I groan, covering my face with my hands before letting them slip down. "You know what? From the moment I first saw her, I knew I was going to break that oath one day. We were going to collide eventually, like it was written in stone or something. I hoped I'd have been strong enough to resist, and maybe just get over her, but it never happened. Then she started showing signs that she was into me too, and well… I'm a weak man, I guess."

"You're not," Roxie hums softly. "Does she feel the same way?"

Her question feels like a knife twisting in my chest, and I unconsciously rub the spot over my heart. "I … I don't know, honestly. She's never directly told me about her feelings for me, but it's clear she said those three words to Johan. Maybe that's why Andries wanted to do that oath because he knew she loved Johan even back then. Who knows…?"

Roxanne scoots closer to me on the stone bench and leans her head on my shoulder in a show of sister-like affection. Had my heart not been so shattered, it would have meant a lot, but as of right now, I'm just numb.

"You can't force someone to love you, no matter how good the sex is or how strong the lust is between the two of you. I know it seems odd, but lust and love only come hand in hand on very special occasions." She sighs. "I should know. I was an escort, remember? Many men fell in love with me, and it was a really complicated and delicate situation to navigate out when that happened because it was always just work for me."

"It's just… there are these moments between us when I'm sure she's about to tell me that she loves me. There's this look in her eyes or the way she touches me…"

"Maybe Elise feels like she should love you because of those types of moments, but you can't force her to love you if her heart is somewhere else," Roxanne says.

The imaginary knife in my chest twists again—hard. "Do you really think she could have held a dwindling flame for this guy for three years with zero contact?"

Roxie shrugs. "I've heard stranger things."

"Fuck," is all I can say.

This is exactly what I have been afraid of. She's always been such an ice queen, but I really thought it was different when she was with me. When I spend time with Elise, she's warm, sweet, kind, and always desires me fully whenever we have sex. To me, that feels like love, but what if coming from her it's not? The idea that she's just been using me for fun and pleasure makes me feel ill.

The worst part about it is that I can't even be mad at her for it. She never promised to love me, and when I confessed my love to her, I even assured her that she didn't have to say it back. I've given her every signal that what we're doing could just be a friends with benefits setup if that's what she really wanted. I should have never given in to her when she came on to me at the party. If I hadn't, we would be pretty much separated by now. Sure, I had made advances toward her in the heat of the moment before the first night we had sex, but that night when I took her virginity changed everything. We're connected, and I can't separate love from lust when it comes to her. Hell, I had even commented to her on her birthday that I knew she was using me, and she didn't even deny it. Elise has been waving red flags in my face for weeks now and I've been more than happy to ignore them just to spend more time with her.

Andries is right. I'm a fool.

Roxanne lets me process things, but eventually, she raises her head from my shoulder and pats me on the knee again. "I've got to get back to the party before Andries comes looking for me. Dan...?"

At the sound of my name, I turn to face her, finding a wealth of sympathy and understanding in Roxie's eyes.

"Andries will be better tomorrow after he's had time to digest the news. I know he already knew, but the confirmation is a lot more shocking than having a hunch. Regardless, I'm here if you need me, okay? And I bet Andries will be there for you too... once he's gotten all the angriness out of his system."

I give her hand a quick squeeze as she leaves but don't offer her any other words. I'm thankful for her company, and the hard truths she's made me see, but there is a lump in my throat that makes it hard to speak. What a tough guy I am, getting all choked up in a garden over a girl. I hate myself sometimes.

The garden is secluded, but I can still hear the music and laughter coming from the terrace. I briefly consider leaving and going to a bar downtown to drown my sorrows. I'm sure it wouldn't be too hard to find someone to buy some cocaine from, but something makes me hesitate. Being inebriated in any way is going to make me more impulsive. With a man I want to beat the shit out of staying under the same roof as me, it would surely be a recipe for disaster.

Maybe I'm starting to realize that I have to actually face my emotions and not drink and snort them away. Is it possible that I'm maturing? I laugh to myself at the thought.

There is one person that knows what's going on with Elise and me, and it just so happens to be the person I trust most in the entire world. Thinking about calling my dad for advice in my twenties makes me want to cringe, but as soon as the idea crosses my mind, I can't shake it. He'll know what to do, even if it isn't what I want to hear. Plus, I really want to hear his voice. I think it will ground me.

Dad picks up on the first ring, no doubt scrolling through Instagram—where he follows hundreds of classic car pages. He accepts my FaceTime, and I can see him now, sitting at the kitchen island while mom makes herself a post-dinner cocktail. His reading glasses are perched on the end of his nose. It makes me feel better… like home isn't so far away.

"Hey, kid," Dad says with his usual warm voice causing me to smile. "How's Capri?"

"It's… uh… well, Capri itself is great. But if you're asking if I'm having a good time…"

"Uh-oh. Let me guess, this has something to do with being in a crucible with your best friend and his sister who you've got a thing for even though you've sworn never to even look at her flirtatiously. Am I right?"

I roll my eyes, even if he can see it. "Yes, but even worse, somehow."

"Okay, well fill your old man in and I'll give you some sage advice."

So I do, telling him everything I can while still keeping it appropriate for a father-son conversation. From Elise sleeping over after my party to the chilly flight and arrival at Capri, my brief fake interlude with Mia, and then my reconciliation with Elise. Skimming over the more lurid details, I admit that I confessed my love to her, and the escape we had in the private cove before Andries invited Johan. Once I explain that Johan is not only Elise's ex, but connected to the British royal family, Pops lets out a long, low whistle.

"Wow. That certainly is a lot of trouble for the few short days you've been there. How are you right now?"

"A fucking mess," I admit, raking my hands through my hair. "I love them both, you know? I love Andries like a brother, and I love Elise so intensely that I could see myself being with her for a long, long time. But now, I feel like they're both using me. Andries is getting this trip, not to mention the engagement party, and Elise is getting…" I trail off, not sure how to say it.

"I know you're having sex with her, Dan," Pops deadpans, and I want to sink into the ground and disappear. "You don't have to sugarcoat it."

"Okay, fine. Andries is getting all the perks of our friendship, and Elise is getting all the romantic Capri moments, but now I'm on the brink of losing them both even though I've given them *all* of me."

I'm embarrassed about the emotion in my voice, but I'm glad that if anyone has to hear it, it's Pops.

"Ah, Daniel. I hate that you have to learn these lessons, but sometimes people may hurt you without even realizing it. I'm sure Elise and Andries are so wrapped up in their own minds that they haven't even seen how their behavior is affecting you, a loyal friend and romantic partner. I think they'll come around in time."

"But what if they don't?" my voice sounds small.

"They will." Dad's voice is firm and sure, and despite everything, it reassures me. "Get some sleep, son, and don't do anything crazy. That will only make everything worse."

"Okay," I swallow past the tightness in my throat, nodding. "Thanks, Pops. Just being able to tell someone really helped."

"Call me tomorrow," he says. "I want to make sure you're doing okay."

"I will. Talk to you later."

I hang up and slip the phone back into my pocket. During my time out here in the garden, the sun has sunk below the horizon and it's nearly full dark. Even though I can hear the party still going on the patio, I decide that I'm just not in the mental place to deal with seeing Elise and Johan around each other. Like my dad suggested, I'll just go to bed and try to make up for some of the sleep I've lost because of Elise and our activities together.

It's a noble thought, and I'm able to hold onto that plan throughout showering and brushing my teeth, but the moment I crawl under the covers and turn the lights out I'm once more assaulted by all the intrusive thoughts in my brain. The sounds of everyone on the terrace haunt me like ghosts, and I'm likely to drive myself insane trying to pick out Elise's and Johan's voices from the cacophony. Is that them laughing together? Or is that her squealing as he throws her in the pool?

Logically, I know there are numerous established couples out there that could account for everything I'm hearing, but as soon as I close my eyes, it's only the woman I love and her ex that I see.

I toss and turn, desperate to find rest and an escape from the hell that I've put myself in. I can't stop thinking about how Johan, the only man Elise has ever said those three words to, is sleeping under the roof I paid for. Not only that, but Andries knows how much that pisses me off, but he still took Johan's side and made sure he was able to stay, instead of considering how it all made me feel. I had done everything in my power to make sure he and Roxanne pulled through when their relationship got tough, and he couldn't even do me the favor of throwing out this guy that he is only acquaintances with. All so he can get back at me for daring to love his sister.

Enraged and heartbroken, I throw the light blankets off of my body and stomp to the bathroom, digging in my bag of things until I find some sleeping pills I had packed just in case. I pour more than the recommended dosage into my hand and toss them back with a handful of cold water from the sink.

With the pull of the sleeping pills now dragging me down, my last miserable thought is how Elise won't be coming to bed with me tonight. Surely she wouldn't go as far as to hook up with Johan, would she?

With that terrible visual weighing heavily on me, I finally fall into a fitful, drug-induced slumber.

CHAPTER 2

Elise

"You can do this," I tell my reflection, despite my racing heart and overly palpable anxiety. "People interact with their exes all the time, and it's going to take more than Johan being here to shake you up. You've got this."

Hands planted on the marble counter, standing on my tiptoes to lean in close to the lit mirror, I'm so out of options to force myself out of my room that I've resorted to affirmations. Unfortunately, my reflection doesn't look any more confident about the day to come than it did at the beginning.

I don't have to go to breakfast, really, but appearances are everything, and the last thing I want to appear to be is nervous or afraid. It isn't Johan's fault that my brother dragged him right into the center of our drama, and I know he wants to spend more time with me.

The bombshell about his number being blocked on my phone has made me rethink, well… everything. It's made this lost, hypothetical past unfold behind me, and I can't help but wonder what life would have been like if Johan had always been around. I was more than smitten with him back then, and while the sight of him still gives me butterflies— especially now that I know he didn't ghost me—I have true, deep feelings for Dan. Not to mention the fact that my brother's best friend and I are sleeping together. It's all so tangled up that I don't even know where to begin untangling it.

I can't just keep hiding in my suite and talking to myself in the mirror. Breakfast isn't nearly as tightly scheduled as dinner, but there's no point in showing up if everyone has already finished eating and moved on. It has to be now or never.

Hanging my head, I take a few deep breaths to reassure myself, and finally leave the safe haven of my suite, straightening my breezy, floral maxi dress as I go. As soon as I'm past the threshold of my door, I can feel myself tense up, but there is nothing to do about it now.

Like usual, I can hear voices coming from the terrace already and figure that's where breakfast is laid out. A server standing by the door of the terrace is waiting with a coffee cart, and after pausing for a french press cup, I step into the sunshine of the early morning. Everyone is spread out talking and tearing at scones and croissants with their fingers as they do, servers hovering around to refill coffees and mimosas as everyone breaks their fast.

As I'd expected, Andries and Johan are sitting together, looking like they've been the best of friends for years and not just distant acquaintances. Since bringing him here was my brother's idea, it seems fitting that he play host. Neither of them notices me at first, and I tap my foot on the stone floor as I scan the terrace for the only person I really want to sit with this morning. It's just my luck that Dan is absent.

Flicking a gaze over to my brother and ex, I try to walk the perimeter of the terrace to sit with Lili and Robin, but the sound of my sandals on the ground catches Andries' attention, and his face brightens.

"Elise! Come sit with us. Johan was just telling me all about the equestrian camp you two attended. Do you know he sponsors the place now so more kids can attend on scholarships?"

"How very altruistic of you," I say, turning to Johan as I sink into a seat next to him. There isn't any escaping him now, but I'm actually less annoyed with him than I am with my brother.

Johan seems even more glad to see me than Andries does, and it makes my chest feel tight. He really is so handsome, and when I look at him, I can't help but think of all the wasted years between us. Who would Johan be to me if things were different, instead of the almost stranger he is to me now?

"I enjoy giving back," he comments, his tone casual, pivoting in his seat so he can give me his full attention. "Scholarships are an easy way to do that without actually having to show up and play teacher to a bunch of children."

I laugh, despite my negative mood, and feel some of the heaviness on my shoulders start to lift. "But I'm sure you'd be an exceptional teacher!"

"You'd be mistaken." Johan picks up his glass, a tall ordeal filled with what looks like a green smoothie, and takes a draw of the thick liquid. It's not a surprise he eats healthy even on vacation, considering how fit he is… which isn't something I should be thinking about, but the thought creeps in anyway.

"Well, what else have you boys been discussing besides fun childhood camp memories?" I question, crossing my leg and cupping my coffee mug in my hand, absorbing the heat through my palm.

"Actually, we just strayed off topic. Johan was telling me how unprepared he was for the—" Andries leans forward and lowers his voice theatrically, a smirk gracing his lips, "secret societies and weird rituals at Oxford. Apparently summer camp didn't exactly prepare him for anything like that."

My interest is piqued. "What kind of secret societies and rituals?"

It might be my imagination, but I think Johan looks slightly uncomfortable when he responds. "Oh, you know, the same sort of clubs you find at all the big universities. Invite only, secret meeting places, things like that."

"Are you a member of one?" I press.

He rubs the back of his neck. "Even if I was, I'd have been sworn to secrecy and not be able to tell you anyway."

"He's definitely in one," Andries concludes, leaning back in his chair and looking smug. "Our Johan here is too big of a public figure not to be invited to the most elite groups, I'm sure. What I'm interested in is what you had to do to get in?"

"I don't know what you're talking about," Johan insists, but there is a hint of a smile at the corner of his mouth that gives him away. Maybe when we're alone he'll tell me more.

My brother huffs and leans back in his chair, taking a sip of his orange juice. "You're no fun."

Flicking his gaze in my direction, Johan gives me a quick wink before saying, "I can be plenty of fun, under the right circumstances."

Blushing, I look away and sip my coffee, suddenly wishing it was iced.

As breakfast continues, everyone that is scattered about the terrace makes their way over at least once to talk to the newest guest, Johan, and discuss plans for the day. Roxanne makes her way over eventually and bends down to kiss my brother on the cheek, telling her to meet her in their suite once he's done talking to everyone. He gets up to follow her, but I grab his hand to stop him.

"Can we talk alone first? I promise I won't take up too much of your time."

His gaze follows his fiancée, but he shrugs. "Sure, just make it quick."

We meander over to the side of the pool, sitting down and dipping our feet into the warm waters. If he hadn't been such an ass and brought Johan here, it'd have actually been nice to bond with my brother again, but Andries always has to stick his nose where it doesn't belong. Now, things have to be awkward.

Turning to him and realizing he isn't going to be the one to start the conversation, I take a deep breath and speak instead. "You know you need to apologize to Dan, right?"

Andries snorts in amusement. "For what? He's the oath-breaker and liar, not me."

"You know that makes me a liar, too," I respond, kicking my feet in the water so it swirls around my legs.

"It's not the same."

"It's only not the same to you because I'm your sister, but might I remind you that even when you and I weren't speaking, Dan was there for you. Admit it, yesterday was a shit show, and you did it on purpose."

He looks down at me and the stubborn look on my face, which is consequently mirrored on his. "Dan made it a shit show by messing around with my sister, not me. He didn't care one bit which friends I invited until it was someone who was interested in you, and vice versa. If Johan was anyone else but your old summer crush, there would be no issues, besides that, you and Dan would still be lying to me under my nose."

I glance over my shoulder at where Johan is still standing and talking to Robin and Lili and feel a pang of guilt. Poor Johan... he's only here as a pawn in my brother's game, but my brother is right about one thing: if Dan and I hadn't been hiding this from him, none of this drama would have happened.

"You're looking at Johan an awful lot for someone so concerned about Dan and his feelings," Andries drawls, nudging my shoulder with his. I shove him in return.

"Shut up. This is not some star-crossed love story that you are concocting by inviting him. It just makes things weird for everyone, and now your best friend's feelings are really hurt. I mean look at this place—" I wave my arm over the horizon and the pool we're currently lounging in front of. "Dan brought us here and did all of this because of his love for *you*. Are you even thinking about that?"

A look of contriteness moves over his face, but he shakes his head and it's gone. "You're not going to make me feel bad for being pissed that Dan broke the oath he made to me."

I groan in frustration, rubbing a hand over my face. "Andries, I'm an adult! It's my decision whether I want to be with Dan or not. That decision has nothing to do with you or any stupid oath you and Dan may have made."

He cocks his head to the side before turning around at the waist and nodding over where Johan is standing. "Do you really want to be with Dan, though? Especially now that Johan is here with you? I bet there are all kinds of things left unsaid between the two of you."

Andries's question makes me uncomfortable, causing me to tap my fingers on the concrete edges of the pool to disperse the nervous energy. I'm not ready to face my feelings for Johan or Dan when I put them side by side to compare them. This change in the situation is too new and fresh, and I need more time to mull it over. But there is something my brother says that makes me think…

"Speaking of unsaid things… Johan and I had a little time to talk yesterday and it turns out that neither of us actually ghosted the other one. Someone blocked him in my phone and changed his number, so even when he did reach out, I never saw it." I narrow my eyes, studying his expression more attentively. "Do you know anything about that?"

His expression is completely blank. "You probably did it in a fit of teenage jealousy or something. Who knows."

"I'd remember if I blocked and changed his contact, Andries! I'm not an idiot. Plus, that's not all, whoever changed the number made sure to send one text to Johan before blocking him telling him to leave me alone or they would report him to Dad. Does any of that ring a bell?"

My brother shakes his head. "Not at all. Why would I do that? I like Johan quite a bit and he seemed popular with the rest of the family, too."

I kick at his foot under the water, my suspicions growing by the second. He's giving me no indications that he's lying, but having spent my whole life with Andries, I feel like I'm able to read him better than most. Maybe I'm just looking for someone to blame, or maybe he's lying to me. And if so, he has no right to be mad about me lying about Dan. We'd be even.

"I don't believe you. I know you, Andries. It's so perfectly in character for you to want to play the protector even when I don't need it," The look I give him is meaningful, "Like now, for instance."

My brother just rolls his eyes and makes a show of checking his watch. "I really need to get back to Roxie."

"But you never promised to apologize to Dan. That's the whole reason I brought you over here, not to talk about my love life."

He moves to stand, stretching as he does, rocking back on the heels of his feet and lifting his arms above his head. "Good thing you're not the boss of me, then. Because I'm not doing it."

I stand too, hands on my hips. "Yes, you are. Again, do I need to remind you that everything you're currently enjoying is all thanks to him?"

He tries to wave me off, turning to stalk back into the house, but when we both pivot, Dan is hovering around the breakfast table, hair mussed and dark circles under his beautiful eyes. It makes my heart ache, but at least his timing is impeccable.

"Let's go," I insist as I grab my brother by the arm and start to haul him over to his best friend.

He tries to hold firm, but I've caught him by surprise, so he stumbles forward with me anyway.

"Knock it off, El," he hisses.

But it's too late, and Andries and I are in front of Dan within just a few steps. He looks at the two of us in confusion but then shrugs. "Have you guys had breakfast yet?"

"Yes, but I was just about to have another cup of coffee before going in," I say cheerily, trying not to make it too obvious that I'm forcing Andries to sink into the chair next to me as I sit. I don't let him go until we're both seated, my brother looking grim while I wear a smile that is much brighter than I currently feel.

Dan shifts his gaze between us, one eyebrow creeping up before he shrugs a second time, clearly not bothered by what either of us is doing. Or at least trying to appear like he doesn't care. "Whatever. I ordered some blooming tea if you'd like a cup."

"I'd love one," I answer immediately. "So would Andries."

"Uh, sure," my brother says, crossing his arms and looking away. The air is almost painfully tense.

The server brings the blooming tea, quickly leaving and coming back for two more glass cups for my brother and me. We all watch the dried lily flower open, coloring the water and filling the air with the scent of herbaceous florals, but there isn't any shared conversation. Dan holds my gaze as he pours for me, a million words in that glance, but none of them come to his lips. We are all still drowning in silence.

Sipping the tea, memories of all the times Dan has shared similar teas with me come rushing back in a barrage of images, both happy and sad. We've got so much history, and he and Andries have even more than that. This can't stay the way it is now, with all of us acting like strangers.

I elbow Andries, who is holding his glass cup and swirling it in his hand to keep busy. He jumps, almost spilling the hot liquid as he looks at me, and I jerk my eyes toward Dan. Andries looks like he wants to complain, but after glancing at Dan and taking in his tired appearance just like I had earlier, something passes over his face. To me, it looks like concern for his friend.

He sucks in a huge breath, letting it out slowly before speaking. "Dan, look... I'm sorry for inviting Johan to the villa without asking you first. It was a spur of the moment decision that I really didn't think much about, and I understand why it'd be frustrating for you." He pauses, giving a glance at me before returning to Dan. "Since I did it just to mess with you and Elise's little... thing... well, it was petty. I'm sorry."

Dan blinks a few times, surprised, but after a few seconds pass he nods. "I appreciate it. I want to apologize for acting out the way I did and immediately trying to throw your friend out. I just recognized him from a picture and—" he looks over at me, his expression uncomfortable. "Never mind. Just know that I'm sorry."

Andries swallows, looking like he wants to be anywhere but here. It seems like they can't talk freely with me here, so I finish my tea and stand, straightening my clothes as I do so. "I'll give you boys some space to talk, okay?"

Before either of them can insist that I stay, I leave, wanting to go to my bedroom and plan for the rest of my day anyway. There had been talk of going to the blue grotto, among other attractions, or maybe going sailing again, but I'll leave it up to my brother and his fiancée to make the final decision.

It's quiet inside since nearly everyone is lounging by the pool and enjoying the sunshine, but as I walk down the long hallway to my suite, I pass the room that Johan had been given and pause. Outside of the partially open door is a set of luggage that is black with silver accents, all perfectly packed and lined up. Curious, I peek into the room and see Johan packing his toiletries into another, smaller bag.

My hip hits the door enough for it to creak open slightly, and Johan turns to see me. Caught, I give a small wave. "Hey. You sort of just disappeared from breakfast. What are you doing?"

Johan looks down at the things he's packing, a sad cast to his features. "I've clearly made a mess here, so I'm just going to go stay at a hotel and make it easier on everyone."

"You don't have to do that," I tell him quickly, making my way toward him. "Sure, Andries was a little quick on the jump with inviting you, but he and Dan are working it out as we speak."

He shakes his head. "Dan hates me, El, and it's clear it's because of what happened between us. I don't want to ruin everyone's vacation by staying here."

I give a few more steps until I can lay my hand on his bicep, trying to ignore how firm it is. "Johan, Dan overreacted and he admits it. He's out on the terrace apologizing to my brother right now, like I said." I grin up at him and try to tease. "I'll make sure you two get along."

He smiles, but it doesn't reach his eyes. "El, I know I already asked you this yesterday but… are you sure nothing is going on between you and Dan? He didn't even show up for breakfast."

The urge to lie and tell him nothing is going on is immediate, but lying has gotten me into so much trouble lately that I resist. Even though I know it will hurt his feelings some, I have to be honest.

"To tell you the truth, Johan, Dan and I have hooked up a few times, but it's not like we are officially together or anything."

Johan clearly doesn't enjoy this information, frowning while he takes my hand from his arm and holds it in his instead. "If you two aren't really together, why does Dan seem so fond of you?"

I sigh, squeezing his hand, my eyes switching between the floor and his gaze. "It's complicated…we've been around each other for years—since he's my brother's best friend. He already cared about me before our *fling* started."

His thumb skims over my knuckles, and I shiver as he moves closer to me. "You can trust me, Elise. Don't sugarcoat anything on my account."

"Honestly, I don't know what I want out of that relationship. Maybe I'm just scared, maybe the fact that the last time I said I loved someone and showed vulnerability that person disappeared from my life…"

Johan moves slowly, taking me by the arms gently and running his hands up and down in a comforting motion. "I'm so sorry for that. If I could go back in time, I'd have tried calling your mom or your brother before giving up. I just truly thought you wanted me to leave you alone."

It's still hard for me to believe that he let what we had go so easily. I shake my head, asking him, "After the time we spent together, how could you believe that? How could you be so naive?" He opens his mouth to respond, but I realize that it doesn't matter what he says. The years are lost no matter what. "Stop," I interrupt before he can speak. "What's done is done. There's no coming back."

Looking troubled, Johan looks deep into my eyes, like he's trying to suss out the truth in my words. "Are you sure you even want me to stay, or are you just being polite? I don't want to cause you any more trouble."

He's trying to move away from the subject of our time apart, and I can't really blame him, so I just nod instead. "Positive. I will speak to Dan and make sure he is more welcoming."

Making a contented noise in his throat, Johan pulls me forward and leans down to plant a kiss on the crown of my head. I feel a blush rushing up my neck right as, at the worst possible moment, a curt knock sound echoes from the open door frame. I jump back from Johan, already knowing who must be there even before I confirm it with my own eyes.

Dan, leaning against the frame with his arms crossed, looks us over before saying shortly, "We're going to the Blue Grotto. Are you guys coming?"

I'm frozen in place, Johan's hands still on my arms even though I've moved away. Luckily, he answers for us both while I try to get my brain back online. "Sure. Sounds great."

Dan nods once and leaves as quickly as he arrived. I crane my neck to watch him go, my heart sinking to my feet out of guilt and shame. Johan and I were so close to each other that we might as well have been embracing, and then that head kiss… oh no, I'm in trouble.

Johan must be able to see the stress I'm experiencing because he lets his hands slowly fall away. "I guess I should unpack. Maybe you should, uh, get the itinerary from Dan or your brother for the day?"

I swallow hard but nod in agreement, reaching out to give his hand one last quick squeeze before rushing out into the hallway, heading straight for Dan's room. I can't let him think that I'm already falling for Johan all over again, not after he and I have just spent the previous evening together drinking champagne and making love…

Dan has left his door open, too, and is angrily cramming his scuba gear into a carry bag, his expression dark. I'm relieved to see that he hasn't locked me out, but the way his face looks doesn't bode well for me.

"Dan, that kiss was just—"

"I don't give a fuck," he snaps, not even glancing at me. "I already figured you and Johan were meant to be together. I should have known better, anyway."

"You're not even giving me time to explain," I insist, stepping towards him.

"Whatever, Elise, I hope you both enjoy the island. Maybe you can take him to the private bay I showed you yesterday?"

Indignation surges up inside me and I resist the urge to slap him. "Why are you being such an asshole!" I yell, fists clenched. "Johan and I are just friends with a romantic past, that's all. I don't have any interest in him. I… you don't even deserve me saying this with the way you're acting, but I'm only interested in you, Dan."

He wavers, raising his head to look at me, hope flashing in his eyes before disappearing. He snorts, looking back down at his scuba gear. "Of course. That's why you want him to stay, huh? Makes sense. Or maybe you're only here to make sure we get along?"

"He's a friend of the family and Andries likes him. That's it! For fuck's sake, Dan, why are you behaving like this with me?"

He throws the flippers on the bed, where they hit with a soft thud as he rounds on me. "Because I think you want him to stay for your own selfish interests. So you can finally see how the rest of the stay plays out for you two."

Now I'm so close I can reach out and touch him, but I hesitate, seeing how he's almost vibrating with anger. "I swear that's not the case. Johan and I are just friends. You've got to believe me on this, Dan…"

"Really? How am I supposed to believe you after what I just saw?"

Getting him to see logic isn't working, so in a fit of inspiration, I soften my stance and loop my arms around his neck, locking my fingers together on the back of it. "I don't want to lose you." I let all the desire I feel every time I see him seep into my tone, making it sensual and low, "I want us to continue whatever is going on between us."

"You mean…" he tilts his head as he comes closer, and for a brief flicker of time, I think he's going to kiss me. "You want to continue enjoying some good sex and letting me romance you while you figure out whether or not you're still in love with your ex?" He jerks his head to the side and steps back, breaking my hold. "We are done here."

"Wait—" I breathe, feeling tears in my eyes, but before I can even get the entire word out Dan is gone, leaving me alone in his room.

Feeling shocked, I slowly sit on the side of the bed, surrounded by the scent of the man I want so badly, but with the real thing nowhere to be seen.

CHAPTER 3

Dan

As much as I hate to leave Elise so hurt back in my room, I just can't stay. When she looks like that, eyes big and shimmering with tears, her perfect mouth pulled down at the corners... fuck. I just want to hold and comfort her and make sure nothing in the entire world can hurt her. Elise is a sneaky, conniving harpy at times and I take great pleasure in making her angry from time to time, but her being hurt is a completely different thing altogether. That, I hate and want to avoid at all costs.

If I had stayed, I'd have forgiven her, and that's something I absolutely refuse to do.

Adjusting my bag on my shoulder, I walk out of the front door and into the bright light of day. Instead of the one long SUV that usually transports our entire group from place to place, two smaller vehicles are idling, both identical. I hesitate on which one to go to, but the passenger window on the closer car rolls down and Andries waves me over.

Opening the back door, it takes my eyes a moment to adjust until I can see who is seated inside and that I'll be sharing space with. When I can see that it's Johan, I mumble a curt apology and go to back out and head to the other car.

"No, no," Johan says, causing me to pause. "Get in here, man. No reason to leave."

I hesitate. I really don't want to share the back seat with Johan even if the drive is short, but bailing would make me either look like a coward or an asshole, and I've already been quite the asshole to this man. I feel plenty guilty about that already, so I slide awkwardly into the leather seat after stowing my things in the trunk.

"Good to see you, buddy!" Andries crows, turning around in his front seat, as if we hadn't just been talking during breakfast. His chipper attitude strikes me as odd, but I brush it off. "Ready to go to the port?"

"Sure." Going to the Blue Grotto would be amazing if I wasn't crammed like a sardine in a car with Elise's ex and her brother who may or may not still hate me. I had imagined visiting it with Elise, watching her sleek body cut through the water with her flippers and the way she'd look, slicked with seawater and aquamarine light illuminating her face. What I hadn't envisioned was being part of the loud, overly-eager group that had come to Capri with Andries and me.

"I think you're going to have a better time than you think," my friend chuckles.

The driver pulls out onto the road, and the air is heavy with silence. I'm tired of feeling like an interloper during the vacation I planned and paid for, but thankfully, Johan speaks first.

"Hey, Dan," he starts rubbing the back of his neck as if uncomfortable. "Look, I just want to say that I'm sorry for any kind of ruckus I've caused by coming to the villa. I had no idea that anything was going on between you and Elise, but she told me that you two were involved somewhat, so I can absolutely see why you'd be pissed that I showed up. I can leave the villa at any time if you want me to."

Part of me wants to tell him to just pack his shit and leave as soon as we get back from the tour, but I have to hold on to at least some of my reputation as a good host. Plus, it isn't Johan's fault that Andries was trying to pull something over on Elise and I. Even if Andries seems to be better friends with Johan than I had expected, it's still undeniable that he was first invited to the villa to drive a wedge between me and Elise. He seems like a decent man, and probably feels painfully out of place right now.

"There is no need," I tell him, forcing a smile to stretch up from the corners of my mouth. "It's all good. I'm sorry for reacting the way I did when you first arrived. I had been drinking quite a bit yesterday and it made me freak out when I shouldn't have."

Andries turns around again, his expression bubblier than ever. "You know what? I'm sure the two of you could actually be good friends if you didn't both have feelings for my sister."

Easier said than done, I think sardonically.

Both Johan and I give forced chuckles, but I don't entirely disagree with Andries. If he and his sister both had reasons to enjoy Johan's company, then he couldn't be all bad. Andries has a good talent for reading people and figuring out their true intentions, and Elise is too stuck up to waste her time with anyone that doesn't meet her excruciating standards.

I hazard a quick look at Johan, and I have to admit he is a handsome guy. Damn Elise, why does she have to complicate things so much without even trying?

It doesn't take us long to reach Marina Grande, the drive being filled with surface-level conversation about Capri, the weather, and everything in between. The main portion of the port stretches out far and vast into the water and beyond, while the opposite side curves more gently inward. The sky is cornflower blue, dotted with sparse white clouds, while the sea is an endless turquoise. It's so stunning that it almost breaks me out of my reverie. Strangely, our driver takes a different turn than what I expect, and doesn't stop the car until we are parked in front of a small sailing club. There are boats of every size, white sails flapping in the wind and shining, brilliant paint jobs sitting like jewels on the water.

"I don't think this is the right place," I say, craning my neck to look at what I can see from the car.

"It is," Andries assures me, his tone laced with excitement, before stepping out of the vehicle. Johan follows suit.

"Where is everyone else?"

My friend walks up next to me as I also exit the car, clapping me on the shoulder. "They are going to the Blue Grotto on a private tour," he tells me with a mischievous smile.

Johan then joins us, stepping to the other side of me and holding up his hand to shield his eyes as he looks over the sea, letting out a low whistle in appreciation.

"If they're going on the grotto tour, then where are we going?" I ask Andries, who seems to revel in my curiosity.

He is baiting me, I'm sure of it, and it's starting to get on my nerves.

"We are going to do something a little bit different." He smirks, raising his hand to wave at a man that is approaching us. Dressed in a solid black wetsuit, I've never seen this new person before, and it's becoming clearer by the second that my friend and his new companion Johan have something up their sleeves.

"Ah! You're finally here!" The man in the wetsuit yells as he gets close.

Andries holds out his hand and shakes his hand enthusiastically. "Thank you so much for having us," he all but gushes, more excited than I've seen him in days. He turns to me, eyes glinting with anticipation, and tells me, "We're going to sail on our own! We'll be on a Persico 69F."

He jerks his head towards the docks where a number of matte black sailing foils are bobbing in the water, and I frown. They look too small for all three of us, but I am certainly not taking one out on my own, either. "What do you mean on our own?"

The other man steps up and holds his out for me to shake. "I'm Antonio, and I'll be teaching you boys some sailing today. I'm actually here with my team which is training for an upcoming regatta in October, and you all are going to have the exact same training as they are. I'll record you all with my drone so we can discuss form and posture once everything is all over. Sounds like a good time, yeah?"

"Uh," I pause, once more trying to figure out how all three of us are going to fit on the foil. "I'm sure it will be a great time."

We all walk down the incline towards the docks, where a small group of sailors are getting their own wetsuits on and preparing for what I can only assume is practice. Everyone is in high spirits, and Andries and Johan are chattering amongst themselves about the day ahead, using terminology that I am wholly unfamiliar with. I'm not usually a nervous person, and I'm always up for a new experience, but I've never sailed on a foil before. I'm also not looking to embarrass myself in front of Elise's ex, while potentially drowning in the process.

I interrupt my two companions, pausing in my steps. "So, just so you know, I've never done this before in my life. I mean I've sailed, but never on anything like this."

"Relax," Andries pats me on the back, "the Persico 69F is a great boat for first timers, and Johan and I both are old hands at this. We'll make sure you don't fall behind."

"You're going to love it," Johan adds as we resume our walk, which I'm somewhat afraid might be my last. "It's a thrill like no other. Foil sailing takes real skill and quick thinking. Andries says you're well suited for it!"

I slide my friend a suspicious glance. "Oh, do you? How can I be sure this isn't some plan to murder me out on the ocean for seeing your sister?"

Andries throws back his head and laughs. "If that was the case, I'd be drowning you both, wouldn't I? Plus, I need at least one of you to sail the Persico back with me, so at least one of you is safe from my wrath."

Still rankling from the change of plans that I had no part in, I take the wetsuit the instructor offers and head inside the sailing club to change in the locker room. Inside, everything is decorated in light wood and navy blue, and there are numerous photos of the sailing team on the water, their foils so high out of the water that it makes my stomach clench. Oh boy, I might be in over my head.

Once we're all dressed, the instructor shows us to our Persico 69F, which really is the exact same model that the sailing club is using. Andries and Johan board without hesitation, and after a second, I follow them. I might be unsure about all of this, but I'm not about to back down from a challenge. As some of the sailing team takes to the water ahead of us, I watch them closely and have to admit that it does look like a good time.

"Are you sure about this? I'll haunt you forever if I die," I hiss at Andries.

"Oh, me and not my sister? I'm flattered."

I punch him in the arm. "I'll alternate days. You both piss me off in spectacularly different ways."

Johan peeks around Andries' shoulder and gives me a cheery thumbs up. "Don't worry! It's going to be fun. I've done regattas my whole life."

"I haven't sailed much at all," I admit again, in case he didn't hear me talking with Andries about it earlier. "But I guess I'm a little excited."

Both of the other men grin wide, teeth white and expressions mirroring one another. Johan isn't just a better match for Elise than I am, but he looks like a better friend for Andries, too.

I can't think about that now. Hell, I shouldn't be thinking about it at all. I want to enjoy the rest of my time in Capri, even if I have to do so alone.

With a heavy breath, I tell them, "Alright, let's do it."

The Persico is larger up close, but the arrangement of the seats still didn't inspire much confidence in me. On the sides of the black boat, adorned with neon green sails in a loose triangular shape, the long, thin bench-like seats have enough space for two sailors to be able to perch. The sails are connected to so many ropes that it boggles the mind, but Andries and Johan board the thing like they're born to do it.

Andries takes a seat on one side of the foil while Johan takes the other, and after some clear hesitation from me, Johan waves me over to his side. I look at Andries, wishing I didn't have to sit next to Elise's ex for the entire day, but he shakes his head, already knowing what I'm about to ask.

"Johan is the more experienced sailor on these types of boats, so you should stick with him."

Repressing a sigh, I sit next to Johan and strap the helmet I'm given under my chin and pull on a pair of gloves meant to save the skin of my palms from the rough ropes.

"We'll be moving around the boat anyway," Johan points out, tugging and pulling at parts of the sail rigging while he speaks. "So we'll be all over the place before long."

"Great," I grumble, buckling the thin life jacket over my wetsuit and settling in. "Sounds safe."

"It's not," Andries says, his grin wolfish across the boat. "But that's the fun in it, right?"

With that, we follow the rest of the sailing team out into the open ocean, all of us constantly in motion to keep the Persico 69F moving in the right direction. I've sailed before, but not on anything like this small racing boat. Everything moves like we're in fast forward; what would have taken a few long moments of adjusting the rigging on a normal sailboat happens in mere seconds on the Persico, and for Andries and Johan, it's like the boat has become a part of them. They move with it like they can anticipate its next move before it's even necessary, and I have to admit that they work well together for only being acquaintances.

That's nothing compared to the guys on the racing team, though. They barely speak to one another, just moving, tossing ropes, and pulling in one direction or another with hardly even a glance, they're entirely in tune with the boat and their teammates. I'd have been happy just watching them work—it's so incredible—but there is zero time for leisure on our foil, even if I am a novice.

I do what I understand, but with everything moving at light speed, I can't help but feel like I'm two moves behind everyone else. I am thankful, though, that I took the seat next to Johan and not Andries, because where my friend would have loved the opportunity to poke fun at me while teaching, Johan took it all very seriously and is a perfectly patient instructor for me. Every once in a while the team coach would come up beside us in his own foil and call out some instructions, which we would put into action in a snap.

I fumble and struggle to catch up for the first thirty minutes or so, but suddenly, everything starts clicking into place, and it all just works. After that, it stops being just a frustrating learning exercise and becomes fun.

I'm not exactly as in tune with everything as everyone else, but sooner than anticipated, I'm able to get into a sort of groove with everyone. Johan continues to be a stellar teacher, and even Andries manages to help me when I'm finally ready to move from side to side on the boat when the course demands it, and eventually, the ropes stop all looking exactly the same and I'm able to pull and let out what I need to with a decent amount of accuracy.

The foil rises so far above that water at times that it should be terrifying, but really, I'm feeling exhilarated, even letting out a few enthusiastic yelps when we get a particularly large amount of air, splashing back down with a controlled slap into the water before going upwards once more. I'm soaked, the salt water sticking to my eyebrows and eyelashes, but I love it. I haven't been able to work out since we've been in Capri, and my muscles are happy to be awake and put to use once more. The slight burn is a welcome sign that I really am giving the Persico my all.

About halfway through the practice, I see a drone zipping above us here and there. It's white and difficult to see against the bright sky, but the blinking red light gives it away occasionally. I hope the footage doesn't make me look like a fool.

"You're a natural!" Andries laughs right as I get a mouthful of seawater.

I sputter and spit the water out, letting go of the rigging just long enough to flip him off before getting back to work. My friend laughs again just as one of the racing team foils comes up next to us, bouncing on the waves. Waving, it almost seems like they're issuing us a challenge. We've been keeping up with them better than I would have thought, but there is still a subsequent gap between the professionals and us hobbyists. Regardless, I know I'm not one to back down from a challenge, and neither is Andries. Johan throws the other boat a thumbs up, so I guess he's in for a little friendly competition, too.

There's no way we would ever beat any of them in a full sprint, but there are a few times we catch up and even pass them before they overtake us much more, and it makes my pulse thunder in my chest trying to keep pace. I don't even notice the way the ropes heat my gloved hands as they whip through my grip or the way my arms and legs start to shake with the strain of it all.

After about three hours, a shrill whistle pierces the air and the coach waves us all back towards shore. I'm initially disappointed that it's over already, but Johan sighs happily as we maneuver the boat around.

"I thought lunchtime would never get here. I'm starving," he comments, almost as in relief.

His words go straight to my stomach, and if it wasn't so loud out on the water, the angry growl it gives off would be quite audible.

* * *

Once the boats are docked back at Marina Grande, the coach lets us all strip off the wet gear before we all make our way to a seafood restaurant called "Lo Smeraldo" which looks out into the beautiful water. One would think I'd be sick of the ocean by now, considering I must have swallowed a few gallons of seawater, but I don't think I will ever be able to get enough of these views.

While the staff pushes tables together for us on the patio, I take a second to pull out my phone, chuckling at the string of increasingly angry messages from Elise as we choose our seats. I pull out my chair with my hand on the back of it, shaking my head and grinning as I do so.

"What's so funny?" Andries asks, all but falling into his seat beside me, and Johan next to Andries.

"Man, your sister is pissed." I hold out the phone so he can read the message.

Elise: *Where are you guys? I can't believe you left us to do the tour alone! I hate you!*

He waves his hand in the air with a scowl. "If you want to annoy her even more, just ignore her."

I actually agree with Andries, so with a shrug, I re-pocket the phone and turn my attention to the sailing team and coach as they fill in the other seats around us. The practice has taken a lot out of everyone, both from the intensity of the workout and the hot sun that has colored everyone's cheeks red, but the energy is still lively. Before the coach sits down, he makes sure to shake all of our hands and pat us on the shoulders.

"You boys did great out there. Seriously! You kept up better than I'd hoped. I'll send you the footage as soon as it's done uploading."

We all thank him, as well as the other team members. The general consensus is that they won't underestimate us so much during the second half of the day, and they definitely won't be taking it easy on us.

The wine that I see going out to other tables calls to me, but with the post-lunch sailing plans looming over me, I order sparkling water and a light meal of white fish and rice when the server comes by. After thinking for a moment, I wave him back over and add a double espresso to my order. I might need it to get through the rest of the day.

Elise keeps trying to reach me, but I'm happy to click my phone onto *Do Not Disturb* mode and immerse myself in the present. Good food, new people to meet, and new experiences to share ascertain that there is never a lull in conversation, but my ears perk up when I hear Andries tell the coach that the drone pictures and videos have finally come through. He passes his phone around the table so everyone can see, and by the time it gets to me my palms are almost itching to get my hands on it. I'm afraid that how much of a novice I am will come through in the pictures and recordings, but after a cursory scroll through them all, I'm pleasantly surprised at how confident I appear.

My viewing is interrupted when a message from Elise pops up on the top of Andries's phone screen, and while her constant bombardment is annoying, it does give me an irresistible idea to pick at her just a little more.

I hand Andries his phone back, asking, "Can you Airdrop me all of those?" to which he nods absentmindedly, hitting the buttons while still engrossed in his own conversations.

Once everything has come through, I unmute Elise and send her the best picture from the lot that I can find on short notice, making sure that it has Andries, Johan, and myself all in the frame sailing our majestic Persico.

Dan: *Having fun with your ex. You were right. He's pretty nice actually... much nicer than you'll ever be. Don't wait up for us to have dinner, we might be pretty late.*

I immediately mute her again with a wicked grin, knowing just how pissed off she will be. Slipping the now-silent phone back into my shorts pocket, I jump right back into the conversation, and put Elise out of my mind the best I can. At least for the time being.

CHAPTER 4

Elise

I really never imagined that someone could piss me off this much while in paradise, but if there is anyone that can accomplish it, it's no surprise that it's Dan O'Brian!

"You're gripping your phone so hard I'm afraid you might break it," Roxanne points out, turning her spoon upside down and licking the cherry sorbet off. "And I don't think they have an Apple store on Capri."

"Sorry," I say, setting the phone back down on the cushioned bench seat beside me and taking a grape from the shared food bowl, popping it into my mouth. "I could kill Dan and Andries for ditching us," I explain after swallowing.

Roxanne, in a maroon, high cut one-piece, shrugs one sun-kissed shoulder. "Eh. It's a little more peaceful without them though, don't you think?" She pauses as her gaze scans around the anchored yacht we are currently on, floating near the grotto. "Also, I noticed that you blamed Andries and Dan, but not Johan, who is also suspiciously absent."

"Johan has been here for less than twenty-four hours," I snap. "Something tells me that he hasn't used that time to find ways to piss me off. On the other hand, I could totally see my brother or Dan taking time out of their precious days just to push my buttons. It's like a favorite activity of theirs."

One of the servers on the yacht comes by and refills our champagne flutes, and I sit up long enough to take a long drink before lounging back.

Roxie and I have already swam through the Grotto and are stretched out on the sinfully comfortable seats on the front deck, letting the sun dry us and give us a bit of a healthy glow. Sorbet, champagne, and chilled fresh fruit were served when we climbed back onboard after our snorkeling, and it was the perfect compliment to the hot temperatures and my aching muscles after all the swimming.

I exhale slowly, knowing that Roxanne is still sitting up and watching me with an amused expression on her face.

I pull my sunglasses down just enough to look at her. "What, Roxie? Just say whatever you're thinking."

"I'm just thinking that Andries messes with you all the time as a way of showing his brotherly love. Lili and I used to do just the same when we were younger. But if Andries is picking at you because of that, why is Dan doing the same? Friendly love? Or something else?" Her tone turns more inquisitive as if she's trying to imply something.

"It's just because he's an asshole. Nothing else." I go to put my glasses back on and return to tanning, but she isn't done talking apparently.

"The two of you have been circling each other like sharks in the water since we got here. At first, I was sure it was just a hookup thing, but now I'm starting to think it's something more." She takes another bite of her sorbet while she waits for me to answer, but instead of saying anything else, I just sit up, open the messages on my phone and hand it to her.

"There. See for yourself. He's just a jerk."

Roxanne reads the messages with a contemplative look on her face before handing the phone back. "You can't seriously sit here and tell me that there isn't a bunch of emotion loaded into those messages, El. Get real."

I just shrug as I retrieve my phone and lay it beside me.

"Do you love him?"

Her question is so random that I'm caught totally off guard. "Who?"

Roxanne rolls her eyes. "*Dan, of course.*" Since I don't reply, she asks again, "So? Do you love him?"

I'm torn. Roxie and I have had a tumultuous relationship, to say the least, but she's the only one thus far to figure out what is going on between Dan and me and not have any harsh judgments about it. After I got hit with the volleyball, I'm sure Roxanne had an inkling that I liked Dan more than just as a hookup, but I'm not sure if she has really figured out the full extent of it or not. But it would be nice to have someone to open up to....

I sigh, pondering where to even start. "The truth is I don't know what I feel," I tell her sincerely. "All I know is right now I'm super mad at him. I thought we were moving in the right direction, but as soon as Johan showed up he started acting like an asshole all over again."

"Can you blame him, though? I mean, look how upset you were when he pretended to be flirting with that girl the first day we arrived. This has to be worse than that for Dan, since you and Johan actually have history." She slicks back her blond hair with her hand as she speaks, but never stops giving me her full attention. I'm infinitely relieved it's just the two of us on the boat while her sister and boyfriend are still out on the water.

"But Dan was flirting with that girl just to piss me off, like he always does. Andries invited Johan hoping that he'd come between Dan and me, and that's exactly what's happening. I'd think since it's so obvious what my brother is doing that it wouldn't bother Dan so much, but I guess I'm wrong..."

"Well, maybe he's acting like that because he loves you but you seem to be still holding onto some feelings for that first crush of yours." Roxanne crosses her arms, waiting for an answer from me, but I just can't come up with one. "Are you?" she prods when I stay silent.

I blow out a breath before downing the rest of my champagne. I'm going to need more than just one glass if I'm really going to have this conversation. "Johan was more than just my first crush. He was the first man I said I loved. He even met my family, and you of all people should know how daunting that can be." I laugh awkwardly, but Roxanne just waves at me to continue speaking. "Anyways... I was young and stupid. I should have never done that."

"Did Johan say it back?"

The memory of Johan's response, and then his subsequent lack of communication, makes me feel cold despite the blazing sun. I rub my arms, trying to shake myself out of the negativity it makes me feel. "Not quite. He said I will always have a special place in his heart, and then he left and went back to England. Not long after that, he stopped texting me back."

Roxanne snorts, pausing with her spoon halfway to her mouth. "Typical man."

"No, it wasn't like that," I insist, causing her to pause and look back at me, her eyebrows drawn together. "I thought he had ghosted me, but in reality, someone took my phone and, pretending to be me, told him never to contact me again and then blocked his number. Whoever it was went as far as to change his contact, and I never noticed because I was too ashamed about how I confessed my love to him and I refused to make the first move and text him. I figured I weirded him out and he didn't want anything to do with me anymore."

"Woah," Roxie leans forward, completely invested in my story now. "Do you think it was Andries that blocked Johan and sent that text?"

I give her a long look. "I don't know. He denies it, but... isn't it weird that we both thought the same thing immediately about my brother being guilty? That makes me think even more that he did it, which is so in character for him."

"I mean... yeah, I can't exactly deny that it sounds like an Andries move, especially younger Andries." Her tone turns gentle. "I suppose it must have been tough to be ghosted by the man you love for three years."

I can feel the familiar lump building in my throat that always seems to appear whenever I think of what Johan and I shared that summer, and his abandonment afterward. Even if I know now that it wasn't his fault, it doesn't erase the hurt I felt back then, or all the years we missed out on. By now, Johan has probably been with other girls, maybe even loved some of them, but I can't even be mad about it because I've been hooking up with Dan! Johan and I could make up, but it wouldn't ever make up for what was lost. If only one of us had been a little less stubborn and tried harder to reach out, or, in my case, reach out at all, it could have all been avoided.

"He even told me he would come back for next year's summer camp, but of course he never did… so yeah. It hurt a lot. It felt like he dropped off the face of the earth, but what made it even worse was seeing him go about his normal life on social media whenever I looked him up. If he missed me, it didn't show. He says now that he did, but it's still so new, thinking that Johan might have missed me that entire time."

Roxanne's face is soft as she stands, coming to sit on the bench seat beside me. "So where does Dan fit into all of this?"

I cross my legs, my foot bouncing as I try to bleed off some of the nervous energy this conversation is building up in me. Spilling my feelings out like this is *rough*. "That's hard to say. Dan has always been around it feels like. When I was going through my stuff with Johan, I kept it to myself, even though I thought he was the one, you know? My family loved Johan, and Dad and Mom were so happy and proud to meet him. It felt meaningful. But the whole time Dan was there in the background, being annoying and goofy… I can't pinpoint when exactly it happened, but the way I looked at Dan changed, and now I feel like he's filling that gap that Johan left behind."

"You don't sound happy about that last point," Roxie says.

"No, not really," I sigh. "That isn't fair to Dan. He's not a replacement for Johan, but I can't help but feel like he helped heal that hurt in me, and it's impossible not to compare the two men I've had such deep feelings for."

"Are you afraid that since Johan broke your heart, Dan might do the same?" she queries, reaching forward into the fruit bowl and pulling out a clementine, peeling the orange skin back.

"I wasn't at first." I take the piece of the clementine Roxanne offers, chewing it thoughtfully as the sweet juice coats my tongue. "I was more worried that Dan would never ditch his playboy lifestyle, but he proved pretty quickly that he would without issue. But now Dan is convinced that I will go back to Johan so he already ended whatever we had going on."

Tears prick the corners of my eyes, and I bring the corner of the towel I'm laying on up to dab them away, not wanting to touch my eyes with my salty fingers. "I know the situations are completely different," I continue as I focus to keep my emotions at bay, "but neither man has given me any control over how our relationships have ended. It's stupid. They're stupid."

To my surprise, I feel Roxanne's small hand take mine. Her skin is soft and warm from the tanning, and the gesture is more comforting than I would have expected. The tears threaten to make a second appearance, but I blink them away.

"Maybe it's for the better," she tells me quietly, squeezing my hand.

We sit there in the quiet, only the sounds of the sea birds and the background chatter from other people touring the Blue Grotto cutting through the air. The sailing yacht bobs gently in the water, the motion making me a little sleepy after spilling all my emotions out to Roxanne, but the calm of it all is interrupted as Lili and Robin return, climbing onto the boat. They're all smiles and excitement, Lili's eyes wide as she gushes about how incredible it all is.

"Go swim again before we leave," she insists as she reaches her sister. "You'll regret it if you don't!"

I look at Roxanne, who nods in agreement. "Yeah, I could go again. I want to make sure I see everything so I can really rub it in Andries's face when we get back. This place has to be better than some dumb racing boat."

Our masks, snorkels, and flippers are sitting in the back of the boat, so we sit on the edge as we put them on for the second time today. Having my nose covered and the smell of the plastic and rubber is unpleasant, but once we tilt ourselves into the sapphire water, the small inconveniences fade away in the majesty of it all.

There are none of the colorful fish I've seen while snorkeling in other places here. The main draw is the otherworldly Blue Grotto itself, accessible from a small cave entrance that would make me claustrophobic if I didn't know what waited beyond it. Where the sea is deep blue and stunning on the open water, here in the grotto it's bluer than seems possible, almost glowing with radiance. Above, the ceiling, which had been carved by the waves long ago, ripples as the glowing water and sparse sunshine dip into crevices. Here, it feels like we really are on some alien planet.

I surface, noticing Roxanne is still swimming beneath the water, visible only by her snorkel above the soft waves. Taking off my mask and snorkel, I hold onto them tightly as I float onto my back, buoyed by the salty ocean. It's so beautiful here that it makes my heart ache, and as I spread my arms, I imagine there was a hand there for me to take. A man floating next to me, intertwining our fingers together and pulling me closer to him so we can share the moment together. In my fantasies, it's Dan with me, not Johan, but when I close my empty fist I'm brought back to reality.

Damn, I miss him. I really do wish he were here, even if he is a jerk.

CHAPTER 5

Elise

Sunset is quickly approaching as the driver pulls the car around to the villa. Despite the low light, it's still pretty quiet inside and the sight of it makes annoyance bubble up in me again.

"Are you kidding me?" I say, more to myself than anyone else. "They still aren't back yet?" I rotate in my seat to look at Roxanne, who is sitting beside me with her eyes closed and head leaned back against the headrest, clearly worn out from the day. "Did Andries tell you when they would be back?"

She doesn't open her eyes, just makes a noise in her throat. "He just told me that they were going to spend the day sailing and would be coming home late. Otherwise, I haven't spoken to him today."

"I'm going to call him," I huff, digging my phone out of my beach bag and pulling up my brother's contact. Dan's unanswered text is still sitting there burning a hole in my inbox, but I refuse to give him the satisfaction of responding to his vitriol with more negativity.

The line rings and rings, eventually hitting my brother's voicemail. With a growl, I toss the phone down on the seat beside me and massage my temples, trying to dispel the headache that is threatening to creep in.

"Just give the boys some space," Roxie adds. "If you let them know how much this bothers you then they are bound to do it again at the first opportunity."

"You talk about them like they are naughty children," Lili laughs from the back seat.

"They are," Roxanne and I answer at the same time. A reluctant smile tugs at my lips as everyone else cackles, but even this doesn't do anything for the anger I feel creeping in. How dare they! I expected it from Dan and Andries, but Johan, too? Ugh.

My skin and hair feel crunchy from the salt water, so after we park I grab my bag and make a beeline for my room, hoping that a shower will clear my mind as well as clean my body. I throw the lever on and let the hot water steam up the room as I undress, tugging a brush through my hair to make it easier for the shampoo to do its work. As I do so, I hear my phone vibrate in my bag, the familiar sound of a new message, and I scramble to grab it, hoping that it's the boys.

Instead, I'm surprised, and feeling sort of guilty, to see that it's my dad instead. I have done less than nothing to split Andries and Roxanne on this trip, and at this point, I'm not even sure that it's in my plans anymore... even though that was the entire reason Dad was okay with me going to Capri instead of the on a family trip in Lake Como. No doubt he wants an update since I've been radio silent for days.

As I check his text, though, I realize I couldn't be more wrong about his reason for reaching out.

Dad: *Have you seen this?*

Following his question is a link, but the preview cut off the headline at "Bar Rouge", but that's more than enough to make my heart rate kick up. I can't click the link fast enough, and once the page loads, it's even more shocking than I could have ever imagined.

It reads, "*Bar Rouge Under Investigation: Video Shows Dancer Sucking Off Client on Stage*"

Right below the headline for the seedy online tabloid is a link to the video itself, and after a quick deliberation about how much I really want to see, I click the link and wait for the video to load.

It's shaky camera phone footage, and there is so much loud talking and yelling in the background that it seems like it must have been taken at a normal strip club or bar and not the subtly seductive Bar Rouge, but the decor gives it away. It really is at Roxanne's cabaret. On the stage, there isn't a burlesque show or anything of the sort going on. Instead, there is just a single dancer in a black g-string and matching thigh-high leather boots. She has a mic in her hand, and with a wild look on her face, she holds it to her mouth and asks the raucous crowd, "Who wants a blowjob!?"

Cheers and whistles of excitement follow her query, and it makes my jaw drop. I'm more than familiar with Amsterdam, but the pure audacity of this dancer is astounding! I remember talking to Roxanne about how some of her escorts were given jobs at the cabaret when she took over Bar Rouge, and I can't help but wonder if this girl is just trying to drum up new clients, not satisfied with the more steady if less lucrative pay of the cabaret.

A man, cheered on by his friends, approaches the stage, already undoing the button on his pants. He climbs onto the stage to applause and lays on the floor when the escort asks him to. My lip curls up, wondering about all the unpleasant things that must have been on that floor in the past, and how comfortable this man seems to lay in it just in the hopes of getting his dick sucked. The dancer straddles him, her back a perfect arch as she leans her head down, her nearly bare ass in the air. All that can be seen on the video is her back, but after a second she holds up her hand with her thumb and forefinger only a few inches apart, apparently telling the crowd that the poor man wasn't very well endowed. The entire club laughs, and after about thirty seconds more and some enthusiastic movement by the dancer, the man's feet can be seen jerking right before the dancer jumps to her feet, ridiculously nimble in her high heels, with his seed clearly present on her chin and lips before she wipes it off. The dancer takes an exaggerated bow as the crowd erupts in cheer and the satisfied man makes his way back to his seat. It all happens in a matter of minutes, but I know that the repercussions of this video are going to echo far and wide and that her cabaret's reputation is over.

My mouth dry, I close the video and scan the article as quickly as I can. It's only a few hours old, so there's no way Roxanne could have known about it during our trip to the Blue Grotto. I barely saw her with her phone anyway, which means she's probably receiving texts and voicemails about the incident right this second. At the end of the article, a line reads, *"Reporters tried to reach out to the owner, the infamous ex-madame Roxanne Feng, for comment but have been unsuccessful in their attempts."*

Oh man. This was bad news for Roxanne. Andries is going to lose his mind when he finds out she still owns the cabaret. Had she told him when everything was still above board and functioning just as a normal cabaret, he would have been pissed, but I'm sure he would have gotten over it with time. This, though… it looks like Bar Rouge is selling sex work, even if this is a one-time incident, and that's exactly what Roxanne had promised Andries she was done doing. This could be the end of them, if she doesn't handle it correctly.

I switch off the shower, grab the silk robe off the hook on the back of the bathroom door, throw it on, and go to sit on my bed. My phone feels like it weighs a million pounds in my hand. My mind is racing, and I just can't figure out how I feel about all of this. Just months ago I would have been over the moon about getting such good dirt on Roxanne, but now things have changed drastically between us. My brother's fiancée has such a wellspring of forgiveness in her that it has completely changed everything. Not only did she forgive me, I'm sure now that she cares about me, too. I think of her hand taking mine this afternoon as thoughts about Dan threaten to overwhelm me, and curse everything about what I've done to her in the past. And, maybe, what I'm about to do now.

Maybe Dan is right about the things he said a long time ago. Maybe I am a terrible person.

Knowing that I can't avoid it, I call Dad. He answers immediately, which tells me that he was waiting for my call.

"Looks like fate has just dropped a golden opportunity into your lap," he chuckles, and I roll my eyes.

"When did this all go down?" I ask, ignoring his smug greeting.

I can hear some jazzy music in the background of the call as he speaks and that makes me wonder if he's really alone. "To the best of my knowledge it was last night, but the video only really started going viral when they made the connection between the scandal and Roxanne being the owner."

I cross my legs, pursing my lips. "How did you see it?"

"Karl sent it to me a few hours ago. It's viral everywhere you go now." His voice is gleeful, as if he can't get enough of this unfortunate situation, but Karl's name makes my skin crawl. It figures that he'd have something to do with all of this. "Looks like that girl just wanted her moment of fame and she definitely got it. I just read that she's even going to go on national TV to try and explain herself."

"Explain herself how?" I say incredulously. "It's all on video, and I highly doubt that's the only angle! Everyone has phones, so who knows how many recordings there are."

"According to her it was staged and fake, but who knows? The establishment doesn't have a license to offer such services to clients so they might even shut down if it turns out there was really sex involved."

"Does Andries know?" After all, they are out later than I expected them to be. What are the chances it's because Andries is avoiding facing his soon-to-be bride will all of this new drama? I can't imagine how it would feel to him to see the video on television or from some acquaintance and not hear it from his fiancée herself. If she hasn't told him, she has to as soon as possible. Otherwise, the fallout is going to be astronomically worse.

"Not yet, from what I understand," he sounds almost giddy at the prospect. "I'm hoping you'll be the one to deliver the news."

His words sink down into my gut like a stone. "Dad, I um…" I don't want to do any of this anymore. I want Roxanne and Andries to be happy, but alas, that isn't what I say. "I don't know if I can do it."

"Why not?" he demands.

"I know you want to split them up but this is his bachelor's party and everyone is here. Even Johan came! I don't want to ruin everyone's vacation or humiliate my brother in front of all his friends. That isn't fair and it's not the goal here, anyway."

"Either you share the news, or I will." His tone is stern now, and I wince.

Dammit, what am I going to do now? Of course, Dad would want to pile this on me now while I'm already dealing with so much in my own personal life. "Just… give me a few days, okay?"

"Fine. But just so you know, I really expected you to have accomplished more at this point… Did you say Johan is there?"

It's the perfect opportunity to change the subject, even if this subject is one I dread nearly as much. "Uh, yeah, actually, Andries invited him."

"You must be so excited to see him again. Did you have any idea he was coming?"

"No, it was sort of a last-minute addition." I cringe thinking about Johan and Dan's first meeting. "It's complicated…"

"I'm sure it is, but what a wonderful opportunity! You know your mother and I always thought he was the best match for you. If the two of you manage to rekindle something that would just be the icing on the cake after getting your brother to dump his prostitute girlfriend."

The urge to tell him to shut up is strong, but instead, I just make an excuse to end the call. Dad seems reluctant to do so, but after a few excuses, I'm finally able to say my goodbyes and hang up. This is really, really bad, and even though he was only briefly mentioned, I'm getting this feeling that Karl has his hand in this somehow.

I stand, pacing restlessly around the room while I consider my options. First and foremost, I have to talk to Roxanne before anything else. If she's somehow already spoken to my brother, then this all becomes much easier for me. Still awkward beyond belief, but I'll be able to honestly tell Dad that Andries already knew before I could get to him. Something tells me she's going to hesitate, though, considering how terribly Andries has acted in the past concerning Roxanne's career. A cabaret isn't an escort service, but if her cabaret employees are acting as escorts anyway, well… What's the difference? I try to call Roxanne, but it only rings once before going to voicemail, an indication that she's on the line with someone else and not willing to switch over to me. Stripping the robe off, I go and take my shower, making it quicker than I had anticipated. Such a big part of me wants to just pretend I never saw the video and let it play out naturally between Roxie and Andries, but I know that just isn't possible. I need to face my fears head on, but I don't think I'm going to run to tell Andries straight away like Dad wants. If I can convince Roxie to do the right thing, then maybe—just maybe—this will all be okay in the end.

I towel dry my hair and braid it loosely behind my back. No time to do my normal routine, not with this video going more viral with every passing minute. In a hurry, I pull on a yoga outfit—dark olive bike shorts and matching sports bra crop top—slide my feet into a pair of sandals, and start my hunt for Roxanne.

I hear voices by the pool, but when I walk out onto the terrace it's just Lili and Robin, lounging away their evening after the long Blue Grotto tour today. It strikes me as funny, if only for a second, that these two might be the only totally happy couple in the entire villa.

"Lili, have you seen Roxanne?" I ask as I approach them. Lili tilts her head down but doesn't rise from her lounge chair.

"She was here earlier but her phone kept ringing and ringing so she went to the garden to return a few of the calls, I think. It sounded urgent."

My stomach drops. There's only one subject all these people could be calling her about. "Okay thanks, Lili."

She raises herself to her elbows, eyebrows furrowed. "You look a little freaked out. Is anything wrong?"

"No, no," I try to assure her, even if it is a lie. "I just need to talk to her about my brother, that's all."

"Alright…" Lili lays back once more, but she doesn't look convinced. "Come get me if you guys need anything."

"We will. Thanks."

The garden isn't far, and in the waning light of day, it would almost seem magical if it wasn't for my future sister-in-law pacing the area, her phone held to her ear and an angry flush to her delicate face. I can't quite make out what she's saying as I approach, but her voice is pitched low and her words are acidic. Roxanne is talking not just with her mouth, but with her hands, even though the person on the other line can't see her. It sounds like she's rebuking someone, which makes me think she must be talking to the dancer. That means she really must have just found out, probably around the same time I did.

I come into the garden slowly, giving her ample time to see me so she knows I'm not trying to invade her privacy. Her eyes flick over to me, and although she looks mildly annoyed at seeing me, she ends the call quickly enough.

The total antithesis to the sweet woman from the boat this afternoon, Roxanne crosses her arms, putting her weight on one hip and narrowing her eyes as she looks at me. I'm transported back to when she and I were fighting, and how defensive I had forced her to be. She's defensive like that now, and a big part of me hates it.

"I suppose you already know what happened, right?" she snarks.

"My Dad just told me," I tell her honestly, not wanting to lie and break her trust.

She barks out a sarcastic laugh. "Ha. Looks like your dad was faster since I just got the news minutes ago."

I don't tell her about how Karl shared the video with Dad, knowing that will just be rubbing salt in the wound. "He has a lot of employees, so a lot of people are looking out for the company's best interest."

Roxanne resumes pacing, waving her hand dismissively while she looks down at her phone again. "Whatever. Anyway, you don't have to worry about it. This will be fixed very soon and your brother won't even have time to find out."

"You aren't going to tell him?" Alarm bells start to go off in my head. This is the worst sort of damage control for her to do. "What if Andries already knows? Has he texted you since we left this morning?"

She pauses, uncertainty flashing across her features before she banishes it, the haughty expression returning. "No, but I didn't expect him to text me during his guys' outing anyway. He doesn't know, or else he definitely would have called me. And we're going to try to keep it that way."

"Roxie," I plead, coming towards her even though the vibe she's putting out is pure ice. "Maybe he's getting drunk with Dan and Johan and venting about what a liar his fiancée is. Did you ever think about it that way?"

I know I've worded it wrong when she whips around, fire in her eyes. "I didn't lie!" she spits out like an angry cat. "He never knew the cabaret was mine because he never asked about it. If he had, I'd have told him the truth, but he didn't. That's it."

I roll my eyes. "How convenient he never asked." Sparks of fury are in the air between Roxanne and me, and I realize with a start that this is going so terribly. I didn't want any friction like this at all, but she had just come at me so hot that I responded in kind instinctually. I inhale deeply, letting out a long exhale, which takes some of my annoyance with it. "Look, I'm not trying to fight with you. I'm worried about you, Roxie. I can call him if you want and try to see if he knows already."

She doesn't calm down like I have but smiles strangely. It almost feels patronizing. "I will call him Elise. Don't worry."

We stare at one another for a long moment. I'm confused by her all over the place behavior, but I feel like she's just waiting for me to leave. Shifting from foot to foot, I don't back down. This conversation isn't over yet. Roxanne keeps checking her phone, and I wonder whether she's still getting bombarded with messages about the video, or if she's anxiously waiting for Andries to confront her.

Figuring that she isn't going to be the one to back down first, I sigh and walk over to the stone bench in the middle of the garden and pat the empty space beside me. Roxanne clenches her jaw in annoyance, but comes and joins me anyway, even if she doesn't turn in my direction.

"I'm not trying to crowd you," I tell her after a long moment of silence between us. "But I want you to know my dad wants me to be the one to tell Andries." She stiffens beside me, but I continue, "Don't worry, I'm not going to."

Her posture softens as she turns to look at me. "Thank you, Elise. Really."

"The biggest reason I'm not telling him is that I think he should hear it from you. *You* should tell him as soon as you can if he doesn't know yet."

She shakes her head, crossing her arms again as if she's trying to hold herself. "I don't think so, no."

I lay a hand on her shoulder. "Roxanne, sooner or later he's going to find out. My dad isn't going to let such an opportunity get away. You know they want to make sure the wedding won't happen, and this incident is the perfect pawn for them. You have to beat them to the punch."

She laughs sardonically. "It's so convenient, isn't it?"

I frown in confusion. "What do you mean by that? What's convenient?"

Changing her attitude again in a flash, she glares at me acerbically. "Everything was going so damn well between Andries and me, and all of the sudden the only secret you have against me blows up on the news and goes viral."

My mouth falls open in shock. "Roxie, I've been here the whole time! How would I have orchestrated such a thing? I've got nothing to do with this, you have to believe me." I pause, considering if I want to show my hand or not, but I'm already in this deep. Might as well jump all in. "This sounds more like Karl's doing than mine."

"Why do you mention him now?" she demands.

"He's the one that sent the video to Dad first. Other people did, too, but Karl was first."

Roxanne searches my eyes, looking to see if I'm lying to her, but apparently whatever she finds satisfies her. Shoulders slumping, she nods. "Fine, I believe you. But I'm still going to tell Andries on my own, in my own time."

Looking towards the villa and then back to me, I get the cue that Roxie wants me to leave. Having said my piece, I relent, wishing her good luck and really meaning it before I exit the garden.

As I stroll back to the villa, in no rush, I decide to try and call Dan again. With all of this going on, he's really the one I need to speak to. Not because I want to talk to him personally, which I do, but because he's always the best person to have around in these sorts of situations. Andries may have taken a shine to Johan, but no matter what he says no one will ever be able to replace Dan, and if Andries hits the roof when he finds out about the video, he's going to need Dan more than ever.

I try to call him, but as I expected, there is no answer. I swear I feel like throttling him when he gets back, but there's no time to waste seething about it. Calling Andries is out of the question since he's the one I need watched, so after a moment of deliberation I call Johan.

Miraculously, he picks up. "Oh thank God you picked up. Is everything alright?"

"Hey," Johan sounds confused. "How are you, El? Things are all good here. We just finished sailing for the day and are having dinner at the bar with the crew. How are you?"

"Fantastic," I lie. "How is Andries?"

He pauses. "Oh, uh, he seems to be doing okay. Why?"

"Can you call me if something changes on that front? And please don't let him get drunk."

"Sure," he sounds more bewildered than ever, but it's a blessing that Johan is such a good sport. "I'll be over watching him, for whatever reason…"

"I can't explain right now, but I promise I will when I am able to. Can you trust me on this?" I need to know he isn't going to go straight to Andries and report this phone call, but who knows?

"Yeah, El, I've got you. Don't worry." Another pause, before he continues. "Will I be able to see you tonight when we get back?"

"Probably, yeah." *If shit hasn't hit the fan by then*, I think.

"Great," he responds brightly. "See you soon, then."

I hang up without saying anything else, a pit in my stomach. I'm glad Johan answered, but I had really been hoping to talk to Dan. That he would still be ignoring me right now, when I really need him the most, is breaking my heart. It's not like he knows what I'm dealing with, but it could be any sort of emergency, and he would never know! Does he really care that little about me?

I lean against the front of the villa, not wanting to go back in yet as I contemplate my next move. I have a feeling Roxanne doesn't really intend on saying anything to my brother. I think she's hoping to keep it a secret till we're back home so she can tell him in private instead of around everyone, or maybe she's hoping it will all have blown over by the time we return to Amsterdam. I guess I'll just have to keep an eye on her and my brother and watch for any changes in behavior. He, Dan, and Johan being out so late is already weird, considering the timing of it all, but I have no proof that it's connected to the Bar Rouge incident.

I jump when someone touches my shoulder, whipping around to see an apologetic-looking staff member. I had been so lost in thought that I hadn't even heard him come outside. He asks if I'll be joining Lili and Robin out for their dinner, or staying at the villa for dinner instead. Once I find out that Roxanne is staying behind, I decide to do the same, feeling bitter about the couple and their lovely date while I have to sit here and wonder why Dan isn't answering me. As annoyed as I am, Roxanne must be feeling even worse, sitting on this secret of hers. Add that onto the fact that her fiancé has been gone all day, and I bet she's feeling especially jilted.

It's not that I don't believe that they were out sailing, but it seems so odd for Andries to plan an entire day away from his fiancée. I was under the impression that he wanted to spend every moment with Roxie while we were here.

Maybe he wanted Johan and Dan to bond and get along for the rest of the stay, I think as I go to my room to freshen up for my dinner on the terrace with Roxie. *But what sense does that make, if Andries wants me to end up with Johan?* I would think he'd want Dan out of the picture as much as possible. I wish my brother was easier to understand!

Once I make it to the terrace, I see Roxanne sitting there, a bottle of red wine open on the table beside her. She isn't exactly the person I'd like to be having a private dinner date with, but in a way, she and I both have been ditched by our men, so I feel some kinship with her there. It's a stunning evening, the sky painted pink and burnt orange as it reflects off the sea and the water of our infinity pool.

The server pours a glass for me as I sit before disappearing to give us some privacy. The first drink is delicious and jammy, but I've been drinking quite a bit since we arrived, and make a mental note to order a Perrier as well when the server returns. Roxanne is already most of the way through her glass, but she doesn't look nearly as upset as she did earlier.

"Guess we're just two introverts tonight," she comments, holding up her glass for me to clink mine against it.

I do so, taking a drink afterward and set the glass down. "I really thought the boys would be back by now. I don't know what Dan is up to, but I was sure Andries wouldn't have left you alone for dinner."

Roxie shrugs one shoulder, and I can't tell if she's hurt or really just doesn't care. "It's fine. I don't care that he's spending time with his friends. I just hope he doesn't drink too much."

"I managed to get a hold of Johan and told him to keep an eye on him," I assure her. "But have you talked to any of them?"

She nods as the server brings out a fruit and cheese board, spearing a piece of white cheese with her fork once he departs. "Andries answered my call, but he seemed distracted. Affectionate, but distracted, so I'm positive he doesn't know about Bar Rouge yet."

Silence stretches between us as I nibble on a piece of pungent cheese and sweet candied pecans between sips of wine. Roxanne isn't meeting my eyes, and I know she doesn't want to talk about the cabaret incident anymore. Well, too bad. I still have more to say.

"Roxie, are you going to tell him while we're still here or are you trying to drag it out until we're home?"

She sighs, rolling her eyes to the sky as she does so. "You're being so nosy, Elise. No, I don't plan on telling him while we're here. It will just make things more awkward for everyone, and I don't really care what you think about it. I actually want us to enjoy the rest of our time in Capri."

"I'm not being nosy when people are sending me the video! That's the opposite of nosy; it's being thrown in my face!" I resist the urge to flick one of the nuts on my plate her way to emphasize my point, popping it in my mouth instead. "Every second you don't confess is another chance for someone else to tell Andries. You're really playing with fire here. Especially when my father has threatened to tell Andries himself."

We're interrupted when the server returns with two plates; beautiful fig and pear salads with a basket of crunchy fresh bread placed between us. The entire time the table is set, Roxie glares at me, daring me to say anything else about the incident in front of the staff. I have no plans to, even if my anxiety about it all is rising by the minute. There is no possibility of a good outcome if she doesn't tell Andries the truth.

Once the server departs, she relaxes, pouring her own wine refill, apparently not content to wait for someone else to do it for her. While she drinks deeply, I sip my Perrier, squeezing the accompanying lime beforehand. One of us needs to be fully sober for the upcoming evening.

"Now," Roxie says, picking up her fork and smiling as if nothing is wrong, "Let's drop the subject and enjoy our dinner, shall we?"

I pick mine up too, but I don't have it in me to answer her, because Roxanne doesn't want to hear what I have to say. I just hope that I'm wrong and she's right because otherwise, this entire trip is going to implode around us.

CHAPTER 6

Dan

As exhausted as I am, I can't help but cheer just as loudly as everyone else. After all, I've had a shit couple of days, and this is a welcome reprieve after being the scapegoat for everyone.

We've made fast friends with all the other sailors, and a large portion of Le Grottelle is now filled with the bulk of us who were on the water today. And this isn't a sit down kind of dinner, either. Everyone is up and moving around, laughing and watching the drone footage from today to critique each other's form. This restaurant, picked out by the coach, sits high on a rocky cliffside of Capri with stunning, almost frighteningly high, ivy and olive vines crawling up the railing and trellises, keeping everyone safe. The boats still on the water are turning on their lights, and look like little stars in a deep blue sky as they float.

As it gets dark and the overhead lanterns flicker to life, the coach holds his beer stein in the air and proposes a toast, his arm slung around Andries's shoulders.

"I want to make a toast to Mr. Andries van den Bosch here, who has been our student today, along with his friends!" The rest of the team cheers, whistling, and clapping. "Andries here is not just a savant at sailing… this is also part of his bachelor's trip. He's getting married, and still made some time to come hang out with us!" More cheering arises from the drunken athletes, a few of them coming up to slap Andries on the back. "So, let's all wish him good luck and a long, prosperous marriage. To Andries!"

"TO ANDRIES!" the room echoes back. I join in, too, glad that my friend is enjoying himself even if he is a pain in my ass.

Andries holds his pint glass up in return. "Well, I want to toast to you all, and how welcome you made us feel. To the team, and more regattas!"

"TO MORE REGATTAS!"

I find Johan amidst the crowd, sidling up to him and nudging him with my shoulder. "This is a lot, eh?"

Johan just laughs. "I think it's nice. Andries seems like he might not be the most social person on the planet. I bet he's loving this."

"Yeah, you're right. I hardly ever see him let go like this. We call him a broody poet for a reason."

The broody poet himself makes his way over to us after finishing celebrating with all his new friends. There's color in his cheeks and he's grinning so widely that the corners of his eyes crinkle. As he saunters over, he throws his arms around our shoulders so he's in the middle of us, giving both Johan and me a shake.

"You know, I wasn't sure how you two would handle being together all day, but I'm really impressed. I've had so much fun. In fact…" Andries looks around until he finds a server, waving him over. "Another round of drinks for everyone! I want to make a toast to my two friends here!"

The coach and the rest of the team seem plenty happy to have another round on Andries, and the harried restaurant employees slowly manage to get a new drink in everyone's hand. Andries toasts to us, his message nice enough but his words slightly slurred from all the alcohol. This makes me pause with my drink halfway to my mouth and really examine my best friend. Has he been drinking more than I thought? I don't want to bring him back to Roxanne in a blackout drunk state.

"A toast to my two amazing friends, Johan and Dan, who have been by my side all day. You both are incredible. Sorry my sister has to come between us all. Cheers!"

There are a few confused looks exchanged from the rest of the team and other people around us, but no one seems too bothered by his odd toast. Or maybe they're all just too drunk to understand what my friend is on about. Johan, though, is immediately embarrassed and goes to get Andries away from the toasting crowd to keep him quiet.

"Maybe we should slow down," Johan tells him with a stiff laugh. To make his point across, Johan tosses back the rest of his beer and gives the glass to a passing server. "That's definitely my last drink, anyway."

"What!" Andries exclaims, shaking his head. "No way, man. You need to drink with me tonight!"

"I'm just not a big drinker is all," he explains.

"Are you sure you're not just a lightweight?" I tease, but Johan shakes his head. I notice that he's keeping a hand on Andries's arm, as if he doesn't want to lose him in the crowd.

"Let's leave him alone, Dan," Andries cajoles. "It will be good to have someone here that's sober, since I intend to get wasted tonight."

I exchange a look with Johan, who is frowning now, his grip on Andries growing tighter. There's something about the way Andries is acting that is setting off alarm bells in my head. He usually isn't like this at all, and this goes above and beyond the normal way that alcohol loosens someone up and makes them more comfortable in the crowd. Andries seems like he's drinking to be self-destructive, not to have fun. All at once, I have a rush of memories about how dark his drinking habits had become when he and Roxanne split for the first time. I had never seen my friend like that before, and Elise and I had been truly scared for him until he put himself into self-imposed exile at his family's estate to detox. I'm seeing shades of that Andries tonight, and I don't like it one bit.

"Why do you want to get wasted?" I ask as carefully as I can over the din of the restaurant. "You know that's bad for you, man."

Andries brushes Johan off dismissively and waves his hand at me. "Because I'm in Capri and I want to enjoy it! Stop trying to babysit me, both of you."

Johan catches my eye and jerks his chin toward the door leading back inside. I get the hint and follow the taller man through the crowd and to a quieter corner of the bar inside. I take one look back at Andries as we go, but I don't think he's likely to leave the group of sailors, so at least he won't get lost while we're gone.

"What's up?" I ask Johan as we reach a quieter area. "Andries acting like an asshole."

"About that…" Johan leans against the bar, looking stressed. "I don't know if I'm even supposed to tell you this or not, but Elise called me earlier. She told me to keep an eye on her brother and to make sure he didn't drink a ton. She was being oddly vague so I'm not sure what is going on, but she seemed really worried."

Guilt churns in my stomach knowing that Elise had to call Johan and not me. My phone is weighing itself down in my pocket now. I know she's tried to call, but I've ignored her all night… now it turns out she might have really needed me. *Fuck.*

"Does he usually drink like this?" Johan asks when I don't answer him right away.

I rub the back of my neck, a headache threatening to build in my skull from the stress of all of this. "Not so much anymore. The last time he got really drunk was at his engagement party, and I sort of wrote that off because it was a time to celebrate. But before that…" my words trail off, as I hesitate whether or not to open up to someone I barely know.

"Share whatever you're comfortable with," he says, noticing how torn I am.

"Let's just say when he and Roxanne split up some time ago—which is a long story in itself so don't ask—he got drunk almost every night. We were all pretty worried about him, but I really thought we were past all that."

Johan looks over his shoulder at the patio area where Andries still is. He doesn't look convinced by what I've told him. "I see…." He nods, his expression is thoughtful. "I think he might have just had one too many and things are getting out of hand. Let's just try to get him home."

"That's where you and I are in agreement." Despite telling me that, I can't shake off the fact that Elise had specifically wanted to make sure that Andries didn't get wasted, and she hasn't ever been overly concerned about what her brother was doing until now. It makes me think she's up to something sinister, which means that either way we need to get Andries home. Both for his own good and so I can see what scheme she is cooking up.

"Something tells me that he isn't going to be thrilled about leaving."

My phone pings with a new text message. This time though, I decide to retrieve it and check it out. "Give me one moment."

Turning around so Johan can't see my screen, I pull my phone out and wince when I see how many calls I've missed from Elise. There is a barrage of text messages too, but it's the most recent one she sent me that strikes the hardest.

Elise: *Of course Johan picked up his phone. He's a gentleman. Not like you! Have fun!*

I'm such a dick. She needed me, reached out to me, and I failed her. Of course, Johan answered when she called and provided her with the help that she needed. He continues to prove that he's the right man for her and that I am anything but.

And yet... on the other hand... I can't help but get a little bit of enjoyment from how annoyed Elise must be from having me ignore her all day. It gives me an ego boost to know that she misses me enough to continue to reach out even before she made the call to Johan about Andries. I wonder if she called him at all before that, or if he had been her last resort. If she wants to play with my heart so badly, then she can deal with a little taste of her own medicine.

I can feel Johan looming behind me, waiting for me to join him in wrangling Andries outside so we can take him back to the villa. My friend might be drunker than he needs to be, but he doesn't seem to be getting into too much trouble, and thinking of Elise calling Johan for help is making me feel on edge. He's a good person, I'm sure of it now after he helped me with the sailing all day, and I think I need to set some things straight with him. The sailing team can babysit Andries for a little longer.

I turn around to Johan's expectant face, and he immediately makes to go back out onto the back patio to grab Andries. I grab his upper arm to stop him. "Hey, man, can we go out front and have a conversation? I think it's long overdue."

"But Elise said her brother—" Johan protests, obviously not keen on the idea of the two of us having a private chat.

"He's an adult. He'll be fine." I make a dismissive gesture toward the back patio. "Plus, if she's that worried about him she can come get him herself. We aren't her lackeys."

"If you think he'll be alright…" Johan sounds reluctant, but I don't give him any room to argue, moving through the crowd and out through the front of the restaurant. The night air is cool and much less oppressive out here where we aren't surrounded by dozens of other bodies.

"What do you need?" he asks, exiting behind me. I walk us over to the side of the restaurant, leaning on the brick wall of the structure.

"I just wanted to talk to you, man-to-man, about this whole thing with Elise." Shoving my hands in my pockets, I turn my face to the sky, breathing deeply. This is stressing me out more than I thought it would. "I just need to know… what are your intentions with her, and are you still in love with her?"

For the first time today, Johan's expression shutters and his posture becomes defensive. "Elise told me that you and her weren't anything official, so I'm not sure how my emotions towards her are any of your business."

"I respect you enough to talk about this in private, Johan. I'm not trying to corner you and give you any grief, so chill out." I hate giving him any sort of insight into my own feelings toward Elise, but if I want honesty from him, I'm probably going to have to give it in return. "Look, I'm not going to pull any punches here. I love her, and before you arrived, we were basically acting like boyfriend and girlfriend—just without the title. So can you see why it would be important for me to know what you want with her."

Johan exhales slowly, sounding disappointed. "I was afraid that was the case. To be completely transparent, I feel just as strongly about her as I did three years ago. If it isn't love, then it's as close as an emotion can be to it. But… I think we just met at the wrong time in our lives, and it wasn't meant to be back then."

"And now?" I demand, standing straight and facing him head-on. "Be real with me, Johan."

He sighs. "I don't know. This could be the right time. I thought it might be, but the fact that you two were basically together when I arrived tells me that it really isn't. Maybe it will never be, no matter how strongly I feel about her. Elise might be destined to be the right person at the wrong time for me, forever."

There is a long pause of silence between us, before Johan adds. "She's a special woman, Dan. I just want her to be happy."

"Same here, even if she pisses me off to no end sometimes. I think... well, I think we both know what we want, but it's going to be up to Elise to choose. If we both just want her to be happy, then we have to give her the space to make up her own mind."

"Agreed." Johan sticks out his hand, and I shake it, sealing the deal with a man that I thought I hated only a day ago.

I've had real thoughts about how much easier my life would be if I could just kill Johan and make him disappear from the planet. Elise would never have to know, and with her perfect prince Johan out of the picture, there would be nothing standing between her and me. But on the other hand, like Andries had said earlier, if Johan and I weren't in love with the same woman, I really do think we could be great friends. He's an easygoing, capable person with a good sense of humor—just the kind of friend I look for in life. Elise, though... she's more important than anything else in my life, and no friend, good or bad, would be worth losing her for.

He must be on the same mental wavelength as I am, because after a pause Johan says, "Listen, Dan, no matter who Elise chooses to be with, even if it's neither of us, I've enjoyed getting to know you better. With how much Andries appreciates you, and all the things you've done to celebrate his upcoming marriage, it's clear you're a good man—"

I hold up a hand to stop him. "I know what you're getting at, and I can't speak for you, but if Elise chooses you instead of me, we cannot be friends. Sorry, that might make me a prick, but I love her too much to spend my days watching her be with someone else. I won't get in your way, but I also don't want to have to be around to see you with the woman I love."

"Understood." The air is tense between us, and Johan rubs the back of his neck while we both struggle with what to say next. "Should we, uh, go back and check on Andries? We've been out here for a while at this point."

"Shit, you're right!"

I refuse to be responsible for Andries's drinking habits, but I also don't want to drag him back to the villa blackout drunk. I hope he hasn't managed to get into too much trouble while we've been away. Knowing my luck, though, he'll be passed out somewhere, totally shitfaced, and somehow it will be all my fault.

I breathe a sigh of relief seeing Andries still standing with the rest of the athletes, arms slung over their shoulders as they all laugh. There's an empty shot glass in one of his hands, and with his heavy eyelids and flushed face, it's a safe assumption to say that my best friend is pretty inebriated. Whether we're past the point of blackout or not, I'm not quite sure yet.

The relief of seeing him on his feet is quickly banished when one of the other sailors comes by with a tray of shots he stole from a passing server, handing one to Andries as he untangles his arms from around the other men. Before I can even open my mouth to tell him to take it easy, Andries has thrown the shot back, swallowing it without even a shiver from the taste, and it begins to dawn on me how bad this can get if we don't get him out of here as soon as possible.

Grimly, I turn to Johan. "This might be difficult."

His mouth thins as he nods. "You're probably right. Let's get it done."

Andries looks happy to see us at first, but when he realizes what we're there to do, he frowns bitterly and tries to shake us, moving back into the press of people to keep away from us, but in his drunken state he isn't nearly as fast and nimble as he thinks he is. With me on one side of him, and Johan on the other, each of us having a firm grip on his arms, we began to maneuver him out of the restaurant.

"I'm not done!" he protests as we start dragging him outside. "We were just getting started!"

"Man, you've gotten started and finished. Now you've overstayed your welcome. Let's get out of here." He's hard to keep a hold of, and I struggle to get the words out from the effort. My body is still exhausted from sailing and wrestling the over six foot tall Andries out of a crowded restaurant is just adding to my discomfort.

"How are you not miserable?" I ask him. "I feel like I've been run over by a team of horses and you're here getting wasted."

"I'm in better shape than you!" my friend declares confidently. "I always have been."

Rolling my eyes, I can't help but laugh as we maneuver him out the front door. "Whatever you need to tell yourself. What on earth makes you think that it's a good idea to drink this much, huh?"

Once we have him on the sidewalk outside, the cool evening breeze a balm to how sweaty I've become under the collar from the exertion, Johan goes back in to take care of the tab while I keep a hand on Andries's shoulder and call the driver with my free hand.

"I have to drink to get through all of this," he confesses, finally letting up in his struggles. "I feel like I can't trust anyone. You betrayed me by fucking my sister, and my sister betrayed me by both fucking my best friend and going behind my back to please our dad. And Roxanne... well, God knows when she's gonna pull a fast one on me."

I'm pissed about his comment about myself and Elise, but a pang of guilt stabs my heart when he mentions Roxanne. For all Andries knows, they're perfectly fine right now, but the fact that she owns that cabaret is hanging over them like a storm cloud and he doesn't even know it. If I was in his shoes, I wouldn't care about the cabaret itself, but the lying would hurt like a knife in the back. With the way Andries feels about sex work and things like cabarets, plus the lying... he's right. She's currently pulling a fast one on him and he's none the wiser.

"People aren't perfect, my friend," I tell him, trying to sit aside what an asshole he's being concerning my own sins. "Your expectations for your friends and family are so high that meeting them is almost unattainable. Just because people make mistakes doesn't mean that those mistakes are a personal slight against you."

"Did I ever backstab you?" he snaps, maudlin attitude switching to anger in a snap. "Or my sister? Or Roxanne? No, I didn't! I've got morals, unlike all of you. Except *you!*" Andries cranes his head and points behind us, where Johan is walking out to us with a confused look on his face. Andries pulls away from me and moves to Johan, throwing a loose arm over his shoulders and patting him rather hard on the chest. "You, Johan, haven't betrayed me yet, right? You're a good lad."

Johan meets my eyes, bewildered and slightly alarmed, obviously hoping that I'd take the reins so he didn't have to get involved in whatever fit Andries is having. "This is getting fucking ridiculous, man," I grate out, temper flaring despite how hard I'm trying to control it.

I can't stop myself from getting pissed off. Johan is a 'good lad' but he's just as interested in Elise as I am. Hell, if he had been here with her from the beginning and I wasn't in the picture, there's no way to know how close the two of them would have gotten! But somehow, Andries is sympathetic towards Johan and his desire to be with Elise. Me, though? He treats me like shit, and it isn't some silly teenage crush I have for Elise, either. I love her.

Looking at Andries hanging on Johan, I feel another seed of jealousy planting itself in my chest; Johan has Elise's attention and Andries's trust and blessing.

"Johan didn't have to put up with your bullshit of an oath. He could have fucked your sister and you wouldn't have even been bothered!"

"Come on, Dan... that's not fair," I hear Johan say quietly, but Andries snicker on my face, drowning out whatever else he has to say.

"Because Johan isn't a fuckboy like you are! He's got standards!" Andries raises himself to his full height now, pulling away from Johan and coming at me faster than I would have expected in his inebriated state. He pokes a finger into my sternum, opening his mouth to say something else, but before things can get physical Johan is there, inserting himself between us.

"Enough," he snaps, pushing us apart. Andries stumbles but manages to keep himself on his feet. "Aren't you two supposed to be best friends? This is supposed to be a celebration!"

"Dan seems to think that throwing money at our friendship gives him a free pass to do whatever the fuck he wants, so I don't know anymore. Are we best friends, Dan?" his voice is tight and furious.

I'm so angry that I can hear the pulse of my blood rushing in my ears, but I'll never be able to forgive myself if I kick my best friend's ass when he's both drunk and on his bachelor's trip. I clench my jaw, but still manage to force out a response. "As of right now, yeah, we are. If you're still this much of a dick when you're sober though, we can reevaluate."

"Enough," Johan repeats again, more calmly this time. "Shake hands like gentlemen and let's get back to the villa. This night has obviously gone on a little too long." When neither of us moves, annoyance creeps into his tone. "I said shake hands!"

We both reluctantly extend our arms and shake brusquely just as the cab arrives. I exhale in relief that we won't be fighting like hormonal teenagers out in public anymore. Johan works to cram Andries's tall frame into the backseat of the cab, climbing into the middle, and I take the other side. I feel like Johan is a parent separating two naughty siblings, and the thought almost makes me laugh. Andries tries to broach a conversation a few times, but Johan shushes him before he can speak, and as the short trip continues a lot of my best friend's rage bleeds away and all that's left is his drunken stupor. He looks significantly worse for wear as we pull up to the villa, but at least we're only feet away from salvation and being able to turn Andries over to his fiancée. Poor Roxanne. Cabaret or not, she doesn't deserve Andries in this state, but I've already put in my hours taking care of him today.

Seeing how he's nearly passed out, his head leaning on the window and breath fogging up the glass, I figure that we might need some backup.

Dan: *Hey, Elise, not that I want to talk to you, but we might need some help getting your brother inside.*

At that, I tuck the phone into my pocket and open my car door. "Hold him steady so he doesn't fall out when I open the other side," I tell Johan, who nods, grabbing Andries by the shirt so he doesn't slip away.

I walk around the vehicle and open the other back door. Johan lets me take Andries's weight long enough to unbuckle and extricate himself from the vehicle out the door I had originally exited. He comes around to join me, and as a team, we shake my friend to semi-consciousness and tug him out of the car.

"Good God you're heavy," I groan, helping him to sling an arm over my shoulder. Johan does the same on the other side of Andries.

"It's all muscle," Andries slurs. "You can ask Roxie."

As angry as I am with him, it's still pretty funny. "I'll pass. Thanks."

"Did you know I'm getting married, Joe?" Andries gasps in excitement to Johan as we drag him up the driveway. He takes one step for every three Johan and I take, and it's like maneuvering a large, clumsy toddler.

"It's Johan," the other man corrects, his tone deadpan. "And yes, I've heard."

"One of you is going to marry my sister I bet. I don't know why, she's such a brat sometimes..." Andries sighs, almost going limp before we shake him again.

Where the hell is Elise?

"Come on dude, you have to walk," I groan.

"I am!" he insists.

Finally, Roxie and Elise rush out of the house, both of them in what appears to be their pajamas; Roxie's wearing a white floor length robe with cherry blossom trees curing up from the bottom and over the sleeves, while Elise is in a silvery nightgown that hits right above her knees, her bronzed, long legs bare, and a matching short robe is thrown over it but untied. I guess they had an early night, and part of me is jealous because an early night sounds way better than trying to corral pissed off, overly-tipsy Andries.

"What the fuck, Johan!" Elise snaps as they meet us at the top of the driveway. "I told you to keep an eye on him, and now here he is, drunker than I've ever seen him before! All I needed you to do was watch him and you couldn't even accomplish that simple task?"

I soak in how Johan looks like a whipped dog at her rebuke, but before he can apologize I speak up. She's already mad at me, so what's a little more going to hurt? "It was my fault, okay? Not his. I needed to speak to him so we went outside for a minute and when we came back in, your brother was already doing shots with the rest of the team."

Elise goes red, but she's interrupted in her diatribe by her brother, who is looking at Roxanne with stars in his eyes.

"You are so fucking hot, damn. Are we really getting married?"

She lets out an amused laugh that sounds oddly relieved, going to Johan's side and taking Andries's arm onto her shoulder instead. With the love of his life so close, Andries tries to stand under his own power, and she's able to start to lead him away without too much trouble. "I think so. Now come inside, lover-boy, and we'll get you some water and Advil."

"That's not all I want you to get me," he replies, trying to sound seductive while sliding a hand over her ass. She slaps his arm, but the expression on her face is full of nothing but affection.

Once the couple is inside fully, I have to face Elise, who is so annoyed that she's almost vibrating with it. Her eyes are fixed on me, so full of fire, that even Johan senses the tension in the air. There is a crash from inside, and he takes the opportunity to flee.

"I'm going to go make sure Roxanne doesn't need help!" he proclaims, pushing past me and into the dimly lit villa. I sigh, rubbing my temples, not looking forward to the lecture I'm about to get. Making Elise angry is fun, but dealing with the aftermath is less so.

"Why did he get drunk?" she demands, crossing her arms over her chest. "What the hell happened?"

"You're not going to like the answer, so why don't we just go in and call it a night."

She puts her hands on her hips, refusing to move. "Absolutely not. Tell me what is happening."

I look at her a little more closely. I think there is something else she isn't telling me, because the amount of tension in her body is way more than is necessary for something as small as her brother getting drunk. I wonder what secrets little Elise is hiding from me? If I want to figure it out, I guess I'll have to give her a bit of information, too.

"He's still really pissed off about the both of us. I guess he's been trying to fake it for the sake of the vacation."

Elise cringes. "Ugh. It's his vacation!"

"I know. But we can't control how ridiculous his reactions to things are."

She nibbles at her bottom lip, and I have to shake my head so I don't get distracted by it. Elise is thinking hard about something, but I'm positive she's only going to give me bits and pieces about what is on her mind. "Did... did he mention anything about Roxanne or the cabaret?"

There it is. This is what Elise is worried about, something related to Bar Rouge. Her hesitation gives it away. Now I just have to get to the bottom of it. "He was ranting about how everyone he loves betrays him and how he's expecting Roxanne to disappoint him sooner or later. That boy has some sort of sixth sense about those sorts of things, I'll tell you that much."

Elise rolls her eyes to the sky and exhales. The wind picks up the hem of her dress, exposing even more of her perfect, glowing skin, and my pulse starts to pick up despite everything. "My brother is very intuitive," she points out. "He knows when something is up. Always has."

I take a step closer to her, clenching my fists to fight off the urge to touch her. "Elise, what exactly are you getting at here? Is there something I should know about Roxanne or the cabaret?"

"I didn't say there was," she replies stubbornly. "You're reading too much into things."

One more step forward, and there is less than a foot separating us. "Spill it, El. I'm not stupid. I'm your ally here, at least in regards to all of this."

Crossing her arms, Elise considers my words. I know she feels alone here with everyone else, and I think that's why she gives in so quickly to me. "Fine." She heaves a long sigh, measuring carefully her next sentences. "Dad messaged me this article from a tabloid when we got back from the Blue Grotto. There is a huge scandal back home with Bar Rouge and it's all going viral."

"Shit. What kind of scandal?"

She looks over her shoulder and around us, to make sure no one else is close enough to listen in. "There is a video of one of Roxie's cabaret workers giving someone a blowjob on stage. The girl is claiming it was staged and she didn't actually do it, but it doesn't matter, the video is already everywhere. All these news outlets have been trying desperately to get into contact with Roxanne but obviously, she's here and not responding to them."

Elise is shaken by all this, which surprises me. I take her by the arm and walk her to the garden on the side of the villa so she can sit and we can have some privacy to talk. To my surprise, she comes without a fight, and it strikes me that she's probably been overwhelmed with all of this.

Once we sit on the stone bench, Elise lets out a long breath, her body relaxing. I wish she would lean on me, but I can't initiate anything. Not with how much she's been messing with my feelings. "I'm assuming Roxanne is now aware of the video too?"

She nods. "We found out at exactly the same time. I found her out here in the garden talking to someone on the phone. She was pissed at them, so I think it was the worker she was speaking to, not the media."

Oh, this is going to be trouble. It's already gotten out of hand, and it's only a matter of time before the storm that this situation is causing reaches us here in Capri. "She has to tell him." My tone comes off as more serious and worried than I aimed for. "There's no way she can hide this anymore. He's going to be irate, but—"

"You're wasting your breath," she cuts me off. "I've already told Roxie the same thing, about how he needs to hear it from her and not someone else, but she is refusing. I think she wants to try and keep it under wraps until we get back home so she can enjoy the rest of the vacation with him, but she's delusional if she thinks people aren't going to send that article to him."

"I agree with you. She's in denial, this is all about to blow up in her face."

Elise clasps her hands in her lap, looking down at them, the sheet of her golden hair partially covering her face. "There's more. Dad wants me to deliver the news to Andries before Roxanne can make it as dramatic and scandalous as possible, but…"

I pivot my body towards her, all my attention now on the woman beside me. This will be a telling moment; has Elise really started to change for the better, or will she still backstab anyone to get ahead in the world and please her father? She looks up at me with big eyes, and she's so beautiful it almost hurts.

"But what, Elise?"

"I don't have the stomach for it," she admits, causing my lips to curve up with pride. "Not with everything I've already done to the two of them, plus all the nonsense that Dad has put him through as well. I just can't do it."

The lovely ice queen, Elise, is growing as a person, and every ounce of me wants to be there to grow with her. I lay a hand on her shoulder, and I'm able to feel the warmth of her skin through the cool silk. "I'm proud of you. You can count on me for any help that you might need."

At my praise, she smiles softly. Our bodies move of their own accord, my lips were drawn to her as if by gravity, but as her eyes flutter closed I remember that just this morning, Johan kissed her forehead while she was in his bedroom with him, and this recollection snaps me out of the trance that she has put me in. She's growing as a person, yes, but Elise still hasn't told me that she wants anything more than just a friend's with benefits relationship with me. I need so much more from her. I turn my head at the last second, lips grazing her cheek in the ghost of a kiss before I sit up straight once more.

She's visibly disappointed, her bottom lip stuck out in a pout and hurt in her eyes. "What?"

"Goodnight, Elise," I tell her, standing and leaving her there in the garden before I can change my mind and pull her into my arms. Elise is everything to me, but I'll be slowly killing myself if I continue to hook up with her without receiving any love in return. What I feel for her is real, and what I want from her is a real relationship to match. She can't give it to me, so I can't give her the physical portion that she wants. Even if it is unimaginably painful to deny her.

"Wait!" she calls behind me. "Dan!"

I don't respond.

Inside the villa, I can hear movement from Roxanne and Andries's suite, but leave them to it. I don't bother to check in on Johan and make sure that he was able to help Roxie get Andries down for the evening. He was a good man today, helping me at every turn, whether it be on the boat or with my drunk friend, but that doesn't mean I can tolerate seeing him right now. Not after turning Elise down and remembering their moment in his suite this morning. I guess I'm not as big of a person as I thought I was.

During my nighttime ritual—brushing my teeth and showering while desperately trying to ignore the sound of Elise moving around on the other side of the wall—I can't help but remember the vitriol-filled words Andries had spewed at me earlier in the evening.

The worst part is, he isn't exactly wrong. I have been a fuckboy for a good part of my adult life, at least if you were to ask some of the girls I've slept with and left behind. Before Elise, I never wanted a relationship with anyone, and it's awful to think about all the pain I probably left in my wake by refusing to have any sort of emotional connections. So I played with girls' emotions, and now Elise is playing with mine. Is this some sort of karma for my past mistakes?

I don't just want Elise. I love her, crave her... if the universe is punishing me by making sure that she will never be interested in me as anything other than a fling, then it has to be the worst fate I can possibly imagine.

I crawl beneath my blankets, body tired but mind restless. She's only feet away, in the suite right next to me, but Elise and I might as well be worlds apart.

CHAPTER 7

Elise

I'm in paradise and could be doing anything I want right now... so why in the hell am I laying on the cloud-like bed in my luxury suite, only thinking of Dan?

Telling him about everything with Roxanne and the viral video scandal has made me feel a little bit lighter, and I'm grateful for it, but I can't help but be bitter at how close we had come to kissing when he pulled away. He's occupying every portion of my mind right now, and I just want to be back on that stone bench kissing him right now. Not here daydreaming about it instead.

I pull a pillow over my face and scream out my frustrations into the soft fabric, the shrill sound of it muffled. I hate him so much sometimes, even if I'm falling for him at the exact same time.

At the thought of falling, an idea occurs to me. Dan had jumped the distance from his own balcony to mine so he could spend the night with me, so why can't I do the same?

Surely such a romantic gesture would change his mind and encourage him to kiss me like I'm craving so badly.

Well, I want more than just a kiss, but it would be a good start.

I hop up from the bed and go open the double doors to the balcony, the diaphanous curtains flowing around me in the breeze. The night is lovely, dark out towards the sea but illuminated by the many lights of the island, making me wish I had an excuse to be outside instead of cooped up thinking about a man who keeps rejecting me.

I'm full of adrenaline thinking about his reaction to seeing me on his balcony, but when I walk to the edge and grab the rail, gauging the distance, my mouth goes dry. Oh, no... that is way too far for me to jump. Dan must be insane to have done so! He wanted to be with me so badly that he had put himself in danger like that... and now he wants nothing to do with me. It hurts.

Still considering the jump, I hear a knock coming from the door, and my heart leaps. It has to be Dan! Maybe he's coming to actually kiss me goodnight this time. Even if it goes no further, I'd be able to settle for just a kiss. Anything but the cold shoulder he's been giving me.

I'm so certain that it's Dan, but when I open it to see Johan instead, I can't hide my disappointment. I clear my expression to something neutral as soon as I notice how grumpy I must look, but thankfully Johan is gentlemanly enough not to mention it.

"Hey," he drawls, leaning against my door frame. "I just wanted to let you know Andries vomited, but he's sleeping peacefully now. Poor guy, he's going to regret all of that in the morning."

"Thank you for telling me." I smile up at him, feeling bad that my brother had been the last thing on my mind before Johan knocked.

"Elise," he begins, rubbing the back of his neck as if he's nervous. "What are you doing right now? Do you want to go outside and enjoy the night air with me? Maybe look at some stars?"

"Well…" The invitation catches me off guard, and I twist the edge of my silk robe in my fingers while I consider the request.

"Oh, come on. Remember when we did the same thing at camp, and the moon was full? It was so dark that we could even see satellites go by, except near the moon. I've never seen the sky look so beautiful ever since that night." His gaze is meaningful, as if he isn't only talking about the sky. "Let's go. When will we have another chance like this?"

He's right. After this trip, it's unlikely we'll have time to sneak away to stargaze. Thinking back to when we did so all those years ago, and how magical it had felt laying beside him in the cool grass, I'm overcome by a wave of nostalgia.

"Okay," I give in. "Let me find some shoes and we can go."

There is no soft summer grass this time, or giddy laughs shared between two people young enough to still find something so small as sneaking out at night to look at the stars exciting. This time, there is a lot of heaviness between Johan and me as we stretch out on the loungers by the pool, our two seats pressed together so it forms a sort of loveseat for us to recline on and look at the deep dark sky.

Of all the serious things he and I should talk about, I can't decide on a single one. I don't want to broach the subject of what we are to each other now, or how to repair a friendship that has been nonexistent for three years. Instead, I find something else to talk about. I can't deal with much more seriousness tonight.

"So how was your day away from all of us?" I ask teasingly. "Was I that unbearable that you had to go hang out with Andries and Dan?"

"Of course not," he assures me, his lips twisting into an amused smile. "But we did have a great time, all things considered. Things didn't start to go off the rails until all the sailing was done with."

I prop myself up on my elbow, head in my palm. "You've done that kind of sailing before, haven't you? I know my brother has, but I'm almost positive Dan hasn't."

Johan nods. "Yeah. We knew Dan was a rookie, but he kept up surprisingly well. Do you want to see the pictures and videos?"

"Yes!" I exclaim, sitting all the way up and leaning forward as he pulls out his phone and begins to show me some of the footage taken from the day. From the drone footage, it seems much more fast-paced than I would have thought. The foils lift so high out of the water that I audibly gasp watching the three of them maneuver without panicking. "That's so crazy! I can't believe Dan let himself be coaxed into doing this."

"He did great, actually. He was a really good sport. We had to help him get the hang of it but afterward he was a great teammate."

I snort, laying back down on the lounge and turning my eyes skyward. "That's something I never thought I'd hear you say about Dan. How did you guys manage the entire day without killing each other?"

"When I say he was a good sport I really mean it. Dan is a true gentleman; he apologized to me for his behavior yesterday and we came to an understanding. As of right now, there isn't any bad blood between us." Johan turns his body towards mine, but I don't do the same, processing what he's just told me.

I'm shocked that Dan would apologize all on his own, but it makes me feel warm inside to know that he would. We spend so much time antagonizing each other that it's easy to forget that Dan is a good, generous, caring man at his core.

"In fact," Johan continues. "Your brother said something about Dan and me that I totally agree with."

My interest is instantly piqued causing my gaze to meet his. "What did my brother say?"

"He said if we weren't interested in the same woman, then we would be great friends."

Feeling thunderstruck, I close my eyes. "Are you saying that it isn't you coming between Dan and me, but *me* coming in between you and Dan becoming best friends?"

Johan chuckles, his voice low. "I don't know about best friends, but he's a guy I could definitely get along with. He's definitely less dramatic than Andries, that's for sure."

Now I do laugh, despite being a bit shaken up by this conversation. "Yeah, well... isn't everyone?"

With nothing left to say, there is a long period of silence between us, and things have just started to feel awkward for me when Johan breaks the silence. "How is the rest of your family doing, El? I don't know all the details, but I've picked up they didn't attend the engagement party. There is some tension between Andries and your parents, huh?"

"Ugh. That's an understatement." I throw my forearm over my eyes. "This is a really long story, are you sure you want me to get into it?"

"I feel like it isn't going to make sense unless you describe it fully, so yeah, go ahead."

I peek out from under my arm at Johan, and his open, earnest face. He's such a gentleman that I know I could tell him about Roxanne's past jobs without him being judgmental, but it's not really my story to tell, so I decide to keep that part of it vague at least.

"Let's just say that my parents aren't very fond of the bride-to-be. So much so, that they're boycotting the wedding, just like they did the engagement party. When everyone realized that they weren't going to celebrate their oldest son's engagement, Dan stepped up and threw Andries and Roxanne a huge engagement celebration and then booked this trip. No matter how much Dan tries to make up for it, I know my brother is still hurt and missing our parents."

"That's awful," he says, sounding genuine. "Roxanne seems great. I'd like to say it's their loss, but even though that's true, I'm sure it doesn't make Andries feel any better."

"No, it doesn't." I sigh deeply. "Andries has always said he will only ever have one love and marriage, and if he sticks to that, then my parents will miss out on the most important event of his life thus far. At least as far as Andries is concerned."

"I take it since you are here that you are on your brother's side?" Johan asks carefully. There's no way I can tell him the honest truth about how I'm balancing so carefully between both warring parties, and I have to think quickly about how to explain it.

"It's complicated. I work at Dad's company now, which muddles things a bit, but yes, I'm supporting my brother right now."

"Huh. That makes sense. Well… how about your other siblings? How is everyone else? Does Hannah still collect random things she finds?"

Now I do sit up and look at him fully, not having any idea what he's talking about. "Does Hannah do what?"

Johan tucks his arms behind his head, a smirk on his face as he recalls the story to me. "When you introduced me to your family Hannah showed me her collection of random treasures. It was all just little things that she found interesting enough to bring home—fossils, coins, broken jewelry, things like that."

"Uh, wow…" I'm thrown through a loop at this new information about my sister. How is this all a surprise to me? "To be honest, she's never told me about it. Hannah is the most reserved child in the entire family and the fact that she opened up enough to show you something like that is impressive." I wrinkle my nose at the next thought. "Even if it does make me feel like a crappy sister."

"Maybe she has a sense that I was someone special and not just a random stranger," he teases. "I have that effect on people."

"In that case…" What I'm about to do is totally out of the blue, but it just feels right. Dan will be pissed, but he isn't exactly paying me any attention right now. "Why don't you come over for dinner when we get back to the

Netherlands? I'm sure Hannah and the rest of the family will be delighted to see you again. Especially now that you and Andries are friends."

Johan reaches over to touch my arm, and I feel a flutter of something inside of me. "I'd be delighted to join you all for dinner. I look forward to it."

I swallow, sensing that this moment can go one of two ways; I can lean forward and touch him back, maybe even leading to a kiss, or I can back down and we can continue stargazing as just friends. With my mind still preoccupied with Dan and our almost-kiss this evening, I simply can't imagine pushing forward with Johan. This is a deciding moment, even if it is just a split-second decision, but even with that in mind it's easy for me to make my choice.

I settle back down on the lounge with a slow exhale. The potential of the moment fades away into the night, joining the sound of the sea lapping against the rocks and the constant hum of the living, breathing city beyond. Johan stays in place for a beat longer, maybe mourning what couldn't be, before he too lays back down.

Johan might not be completely ready to let this all go, though. "I missed this," he whispers, and even though I'm not sure it's the right thing to do, I answer honestly to his heartfelt confession.

"I missed it too, Johan."

It feels like the closing of a book, a chapter of my life, but it doesn't make me sad. I'm happy, in a subdued sort of way, to be out here watching the sky with Johan tonight after all the drama of the day. Content is the word, I think. He doesn't pressure me to define our friendship or question how

I feel about him all these years later. Johan is just happy to be with me, and be my friend. At least for now.

The night is as clear as it could possibly be, and the breadth of all the stars is almost impossibly huge. We point out constellations and the red speck of Mars, marveling at how it's all identical to the way it was three years ago. Everything else has changed in our worlds—in our lives— but at least the stars are still the same.

Minutes pass into hours, and it's so dreamlike that I almost don't register Johan's knuckles brushing against the back of my hand. It's a question, asking if I would link my fingers with his, but with a squeeze of guilt in my heart, I keep still. After a second, his hand retreats.

The energy between us is feeling awkward, so I decide to try and fix it. "My brother doesn't have many friends, Johan," I speak into the quiet. "I know I tease you about how much he likes you, but it really is something special that he trusts you so quickly. I'm glad he took you and Dan for that day trip."

Johan turns and looks at me for some time, searching for some display of emotion, but he doesn't find it. Finally, he answers with a sigh, "Yeah, I'm glad too."

After a few more minutes, I can sense that this meeting between Johan and me has run its course. I stand, stretching my arms above my head before leaning over just enough to give Johan a quick kiss on the cheek. He smells like evergreens, and I feel his hands ghost over my sides in an unconscious reaction to touch me, but he lets them fall to his sides without actually making contact.

"I'm heading to bed, Johan, but thank you for this. It was lovely."

Once more, he looks me over head to toe, a soft look in his eyes. "It really was, Elise. It really was."

CHAPTER 8

Elise

All things considered, I slept pretty well last night and woke up with my stomach growling and the slightest headache building in the back of my skull. It's another perfect morning, if the view from my window is any way to judge. By the time I've showered and I feel a little closer to alive, I can hear everyone on the terrace already having breakfast. My stomach lets me know a second time, even louder now, that we only picked at our dinner last night, and that there is hot food waiting on us if we can only leave our suite.

Wearing a white linen shirt and denim shorts, I throw on a pair of sunglasses and go to join everyone else. Lili, Robin, Johan, and Dan are all here, but my brother and his fiancée are suspiciously absent. Considering how drunk Andries was last night, it's no wonder they're both sleeping in. I'm sure he wasn't the most peaceful bed partner... poor Roxanne.

"Well, has anyone heard news about my brother?" I ask, sinking into a seat next to Dan and across from Lili. The other woman rolls her eyes and laughs.

"Oh yes. Roxanne says he has the hangover of the century, and that they probably won't join us for quite a while. I'm sort of sad that we missed it all last night! It sounds like it was hilarious."

I order an espresso and glass of cucumber water when the server comes by, as well as a *pain au chocolat*. I shake my head at Lili's comment. "I'm sure it sounds funny from the outside looking in, but Andries is a pain in the ass when he's been drinking."

"You're telling me," Johan mutters into his cappuccino cup.

"Enough about our absent companions," Robin pipes up, leaning forward and fixing us all with a playful gaze. "Are you all ready for volleyball in the pool?"

I feel the blood drain from my face, remembering how hard I got hit last time. "Volleyball? At this hour? Absolutely not."

"It's never too early for volleyball!" Johan adds, clapping his hands together.

"No thanks… I'm good. I'm just going to eat my breakfast. I'll watch."

I feel Dan kick me gently under the table. "I bet you are all set after that hit you took last time," he teases.

I turn my nose up at him, sipping my espresso without even giving him a glance. "Oh, you mean the blow to the head where you didn't even come to check on me?"

"That's only because I know that your head is hard enough to take more than a volleyball hit to be hurt," Dan stands, stripping off his t-shirt and laying it over the back of his chair.

I force myself to look away at his shirtless figure, only for my gaze to land on Johan instead, who is equally undressed. Everywhere I look seems to be a minefield, so I just pull out my phone and start scrolling social media instead. Looking up discretely from under my lashes, I'm surprised to see that it's Johan and Dan on one team, and Lili and Robin on the other. I guess they really have become fast friends despite the odds. If my brother was here, I'm sure he'd be more than happy to tell me how I ruin everything—including this potentially strong friendship between the two men.

Refusing to sink into melancholy before I've even had my breakfast, I watch them play absentmindedly while checking my emails and other accounts. At first, I feel bad for Lili having to be stuck in the pool with all the men. It's soon revealed that the little bookshop keeper is quite the competitor, and it's fun to watch her come out of her shell.

Quickly, though, I realize that while Johan and Dan are on one team, it's really just an excuse to compete with each other differently. Instead of using some sort of tactic to win the game, they spend all their time trying to outplay one another, rushing to the ball at full speed and pushing each other out of the way when necessary. Their showboating leaves plenty of room for Lili and Robin to play more skillfully, which makes me happy. Dan and Johan could both stand to be knocked down a few pegs.

While I'm still perusing apps on my phone, a text comes in from Mom, asking if we can video chat. Since Dan is occupied and Andries is still asleep, I figure that there isn't anyone to humiliate me around and tell her to go ahead and make the call.

Mom looks lovely and well rested, and she's excited to walk the phone out to their balcony and show me the stupendous view of Lake Como.

"I wish you were here, darling," Mom sighs. "But are you having a good time? I was so afraid you'd feel left out."

"Not at all," I assure her, even if she's partially right. "It's so beautiful here. I'm having a good time."

Mom tilts her head to the side as she considers how to be delicate with her next inquiry. "And your brother? He's doing okay?"

"Better than okay now that Johan is here. They've become the best of friends it seems like," I tell her, exasperation in my tone. Mom laughs.

"We all always liked Johan, so that's no surprise. But it must be making Dan jealous for Andries to have a new close friend... or is it something else he's jealous about maybe...?" She's fishing for information, but unfortunately for my mother, she isn't going to get much from me.

"I have no idea what you mean, Mom."

She huffs. "Yes, you do. I'll just ask plainly, then. How are you doing having both Dan and Johan there? It must be strange."

"It is," I admit. "But Johan is just a friend. We've established that. He and Dan didn't hit it off right away, but they've been warming up to each other. At this point, Johan is here for Andries, not me. I hope you don't mind, but I invited Johan over to have dinner at the estate once the trip is over."

"I don't mind at all!" Mom chirps. "That sounds lovely. Will he be around, though? That's quite a long trip for him to make just for dinner."

"Actually, he's going to be in the Netherlands anyway for Andries's wedding..." I look around to make sure that my brother hasn't made a surprise appearance. I don't want him to overhear me. Bringing the phone closer to my face, I continue, "Speaking of the wedding—"

Mom's face shutters. "Elise. Don't."

"Come on, Mom. Are you sure you want to miss your oldest child's wedding? I know you and Dad are trying to make a point, but by now you have to see that Andries isn't going to change his mind."

"You know why it's difficult."

"Honestly, Roxanne isn't nearly as bad as you and Dad want to believe she is. Andries got wasted at the bar last night with Dan and Johan and Roxanne immediately took care of him when they got back to the villa. She's very caring and protective of him... there's real love there. Isn't that what you want for him, to be loved?"

I can see Mom lowering herself into a seat on their balcony with a heavy exhale. The stress of thinking about the wedding seems to weigh her down, even the corners of her mouth falling. "Yes, darling, but I want more for him than that, too. Your father—"

"I know plenty about Dad. We're talking about *you*, Mom, not him." I hate to interrupt her, but given the chance, Mom will just talk in circles until I get tired of hearing it and just give in.

Her eyes flutter closed, and to my surprise, she gives a small nod. "All I can promise you is that I'll think about it, okay? No promises." She opens her eyes again, her mouth thinning. "Just make sure you keep an eye on your brother.

You're the more responsible Van den Bosch child, Elise, and I'm counting on you."

"I'll try my best, Mom." Truthfully, I've been just as wild as Andries, I just hide it better than he does. But Mom doesn't need to know that. "I love you."

"I love you too, dear."

The screen goes dark. I sit my phone beside my pastry plate, tearing into the flaky treat with my fingers before it cools off fully, the dark chocolate pairing perfectly with the bitter espresso on my tongue.

Mom didn't exactly say that she was going to come to the wedding, but she didn't explicitly say she wouldn't either. It's a better response than I expected, and it gives me hope that at least one of our parents will attend. If neither of them come... well, it will be a long time before Andries forgives them. Our family can hold grudges for a long, long time.

Please come through, Mom, I think desperately, *I really need you to show.*

As if he could sense that I was talking about him, the silhouette of my brother appears in the terrace doorway, shuffling out into the daylight like a zombie, and groaning like one too. Right behind him, with a steadying hand between his shoulder blades, is Roxanne with a bemused look on her face. Andries is wearing sweatpants and a wrinkled t-shirt with an enormous pair of women's sunglasses on his face which I recognize as Roxanne's.

"Well if it isn't the man of the hour!" Dan hollers from the pool, clapping his hands while everyone else whistles and cheers. "Welcome back to the land of the living, my friend!"

Andries gives Dan the middle finger, causing everyone else to erupt in laughter. My brother falls heavily into the chair across from me, immediately folding his arms in front of him on the table and pillowing his head on them. Roxie sits next to him, waving the server over and ordering a spread of bland food for my hungover brother to attempt to keep down, as well as an entire carafe of French roast coffee.

"Poor baby Andries," I coo, poking him on the top of his head, mirth bubbling up in me. "Did you have a little too much to drink last night? Are you a lightweight now, brother?"

"Fuck you, Elise," I hear coming from his folded arms, his voice muffled.

"He really is exhausted," Roxanne tells me gently, stroking her fiancé's back. Soon enough I think I hear snores coming from his direction. "I wouldn't have brought him out here except I knew if I didn't get him moving he'd just sleep the day away and then be pissed that he wasted a day of vacation."

I shake my head, chewing on a piece of croissant while I observe my brother. As introverted and private as he is, seeing him like this around all his friends is really out of character. Even when he had a drinking problem before, he'd spend his time drinking all on his own. This tells me that Andries didn't intend to get so inebriated last night, and if I wasn't already mad at him for how he has been treating Dan and me, I might even have some sympathy for him.

"Is he sleeping!?" Dan yells from the water, his tone filled with amusement. "That's bullshit! This is his bachelor trip. Wake him up!"

"As if I care that he's asleep," I scoff. "He's the most tolerable like this. It's much worse when he can talk."

I watch, holding my espresso cup in front of my lips to hide my smile, as Johan and Dan talk quietly among themselves in the water, the volleyball game all but forgotten. There's an empty juice glass sitting on the edge of the pool that Robin has just finished, and when I see Johan grab it and fill it with pool water, I already know what is about to happen.

I slide a glance over to Roxanne. "You might want to move."

"What?" She leans to the side to see past me, and her eyes go wide. "Oh, no. No no. Do not do that!" She admonishes the two other men, but they aren't listening to her at all. In seconds, Dan and Johan have poured water down on my sleeping brother, who shoots up, sputtering and wiping pool water from his eyes. He's vibrating with anger, cursing them up and down while he tries to peel his wet shirt off over his head.

To add insult to injury, Dan calls out, "It's a wet t-shirt contest!" and everyone but myself and Roxanne join him in whistling and cat-calling Andries as he gets his shirt off.

"Take it all off!" Johan laughs, and Andries launches the wet shirt at him, stomping towards the door leading inside. Roxanne rockets to her feet, pointing a finger at her husband to be with her other hand planted on her hip.

"Absolutely not, Andries. Do not take your soaking-wet self to our suite and get everything damp." Her voice is stern, and to my surprise, Andries obeys, muttering in annoyance as he chooses a random lounge chair and throws himself down on it, rolling onto his stomach and hiding his face in his arms. Within seconds, he's asleep again, much to everyone's amusement.

With a frustrated sigh, Roxanne sits back down, pouring a cup of coffee out of the carafe that Andries will obviously not be using now. Something about her manner makes me smile fondly, and with a start, I realize that I'm not just tolerating Roxie anymore. I *like* her, and because of that, and the way she both bosses my brother around and loves him at the same time, I'm also starting to warm up to the idea of them getting married. Not just because it will make Andries happy, which is what I've been telling myself for weeks now, but because I think they're good for each other. I genuinely wouldn't mind having Roxie as my sister-in-law. If I can feel this way, even though there is so much of me that is more like my father than my mother, I just know Mom will be able to see the idea of the wedding from the same point of view I am now. She just needs to be exposed to the idea more. Putting my chin in my hand and glancing over at my passed-out brother, I wonder how much pain he's hiding from the rejection of our parents, and how all of this will play out once we get home and it becomes clear that he and Roxanne aren't splitting up.

As I ruminate on all of this, the other four resume their volleyball game, leaving me and Roxanne at the breakfast table. She nibbles on a piece of buttered sourdough bread, slathering it in grape jam between sips of strong black coffee.

"At least he made it through the night," I joke, jerking my chin towards Andries.

"Don't repeat this, but there were moments where I was hoping he wouldn't," she laughs. "What an absolute monster he was to deal with! At least we finally got him to sleep."

"Was he in good spirits all night at least?"

She nods. "For the most part, when he wasn't whining about how bad he felt. Other times he was trying desperately to hit on me even though he couldn't even keep his eyes open." She snorts, thinking about it all, and shakes her head in disbelief. "I am never letting him live this down, I'll tell you that right now."

"So he wasn't angry or upset about anything?" I prod at her gently, wanting to gauge if Roxanne has come clean about the cabaret. I don't think she would do so when he was intoxicated, but there's the chance she told him before breakfast.

Roxie's amusement fades from her face, and her expression turns stony. "No, Elise, he wasn't mad about anything. I know what you're getting at, so drop it. Now."

Exasperated, I still try to push. "He might not know yet, but when he sobers up and gets his phone, there's no way he won't find out. Don't you want to get ahead of the story?"

"Look," Roxanne exhales, shoulders falling. "I talked to my manager this morning, and the investigators that law enforcement sent found traces of cocaine in the backstage area. Now they might just close the entire cabaret down, all because a dancer might do a line before performing. It's ridiculous, and it also means that I'm dealing with way too much right now to spend any extra energy talking to Andries about it. So please, can we change the subject?"

My mouth has been hanging open since she first said the word cocaine, and it takes me a moment to find my words. "*Cocaine*? How can that be?" My mouth is running faster than my brain, and my next words are out of my mouth before I can stop them. "Do you have a bunch of junkies working there?"

Roxanne's expression turns thunderous. "How dare you? They aren't junkies, El. A few of them just do the occasional line before going onstage for a show. If you had ever worked in the industry, you would know that it's a pretty standard thing to do, so get off your high horse."

"How am I on a high horse for being shocked that you have employees doing illicit drugs backstage while other workers suck off customers?" I ask her, keeping my tone as low as I can so that no one else can hear us. "It sounds like way more trouble than it's worth. Maybe you should just let the place close down and wash your hands of it."

She barks a sarcastic laugh. "Get real, El. This is how the world operates. Get high up enough at your dad's company and you'll see way more than a few lines of coke, I can guarantee that."

I can feel the blood rushing to my head at her words, and I slap my hands down on the table in front of me. "Don't you dare talk as if you know how our family business works, Roxanne. We aren't some sleazy cabaret, so no, I'm not worried about any of us doing lines of coke before a business meeting!" My voice is becoming shrill, and I struggle to keep it down. "Why are you so defensive about this, anyway? Have *you* done cocaine before a job?"

Roxie's cheeks turn pink, and she avoids my eyes. "Worry about yourself. There's plenty there to keep you occupied."

Her immediate avoidance makes my head spin. Here I had just been having such warm thoughts about this woman, and now she's all but admitting that she's done cocaine before!

"Holy shit," I breathe, unable to look elsewhere but at her. "You have, haven't you?" Repulsed, I reel back in my seat.

Roxanne's jaw works, but she still doesn't answer me. Mastering the art of ignoring me, she proceeds with breakfast like I'm no longer here.

I try to imagine what would drive someone to get high like that before a job, but I'm quickly reminded of how Roxanne wasn't doing burlesque shows or serving tables. She was an escort, and then a madame, selling herself and other women for profit. It almost makes sense that she would need to do a line or two in order to get through the day as a coping mechanism. Still, it doesn't excuse her behavior or the way she's trying to make light of her dancer's behavior now.

Having had enough, and wanting to flee before I figure out what to say next, Roxanne stands brusquely, her chair scraping the concrete loudly with the force of her movements. My stomach is roiling, head aching with this new information. How could I get so close to letting my guard down with Roxanne?

When she turns to go, desperate to get the last word in, I blurt out, "Maybe it's a good thing that they're going to shut down your cabaret. That place is trash, anyway."

Slowly, Roxanne turns around to face me once more, her chin held high and a flash of prideful anger in her eyes. Her words are loud enough for everyone to hear but steady. "Don't you ever get tired of hurting people like this? Is it because daddy dearest didn't give you the same attention growing up as your brother, so now you feel entitled to be mean to the rest of us?"

Her words drop like an anchor in the ocean, and all other activity on the terrace ceases. The volleyball that had been in flight falls to the water with a plop. Everyone has gone pale, their eyes wide, and Dan is climbing out of the pool. I run a gamut of emotions in the space of a second, seeing red from rage before it all drains away and leaves me cold and humiliated, every part of me chilled except for my hot, flushed cheeks and neck. Like a robot, I stand, turn on my heel, and stomp back inside without looking back. I don't even glance at Roxanne when I pass her. She's won and driven me off, so now she can live with the consequences.

I can still feel everyone's eyes on my back as I disappear out of sight, the humiliation weighing on me like a ton of bricks. How could Roxanne say that to me? I know what I said to her was out of line, but not nearly as out of line as her loud proclamation to the entire terrace. At least I had spoken to her quietly. Now everyone knows me as a spoiled brat, and the worst part is, I don't completely disagree with what Roxanne accused me of. Still, I'm not going to stand outside and let myself be a punching bag for everyone else.

Despite enjoying the quietness of my bedroom, I don't want to stay in this house the whole day, knowing that everyone will be tiptoeing around me and my bruised ego. I'm going to take the entire day for myself and run away somewhere private to get my head straight. I don't need anyone here, and I certainly don't need their sympathy.

In a trance, I strip, pulling on my olive green two piece and throw an off-the-shoulder ivory cover up over it. Then I shove a beach towel, sunscreen, and a few bottles of water into my beach bag and haul it over my shoulder, sending out the request on my phone for one of the drivers. I can't get out of here fast enough at this point.

My eyes are fixed on the floor as I leave my room, focused on the lines of grout and the veins in the marble, afraid that if I look up there will be more pitying, awkward glances cast my way. I'm almost free of the place, the door in sight when I run face first into another human body.

"Easy there," Dan says, taking me by the shoulders so I don't knock us both over. "Where are you headed, El?"

"None of your fucking business, Daniel."

"Ouch, you're a little spicy I see," he replies, jogging behind me to keep up as I continue on my escape path. "But seriously, where are you going?"

"Anywhere but here," I admit as I head to the gates. "Without you, by the way, so go back inside."

"Don't be such a brat," he calls behind me as I reach the front gate, the black sedan I called idling there waiting for me. Dan sprints in front of me and opens the back door like he's taking me on a date, waving his hand to indicate that I should get in, as if that wasn't what I was doing already. Annoyed beyond reason, I crawl into the leather seats, feeling Dan's weight on the seat beside me as he follows me in. I hold up an arm to block him, still not looking in his direction.

"Dan, leave me alone," I beg.

Now, his tone is genuine. "After what Roxanne told you? Not happening. I don't want you to be alone."

"But I *need* to be alone," I insist, those damned tears threatening to pour forth again. "Please, Dan, can you—"

Dan, of course, interrupts me and speaks directly to the driver. "Lido del Faro, in Punta Carena."

The driver gives a tight nod, and then the car, to my chagrin, starts to move. Dan sits back smugly, folding his hands behind his head as if he's won some great victory.

"Where the hell is that?" I demand, feeling my perfect day alone unraveling in my hands. "I want to get far away from here and go to the beach."

"That's exactly where we're going," he tells me, the corners of his mouth twisting up. "It's a little bit of a drive, though, so why don't you talk to me?"

I cross my arms, falling back against the seat in defeat. "About what, exactly?"

He unfurls himself and turns his body towards mine. I can feel his eyes roving over me, concern creasing his brow. "Don't play dumb, El. About what happened. I didn't catch any of the conversation until Roxanne spoke up. How did you guys get to the point of arguing like that so quickly?"

"I asked about the cabaret video scandal again," I admit, looking out the window, a sigh rolling off my lips. "I know it wasn't the right thing to do, but Roxanne is being ignorant if she thinks this is going to stay hidden, even for one more day."

"But you said you two talked about all of that yesterday and it didn't make her this angry. What changed?"

I feel Dan's hand graze mine, and it reminds me immediately of Johan brushing his knuckles against mine, trying to initiate holding hands. With Dan, though, it's different, and I'm happy to let him lock his fingers in with mine, his touch a grounding comfort in my time of need. "I might have been a little harsh, but not nearly as harsh as she was.

There's a glint of humor in his gaze as he asks, "What did you say?"

"Well, I might have called her cabaret trash…"

Dan winces. "Elise… it cost Roxanne a lot to give up her escort business, which, might I add, she built from the ground up. The cabaret is her last connection to her successes as a single woman, and now it's all in danger, so of course you insulting it would offend her."

"But she told me they found drugs in the backroom there. Cocaine!" I whisper, as if the driver is eavesdropping on us. I don't want to take any chances.

To my surprise, Dan doesn't seem affected at all by this news. "Okay, and? That's pretty much normal stuff for the hospitality business anywhere. Not that I'm saying she's in the right… but it's just cocaine."

My mouth gapes open at this. "Are you serious right now? *Just* cocaine?"

"Yes, my sheltered little ice queen, just cocaine. It's not the end of the world, but…" he squeezes my hand to let me know we're still connected, "I can see why what she said to you might actually feel that way. Like the end of the world, I mean."

I can feel my cheeks getting warm again. Dan is the last person I should be embarrassed in front of, considering our intimate history, but I can't help it. What Roxanne said… it's my deepest, darkest secret and insecurity. And she just bared it all to the world like it was nothing. I know I've been a bitch to Roxanne in the past, but this is something more entirely.

"Do you think my brother told her that? I don't know who else could have possibly known." My voice is small, but Dan doesn't push me to speak up, which I'm thankful for.

"Who knows?" He shrugs. "She might have just figured it out on her own. I doubt your brother even thinks that way. Andries for all accounts thinks he's the victim, remember? Which, in reality, you both are." He pauses for a beat, his expression thoughtful. "I'm sure she's just reeling from the investigators finding the cocaine and lashed out without thinking."

"I don't know if I can forgive her, Dan…" voice shaking, I lean into him.

"You can. You will. I know you, El, and you've grown so much in such a short time. But for now, maybe it's best we leave Roxanne alone and let her deal with all the nonsense occurring at her cabaret, especially if she's going to let the stress of it all color how she treats everyone. If it shuts down for good… well, it will break her heart, but she's going to have even more heartbreak I think if she doesn't tell Andries what's going on."

"I agree. He's going to lose his mind over it, I just know it, and she's running on stolen seconds right now. Any time he picks up his phone she's in danger of him seeing that viral video."

Dan hums in agreement, his thumb stroking over my knuckles in a comforting rhythm. "If Andries doesn't find out, it'll be nothing short of a miracle."

CHAPTER 9

Dan

"A lighthouse? I thought you said you were taking me to a beach?"

Elise is indignant, but I don't give in to her whining. "Will you just calm down and trust me for once in your life? I wouldn't lead you astray."

She snorts. "Now that's a lie. But seriously, what is this place?"

"Let's just get this out of the way before you freak out anymore; it is a lighthouse, but there is a beach, too. Satisfied?"

She presses her hands to the car window like a little kid and looks outward, examining the location I have brought us to and deciding if it meets her exacting standards. Finally, she nods. "I guess it will work. Let's get going, then."

A small peninsula sticks out into the sea. This part of Capri is topped with a century-old lighthouse, known only as the Lighthouse of Punta Carena, built from red brick and white stone. Amazingly, it's still actively used to warn ships of the stone outcroppings.

Down lower is an extensive beach club, with a full-service bar, dining options, lounge chairs, a freshwater pool, and all the amenities someone could possibly need to make a beach trip into something much more luxurious. It's only steps from the ocean, which checks off Elise's demands for a beach trip, but some creature comforts will make the day even more relaxing for us.

She waits for me to help her out of the car, which amuses me. I'm fully aware she doesn't do this with everyone, but Elise knows at this point that I'll be there to open her door or help her to her feet. She has me wrapped around her little finger—even when I know that it's a bad place to be, considering I'm in love and she isn't.

The path to the lighthouse is long, and when I try to tug her in that direction, Elise isn't having any of it. "My legs hurt from all the snorkeling I did yesterday," she protests. "I don't want to walk all that way to see a damned lighthouse, Dan. Come on!"

Dragging me towards the beach club, Elise does make a good point. I'm still pretty sore, too, but I just want to spend as much time as possible with her before we have to return to the villa. If I can stretch the trip a few hours longer with a lighthouse tour, then I'm all for it. Elise, though, knows what she wants, and it's the beach. Right now.

Resigned, I follow her down the winding path leading to the main beach. It isn't too crowded, but there is a bevy of red and white striped umbrellas with families lounging beneath, the laughter of children filling the air. The constant rushing of the sea and the beachgoers splashing in the shallows adds to the atmosphere, instantly putting me more at ease. Elise pauses halfway down the path, looking at all of them, back at me, and then abruptly she changes course.

With her long, limber legs, it's easy for her to pick a path through the rocky areas to the side of the main beach, but that still doesn't explain exactly where we are going. I yell for her, but she ignores me, her search single-minded in its intensity.

"El, you're going to get lost!" I protest as I try to keep track of her. "You said you wanted the beach, so let's go to the beach!"

"Just give me a second," she insists. "I think I saw something when we were at the top of the path. I just want to check it out."

We walk about fifty more feet, Elise picking her way delicately down a curving pseudo-path behind a tall rock ledge, and then, to my shock, we emerge onto a scene I never expected. It's another beach, but this one is much smaller, tucked into a tiny rocky cove, and almost completely private. Where the water at the main beach of Punta Carena is deep, sapphire blue, it's different here. The rocks, all shades of brown, dark coppery red, and algae-covered green, lurk under the waves and turn the turquoise water into something that resembles an oil slick. The colors roll and morph as the sea moves, but this cove is so deep into the island's face that the waves are so minimal that they are almost non-existent. This place feels secret and wild, as if we're looking back in time to what the island must have been like before it became a tourist destination. I can't explain it, but I can just tell that the water is going to be blissfully warm.

Elise wastes no time in spreading her beach towel out on the sand. As beautiful and special as this place is, I still have some reservations. "Are you sure this is where you want to stay? Back at the other beach, there is a bar and we can rent a cabana, which is what I had planned. There aren't even loungers here."

She waves her hand dismissively, stripping out of her coverup with ease. "We can go over there later. For now, I like it here. I need some privacy to clear my head."

I can't blame her, honestly, considering how scathing Roxanne's words had been. As much as I like Roxie, when she said those things to Elise, I felt a surge of anger surge within me. Elise's face had gone white, and I just knew that she was shocked at having her private feelings laid bare like that. Anyone would need some time to recharge after that, so the least I can do is let her choose where she wants to relax.

"Fine, fine, but just tell me when you're ready to join the rest of the world."

Standing on the edge of the rippling water, she gives me a coy look. "What if I never am?"

"Then I guess we'll both just be beach hermits for the rest of our lives. Whatever you want, El."

My lovely companion laughs, her voice angelic. Little does she know, I mean it. Wherever she goes, I want to go, too.

Sleek and lithe, Elise dives beneath the turquoise waves, emerging with her hair slicked back and her body bathed in sunlight. I follow her as if in a trance, and when I reach her, she's floating on her back, arms out wide at her sides, and her eyes are closed. She appears to be completely at peace, but I know there's more beneath the surface of this little siren than what meets the eye.

Speaking of what meets the eye, though, I can't help but take some time to appreciate her curves and glowing, tanned skin. Floating in front of me, there are just scraps of fabric separating my hands from her breasts and the apex of her thighs, and I have to clench my hands to keep myself from giving into my urges and pulling her bathing suit away.

Let the ocean have it, I want her bare to me, I think wildly, before getting myself back under control.

Elise opens her eyes as if she senses me watching her, irises sparkling. She could be a siren with the way she pulls me in, even just floating here, not touching me or saying anything at all.

Then she parts her lips and speaks, breaking the odd magic of the moment. "What are you thinking? You look very serious."

"Nothing," I lie, knowing that she's not going to accept it but still trying.

She flicks water up at me, just the slightest movement of fingers. "Tell me."

I wipe the water off my face with a scowl. "Stop being childish. I said nothing, so I mean nothing."

Now it's her turn to frown at me, splashing me with more gusto this time to the point I'm sputtering. "You're the most childish adult I know, for one, so don't be a hypocrite. Two, I know you better than that, Dan. You can't lie to me. Tell me what's on your mind."

"Besides drowning you?" I huff, slicking my hair back and out of my face. "I just... can't figure out why your dad behaves the way he does. That's all."

Her expression sobers, the fleeting seconds of playfulness dissipating. "I thought I understood why he acts the way he does, but now I'm not so sure. When all I cared about was advancing in the company and being his heiress, I never questioned him for being so cutthroat and unwavering. I just thought it was how he had to be to get where he was in life and stay there. Preferring Andries over me all those years... well, I just chalked that up to him being from an older generation. That's how things have always been done... the oldest son is the most cherished, or something."

"That doesn't make any of it fair, El. Sebastian is an intelligent man. He doesn't change because he doesn't *want* to, not because he isn't able."

"I know." She sighs, closing her eyes again. "I made excuses for his behavior in my own mind forever, but now I see that it was a mistake. He's acting ridiculous, to the detriment of the rest of the family. Speaking of my family... I spoke to Mom today."

I brush my hands through her hair as it floats in the water. "Yeah?"

"I think I've convinced her to come to the wedding on her own and bring the rest of my siblings. Dad can just stay behind if he wants to so badly." A small smile tugs at her lips. "I'd like to think that it was my talent for persuasion that made her change her mind, but I think she had already decided long before we spoke, and I was just the catalyst for her to say it out loud."

"Is that revenge on your dad or something? Cajoling your mom into coming to the wedding?"

Elise shakes her head, making little waves when she does so. "Not revenge, per se. Just the right thing to do."

"But what about your mission to split Andries and Roxanne up for daddy dearest?" I tease her, and she flicks water at me once more. This time I'm quick enough to dodge.

"Not happening anymore," she declares, and I feel a surge of pride in her. I knew she would make the right call, in the end. "If Andries finds out about the cabaret, it won't have anything to do with me. I'm not going to compromise my brother's relationship."

"See, it wasn't so hard to be a good person, now was it?" I joke, and she rolls her eyes at me. "Really though, El, I'm proud of you."

She blushes, only the tiniest bit, but I can tell she adores the praise. "Thank you, Dan. I haven't had anyone tell me that in a long time."

It would be so easy to scoop her up into my arms and kiss her mouth, her chest, and her neck, that my arms ache with the need to do so. It's clear, from the softness of her gaze and the way she's nibbling her bottom lip that she wants me to kiss her, and knowing that she's grown so much as a person makes me want to give in and reward her with one, but I resist. Elise becoming a better woman doesn't exactly make Johan disappear or her feelings for me change.

It's a cowardly move, but I have to flee, turning around and wading through the water with large strides to go back to shore. Seeing her floating there makes me think of our time in the private cove, and how she had me fuck her in the surf, and I can't take it.

I collapse on the beach towel, the hot sun drying me off but doing nothing to get rid of my arousal. Half erect, I have to reach down and adjust myself when I hear Elise stomping through the water toward me.

I close my eyes, using my ears to tell when her steps hit the sand, and then I can feel her standing over me and looking down. I can almost feel her annoyance in the air between us, and while that would have amused me before, now I'm just tired. Tired of wanting her. Tired of resisting.

I'm interrupted by my melancholy when her chill, wet body drops its weight on me. I grunt in shock as Elise spreads out entirely on top of me, sighing in contentment.

"You're so warm," she says.

"Elise," I bite out. "Get off of me."

Not surprisingly, she doesn't listen. "Why didn't you kiss me? I know you wanted to. Tell me," she pouts, fingers ghosting up my sides. It tickles, and I twitch.

"None of your damn business. Off, Elise!"

My words make her snuggle into me even more. My cock is thrilled with this new development, but that's the only part of me that approves.

"Oh, yes it is. It's my lips, after all."

"I told you that I don't want to hook up with you anymore. There, happy?" I try to turn over to shake her off, but it doesn't work. I grind my teeth together in frustration.

"But why not? Because of my brother? You told me you'd choose me over him—"

"That was before the love of your life came to stay with us, though," I interrupt. Elise freezes, and then finally rolls off of me, sitting on the beach towel and leaning back on her arms as she looks out over the horizon. Her feelings are clearly hurt, which wasn't my intention, but she's so damned stubborn that I don't know how else to get through to her.

"Johan was my first love, that's true," she says after a moment. "But that doesn't mean he is my last, you know."

My heart stutters in my chest. I sit up, looking down at her. She won't meet my eyes. "Are you trying to say you have feelings for me?"

Elise bites her full bottom lip again, making me want to kiss her even more. "I like you, Dan. A lot."

"Fuck, you can't say anything more than like, can you?" I curse under my breath, the little ember of hope in me flickering out.

Turning her head away, Elise inhales and exhales deeply a few times. Either holding back tears or amping herself up, I'm not sure which. After an even longer pause, she tells me quietly, "I told him when I was fifteen that I loved him and he broke my heart. How do I know that you aren't going to do the same thing?"

"Unlike him, I'm not going anywhere, El." Now she turns back to me, expression carefully neutral. "I'm not flying back to England in the fall like he is. I'm right here, and I want to give us a shot."

"Then why have you been pulling away?"

"Because I want something real. Because what I feel for you is genuine. I don't want to just hook up with you for a summer fling. I want you as my girlfriend."

The words hang heavily between us. "You mean like an exclusive, serious relationship?" Elise's tone is disbelieving, but if I'm not mistaken, there's a thread of hope in it, too. "Where our friends and the whole world know?"

I reach down and tuck a strand of her wet hair, stiff with salt, behind her ear. "Yes. Does that scare you?"

"I mean…" She looks away and shrugs one shoulder. "I… I don't know, okay? Everything's happening so fast."

It strikes me that I've known Elise for years, been close to her family the entire time, but it only took her one single summer to admit her love to Johan. We know each other so much better than she ever knew him, and her response annoys me.

"Sounds like it wasn't happening fast enough when it was with Johan," I grumble. Elise falls back onto the blanket with a frustrated groan, rubbing her hands over her face.

"Dan, can you fucking stop?"

"No, I can't," I snap. "You went to his fucking room the day he wanted to leave the villa and begged him to stay."

"Johan was gone for three years," she says indignantly. "It's normal to want to catch up with someone from your past."

"Does he have to stay under the same roof as us in order for you to catch up?"

"My brother invited him, and this vacation was thrown for him, wasn't it? Plus, how rude would it be for him to be invited to stay at the villa and then immediately thrown out?"

I can't look at her anymore, all my emotions are too wound up and confusing for me to make sense of. I want her so badly, but then again I hate the way she shows Johan affection even when I'm near. I gaze out at the horizon, trying to think of what exactly to say. Silence settles between us, and I know I'll have to be the one to break it.

"We can stay friends like before," I finally come up with. "But from my end, I'm no longer interested in hooking up with you for the sake of it. Do you understand?"

Elise shoots to her feet in a flurry of sand, all but running back to the water and diving in. I don't know why what I said was her breaking point, but I need to room the breath, too. Her silent fleeing tells me everything I need to know. I offered her the serious relationship that I want with her, and she was mute, dismissing me with her silence. It can mean nothing else except that Johan is still important to her, and she hasn't made her decision yet. I just can't accept that.

Elise's phone pings in her beach bag, distracting me from my thoughts. I can sit up enough to see her sitting in the water, deep enough that it covers her up to her shoulders, but she has her back to me. On a whim, I grab the phone where it's sitting on top of her towels.

It's Johan calling, and while my instinct is to just silence the call, I look back out at Elise again and decide to answer. Why should I be ashamed of being out here with her?

When I greet him, Johan is shocked enough that he sputters before he gets any words out. "Dan? Why are you answering Elise's phone? And where are you guys?"

"Elise wanted to leave the villa and go somewhere quieter so I just went with her. Why, what's going on?"

"...Can I join you guys, by any chance? Andries is sleeping off his hangover, Roxanne is nowhere to be found, and Lili and Robin just left to go to town. I'm pretty bored here."

I'm momentarily thrown by the odd question. "Uh, let me ask El. Hold on for a few minutes."

I mute the phone, unsure of what to do. Elise is still out in the water, oblivious to the call I'm on, but I'm pretty sure I don't want Johan here with us since I went to all this trouble of bringing us to this private place. Then again, he must be bored to tears there alone, and it's not his fault everyone else is tense with each other. But... what's the point of being in this secluded place with Elise if she doesn't love me? It's not like I can force her to change her emotions, and she has to choose who the best man for her really is, even if that means her being with Johan for good. The idea pisses me off, terrifies me, and makes me sick to my stomach, but it simply isn't my call to make.

With a heavy sigh, I stand and walk the phone over to Elise, who looks up at me in surprise. "It's Johan. He wants to join us."

Elise looks utterly confused. "Doesn't he have my brother to keep him company?"

"Apparently Andries is still dozing off and Roxanne isn't around. Everyone else left to go downtown."

She watches me to see if I will give her any indication of whether I want us to be alone or not, but when I refuse to rise to her bait, she just waves her hand in the air. "Fine. Tell him to come, then."

I unmute the phone, trying to keep the bitterness out of my voice as I tell Johan to come over and join us. He sounds so relieved to be invited that it almost makes me feel bad. Almost, but not really.

"I truly appreciate it, man," Johan says, his tone honest and warm. "Thank you so much."

With the conversation over, and Elise ignoring me again, I head back to my beach towel and lay down once more, tucking Elise's phone back into her bag and ruminating on what I've just done. How much of a pushover am I to be the one to invite Johan here with us? Loving Elise has made me so soft that I don't even recognize myself. It's almost laughable. Elise, of course, manages to notice the second that I'm relaxed again and comes out of the water to torment me once more. I hear her settle on the towel next to me, silent for the moment.

"Your ex is on his way," I tell her, not bothering to open my eyes. "I gave him our location. He should be here in twenty minutes."

Elise just looms for a minute or so more, but then she stretches out on the towel next to me, and my heart rate kicks up in response to how close she is.

"Thanks for everything, Dan," she tells me, her voice low. Then, she plants her lips softly on my shoulder, and before I can comprehend that, she's already kissing my cheek.

I grab her shoulder and hold her in place. "Okay, enough, El."

Elise grabs my hand where it's holding her, prying it off and kissing a path from the palm of my hand back to my shoulder again. My brain is shorting out at the things she's making me feel, but I have to stay centered and not give in. If I let Elise know that she has this kind of power over me, she'll never leave me be.

In one swift movement, I throw my leg over her hips and roll her onto her back, using her shock to grab her wrists in my hands and pin them above her head before she can get her bearings. Elise gasps, eyes flying open wide as she looks up at me, all stretched out and vulnerable. My knees are on the blanket on either side of her body, and again, I'm all too aware of how little clothing separates us—just my swim briefs and her bikini. I smirk down at her, enjoying that I've been able to get over on her.

"I said enough," I growl, making her shiver beneath me.

"Or else what?" she snaps back in a dare.

Elise thinks she has power over me right now, even though I have her pinned down this way. I can see it in her eyes, and in the smug way her mouth is pulling up at the corners. Suddenly I'm annoyed with how no matter what I do, she never feels like I'm the one in control, and her trying to be all seductive right now while Johan is on his way is just more manipulation. How can one woman be so irresistible yet so infuriating, all at the same time?

I want Johan as far from my mind as possible with Elise beneath me like this, but then an idea strikes me that is almost too nefarious to enact. Not nefarious enough, though, that I won't go through with it.

Johan is a good lad and hasn't done anything that I can really take offense to, but the fact that he is still leaving the idea of pursuing Elise open means that he doesn't see me as the threat that I really am. If I want Elise, I can have her, at least physically, and it's about time that I prove it to Johan.

I'll fuck Elise, right now, until Johan arrives and sees us. I just know he'll be too mortified to stay and flee back to the villa. It's a malefic, but brilliant plan, and it will prove once and for all that I am not someone to be fucked with. Too many people are playing with my heart and my friendship lately, and I've had more than enough.

I release one wrist and grab her perfect face in my hand. "Or else I'll fuck you senseless."

She must assume that this is an invitation, because while I'm still working out my plan in my mind, Elise closes the gap between her and me, slanting her mouth against mine with enough gusto that I have no doubt whether she's still playing with me or not. My eyes could almost roll back in my head, it feels so good to be kissing her again, and Elise is pulling out all the stops now that she thinks she has me in her snare. I can't help but enjoy the hell out of it; her tongue dancing against mine, the way she nips at my lip when she pulls away, and the small noises she gives me while we make out. Her mouth tastes so good, but not as good as another part of her body that I plan to explore as soon as possible.

Even though I know that I'm fucking her for my own reasons, there's no denying that she affects me in a devastating way. I'm as hard as iron, rubbing against the soft skin of her belly through my briefs, and her clever tongue has my head buzzing.

Moving her mouth to my jawline, she licks a path from there to my ear, where she sucks the lobe between her teeth and bites down. I inhale sharply, capturing her mouth to dominate her once more, and then I'm the one kissing a path away from her sinful lips.

First her jawline, which I only ghost my lips across, before sucking a mark onto the area right where her jaw meets her neck that drives her wild. When she's breathing heavily for me, her hands restless as they wander over my chest and arms, I scatter kisses across her pulse point and then her collarbone. She takes the cue from the direction I'm heading, raising her back up enough that I can reach behind her and untie her bathing suit, throwing it away in the sand. Her nipples are hard already, and when I suck one turgid peak into my mouth she tastes like salt and something that is all Elise—sweet and spicy.

Her sounds of encouragement turn deep as I work over her nipples with my teeth, tongue, and lips, plumping her breasts with my hands as I do so. I adore her body, even her sharp mouth, which turns so soft when I kiss it.

She's wiggling beneath me, anxious for more but loving all the attention I'm giving her already.

"Dan," she breathes, her fingernails scraping my scalp. "You're driving me crazy. I need more."

"More what, little ice queen?" I ask, letting her nipple pop out of my mouth.

She reaches down and thumbs my bottom lip, her pupils blown wide with arousal. "More of you. Specifically this mouth of yours."

Her words are enough to make me moan, but I hold them back. "You're going to have to be more specific…"

Elise huffs, and then she's pushing my head downwards, and I chuckle to myself. Wrapping my hands around her ribs, I slide my fingers down slowly at the same time I lick a path from her sternum to her belly button, and then the hollows of her hip bones. Elise keeps her hands in my hair, desperate for that layer of control even as I work her over. Little does she know I'm the one calling the shots, even if she doesn't know it yet.

Her bottoms come away just as easily as her top did, and when the scent of her arousal hits me, I can't wait any longer to have my tongue in her. I part her folds with my thumbs, licking a path from her entrance to her clit and then back again. She inhales shakily, but it turns into a full-throated moan when I trace a circle around her clit. It would be so easy to make her come right now, and she's so sweet and wet for me that it's almost an undeniable urge, but a part of me only wants her to come right now with my cock deep inside of her pussy, claiming her in ways only I ever have.

I take it slow as I eat her out, suckling her clit before dipping my tongue into her entrance, repeating the same pathway over and over again until her hips are moving of their own accord.

"Don't fucking stop," she grits out from between her teeth. My hands are running up her stomach to tweak her nipples, and I can feel her muscles there fluttering as she gets close to orgasm.

That's when I pull away, kissing down her inner thighs even as she gasps in indignation.

"I told you not to stop, Dan!"

I give her a quick love bite, laughing against her skin when she yelps. "You don't tell me what to do, Elise. When are you going to learn that?"

"But I'm so close," she pouts. "You were so close to making me come."

Slithering up her body and taking her lips in a kiss again, I can't help but feel a rush of affection for the way she welcomes me, even with her juices still on my tongue. "Oh I'm still going to make you come," I promise her. "Just on my terms."

She raises herself up on her elbows, her face, and neck beautifully flush with passion. Reaching forward with one hand, she caresses my chest, asking, "And what are your terms, exactly?"

"You, my dear Elise, are only going to come on my cock." I thrust into her hip to emphasize my point, and her breath comes out of her lungs like she's been struck.

"Hurry then," she pleads, all of her bravado washed away by need. I feel like yelling from the rooftops that only I can make her feel this way. I'm the only one who can fuck her, no one else. Certainly not Johan.

Remembering that her ex is on his way makes my desire for her even more urgent. I strip my own briefs off, sitting up and straddling Elise again. I remove her hand from my chest and move it down to my cock, and the second she wraps her fingers around it I can feel all my nerves come alive. She strokes me a few times before sweeping the bead of pre-cum from the tip and putting her finger in her mouth, sucking it off.

Fuck, she's so hot I can't take it anymore. "Lie back," I demand, grabbing her thighs and pulling her towards me. She squeaks, falling back on her elbows, her chest rising and falling faster and faster as I pull her legs apart.

I take a second to admire how wet and ready she is for me, glistening and pink in the summer sun, before I fist my cock in my hand and position myself at her entrance. Elise pushes herself up a little more, and we both watch as I slide inside of her to the hilt, bottoming out in her pussy with a moan that feels like it's coming from my soul. Elise whimpers, unable to look away as I begin to fuck her vigorously. I can't take it slow, not with how long I've been wanting her, and how much she's been teasing me. She's so hot and tight that it's a wonder I haven't given her all my worldly possessions just to be able to touch her like this, but from the way she's looking at my manhood sliding in and out of her, her teeth locked onto her bottom lip, I'm sure she's just addicted to me as I am her.

Elise wraps her legs around my waist, her heels drumming against my spine, guiding me to meet the pace that she needs so badly. She wants me deep and slow, stroking her g-spot with each thrust, and I oblige. She falls backward, unable to hold herself up any longer, back arching as I hit all those secret spots that drive her insane. Her pussy is so wet that it feels almost like it's sucking me in, and I have to clench my jaw to keep from coming before she does.

I have to last, even as the sounds of our flesh slapping together fills my ears and I start to lose track of where she ends and I begin. I slow down enough to lean forward, sucking each nipple into my mouth again one at a time, and Elise's whimpers turn into what sounds like sobs of pleasure.

"Yes, yes, yes," she chants, hands gripping hard in my hair again and holding me against her breasts until her nipples are hard and glistening from my attention. Each time I lick her peaks, her pussy flutters around my cock.

I'm not going to last. Fuck, I really want to, but the idea of filling her up with my cum with Johan just minutes away from arriving is too much for me to handle. I grab her hands as I raise my head, pinning her wrists on the towel above her and claiming her mouth in a passionate kiss. I drink down her moans like water, letting my body take over as my mind loses the ability to focus on anything but *her*. Pushing my hips forward so her pelvis tilts up, I piston my cock in and out of her just how I need it, knowing that she's going to come for me regardless. When I feel her hands struggle in my grasp, fingers flexing as her pussy starts to tighten even more, I know she's almost there, and I'm going to make us come at the same time.

With three more powerful thrusts, Elise falls over the edge into an orgasm that has her screaming her satisfaction into my mouth. Her body bucks, pussy milking my cock, dragging me right over that same edge with her. It feels like some sort of band is snapping within me, and once it does, I'm awash in so much pleasure that the world tilts around me. I fill Elise with my seed, coating her walls as I continue to fuck her until we are both spent. She breaks the kiss, pressing her forehead to mine and closing her eyes, legs twitching with the aftershocks of what we've just done.

This is the moment for a romantic declaration of love, or some soft kissing in the afterglow of it all while cuddling. I can see on Elise's face that she's expecting affection and aftercare, her body warm and satisfied, but I'm not quite done with her yet. Because we're still alone here on the beach, and our special guest hasn't arrived yet. That just won't do.

With our foreheads still pressed together, I ask her, "You want to be a good girl?"

Elise nods, and I cup her jaw, making her look at me. "Then I want you to suck me off. Right now."

I raise myself up fully on my knees, back to the ocean, and Elise slides down and props herself up on her elbow. I'm still half erect from fucking her, but seeing how languid and willing she is has me hot, and I feel the blood rushing back to my cock. She reaches out and strokes me a few times with her free hand, head resting on her other one as she holds herself up.

I can see the rocks where we entered the hidden cove, but Elise can't. I put my hand on her head and guide her forward until her lips are touching the blunt head of my member, her tongue snaking out and tasting me quickly. She hums in her throat, as if in approval, opening her pink, kiss-swollen lips and taking the entire head into the hot cavern of her mouth. It's heaven, and knowing that she's tasting herself on my cock makes it even better.

I feed my length into her mouth until I hit the back of her throat. I can see her eyes water, but she doesn't complain, using her hand for the rest of my cock that just can't possibly fit inside, her saliva easing the movements of her palm. She licks and sucks me as if pleasing me is her only purpose on this earth, following my cues exactly when I lay my hand on her head and show her just how I want her to pleasure me. Her eyes flutter closed, and I think the sight of her so well-pleasured, letting me fuck her mouth, will stick with me forever.

I let my moans fall from my lips freely and unabashedly. My balls tighten up against my body, my grip on Elise's hair becoming tighter. I move her head faster with my hand, the increased pace so incredible that it feels like the breath has been sucked out of my lungs. I can't help but close my eyes, soaking in all the sensations her mouth is giving me, but when I open them again languidly, a spike of adrenaline shoots through me like ice.

There, on the rocky path across from us, is Johan. Elise can't see him, her back still turned in that direction, but I can see him as clear as day. He's frozen in place, petrified, all the blood having drained from his tan face. I can't see his expression in detail from here, but I get the feeling that he's in shock.

Johan meets my eyes, his going even wider, if that's possible, and he pivots on a dime, walking away so fast that it might as well have been a sprint.

Fuck yes, I think, pleasure surging through me. *He saw her sucking me, and he ran. Now he knows she's mine.*

The adrenaline and knowledge that Johan caught us, mixed with Elise's hot, perfect little mouth has me cumming again so suddenly that it catches both of us off guard. My body curls forward with the force of it, a strained, helpless noise escaping me. It's so, so good, that it makes my vision white out for a split second.

Elise handles it better than I do, and when I can focus again, I see and feel her swallowing all my come, licking me clean before falling back with a sigh, her eyes closed and her face to the sky. She has no idea what has just occurred, and that makes it even sweeter for me.

"I think I deserve some affection after that," she tells me, not even bothering to open her eyes. "Come hold me."

I'm all too happy to give in to her demands now, laying flat and letting her snuggle up on me, her head pillowed on my chest. She's almost boneless as she lays on me, soaking in the warmth from the sun and my body, letting out a contented sigh. This gives me pause because Elise knows Johan is supposed to be joining us, so why isn't she getting up to clean herself?

I decide, kissing the top of her head, that I don't really care what the reasoning is. She's mine today, her skin silky as I stroke my hand up and down her back in a motion of lazy comfort as we simply enjoy each other's presence. I feel her exhale deeply, and look down to see her eyes fluttering closed.

She's probably a mess down there. Maybe I should have her go clean up, and I'll go with her.

I love thinking about how Elise lets me fill her up raw every time, but this time, something else accompanies that line of thinking. I still, feeling apprehensive.

"El, are you on the pill or something? Not that I wouldn't like having you pregnant with our child to piss off your ex even more, but…"

Now she freezes. "Shit!" she exclaims, raising herself up on her hands to look down at me. "No, um, I've got to take something. The risk is low, but still."

I brush my knuckles down the side of her face. "It's alright. We'll go to the pharmacy later on. For now, just lay back down."

She nods and moves to do so, but then we both hear her phone ring. Her bag is within reach, and it's easy for her to grab the device and open the message. I have a feeling I know who it is, but it isn't until she holds the phone up for me to see that my suspicions are confirmed.

Johan: Never mind about me joining you guys. You seemed busy. I'm heading to Ibiza tomorrow. See you at the wedding.

There's a beat of silence where I wonder if she's going to freak out or not, but when she doesn't, I narrow my eyes at her, the truth hitting me hard. "You knew I fucked you for him to catch us, didn't you?"

She shrugs, throwing the phone back in her bag. "It's better this way. A clean break with my past."

I'm so overcome with emotion for this woman that I feel like it's spilling from my pores. She chose me so absolutely that she made sure Johan got a clear picture of how serious we were. She was unashamed to be seen with me and didn't even care that he was leaving.

"I love you, El. Fuck, I do." I grab her face in my hand and crush my mouth to hers, not even caring that she can't say those three little words back yet. What she's done for me is all the indication that I need about her feelings, and how strong they are.

She's proved that she loves me beyond words, and that makes me love her even more. I didn't think it was possible, but I do.

CHAPTER 10

Elise

By the time we make it to the pharmacy, the adrenaline of what Dan and I have done is starting to wear off. I thought that I would be mortified by what I had been willing to do to make my intentions clear to Johan after the moment had passed, but even now that I've had some time to sit with it I can't make myself regret my previous decisions. They may have been devious in a way, but I'm sure that I have got my point across.

I didn't know until Dan started to kiss me on the beach what I truly wanted, but as soon as we started making out, I was confident that it was him I wanted. Not just confident but totally sure, at least in that moment. It's like as soon as he has his hands, and especially his mouth, on me, I lose all sense of anything else. When I'm with Dan, the thought of ever being with anyone else is absurd.

As we walk inside he takes my hand as casually as anything, linking our fingers together and absentmindedly running his thumb over my knuckle. I am so aware of everything he does—every touch, every breath. There is still salt in our hair and sand on our bodies, but it doesn't even matter to me at the moment. Not as long as everything stays this way.

The overhead lights of the pharmacy are bright and harsh, and we seem to be almost the only ones in the place. Greeting us kindly, the pharmacist waves us over. She's an older woman with dark blond hair, for which I'm thankful. It might seem silly, but I don't want to be asking a male pharmacist for EllaOne.

"Absolutely," the pharmacist tells me when I awkwardly ask for the pill. She fishes it from a shelf behind her, setting the package on the counter in front of me. "Is there anything else I can get for the two of you today?"

Dan squeezes my hand to get my attention. "You really should get on birth control, Elise. Almost every sexually active woman your age is."

"You are starting to sound like my mom," I roll my eyes, snatching the EllaOne package off the counter. "Why don't *you* get on birth control?"

"It's called condoms, sweetheart, and I've got plenty of them in my bag if you want."

"No, not condoms. Something like pills," I turn to the pharmacist, who has an odd look on her face now. "Isn't there a pill or something similar he can take instead of me?"

I hear Dan chuckling as the woman scratches her head, looking uncomfortable. "I'm afraid, at the moment, that the only real option for men is condoms. Or a vasectomy, but that's—"

"Absolutely not!" Dan interjects. "You aren't cutting me. That I can guarantee you."

I look between Dan and the pharmacist. "Wait, are you being serious? It's 2022 and there isn't a single pill he can take?"

"Unfortunately, no." She shakes her head, but there is a look of sad understanding on her expression. "I get your frustration, though. There is certainly a gap in the availability of birth control between men and women, but if you don't like the pill, there are other long-term options that you can look into that you won't have to think about every day. I can give you some pamphlets to look over if you're interested in implants or something of that nature."

"That's just silly," I fume. "I should talk to my Aunt Maud about this. She's a project development manager in a lab in Germany. I'm sure she knows what's up in the birth control field."

Dan raises one eyebrow, "Yes, Elise, I'm sure your aunt is going to stop whatever project she's working on to go and help develop a pill for me."

"It's not just for you Dan," I insist. "It will be for men all over the world."

"Yes, fantastic, but for now we're here for us, not to save the world."

"If you want to get started, I'd recommend this pill which is very light and has the least side effects." The pharmacist jumps into the conversation, "But it will take ten days to become effective. So, you'll definitely need a backup plan."

"She means condoms," Dan says for the second time, nudging me with his shoulder.

"I've got it," I grumble, taking the round, pale yellow pill holder from the pharmacist and dropping it into my purse.

I'll read all the instructions and details later. "We'll try this, but I'm still talking to my aunt about it."

"Good luck," the older woman says earnestly. "Male birth control would certainly be a wonderful innovation."

After paying for the EllaOne and the birth control, we climb into the car that Dan had told to wait for us, and he gives the driver the location of a small coffee shop in Piazzetta. I look at him, surprised because I've been under the impression that we were going back to the villa. Dan's eyes are soft as he raises our still joined hands and kisses the back of mine.

"Just humor me, I'm not ready for my afternoon with you to be over yet."

I smile in agreement and snuggle into his side for the drive over. We don't speak much, even after the little squabble over birth control in the pharmacy, content in just being in each other's company.

The cafe is tucked into a corner of the street, and we seat ourselves at a wrought iron table under a vast umbrella. When the server bustles over, we both get espressos and San Pelligrinos, parched and a little tired from our sexy beach workout earlier. Dan insists on a small piece of tiramisu for us to split, reasonably explaining that it'd be best for me to have some food on my stomach when I take the new medication.

The sugar goes well with the hot, bitter espresso, and I chase the first drink and bite with the EllaOne and a sip of water. I'm a little more apprehensive about birth control, flipping through the tiny pamphlet that is inside the pill case with a frown. It unfolds like origami, with print so tiny that I have to squint to read it.

"How do they expect anyone to understand all of this? Look at how long the list of side effects is!"

"Just take the pill, Elise," Dan drawls over his espresso cup. "You'll be fine."

I pop the pill out of the blister pack, taking it with a swig of sparkling water before I can have any more second thoughts. I don't want to give Dan any reason to back out of us sleeping together again, so I'll take the stupid pills if I have to.

I'm in the middle of scheduling an alarm to remind me to take birth control at the same time every day while glancing at the text on the prescription pamphlet when I hear my phone go off in my beach bag. Dan is reading an article on his phone while I peruse my medication literature, and he only offers me a quick glance as I dig the mobile out and flick the screen on with a touch of my finger.

I still, my chest getting a little tight when I see that it's my father who has messaged me. I expected it to be Andries railing against Dan and I for driving Johan away, but even that correspondence would be preferable to talking with my dad right now.

The message is free of any words from him personally, though. Instead, Dad has simply sent me a link to yet another article about Roxanne's Bar Rouge scandal. I sigh, thinking that it's probably just another rehash similar to all the others, but the tone of this article seems more serious than the others. It doesn't outright say that anything new has happened, but I get the feeling as I read more and more that tensions are rising even more back home.

Then Dad messages me again, and it simply says, *Pretty interesting, huh?*

Dan must see the disturbed look on my face because he puts his phone down and leans in. "Hey, are you okay?"

I swallow hard, switching my phone off without replying and throwing it back into my bag. "Yeah. Fine."

"Don't lie to me, El."

"It's just Dad..." I sigh heavily, tilting my head back and taking a deep breath. "He's still pressuring me to spill all the news to Andries about Roxanne's scandal. It's not even direct, anymore. He just keeps peppering me with articles and Twitter screenshots about how it's all going down back home, and it makes me feel like I can't escape it."

"I know he wants them to split up, but doesn't this seem like an odd tactic to you? Some of this heat is going to come back on Andries, and be associated with the Van den Bosch name, so I would think he'd want to sweep it under the rug more or less."

I bite my lip, thinking. "Actually, I think he has a hand in this. Or, to be more accurate, I think *Karl* is the mastermind behind it all. Maybe because I snubbed him when he wanted me to screw Roxanne over, and now he's seeking out some kind of revenge against me and Roxie at the same time."

"That prick sure can't take any kind of rejection from women, can he?" Dan shakes his head. "What an insecure asshole."

"Agreed. But my fear is that if Karl is responsible for all this, then I feel like Dad has to know at least somewhat. I hate to think it, but it's possible that my dad is involved, and now he's counting on me to complete the circuit and run and tell everything to Andries."

Dan drains his espresso and folds his hands behind his head, looking thoughtful. "Roxanne really screwed herself over on every front when it comes to that cabaret. Obviously, she should've been honest with him from the beginning about owning it," he scoffs. "I mean, what was she thinking? How could owning a cabaret be worse than being an escort? She's—"

"I think we both know the answer to that, Dan. She was giving my brother the truth little by little because she was afraid of losing him. It's what made her lie about her job in the first place. It almost seems like she lies as a defense mechanism."

"Be that as it may," Dan continues, "her second opportunity to come clean came when she found out about this scandal in the beginning. I think Andries would have been pissed, but I think he would have gotten over it, and imagine how mad your dad would be if all the work he and Karl did to sabotage the two of them was for nothing? It would have been great. But now she's dug herself deeper. She *has* to be the one to tell him if there's any hope of her recovering from these lies."

"I'm really afraid it might be too late…" I tap my fingers on the stone table, looking out at the blue sky behind Dan, lost in thought. Dan seems to be thinking, too, but eventually, he speaks up once more.

"Do you really think he'll end their engagement over a freaking cabaret? If you throw a stone in Amsterdam you'll hit one. It isn't even a big deal."

"I don't know… this is Andries we are talking about, so it's a complete tossup how he'll react."

"They are both such idiots sometimes…."

"I know. Obviously, it's the lie that's the biggest problem, not the cabaret, but Andries has standards that are higher than the moon—" my phone goes off once more mid-sentence, and when I lean over to grab it again, I see it's my brother calling me, as if he somehow knew we were talking about him. "Speaking of which…" I swipe the arrow on the screen to pick up the call, but I can't even get the first breath of a greeting out before my brother is fuming at me.

"He–"

"What the hell did you do to Johan? He is once again in his room packing to leave and won't take no for an answer. The man looks absolutely *miserable* and I just know that you're involved!"

I bristle. There's no way that I'd ever admit to my brother what Dan and I had actually been doing, but frankly, it's none of his business. "I didn't do anything. Maybe he's just tired of being here with Andries the broody, drunk poet."

He scoffs. "It's got nothing to do with me, El, and you know it!"

"Whatever. You're being annoying as fuck. I'm hanging up."

"Don't you dare—"

I follow through with the threat, ending the call and throwing the phone back into my bag with more force than is necessary. Dan is looking at me cautiously.

"What's gotten into him?" he asks.

"It's because his precious friend Johan is packing up to leave tomorrow. He can't handle the rejection."

"Does he know why Johan is leaving?" Dan sounds innocent, but there is a gleam in his eye that lets me know he's taking a certain joy in having driven Johan off in such a scandalous way.

I shake my head. "Nope. And Johan is enough of a gentleman to keep it to himself." I blush when Dan smiles at me across the table wolfishly, reaching forward and grabbing my hand, his thumb sliding over the pulse point in my wrist. It's such a small caress, but knowing the secrets we share makes it feel like so much more. "I can't believe I did that. I swear…"

Now Dan's grip on my hand tightens, and his gaze grows more serious. Heated, even, and it makes my heart race. "I know you love me," he declares, and I know he means it one hundred percent. "Even if you find it hard to admit to yourself, what you did on the beach… knowing your ex would see us… that was proof enough for me."

Even though part of me wants to tell him so badly that yes, I love him, there's an even bigger part of me that is still so afraid. "I enjoy this little thing we have going on and I don't want it to end, I already told you that," I say cooly, but Dan huffs and I know he isn't buying into my aloof act.

"Come here, Elise," he commands.

I look around at the semi-crowded street, unsure of what he wants. "What do you mean?"

"Just come here."

I pull my hand out of his and, still a bit confused, walk around the table. Dan grabs me by the hips, maneuvering me until I'm sitting in his lap. I land with a gasp, and his face is suddenly so close to mine that I can feel him breathing, the two of us sharing breaths, and it takes me so off guard that I forget how public this space is.

"Why are you so guarded, Miss Elise?" he asks, his voice low and rumbling in his chest. "Are you afraid that you're falling for me?"

I don't know what to say, but before I can take a breath to answer, Dan's phone starts ringing. It's sitting face up on the table, and when it becomes apparent that it is, yet again, my brother calling, Dan reaches forward around my body to silence the call without a second thought. I raise my eyebrows in surprise.

"You aren't going to answer?"

"I want an answer from you first," he drags his knuckles down my cheek and I shiver. Being so close to him makes it hard to think…

"I need time, Dan," I manage to tell him finally. "But yes, I wouldn't have done it if you were just some summer fling."

He makes a noise of contentment, lowering his hands to my hips again and pulling me forward just enough to press his lips against my forehead. Affection blooms in me, and it's only natural for me to loop my arms around his neck and sink into his body. I tilt my face up towards his, and our lips come together with ease. I kiss him hard, putting all the emotions into it that I'm too afraid to say out loud still, and Dan takes it all happily. Once we pull apart, he brings my hand to his lips, ghosting a kiss on the back of it and gazing at me with so much naked love in his eyes that it's hard to comprehend.

"Promise me something, El."

"What?" I breathe.

"Promise me that you'll let me take you on a real date before we leave Capri. Out to a fancy dinner with candles and a white tablecloth like you deserve. Not that I haven't had fun with all the other types of meetups we've been having, but I want it all. The sex on the beach *and* the romantic candlelit meals. What do you say?"

DAN.

I'm surprised to feel a lump in my throat, as if I might cry, and I'm not even sure why exactly. There's just something about the raw sincerity in Dan's voice, and the overly romantic notions that he's so invested in that makes me melt for him. His words make me think of the two of us together in the future, showing up to events together, me on his arm, and what it would feel like for our relationship to be public.

I think it would feel good. Wonderful, even.

"Yes," I sigh, going back in for another kiss, feeling Dan's hands skim up my back as I touch my mouth to his. "I'd love that."

CHAPTER 11

Elise

A significant amount of time has passed when Dan and I return, but somehow Andries is waiting for us the second we walk into the villa, leaning on the doorframe to the entrance like he knew exactly when we would be arriving.

I groan as soon as I see him, muttering under my breath to Dan. "Here we go. Why can't he just mind his own business?"

"It's Andries. He thinks everything is his business," Dan points out, and I can't help but agree with him.

There's no escaping my brother, but to my surprise he lets Dan pass him by with just a brief greeting. I think I might also be lucky, but when I go to walk inside he grabs me by the elbow. I glare at Dan's retreating back, knowing that he's aware that Andries has stopped me but is continuing to flee nonetheless. Not that I can blame him. I probably would have done the same.

"Let me go Andries."

"Nice to see you too, lil sis," he drawls. "Have a nice afternoon out fucking around with my best friend?"

I jerk my arm out of his grasp, turning my nose up at him. "It was fabulous, if you must know. Now let me through."

He steps in front of me, a stony expression on his face. "You need to go talk to Johan and get him to stay."

"What is it with you and Johan!" I exclaim, throwing my arms up in exasperation. "Is this your engagement trip with Roxanne or with Johan? Because you're obsessed."

"I'm not obsessed. The fact of the matter is that I invited him to the villa and he's been treated so negatively this entire time that it makes me feel like an awful host and friend. He told me he has a last minute birthday party in Ibiza to go to, but I know that he's lying. He doesn't even look like he believes that himself."

"What Johan does is none of my concern, and it shouldn't be yours, either."

"El, can you just go talk to him? Something is clearly going on and I know it involves you."

I search his face, and see beyond the annoyance there is genuine regret that Johan has to leave after having such a terrible time. It makes me pause, and reconsider my own intentions when it comes to making him leave. I want him to understand that I'm with Dan... we might not be in an official relationship yet, but it's clear in every other way. On the other hand, it is nice to see him again, and I don't have any hard feelings towards Johan knowing now that he wasn't the one that ghosted me. Even though I don't want to go talk to him about it—at all—I guess I at least owe it to Johan and Andries both to do so.

"Fine," I grumble, running my hand through my hair in annoyance. "But this is the last time I'm going to let you boss me around."

There is a slight twitch of amusement across Andries's mouth. "Whatever you need to tell yourself."

I shoulder past him, pissed off but still understanding why he wants me to talk to his new friend so badly. Johan has to be hurt, and while I obviously wanted him to catch us, I do agree that it's best that he doesn't leave with a sour taste in his mouth regarding my brother, Dan, and me.

I don't know if I'll be able to get him to be friendly with Dan after what he saw this afternoon, but at the very least I can patch things up concerning my brother and me.

Johan's door is only slightly cracked, but I don't want to knock and give him the chance to shut it and lock me out. I push it open slowly, giving him plenty of warning that someone is entering. When he sees it's me, his neutral expression turns dark.

"What could you possibly want, Elise? I was under the impression you were... *busy*."

"Dan and I just got back," I tell him honestly. "Andries is pretty upset you're leaving and wanted me to come check up on you."

He scoffs. "Yeah, right."

"I'm not lying," I insist, but he's giving me the cold shoulder now, pretending that I don't exist while he folds his clothes and places each item neatly into his suitcase. I cross my arms, tapping my foot as I wait for him to acknowledge me, but it's becoming clearer by the second that he's serious about shutting me out completely. He takes his phone out for a moment, answering a text message, but once he's done the phone goes right back into his pocket and he's back to ignoring me.

"Johan—" I try, but he turns and glares at me.

"The message was clear, El. I'll leave you and Dan alone. I'm sorry that I ever came to Capri…"

I approach him slowly, and to my surprise, he allows me, dropping the shirt he's folding as I come close. His shoulders sag, before he sits on the bed, scrubbing his hands through his hair a few times in clear frustration. I sit next to him, waiting until he lets his hands fall to his sides to the mattress to place one of mine over his.

"Johan, it has still been amazing seeing you again. It allowed us to talk and clear up all the confusion about the ghosting thing, but now—"

"What if it was Dan who did that to screw us over?" he interposes so quickly that it catches me off guard.

Looking at his face, there seems to be a war between understanding and the surprising amount of anger he's holding about what he saw this afternoon. Even though I swore I wouldn't feel bad about it, a little seed of guilt starts to bury itself into me.

"Dan?" I laugh, shaking my head. "Like, on his own without my brother knowing about it?"

"Yes, that's exactly what I mean. That dude seems totally fucked up and super possessive. How long has he had his eyes on you?"

"I guarantee even if he was attracted to me back then, Dan wasn't possessive of his best friend's fifteen year old sister!" My tone is incredulous. "I'm sure it wasn't him. He didn't even know about you until he found a photo of us a month ago or so. Plus he would have no way of accessing my phone back then."

Johan doesn't seem like he believes me, but he's fooling himself. "Are you sure he isn't lying?"

"Positive. Whoever it was, it wasn't Dan."

"Alright…" Johan sighs heavily. "So you and him…. It's not just a summer fling, is it?"

The question gives me pause, and I turn it over in my mind a few times before answering. I'm still not being completely honest with myself, but I don't want to lie to Johan, either. "I don't know what the future holds for Dan and me. For now, I'm enjoying his company, and he's enjoying mine."

"Then why aren't the two of you officially together?" He turns away from me now, looking out the window in his suite and out into the city. "You guys behave like a couple, but just pretending you're a casual fling is going to end up getting people hurt." He pauses, thinking. "It has *already* gotten people hurt, I should say."

That little bit of guilt flares up in me again. "We're just taking our time. Plus, my brother would totally freak out. Dan is his best friend, after all, and with all the shitty things our parents are putting him through I don't want to add to his misery."

Johan huffs a sardonic laugh. "So is it only because of your brother, then?"

"Like I said, we're also just taking our time. I'm not ready to declare what we have going on as something serious yet." I level a meaningful look at him, even if he is only looking at me from the corner of his eye. "You know the last time I was serious about someone, they ghosted me for years."

"El..." he mutters, sounding exhausted.

"I know it wasn't your fault, but it left a hole in me nonetheless. It felt like betrayal, and it still does in some ways. It's still going to take some time for me to move past that."

"I get that," Johan admits reluctantly. There's a long pause in our conversation, both of us thinking about what could have been of us if things had been different. After some time, Johan speaks again. "I'm leaving tomorrow. Tell your brother my decision is final. He clearly didn't know shit about how serious your relationship between you and Dan was or else he would have never invited me here to be the third wheel."

"I'm so sorry about all of this," I wince, knowing he's right. "Can we still be friends, though? My parents really want to see you again, so let's still have that dinner at home when I get back." When Johan doesn't respond, I add, "I'm sure Hannah would be delighted to give you an update on her collection of random things she's accumulated over the years."

"El, I'm not sure..."

"Please?" I bump his shoulder with mine until he looks at me. "My parents really like you and Mom already knows about you coming by."

He still doesn't look at all convinced. "Will your brother be there?"

I shrug. "Probably not. He isn't exactly welcome due to his relationship with Roxanne."

"That still strikes me as so strange," he muses, some of the tension in the room going away now that the subject is changing. "He and your mother always seemed so close. I thought they had a great relationship for a mother and son, so I wouldn't think that she would be so against him marrying whoever made him happy."

"She's on the fence about it," I admit. "I'm making some headway into convincing her to come to the wedding, and I bet if we join forces at dinner we can convince her to go."

Johan rolls his eyes to the ceiling, contemplation written all over his face, before he nods, having made up his mind. "Okay. For your brother's sake, I can come have dinner with you. For right now, though, I think I need some time alone."

"Message received." I stand and stretch my arms over my head before walking to the door. "I'll leave you alone. Thanks for actually talking to me."

He simply nods as I leave, shutting the door fully behind me to give Johan the privacy he wants. I suppose I might as well find my brother and tell him the news, because if not, Andries will just track me down instead.

I find my brother half asleep in one of the loungers on the terrace, a book open on the low table beside the chair. When I approach him, clearing my throat, he sits up and pushes his sunglasses away from his eyes. When he sees that it's me he rotates and stands, most likely anxious to hear about my meetup with Johan.

"How did it go?" he asks.

"He's still leaving for Ibiza tomorrow."

"You were supposed to get him to stay!" Andries complains, pinching the bridge of his nose in exasperation.

"He really wants to leave. There's nothing I can do about that. But he isn't mad at you or anything. In fact, he's coming to the family estate for dinner once we get home. I think Johan and I can work as a team to convince Mom to attend your wedding."

Andries narrows his eyes at me, crossing his arms. "Are you really trying to convince Mom to attend the wedding?"

"Well, yes. Why are you asking?"

"I don't know… I, um, I can't shake the feeling that you might still be on Dad's side." When I don't answer, he stares right through me and then asks, "Are you going to pull a fast one and try to ruin my wedding, or are you really on my side this time?"

I make a show of checking my nails as he rants, waiting until he's finished speaking. "Honestly, Andries, as of right now I'm not on anyone's *side*. Instead, I'm doing what I think is right. But… if you could accept Dan and I seeing each other, I would do everything in my power to convince Mom to come to the wedding." It's a split second decision to try and convince my brother to loosen up on the restrictions he wants to put on us, and I hope it doesn't backfire on me.

He doesn't look thrilled. "So, this is how it's gonna play out, huh? Either I accept your little fling with my best friend or you're going to try and fuck my wedding up?"

I don't rise to his bait, remaining calm. "You can't ask for tolerance if you aren't tolerant yourself, you know."

My brother lets out a huge breath, and when he responds there's more honesty in his tone than I expected. "I just don't think Dan is the right man for you, El. I mean, just a month or two ago he was still fucking Jessica. Do you really think–"

"You are literally about to get married to a former prostitute," I point out, raising my eyebrows. "Shut up, okay? You have no room to talk."

Andries is speechless, and without a word, he turns and walks towards the railing at the edge of the terrace. He leans over it, placing his crossed arms on top of it and gazing out at the sea in contemplation. He's left me just standing here, but after a second I decide to follow him wondering if I was just too harsh with what I'd said. But it wasn't really a lie... Andries can't deny what Roxanne used to do for a living. I wonder if he's still uncomfortable with the fact, and if he is, it doesn't bode well for the future of their marriage.

I approach him, assuming the same stance with my arms on the railing and facing the incredible view. We stay like that for a few minutes, just breathing in the fresh sea air before my brother turns his face towards me. "You really think I'm making a huge mistake getting married to her, don't you?"

His question is difficult for me. My opinion of Roxanne has undoubtedly changed over the past few weeks, and she and I had reached a sort of understanding before this afternoon, but that doesn't mean that I think she's the best match for Andries. But she loves him and makes him happy, so that should be all that matters, right?

It turns out, things aren't that simple, and love might not always be the only thing needed for a successful marriage. The thought of the legal problems Roxanne is about to be deep into crosses my mind, and I sigh deeply. "If you really want to, I'm not going to try to stop you. It's just... you're so damn young, and she's already thirty-six! Who knows how things will be in ten years, or if the two of you will even be the same people you are now?" I shrug, helpless to explain everything that I really feel about this insanely nuanced situation. "It all feels so sudden. Mom and Dad are just worried, even though I have to admit they're handling it terribly."

"You know, Uncle Alex got married to his *goddaughter*, who's like twenty-three years younger than him," Andries points out, but the fact doesn't endear me to his situation anymore. The word 'goddaughter' makes me shudder, even though I know my uncle and his young wife are completely happy in their marriage these days.

"Just because they're married and things are okay between them doesn't make it right," I argue.

"But they're happy," Andries insists.

"But they've only been married for a year or two," I remind him. "That's hardly enough time to base an opinion on." I know that he isn't going to give up on the argument, but I can't help but want to get my own point across, too.

"Mom and Dad have a big age gap too, and yet they've been together for twenty years. Your point about the age thing doesn't stand." Andries doesn't sound smug even though he must believe he's proven me wrong. Instead, he just sounds tired. I feel the same way.

"I just don't want you to regret it," I sigh. "That's all, okay?"

"I know I'm not as cautious as you are, but something inside me tells me it's the right choice. It's not logical, sure, but love isn't logical, and Roxie left the adult industry for me. It's only natural that I want to give our relationship a shot, and I can't picture my life without her." I can feel his eyes on me, but I continue to look out to sea. "Please try to understand, El."

Left the adult industry, he said. It makes my stomach churn, knowing that Roxanne still has secrets she's hiding from my brother, and the biggest one of them being that she is somewhat still in the adult industry. Bar Rouge might not be a full sex club, but the cabaret is still undoubtedly linked to the adult industry, and now it's public knowledge that a dancer was giving blowjobs. Andries is going to be crushed when he finds out, and I can't help but wonder if all these kind words he uses to defend his fiancée will taste like ash in his mouth once everything comes to light. I have no idea how he's going to react, but I know for sure it won't be good.

I'm not going to be the one telling him the truth, so I don't need to worry about it so much, I have to tell myself over and over again. I want to put Roxie's scandal at the back of my mind and focus on the things going on in my own life, but it's so hard. Still, I'm not going to even hint to my brother that something is wrong, so all I can tell him is, "If you're happy, then I'm happy."

"Thanks," he replies warmly. "It's good to hear you say that."

We stay like this for a while in comfortable silence, but I have the feeling that my brother needs some time alone. I don't know if he's thinking about his relationship—or mine—but I decide to leave and give him the breathing room that he needs.

I turn around, ready to go back inside the villa when my brother calls out for me again. I stop in my tracks, turning just enough to watch him swallow and close his eyes as if what he's about to say is painful for him.

"Elise... I need time to digest what happened between you and Dan. I'm not over it yet, but... well, I'm not over it. I can't say I ever will be, but just give me some time."

"I get it," I say, even though it feels like a lie. "Let's put it aside for now and have a proper farewell dinner with our friend. Johan deserves it."

Andries gives me a tight nod, and for the moment, we leave our conversation right there—unfinished, as they always seem to be.

CHAPTER 12

Dan

It's been a long, albeit deliciously enjoyable day, and I think a late afternoon nap before dinner is just what I need to tie it all together. There's something so satisfying about rays of sunshine coming in through the windows and the sound of the ocean coming from outside while I lounge in sweatpants on my bed, eyes getting heavy. The only thing that would make it better is Elise curled up at my side, but I know she has some things to settle with her brother.

The thought makes me chuckle. Better her than me, poor girl. I love her dearly, but nothing on heaven or Earth could make me have all those awkward conversations for her. She's better at being diplomatic anyway. My solution would be to tell Andries to shut the hell up and throttle Johan for even dreaming about being with El. I'm sure she has a much gentler touch.

Yawning, I pillow my head on my arm and start to drift off. It seems like less than a second has passed before my phone goes off. But when I check the time on the bedside clock, it tells me that I've managed to sneak in forty-five minutes of rest before being interrupted.

I expect someone in the house is calling me, but it's a pleasant surprise to see my dad's picture on the screen instead. I probably would have silenced the call had it been any of the villa guests besides Elise, but this call is one I'm more than happy to answer.

"Hey, Pops," I greet after connecting the call.

"Hello," he responds. His tone is cheerful but neutral, and I realize we haven't spoken since the day Johan arrived. He must be wondering how I handled such a delicate affair, and I'm sure it will come as no surprise to him that my fix for it all was anything *but* delicate. Not like I'm going to go into detail, though.

"So how are things?" he ventures. "You weren't in the best headspace last time we talked, and I've been worried about you, my boy. You holding up okay?"

"Better than you might imagine," I confess, sounding smugger than I thought. "Our young lad Johan barely lasted three days here with us, and now he's packing up and leaving for Ibiza, so that problem is out of my head now."

"Hmmm," Dad sounds contemplative. "You haven't gotten yourself into any trouble or burned any bridges to get this Johan to vacate the property, have you?"

"No, I promise. I guess technically my bridge with Johan is burnt, but I don't care a single bit about his opinion over the whole thing."

"So Andries isn't angry?" he prods.

I groaned inwardly. Of course, my dad would know just what questions to ask to make me uncomfortable. "Well, yeah he's angry, but Andries started things, not me. And he would have done so with or without Johan here, so it really isn't relevant to Johan leaving."

"You're being evasive," Dad says before laughing in a resigned way. "I know you better than that. What did you do? I know good and well that you aren't innocent."

An image of Elise between my legs and Johan storming away flits through my mind, and I have to stomp it down before I get too distracted by the thought. Still, a smirk creeps over my face as I answer. "Let's just say I told him implicitly that Elise was already taken."

"Hmmm," he mumbles again. "That sounds ominous, but I'm not going to question you further. I take it to mean that you're having a better time now, though?"

"Absolutely. And once Johan leaves it will be even better."

Dad chuckles. "I almost feel bad for the poor guy. Just be careful not to forget about your friendship with Andries while pursuing his sister, or you will regret it dearly later on in life."

"Trust me, Andries isn't letting anyone forget his feelings—" I jolt slightly when there is a knock on the door, and my instincts tell me who it probably is without me even checking. Just like Andries called Elise while we were discussing him earlier at the coffee shop, chances are that it's him at my door interrupting the conversation that I'm having with my dad about our friendship. "Hey, Dad, there's someone at my door, can we talk later?"

I tell my father goodbye and hang up the call after promising to call him soon. Whoever is at my door knocks again, impatiently, and I yell for them to go ahead and come in.

Like I suspected, it's none other than Andries, wearing a rather sour expression. "Well, you got your wish. Johan is packing up and wants to leave tomorrow."

"I guess he's just ready to leave," I shrug one shoulder, leaning back against the headboard and folding my hands behind my head as I recline. "He's a busy man, I'm sure."

Andries glares at me and the picture of nonchalance I'm trying to give off. "Something tells me that you and my sister have more to do with his departure than you're letting on. She lied to my face about it, so why don't you tell me the truth?"

I almost laugh out loud at the thought of telling Andries what Johan *really* saw at the beach to make him leave. The two of us would undoubtedly come to blows if I did that. "Andries, if you've spoken to your sister, me, and even Johan himself and we've all given you the same answer, then why do you still assume that we are lying?"

"Because just yesterday Johan was having a great time with us. Remember all the help he gave you while sailing?" He crosses his arms. "After all of that, I'd think that you two would have warmed up to each other more, but here you are not even caring if he leaves."

"Man, I've known him for like two days. I don't care what Johan does, but obviously, he has things to do and you're being weirdly over the top about him leaving." I shouldn't say the next thing that comes to my mind, but my best friend is annoying me to no end, and I want this conversation to be over. "Do you think maybe he's leaving because you got so ridiculously drunk last night that he doesn't want to deal with it again?"

"Ha," Andries scoffs. "Fuck you, Dan. It's too bad that, even though I drank until I blacked out, I still couldn't forget the way you betrayed me."

"Back to this, are we?" I take a hand from behind my head and drag it down my face in frustration. "Andries, I'm not going to hurt Elise. I'm even giving her all the space she needs right now to figure out what exactly it is that *she* wants from me, and not the other way around." I swallow, feeling unwanted emotion welling up in me. "Truthfully, if she wasn't hesitant, there isn't anything in the world that I wouldn't do for her, but ultimately it's her choice to make."

Andries pauses, the anger bleeding out of his expression. "If you were any other suitor pursuing my sister, I would appreciate that sentiment more, but it still doesn't erase the betrayal between you and me."

"I don't expect it to," I admit. "I just want you to know that I will never do anything to cause her any kind of pain. You can still be pissed off at me, but I'd like you to know that I respect your sister just as much as I care about her."

Running a hand through his hair, Andries exhales deeply, the stiffness in his frame easing as whatever rage he was feeling when he first came into my room now moves beyond his grasp. "Whatever, man. I'm not over this and I don't think I will be any time soon, if ever. But... you should know we're having a farewell dinner for Johan a little after eight p.m. if you want to join us. Consider this your heads up to get ready."

With that last statement, my best friend disappears out of my suite, shutting the door behind him. I have a little less than an hour before the dinner that I guess I'm expected to appear at, and while there is plenty I could do to pass the time, the allure of returning to my nap is pretty strong. Not that I'm very tired anymore, but dealing with everyone here and the drama that is attached to them doesn't seem appealing, especially when I know I'll be getting my fair share of it during the farewell party itself.

With a resigned sigh, knowing that I have to attend a party for someone I really don't want to see again, I roll over, pulling the thin blanket over myself to try to catch a little more sleep before I have to make my reappearance into the real world.

* * *

Adjusting the collar on my short sleeve linen button up, I walk out into the cooler evening air, surprised at how well-decorated the terrace is considering the short notice. Everyone is dressed impeccably, and there is even a DJ who has the music down low enough that we can all hear each other talking.

I look around for Elise, but even though everyone else is present, she's nowhere to be found. Considering she's the only person I care to see at this party, it's a bit of a disappointment... that is, until I see Johan.

For someone as tall and buff as he is, Johan looks more like a kicked puppy than a man, standing across the terrace with a frown on his face and his shoulders slumped in defeat. He's talking to Lili and Robin, but even from as far away as I am, I can tell his heart really isn't in the conversation.

Even though his sad countenance makes me smirk, I wish he'd have just left tonight. It'd have made everything so much easier.

With the sun just beginning to set, everything is cast in red and gold light, I can't deny that the event is stunning. Roxanne is leaning against the wall next to the entrance in an emerald green dress, and I wonder how Andries hasn't realized that something is wrong with his fiancée yet. There is stress written all over her face.

I make my way over to her, copying her pose and leaning on the wall while we both observe the party going on around us. Roxie clutches a glass of sparkling wine with what looks like a splash of cranberry juice in it, but she hasn't taken a single sip. Her only acknowledgment of me is a quick glance before she's back to staring outwards.

"Your fiancé seems heartbroken that his new best friend is leaving," I comment, nodding to where Andries—looking almost as sad as Johan—is talking to the other man. Roxanne laughs once, but her heart isn't in it.

"If I didn't know better, Dan, I'd say you sound jealous."

"Bitter is more accurate. I didn't exactly book this trip so he could look for someone to replace me with, but here we are." I try to keep my tone light, but there is undeniably some animosity in my voice.

"He'll remember this trip forever, Dan, and once we're back home and he's gotten over this thing with you and his sister, I'm sure he'll think much more fondly of everything and be grateful for his friendship with you." She turns her face to me, and her expression is completely serious. "Promise me you'll give him another chance, okay? He has so few friends…"

"Don't worry. I've weathered my fair share of Andries's dramatic moments. This one may be a little more intense than others, but it's nothing new for me." A thought occurs to me that leaves me feeling cold, and all the humor drains out of me. "Roxanne, you aren't saying that because you think the two of you won't be together, do you?"

She turns her body away from me slightly, indicating that our conversation is done. "Go get a drink or something, Dan."

"Roxie—"

"I said go."

I clamp my mouth shut at her icy tone, but I do as she demands, leaving her behind to join the main crush of party guests. Andries has moved on from Johan for the moment, so this might be my only chance to greet him without an ambush, but at least this should be the last time I have to speak to the other man that thinks he has some pull over the woman I love.

Good riddance, Johan.

I don't even try to wipe the smug look off my face as I approach him, but I see his attention dart to the terrace entrance, his eyes wide, and I turn to see what could have him so distracted. When I see the target he's gazing at, I have to agree that she's worth every bit of attention from anyone at the party.

Elise is wearing a form-fitting silver dress that stops just above her knees. She has her shimmering hair clipped up in a loose twist, errant strands framing her perfect face. Without any hair to hide her elegant neck and the swell of her cleavage, she looks like a goddess that has just walked out of the ocean, flicking a large, ornate fan that matches her dress open to cool herself. Perfectly bronze legs and a pair of strappy, heeled sandals complete the look. Seeing her like this makes my mouth go dry.

Going off of the look on Johan's face, I know I'm not the only one who feels this way. As if in a daze, he starts to walk toward Elise, and I move to intercept him as casually as I can. Johan sees me, and we both stop, shoulder to shoulder, at one of the appetizer stations. I don't bother looking over at him, and I idly order an Old Fashioned from one of the servers that passes by. Finally I speak up, loud enough for only Johan to hear me.

"She's truly something, isn't she?" I ask, nodding at Elise, who is talking with her brother, casually fanning herself as she does so. "Don't worry. I'll invite you to our wedding."

Johan makes a strangled sound at first, but then he laughs, throwing an arm over my shoulder unexpectedly. His grip is almost painfully tight before he relaxes. "Dan, let me tell you something about girls like Elise that come from old money. Just because they have fun with you doesn't mean they want to marry you." He sounds like a condescending jerk, before laughing. "To Elise, you are at best a summer fuck, while I'm still the man she loves." Johan releases me, slapping me on the back in what must look to everyone else like a friendly gesture before I can even respond. "Enjoy the rest of your evening."

I'm so shocked it feels like my feet are glued to the floor as I watch Johan approach Elise with an ease that he doesn't deserve to have. She smiles as he gets close, and my heart sinks to my feet. I try to brush Johan's words away, but they sink into me before I can stop them. I hate that what he's said makes sense, on the surface. The simple fact of the matter is that Johan comes from nobility and the same old-money world that Elise herself does, but what I don't know is if that's something that actually matters to her or not. Will that kind of status play into how she chooses a husband? The idea of it makes me feel ill, and when the server floats back by, handing me the lowball glass that my drink is in, my hands are subtly shaking. I take a long sip to steady myself, and then after a moment, down the entire thing, setting the glass on a nearby table and heading for the bar to order another.

I don't look at Johan and Elise again, wanting to avoid seeing the two of them together if I can, so it's a surprise when Elise sidles up next to me at the bar just as the bartender slides my double shot of whiskey over. She looks at the glass, and then at me, and frowns.

"Why are you drinking such strong stuff already? We just started."

I think about lying and telling her something aloof, but change my mind at the last second. "To forget that your ex is still around."

Elise raises her eyebrows in surprise. "Did he do something wrong?"

"Yeah," I huff. "He exists."

I tilt my head back and take the shot, letting it burn its way down my throat before I glance over at Elise fully. All at once I'm taken aback by how stunning she is, and it almost leaves me speechless. Then I remember that, even though Johan might get to talk to her, I'm the only one here allowed to touch her. If he didn't get the message earlier when he caught us at the beach, maybe he needs another reminder about who Elise is really with.

"El," I murmur, letting my voice fall to a low, seductive pitch. She blinks a few times at the rapid change of pace in the conversation. "You look incredible in that dress."

Elise smooths her hands down said dress, making it hug her curves even more. The curves that she has let me touch and taste, over and over again. The idea of it makes me half-hard already.

"Thanks," she tells me, her smile making her even more beautiful. "You don't look so bad yourself."

I move closer to her. In my mind, we are completely alone, and there is no reason to hold myself back. I want people to know that she's mine. "I really want to repeat what we did on the beach, but in my bed this time…"

She's receptive at first, swaying towards me, but then I take things a step too far by reaching behind her and grabbing her ass firmly in my palm. Elise gasps, offended, her head swiveling to see who caught us in the back before snapping her fan shut and hitting me in the arm with it. I hiss from the sting, but it's not nearly as sharp as the knives she's shooting at me with her glare.

"Behave!" Elise hisses between her teeth before storming away. I almost stop her, but then I notice she's heading towards her brother and his fiancée, and not Johan, so I let her go. I see Johan himself talking to others, but every few seconds he levels a glance at me, looking both smug and annoyed at my existence. The feeling is very, very mutual.

With Elise not looking, I have the bartender pour me another double, and when Johan inevitably looks my way once more, I hold it up to him in a toast.

He's leaving, I tell myself, forcing a smile onto my face. *He's leaving tomorrow.*

Tomorrow can't come soon enough.

* * *

I'm not exactly hungry when it's time to sit down for dinner, but seeing Johan moving to sit next to Elise, I make an effort to do the same. She sits at the end of the table, which means Johan manages to get a seat next to her on one side while I take the other side. I avoid looking at him, knowing how awkward it is, but Elise and Andries at least get a chuckle out of our fierce competition.

I don't want to eat, spending my time instead trying to keep Elise's attention, touching her knee, and engaging her in conversation whenever I'm able. To my credit, she's kind to Johan, but she's interested in me, even taking my hand briefly under the table a few times when Andries isn't paying attention. Andries might be oblivious, but Johan notices, and I can see his expression get darker and darker as the dinner goes on.

I eventually eat, needing something to soak up all the whiskey in my stomach if I want to keep Elise's attention away from Johan. I'm so distracted by her that I don't even pay attention to what I'm putting in my mouth.

Conversations flow naturally through the group, everyone heaping praise onto Johan for how nice it's been to get to know him. Andries is especially invested in his new friend, but I can tell that the only thing Johan is really concerned about is the woman sitting between him and I.

Dessert is brought out—it's creme brûlée with a sugar crust that cracks like glass. I'm not interested in it at all until Elise holds out her fork to me, a bite of the dessert on it, and tells me to at least try it. Making eye contact with Johan, I let

Elise feed me the bite, chuckling in my mind when the other man's face goes red.

What I don't expect is Johan to shoot up from his seat, his glass in hand. He holds it into the air, none of the flustered emotion I see written on his face showing up in his voice as he declares, "I propose a toast to Andries and his beautiful bride, Roxanne!" Everyone at the table claps quietly, Andries smiling sweetly at his fiancée. "I want to thank you for inviting me here. I hate that I had to miss the engagement party, but I swear to be by your side for the wedding, Andries. Unfortunately, I have to leave this lovely villa tomorrow for a birthday party in Ibiza, but I'll be back in Amsterdam before you know it."

Johan is talking to Andries, but in the last sentence, his gaze shifts to Elise, who is just smiling politely. Again, I have to remind myself over and over again that he will be gone tomorrow. I know in my heart that he's only being this complimentary to Andries in hopes of staying close to Elise whenever possible, and potentially getting her brother's blessing, but it still bothers me more than I will ever admit to myself.

Once Johan is back in his seat and everyone is clapping once more, I rise to the challenge and stand to give a toast, too. Instead of toasting to Andries, though, I target mine directly at Johan.

"To Johan, who has only been with us a few days and *sadly* has to leave tomorrow while all of us remain here." I pause, letting my words sink in before continuing. "I don't know Johan very well, but it was nice to get to know you, man. And thanks for all the sailing tips. To Johan!"

Everyone holds up their glasses and repeats my final words while I hold Johan's gaze as long as I can. Elise isn't smiling now, having caught on to our little competition, but on the grand scale of things, a few snarky toasts aren't too harmful in my mind.

Once dinner finishes, everyone starts to peel off and go find their own things to do, talking in small groups and having drinks. The music changes from something just meant for the background to music that can be danced to, and while the thought of asking Elise to dance crosses my mind, my attention is soon pulled away.

I can feel a pair of eyes on me, and when I turn, I see Andries and Roxanne about ten feet away. He's talking to a waiter, but Roxanne is looking directly at me, and when she catches my eye, she pulls out her phone and sends a quick message.

Roxanne: *Hey, can you meet me in the garden for a moment? It won't take long.*

Curious, I decide to agree.

It's easier for me to get away than expected, and I make it to the lovely little garden with the fountain before Roxanne. I have a feeling she wants to talk about the cabaret scandal, but if she isn't willing to tell Andries about it then what even is the point? With the sun having fully set, there is just the slight light of dusk on the horizon, and the automatic lights on the villa are kicking on, subtle and golden, giving the gardens a mystical air that would be nice to share with a romantic partner, but instead, I'm going to have to spend my time here with my best friend's fiancée, sorting through the drama she's gotten herself into, I'm sure of it.

Just as I'm starting to consider going back to the terrace for a drink, Roxanne appears, looking both flustered and tired at the same time. She makes her way immediately to the stone bench and sits down heavily on it with a sigh, tilting her head back to the sky. I take a seat next to her, giving her some time to just breathe before addressing her.

"You doing okay, Roxie? What did you want to talk about?"

"I know you're already aware of the cabaret nonsense, considering how close you and Elise are," she answers, sounding resigned.

I consider lying, but there's no point in it. It won't be too long till everyone in our social circle will know about everything going on with Bar Rouge, so it's useless to pretend that I'm not up to date on the gossip. "Yeah, and? Did you have me come here just to confirm that?"

"I need to know if Andries already knows," she admits. "I haven't told him yet. Every time I think I have convinced myself to do so, I chicken out. Has he given you any indication that he already knows what's going on and is trying to use it to manipulate me or call me a liar?"

I consider her question, combing through my memories of how Andries has behaved since the Bar Rouge news broke. "He *was* acting oddly melancholic at the bar last night. More than usual, if you can believe that, but it's hard to know if he's just still brooding about Elise and me or if something else is going on. I have to admit, it did cross my mind that your scandal had something to do with him getting blackout drunk, but he never said anything that confirmed it one way or the other."

Roxanne groans. "He's so frustrating! If he already knows I wish he would just tell me and get it over with."

"You know, you could put yourself out of misery by telling him. If he does know and is keeping the information secret then he's clearly waiting for you to confess. The longer you wait, the worse it will be."

"I just *can't*," she laments. "The words just won't come out."

"It's the right thing to do either way, Roxie. If he knows, then at least he will be aware that you're willing to tell him the truth no matter what, even if it's tough, and if he doesn't know, at least your confession will give him confidence that you aren't trying to hide anything from him anymore."

Roxanne looks at me, pain in her eyes. "He's just been so cold and distant towards me lately like he's hiding some sort of hurt or something."

"I mean, it's possible… but I don't think he's capable of playing such a convoluted game this close to the wedding. Your marriage ceremony combined with the discovery of everything going on between Elise and me is probably a lot for Andries to handle." I smirk, trying to lighten the mood, but Roxie looks as serious as ever. "Plus, we both know Andries. If he figured out a bombshell like this on his own his first instinct would be to throw a tantrum."

Biting her lip, her brows drawn together, Roxanne looks tortured. I lay my arm across her shoulders, and she scoots closer to me, laying her head on my shoulder with a shaky exhale. "He's testing me, Dan," she says quietly. "I just know it, and it's driving me crazy and tying me up in knots. Can you do me a favor and try to fish for some information? If not, I get it…."

"I will talk to him," I answer back causing her to smile. "I'll see what I can find out without tipping him off."

Roxanne seems to relax, keeping her head on my shoulder for a few quiet minutes longer before sitting up straight and discretely wiping the tears away from her eyes. "Thank you," she says, forcing a small smile onto her face. "I knew you were the right one to ask. Andries might be acting obsessive about Johan but we both know that he's closer to you than anyone else in the world."

"Well, besides you," I point out.

"I hope so," she sighs. "I really do. I know I'm messing up by not telling him right away but it's too late to undo it now. I have a plan for when we get back, but it's all determined by whether he already knows or not."

"Let's get back to the party, Roxie, before Andries finds us back here and accuses us of plotting against him or something," I tease, standing up and straightening my clothes.

She snorts. "That would be just my luck. I'm going to sit here and think for a little longer and then I'll be back."

I turn Roxanne's words over in my mind as I return to the terrace, and the more I consider it, the more I think she might be right about Andries already knowing. I really hope he doesn't, for her sake, but I also know that if she doesn't come clean as soon as possible, that there will be big problems no matter at what point he learns of the scandal. Hell, she's not even going to get away clean if she tells him right this minute... poor Roxanne, she has really backed herself into an impossible corner. I don't envy her at all.

Back on the terrace, string fairy lights are criss-crossing far above everyone's heads and combined with the music floating through it all, the ambiance is soft and enchanting. I see Elise first, and she is so beautiful that she seems to glow from within as her dance partner spins her across the floor. I'm so invested in her every movement that it takes me an embarrassing amount of time to realize that it's Johan she's dancing with, and all the warm feelings I was just feeling flee and are replaced by annoyance of the highest variety.

Even more annoying is the fact that they are the only couple on the dance floor. All the other partygoers are loosely circled, both standing and sitting, around the cleared dining table and mingling. Being so alone gives Elise and Johan a sense of intimacy that immediately pisses me off, and I have to repress the urge to rush and separate them. I don't want Johan to know how much he's affecting me though, so I force myself to walk towards the table where everyone else is, trying desperately to keep the stiffness out of my shoulders.

There is Cointreau, Absinthe, and Limoncello on tiered trays, but I need something with a little more bite. Bypassing the lighter after dinner drinks, I order my third double whiskey for the night. This one is on the rocks so I won't just toss the whole thing back in one gulp. I can feel the alcohol from earlier still making my thoughts just the smallest bit fuzzy, and while I need the bracing alcohol, I need to be coherent, too.

Once I have my glass, I drop into the chair beside Andries, automatically turning it to the side so I can keep an eye on the dance floor. Out of the corner of my eye, I know Andries is watching me, but I can't take my gaze off Johan and Elise… especially with how low his hands are on her back. My anger must be visible in my expression, because after a moment, Andries chuckles.

"I told you that you were a fool," he teases, but there is no room for humor in me right now.

"What the hell does that mean, huh?" I whip around to face Andries, who jumps at my sudden movement. "How am I the fool when he's the one that's leaving tomorrow? It sounds to me like he's the fool, and I'm the man who went the distance."

Andries scoffs, shaking his head. "Whatever, Dan, forget it. I was just joking."

I've had enough, though. I've done so much for Andries lately that his obsession... no, *allegiance* to Johan has gone past the point of bothering me to being downright disrespectful. I've done everything in my power to give him an amazing engagement to the love of his life, and just because the woman that I love is his sister, he treats me like garbage and heaps praise on Johan, someone that he barely knows. It rankles. A lot.

"You know what, Andries? It's very clear where your allegiance lies. If you knew why—" The truth about what made Johan want to leave almost slips off my tongue, but I clench my teeth together to keep the words inside and stand up instead, pushing my chair away with more force than I intended. "Nevermind," I bite out, and if Andries says anything else as I storm away, I don't hear him over the sound of my blood rushing in my ears.

* * *

Back in my suite, I can finally breathe, but I'm still so hot under the collar that I rush to the bathroom to splash water on my face. The cold helps to center me, so I repeat the action before grabbing the face towel to dry myself off with.

In the middle of wiping the water from my skin, I feel my phone vibrate in my pocket, announcing a new text message, and pull it out absentmindedly. To my surprise it's from Dad, even though we just spoke earlier today. He isn't much of a text, either, so I'm quick to open the message and see what he has to say.

He's sent me a YouTube link, then a second message as an explanation, which reads, *Looks like your friend's fiancée is back in the news.*

My stomach drops, wondering what else could be going on with Roxanne. Clicking the link, I take the phone with me to sit on the edge of my bed and watch the video, which is a news broadcast. The anchor explains how the cabaret Bar Rouge is now officially closed for the time being while law enforcement carries out an extensive search of the premises. It turns out that the dubious actions of the dancer onstage is only the tip of the iceberg, and served as a red flag to make all eyes turn to the establishment. While looking into the dancer incident, cocaine was found in the dressing rooms, but even more alarming, some patrons admitted to the police that they had been sold cocaine by employees of Bar Rouge.

The clip cuts to an officer talking about the case while standing in front of the darkened Bar Rouge. He looks somber as he says, "Bar Rouge's revenue streams are now being investigated as well. We think that most of their revenue may have come from drug trafficking and not legitimate cabaret services."

The reporter on the scene asks if this information is just something from a tip or a real concern, and the officer frowns. "We have a strong suspicion that the cabaret is just a front for money laundering. We've tried to get in contact with the owner, Ms. Roxanne Feng, but communication has been minimal. There is still a possibility that Ms. Feng wasn't a part of this trafficking, but until she complies fully with the investigation, it's difficult to know for certain. It'd be much easier once we've interviewed her," he admits, and the video ends there.

I sit in shock for a second, staring at my darkened phone screen. The video link is from one of the biggest news outlets in the country, and if they are reporting on the scandal, then there's no doubt that everyone in our circle knows as well. Which means…

This means that there is no way Andries isn't aware of the Bar Rouge scandal yet. He really is stringing Roxanne along, waiting for her to tell him the truth. Andries is testing his fiancée, that's the only explanation I can think of. And while I can sort of understand his motives, I can't help but think of how cruel this entire thing is.

Unsettled, I realize I can't just sit here and mull over all this new information alone. I have to talk to someone, and while I want to share it with Elise more than anyone else, I did promise Roxie to try and get some information out of Andries. Knowing now that Roxanne can be in serious legal trouble, I'm well aware that she doesn't have the luxury of waiting until we get back home to confess to her future husband.

The terrace has mostly cleared out, and while Andries and Johan are nowhere to be seen, Elise is sitting at the table sipping Limoncello and scrolling through her phone with an intense look on her face. I have a pretty good idea of what is on her screen, but I approach her, pulling up a chair next to her just to confirm. I know she doesn't want to be involved in this disaster anymore, but I have to admit I feel better having someone else to share this with before I tackle it head-on. Like it or not, Roxanne is Elise's future sister-in-law, and she has to be at least tangentially involved in everything with Bar Rouge moving forward.

Elise's brows are drawn together, but when she sees it's me joining her, her expression softens. I'm still annoyed at her for dancing so intimately with Johan, but seeing the affection on her face and the way she instinctively scoots her chair closer to mine does wonders for my bruised ego.

"You've made yourself scarce tonight," she observes, taking a drink and looking at me over the rim of the glass.

"Can you blame me? Johan isn't exactly my favorite person."

"Yeah, I could tell from that lackluster toast." We both laugh, Elise, shaking her head. "It was nice to see him, but it will also be nice to have you back to normal once he's gone."

"It will be good to not have to share your attention too, even if that makes me selfish," I lean in, brushing the quickest of kisses over her cheekbone before moving back. The temptation to let Roxanne and Andries' problems handle themselves and drag Elise back to my suite is strong, but I know we have to be adults and deal with this. "As much as I'd like to talk more about how sad Johan is now, we have other things to discuss." I pull up the video Pops sent me and hand Elise the phone. She takes one look at the screen and doesn't even start the video, handing it back as her smile fades.

"I know. Someone from school already reposted it on Twitter." Her tone is grim.

"We have to make her tell him, or at the very least, find out if he already knows."

She shakes her head. "No. I'm not getting involved."

"Come on, El. You and your brother have all the same friends on socials. If you've seen the video organically, then so has he. There's no way your brother doesn't know."

"And?" She tucks a strand of hair behind her ear, her expression neutral. "It's none of my business."

"Yeah right," I snort. "El, you make everything your business, even if it isn't even close to being so. Now that there is something that is *actually* your business, like your brother's fiancée having potential criminal charges getting ready to rain down, you're going to pretend you aren't interested? I know you better than that."

"Every time I interfere in their relationship it ends terribly for me and everyone's feelings get hurt. I'm sitting this one out, Dan."

"But I need your help," I insist, but this girl is stubborn. "We have to find out what Andries knows."

"I said no. Now, drop it, or I'm going to go find Johan to talk to."

I grit my teeth but stop talking just like she wants. After sticking her nose into Andries's business when it comes to Roxanne for months now, Elise's sudden disinterest is raising some red flags for me. She's sworn to be on her brother's side, but what if she's being tight-lipped because she's still helping her dad on the down low, hoping that the longer Roxanne waits to talk to Andries, the angrier he'll be? It's a nefarious plot, but not only is Elise stubborn, but she's also one of the smartest people I know, and I wouldn't put anything past her.

Still, I want to trust that she's had a change of heart. This reaction of hers is making it hard.

Just before I start to try and convince Elise again, Andries and Johan walk out of the villa and back onto the terrace from wherever they were. Johan shakes Andries's hand and pulls him in to slap his shoulder before the men separate, and Johan disappears around the side of the house—presumably to talk to everyone else before the night is over. Andries makes movements like he's going to come join me and his sister, but I stand, approaching him instead and cutting him off.

"Hey, man, can we talk in private for a minute?" I ask, already taking his arm in my hand and steering him away from Elise.

"Uh, sure?" Andries replies, coming with me willingly but with a confused tilt to his mouth.

I lead us both to the balustrade, as far away from listening, nosy ears as possible. "This was a great farewell party," I tell him, easing into the conversation. "Well done."

Andries waves his hand in the air. "You know good and well Roxie and Lili did most of the planning."

"But I'm sure they needed some of your input to keep them from going overboard, right?"

He chuckles. "You aren't wrong there." To my surprise, his expression then turns sober. "But I know good and well that you didn't bring me over here to talk about party planning."

"I just wanted to check on you. Are you doing okay, Andries?" I ask, dropping any sort of animosity I may have been feeling toward my best friend. I need him to be open with me, so in turn, I have to be open with him.

"I've had better days," he admits. "Why are you asking me this now, though?"

"I know something is clearly bothering you. I have to ask… are you really mad just because of my relationship with your sister, or is there something else affecting you?"

His gaze sharpens. "What makes you ask? Is there something else that should be affecting me, Dan?"

I don't answer immediately, processing his question. Roxanne has me fishing for information from Andries because she's afraid he's testing her trust in some way, but… what if he's doing the same with me right now? It isn't false that, being his best friend, the right thing to do would be for me to tell him the truth about anything that might affect him, like the Bar Rouge scandal, but I also want to give Roxie time to do the right thing herself. It puts me in an impossible situation, and I truly hope he is just being clueless.

I consider just telling him that Roxie owns the cabaret, and keeping the news about the dancer and cocaine incidents to myself so he can find out through his own research, but knowing Andries, he will push and push until I tell him everything. The worst part is that I *want* to tell him. It's eating me up inside to lie by omission to my best friend, but Roxanne deserves the chance to own up to her mistakes.

"I don't know, Andries, you tell me. If something is weighing on you, you can always count on me, even if we haven't been on the best of terms."

A server floats by, and Andries grabs the drink he ordered, which is something that looks nearly identical to the whiskey currently in my hand. He drinks deeply, the ice clinking in the glass, before responding. "After breaking my trust, you still think I'd come to you. Really?" He's clearly being sarcastic, and it grates on my nerves.

"You're being an asshole, but I get it. Look, all I'm trying to say is if anything is troubling you, no matter how humiliating it is, I'm here for you, alright?"

Andries creases his eyes at me suspiciously. "Humiliating, you say? Such as?"

Frustration wells in me, and I know I have to give him a few crumbs of information or he's not going to take the bait. I feel like I'm so close to getting him to fess up that I can't stop now. "Well, anything regarding your and Roxanne's union, for instance. I know it was a big deal for you that she used to work in the sex industry, so it's natural for there to still be friction between the two of you. If anything arises out of that, I want you to know I'm here to support you."

His expression softens and he reaches out, laying one hand on my shoulder and squeezing affectionately. "Well, thanks, man, I really appreciate it, but you don't have to worry about that. She left the industry before we got back together."

Something about his tone of voice rings false, and it's putting me on edge. I feel like Andries is just playing a game with me, and that it's a trust test to see if I will tell him the truth about the cabaret. That would be the right thing for a best friend to do, right? I'm aching inside to tell him, and the idea that he might be totally genuine and in the dark about what is happening makes it even worse somehow. If Andries trusts me, and I fail him like this…

I open my mouth to tell him the truth, the power and guilt of it almost overwhelming me, but then I see a flash of emerald green from the front of the terrace. Roxanne has her hands clasped in front of her nervously as she looks for her future husband, and the words die in my throat. I can't betray her... fuck... I'm going to be screwed no matter how this plays out now.

"I know she left, but I know that some of those feelings might still remain, so again, if you need to talk…" I flick my eyes over to Roxanne again, who hasn't spotted us yet, and lean closer so I can whisper to Andries, "even if you need me to keep a secret from her, I can if you want me to."

Andries smiles again, but it doesn't reach his eyes. "Okay Dan, I hear you. I appreciate you letting me know."

With that, my best friend walks away, and with him, so does all my energy. After the emotional distress of fighting to keep this secret from him, I'm exhausted, and even the allure of beautiful Elise still sitting with her legs crossed at the table isn't enough to make me want to stay. My eyelids feel heavy, just like my heart, and I really, really just want to go to sleep.

I make my way inside, waiting until Andries isn't looking to stop and kiss Elise's cheek and tell her goodnight. She seems bewildered that I'm not staying, but I just can't. My tolerance for all this drama is at its limit.

I tell Andries and Roxanne goodnight as well, Roxie's eyes burning into me as if she's trying to see if I'm hiding any new information from her. I'm so torn on what to do. Should tell Andries the truth to show him how much I care about our friendship, or keep quiet and let Roxanne handle her own dirty work and give the two the best chance to save their engagement? The truth is going to cause serious problems between the two of them, and the best way to mitigate it is for Roxanne to do the talking herself.

The last thing I want to do is fuck their relationship up a month before their wedding, but this scandal at Bar Rouge can't be ignored. If he's testing my loyalty, though, I'm failing miserably, and every minute I keep my mouth shut is another minute that I'm continuing to fail.

I stop and turn back one last time before going inside, and, just like I suspect, Roxanne is still looking at me. I frown, trying to tell her without words that the clock has almost run out. I can see her gulp, and I know that at least part of my message has gotten through to her. She knows I can't keep this up forever, at least.

Roxanne can't hide this shit forever, and she's going to have to tell Andries the truth. Soon.

CHAPTER 13

Elise

After Johan's farewell party, it was hard for me to find sleep. It felt to me like there was so much left unsaid, but at the same time, I'm ready to move on with my life, too. Still… I feel like Johan is leaving too easily, and I think he might have some other tricks up his sleeve before he leaves the villa for good.

I finally manage to fall asleep in the middle of the night, but I'm suddenly jolted awake by the sound of my phone ringing on the bedside table. I consider ignoring it and rolling back over to get some more rest, but almost anyone who would bother to call me will more than likely just call again if I don't answer.

With bleary eyes, I squint at the screen and see my dad's contact emblazoned there. Now any wish of just ignoring the call dissipates, because Dad is certainly someone that will call until I answer. With a groan, I answer, clearing my throat a few times so he doesn't know that he interrupted my sleep, since I don't know how late I've managed to sleep just yet.

"Hey, Dad."

"Good morning, my darling daughter. I take it that you had a nice sleep last night?"

Not really, I think. "Yes, thank you. How is Lake Como?"

"Oh, fine, but that isn't what I called to talk to you about," he pauses for dramatic effect, trying to seem nonchalant. "I was watching the news this morning and just so happened to see that things are really starting to heat up with the Bar Rouge situation. Did you know that they're saying it's just a front for selling drugs and laundering money?" Dad asks, chuckling. "That woman is in every shady deal, from sex work to drug selling. Andries couldn't have picked a worse person if he tried."

"Yes, I've heard," I admit. "But I haven't seen anything saying that Roxanne is directly involved yet, so there's still a chance she didn't know anything about what's going on."

"It's impossible to know for sure since she's been completely silent on the ordeal, but in my opinion, her silence speaks louder than words. Have you told Andries yet?"

I hold the phone to my ear with my shoulder, rubbing my temples. "No, Dad. It's not up to me to do it."

"Of course it is, you are his sister. You should help him come to his senses. If Roxanne is behind the drug trafficking, I'm sure your brother will change his tune towards her."

There's one thing he's not wrong about... I feel terrible about not telling Andries the truth because any other time it would be my responsibility to show him what was going on, but Dan and I are both in agreement that we need to give Roxie space to admit to everything on her own. Dad can't know that that's my reasoning, though.

"Dad, I'm sure that he will find out on his own. It's impossible for him not to. I'd rather keep myself out of this mess."

His tone goes cold and shuttered. "I see... very well. Enjoy the rest of your vacation. See you next week."

I try to put the idea of Dad catching on to me changing alliances aside and sitting up in bed, blankets in my lap and start to do some of my own research on the Bar Rouge situation. Every news outlet is posting everything under the sun that they can possibly find out about the cocaine scandal and the suspiciously silent cabaret owner. The consensus is that she *must* be involved if she's avoiding the media so adamantly, but luckily it doesn't look like anyone knows that she's in Capri, so hopefully, the rest of our trip will be peaceful at least.

It doesn't look like many of the dancers or other employees are speaking out—aside from the one that was recorded giving the blowjob on stage. Upon interrogation, the dancer tells the media that Ms. Feng was most certainly aware of the drugs being sold around the cabaret. "How would the owner herself not know?" she was quoted saying. "Ms. Feng has been working in the red light district for the past 16 years. There's no way she wouldn't know."

On the other side of things, there's also a quote from Poppy, Roxanne's former PA, saying, "There's no way that Ms. Feng knew about it. She was misled by the former owners. This is simply a big misunderstanding."

While it's good to know that Roxanne still has people in her corner back in Amsterdam, I fear that it won't be nearly enough. Even with people like Poppy speaking on her behalf, everything is still going to end terribly if Roxanne doesn't fess up to Andries or make an appearance in the media. All I know is that their relationship isn't going to end well if things don't start improving soon, and I fear for my brother's mental health if this scandal takes him under, too. Nothing is more important to Andries than loyalty, and everyone in this house that knows about the Bar Rouge incidents and are remaining silent are betraying him every second they don't tell the truth.

I text Dan a few of the articles I find, including the ones with the quotes from the dancer and Poppy.

Dan: *Yeah, it's all the same stuff from the article my Dad sent me yesterday. There's no way your brother doesn't know yet.*

I bite my lip, considering diving deeper into my research, but decide that I need a few moments to myself before I engage completely in the drama of everyone else's lives just yet. I call the villa's room service and order some fresh fruit, yogurt, and espresso, enjoying it all while I prepare myself for the day. I pin my hair up and quickly shower, cleaning my legs and applying a little bit of blush and mascara, taking bites of the fruit between applications. I've just finished my espresso when there is a knock on my door, startling me. I guess that's all the self care I'm allowed today... which is unfortunate. I'm not ready to face the day quite yet, but the idea that it's Dan at the door, coming to continue our text conversation in person, makes me feel a little cheerier. Of everyone, he's the one I'd like to see the most.

I pull the straps of my short, burnt orange romper onto my shoulders and slip my feet into a pair of slide sandals before opening the door. My greeting falters when it isn't Dan waiting for me on the other side of the door, though. It's Johan.

He looks so handsome in his pale blue linen shirt with his hair freshly styled and a bright smile that it's momentarily distracting. "Good morning Johan," I manage to say. "I thought you had left already."

"I'm actually heading out, but I wanted to come and see you first." He lowers his voice as if we aren't the only two people standing here. "My driver is waiting outside and I've already bid farewell to everyone else. I saved the best for last, of course."

I can feel a blush creeping up my neck and a shock of guilt shoots through me. I've been trying my best not to feel guilty for what Dan and I did back on the beach to Johan, but I have to keep reminding myself that it was the right decision. Faced with Johan here, though… it's a lot harder.

Johan leans forward slightly as if he wants to be let into my room, but that's just a bridge too far for me. Instead, I walk forward into the hallway with him, and close my bedroom door behind me. The last thing I need is for Dan to see Johan and me in my bedroom alone, even if it is for a brief goodbye. He had been pretty hurt seeing me in Johan's room days before, even with the door open.

"Can I walk you to your car?" I ask innocently, giving him no indication that I'm shutting him out of my room on purpose. I look up at Johan from under my lashes, and any complaints he may have had crumble immediately.

"Of course, El. I'd love that."

We don't hold hands, but I let Johan link his arms through mine as I walk him outside. We try to talk, but the conversation is awkward and stilted now that we're alone once more. I wish it were different, I really do, but things have just changed, and at this point in my life, I want to be with Dan. Even if the ghosting wasn't Johan's fault, he didn't fight for me, either. I know in my heart that Dan would have—just like he is now, in his own grumpy way. That doesn't mean I don't feel bad for Johan, though, or that I don't still grieve what might have been.

It's another beautiful day, and the sun on my skin burns away any lingering sleepiness I have from my restless night. We reach the gate, barely speaking, where Johan's driver is idling and waiting for him.

"I guess this is your stop," I joke. "I don't want to keep you waiting."

"You know if you asked me to stay, I would," he tells me, and when I don't respond right away, Johan sighs and leans in to kiss me on the cheek. It isn't a quick, polite peck, but a slow and lingering kiss that feels much too intimate for where he and I stand right now. I don't have the heart to push him away, though, and after a moment he pulls away, whispering to me, "Once you grow tired of him, you know where to find me."

I open my mouth to say something, though I don't know what, but Johan presses an envelope into my hands before I can do so. He gives me one last tender look, tucking a piece of my loose hair behind my ear, before activating the gates and heading towards his car.

I touch my cheek where he kissed me, feeling dizzy as I watch the car pull away. It's only after the driver turns the corner and the car is out of my view that I remember the envelope in my hand.

I open it carefully, heart beating oddly fast, and shake the contents out into my palm. There are two pieces of paper; the first is the same picture I have in my study, the one of

Johan and me at camp all those years ago. We look so much younger and carefree, none of the weight of the drama surrounding both of our lives weighing on us just yet. Knowing that he kept a copy of this photo too makes my stomach do flip flops, and on instinct, I flip it over, knowing before I even see the words that he must have left me a message on the back.

It says, *"Let's meet in England this fall,"* which confuses me until I bring the other piece of paper to the front and see what it really is. Once I identify what he's gifted me, I can't help but gasp. It's a ticket to the Horse of the Year Show— one of the biggest equestrian shows in England, set in October. Of course, it's a VIP ticket too. The gift causes emotion to swell in me because it's so thoughtful... Johan might be one of the only people to know how much I've always wanted to attend it, and now he's made it a reality for me, if I'm comfortable attending at his side, that is...

I turn the picture back over in my hand and scan over every inch of it. My heart aches for what could have been, and a thread of doubt forms in my mind about what still can be, if I want to pursue it with Johan. I trace my finger over his face in the picture, deep in thought. How can he be such a good man that he'd still want a second chance with me?

There's no way he didn't get the message that I was trying to send him about my wanting to turn the page. Fortunately, we'll have the dinner at my parents' soon to clarify all that.

***

It takes me a fair amount of time to go back to my room, and I spend longer than I'd like to admit staring in the direction that Johan's car disappeared. Checking my phone, I realize everyone else is probably already out enjoying breakfast, and I'm just standing here like a fool.

I start to head to the terrace where I'm sure everyone else is, but then I pause. The envelope in my hand feeling it weighs a million pounds. This is definitely something I don't want Dan to catch me with Andries, so instead I make my way back to my suite. After tossing the envelope in one of my luggage bags, I shut the door behind me and go join everyone else.

I'm obviously late, with a lot of the plates in front of everyone mostly empty, but I had enough fruit in my room to satiate me for the time being. I ask the server for a drip coffee with milk and settle into one of the seats, returning the brief greetings that everyone throws my way.

"I thought you overslept, but you don't look it. What was so important that you were late, little sister?" Andries teases, waggling his eyebrows.

"If you must know, I was telling Johan goodbye at the gate." I look around at everyone else at the breakfast table. "Why didn't anyone else want to see him off?"

"Johan came out here and told us all goodbye earlier, but said he didn't want anyone to walk him out, so I guess it was the plan all along to invite you only," my brother explains, a smirk lingering on his lips.

The implications are obvious; Johan wanted to be alone with me and have time to give me the equestrian show ticket in private, but I don't tell Andries anything else, not wanting to make him any smugger than he already is.

"One more chance to see what he can't have, I guess," Dan muses, leaning back in his chair. "Good riddance, I say."

"Don't be rude," I hiss, and Dan just chuckles. I feel his foot under the table touching mine, and I kick at him instead of accepting the gentle flirtation. He grins at me playfully, and there is an obvious change in Dan's demeanor now that Johan is gone. He seems lighter, and more carefree. I wish it was that easy for me.

Instead, I feel tense and unhappy thinking about the manilla envelope in my room and the sweet words Johan had offered me. I had tried to make it as clear as possible to Johan that I'm with Dan, but apparently he must believe that my affair with Dan won't last, and he's trying to catch my interest so when it is over, he'll be right there to catch me.

That fact gives me a fluttery feeling in my stomach, followed immediately by heavy uneasiness when I look back at Dan. Johan is really making my life unnecessarily complicated, and he's not even here anymore.

"So what's on the agenda?" I ask, reaching over and grabbing a strawberry from Dan's plate. I'm desperate to change the subject away from my ex.

Andries looks away, the humor from earlier disappearing, and shrugs listlessly. I can see Roxanne roll her eyes next to him, which leads me to believe they've argued about something.

"I was thinking about going to check out Villa Lysis," my brother says. "It's supposed to be beautiful, and I could use a little peace right now."

"Well, I'm not going," Roxanne declares. "But you guys have fun."

Is this what is bothering Andries? Not visiting a villa seems like an odd thing for Roxanne to be adamant about. "Why don't you want to go?" I ask her, genuinely curious.

"It was originally the residence of a sex-offender. I don't think that it's a place we should be visiting."

Andries scoffs, annoyed. "The man lived there in the early twentieth-century and committed suicide by overdosing on cocaine. No one visits Villa Lysis to honor him, just to appreciate the scenery and architecture. Can't you just appreciate the art for what it is without over complicating things?"

Roxanne's voice is syrupy sweet and angry all at the same time. "You don't care about any of that, you aren't fooling me. You just care that he was a brooding poet like you."

Andries rears back as if he's been slapped. "That's a new low, Roxanne. I just wanted to go check out the villa. It's supposed to be one of the most beautiful places on the entire island and looks very photogenic, that's all."

With a delicate sniff, Roxanne indicates that she's finished with the conversation, turning her body just slightly away from her fiancé and taking a drink of her water. I can see Andries clenching his fists on top of the table, and I'm worried that we're headed to all out screaming and arguing if I don't intervene.

"I'll go with you," I offer, not having anything else to do with my day, anyway. "It might be fun. I could take some pictures for Instagram."

"I'll go too," Dan pops into the conversation for the first time, trying to diffuse the tension just like I am. "We'll have a good time. How long until we leave?"

We make rough plans that come together quickly. I keep sneaking glances at Roxanne, who eventually rises from her chair and disappears into the house, not wanting to be involved with our itinerary creation since she isn't going to Villa Lysis with us anyway. Andries notices but pretends he doesn't. I'm his sister, though, and I can see the flash of hurt in his eyes all too clearly.

With our plans agreed on, we all split off from one another to get ready for our day trip. I feel a little uneasy with how strange breakfast felt between Andries and Roxie, but maybe a day apart will do them some good. I guess I'm completely lost in my own thoughts, though, because once I reach my suite and try to shut the door behind me, someone sticks their foot in the doorway to stop me.

I open it once more to Dan's grinning face. "Can I come in?"

"No." I try to shut the door, but he comes in anyway, pushing past me and going to sit on the edge of my bed. I roll my eyes, but continue to pack my bag.

"Roxanne and Andries seem to be very tense this morning, don't you think?" he asks, and even though I don't want to talk about it anymore, it will be good to compare notes with the only other person in the same situation I am.

"Yeah…." I nibble my lip, trying to organize my thoughts. "I think my brother knows about the scandal, honestly. The fact that he wants to visit a villa that used to be a poet's self-chosen exile from France after a sex scandal is very telling to me. You know Andries…" I trail off, but Dan easily picks up on my train of thought.

"Yes, he's all about dropping all these subtle hints, and going to Lysis to try and make a point is absolutely something he would do." Dan laughs, but his heart isn't really in it. "He's testing us, Elise, I can feel it in my bones. What if we tell him the truth? It'd be sort of fitting telling him about Roxanne's scandal in a villa that used to be an exile for a guy who ran away from one."

I waver. "I don't know… I think we should wait to see if he tells us first."

"He won't," Dan insists. "This is a fucking test. I've already tried to lead him into confessing but he won't."

"I know!" I throw my hands in the air in frustration. "But Roxanne—"

Dan and I both jump when someone knocks at the door. "Are you two ready to go?" Andries says through the wood. "The driver is here, I messaged you both and neither of you answered."

I shoot Dan a look, annoyed that my brother knows that we are in my room together, but tell Andries that we'll be right out. Once I hear his footsteps retreating down the hallway, I sit on the bed next to Dan and put my head in my hands, taking a few deep breaths while he rubs my back.

"Please don't blindside me and tell my brother without at least letting me know first," I beg him, my eyes meeting his. "I still don't think it's the right call, but if you've got to do it, please give me a heads up."

"We're in this together, El," he promises. "We're both just doing our best, okay?"

Knowing that we can't leave Andries waiting much longer, Dan and I head out to find him and the driver so we can head to Villa Lysis. My brother is already in the front seat, and he gives us a dismissive wave as we crawl into the back seat together.

"Figures that I would find the two of you alone in the same room," Andries comments, and before I can complain Dan scoffs.

"Oh come off it, Andries, we were just talking."

"I didn't even ask anything," he answers.

The awkwardness in the car is high, and our conversations with each other are stilted and rocky. I haven't even had time to look into Villa Lysis, only volunteering so Andries didn't have to go alone, meaning I don't really know what to expect. With Dan and Andries talking about fencing, I decide to do a little research on our destination and see what there is to do once we arrive.

A few minutes into my search, I get a message from Roxanne, who must have just realized that the three of us had already left. The two of us haven't really spoken directly since she tore into me yesterday morning, and I'm not quite ready to forgive her for the way she humiliated me in front of everyone. So when I see that Roxanne is actually asking me for help, it takes me off guard.

Roxanne: El, whatever you do, don't tell him about Bar Rouge. I'm sorry for the harsh words I said yesterday but please don't use your brother to get revenge on me.

I'm a little offended that she thinks I would manipulate Andries like that, but I guess she and I don't have the best track record when it comes to treating each other decently. I don't want to interrupt Dan's conversation with my brother now that they are actually talking normally to one another, so I just sit my phone on Dan's knee with Roxanne's message open. He catches on, asking Andries a question that requires a detailed answer, and while he talks, Dan reads the message.

Groaning, Dan shakes his head in disagreement but doesn't speak anything out loud. Instead, he gives me my device back and pulls out his own, typing up a message for me and sending it over.

Dan: Andries knows about it. He's just waiting to see who will have the guts to deliver the news to him. I can't keep lying to my best friend, El.

"It's none of your business and you have no obligation to be the one to tell him," I reply over text.

Dan: It is my business. He's my best friend, and his happiness matters to me. He's clearly not happy right now.

Elise: If his happiness matters so much to you then keep this information to yourself!

It's then that we both look up from our phones at nearly the same time and see my brother staring at us from the front seat. "You guys are awfully quiet back there. Is everything okay?"

"Fine," Dan and I both say at the same time.

"We were just looking some stuff up about Villa Lysis," I add, trying to distract my brother. "It seems to have a ton of history attached to it, right?"

My plot works, and Andries immediately launches into a brief history of Villa Lysis. "Yes, it has an enormous amount of history, actually. The poet Jacques Fersen had it built to be his main home once he exiled himself to Capri. There were… rumors that Fersen had predilections towards minors back in France, and when everything started to come to a head, he fled to Capri and had Villa Lysis built for him. It's an eccentric building, to say the least, but the gardens and views are unmatched by any other place on the island..." Andries sounds wistful about the Villa, and I wonder if Roxanne was right about this not being a healthy place for my brooding brother to visit.

"What about the... suicide thing you mentioned earlier?" Dan asks uneasily.

"Fersen killed himself at Villa Lysis. In fact, he committed the act by overdosing on *cocaine*." I don't know if I'm imagining things, but it seems like Andries puts a lot of emphasis on that last word. "But don't worry about any of that. Of course, I don't endorse what Fersen did, but the guy died nearly a century ago. The villa is now owned by the municipality of Capri."

"Er... that's good, I guess," I say, not sure how to respond to this new deluge of information. "So it's just a tour we're going on, then?"

"No, we can explore on our own." Andries sounds dreamy and sad. "I think it will be good for me. You guys too, I guess."

When Andries turns back around in his seat, Dan and I share a look that silently speaks volumes. If by some miracle Andries doesn't know about Bar Rouge yet, then there is certainly something else wrong with him, because he is not acting like himself at all.

Even though the history of Villa Lysis is odd, to say the least, I can't deny that the place is heartbreakingly stunning. Once a property that had fallen into disrepair, Villa Lysis has gone through an incredible transformation to preserve it for future generations. Though the stone has been cleaned, the white stone is still discolored in places, giving it an old sense about it. Combined with the tall, pale columns and shimmering gold tile work, those signs of aging mellow the entire place out, taking it from outlandish to charmingly vintage.

The architecture is only one half of the allure of Lysis, though. For all of Fersen's many faults, picking an impeccable place to build his sanctuary hideaway was not one of them. Lysis is built perched on the top of a tall hill, overlooking the Mediterranean sea. We can see the busy marina and boats bobbing on the water, but up here in the villa it's quiet. It sort of feels like observing a movie from somewhere far above.

The grounds are dotted with twisting Italian stone pines, their trunks turned and curved, all topped with a flourish of green and scenting the air with the smell of sap and evergreen.

Like my brother said, there is no tour guide, and we are left to wander the oddly built villa on our own. I'm not sure if he called ahead and paid extra to have it be only us on the premises, or if, like Roxanne, people tended to avoid Villa Lysis because of the complicated history connected to its first owner. Either way, it's peaceful in a way that even the beaches aren't, with soft birdsong complimenting the far-away sound of the sea hitting the rocks so far down below.

Andries stays with Dan and me for a short time, and we climb the wide stone staircase into the main grounds together, but once we're near the gardens my brother goes quiet and when I turn around to ask him a question, he's gone. I look at Dan, confused, and he just shrugs.

"Should we go and find him?" I ask, and Dan shakes his head.

"No, I think he needs some time alone. Walk with me a little while."

I do as he asks, looping my arm through his and slowly perusing the gardens as I let my mind wander. I'm barely touching Dan, and if Andries didn't already know what was going on between the two of us it would be easy to see our interactions as nothing but platonic, but since my brother knows some of the things Dan and I have been up to, I make sure to keep everything casual so as to not upset him. Even still, being in this lovely place with the man I have such strong feelings for is nice, and with Andries somewhere else sorting through his feelings, it almost feels like Dan and I are a normal couple on a date.

A lot of the villa is chaotic in nature—bright, reflective tile-work, mixing of different types of architecture, and winding staircases—but the gardens themselves are tidy and well maintained. There are a number of different statues and art pieces made to withstand the weather out here, and the flowers bloom in shades of reds, oranges, and pinks offering the perfect backdrop.

For a few moments, I'm able to forget all the drama and nonsense going on with not only my brother and Roxanne, but with Dan, Johan, and me too. The two of us take pictures of each other, and a handful of selfies with incomparable views in the background. We laugh and joke, and I feel lighter than I have in days, but eventually, I know it's time for us to track down my brother.

He's on the marble terrace, arms folded on the wrought iron balustrade and looking out into the ocean when we find him. It takes some cajoling but he joins us in touring the rest of the villa and even agrees to take some photos with us. Andries is particularly interested in the inside of Villa Lysis and although he doesn't say it, I know he's also somewhat fascinated by the story of Jacques Fersen.

I try to go look at things on my own, but every time I leave the trio I see Dan moving closer to Andries and talking quietly to him, and it sets alarm bells off in my head. The last thing I want to do is have Dan break the news to Andries here and then have to deal with the fallout during our little expedition. Andries is *not* going to take the news about Roxanne and Bar Rouge well, and if we can avoid an awkward ride home with my devastated brother, I think that will be better for all of us.

Dan doesn't say that he's trying to get Andries alone to spill all the details to him, but I know both of these men well enough to read them and what they're thinking without words. I can tell that Andries is melancholic and distracted, and Dan is being eaten alive by the weight of holding onto all these secrets. I make a silent promise to all of us that this will get handled today... tomorrow at the absolute latest. Roxanne's stalling is making this unbearably difficult for all of us.

Andries and I pull away from Dan while he's observing a piece of art. I don't know where we are going through the building, but Andries seems to have a destination in mind, walking with purpose with his hands shoved into his pockets.

We end up in a room painted in a pale buttery yellow, peeling with age in some places. There are ornate, filigreed columns and the floor is done in a pattern of blue and dark orange tile-work. It isn't a totally unique room when compared to the rest of the house, but there is something strange in the air here. It feels empty and haunting in a way none of the other rooms do. It makes me shiver, and I wrap my arms around myself.

"What is this place?" I ask, and Andries sighs in response.

"The Opiarium," he tells me finally. "It's where Fersen used to smoke opium and consume cocaine while he worked on his poetry."

"It feels off in here, so that makes sense."

"I assume it's also here Fersen died of a cocaine overdose." My brother drops the info like a bomb, sounding sad and distant. "Do you know why he did it?"

I shiver again, hugging myself tighter. "No, I don't. I wonder why, though. As far as exiles go, this is a pretty nice place to be secluded."

"He took a partner when he moved to Capri, but their relationship was tumultuous at times." He seems almost nostalgic as he goes over the tragic death of the controversial poet. "Maybe he was just disappointed in his life and his chosen lover."

His words disturb me at a deep level, and I feel my skin rise in goosebumps as I turn to face him. Andries has his head tilted back, looking at the domed ceiling and ambient lighting. My worry for him spikes out of control. "Andries, is something troubling you?" I step forward, laying my hand slowly on his shoulder. "You can trust me, and I mean it."

He laughs sardonically but doesn't pull away. "Oh really? After hiding your little affair with my best friend from me you expect me to be able to trust you?"

"It's not like I hid it from you for some nefarious reason. I kept it a secret because I *didn't* want to cause any conflict between the three of us. I know secrets aren't okay, but I just didn't know—"

I stop speaking when I see a figure in the open door archway; Dan, looking around curiously. It's obvious he doesn't sense the high emotion filling the room right now, and I internally curse his terrible timing.

"What room is this?" he asks, oblivious.

"The room the poet died in," Andries deadpans, pushing past Dan and out of the room. Dan turns to watch him walk down the hallway, bewildered.

"What's his problem now?"

I've still got a huge sense of fear for my brother, so Dan's aloofness rubs me the wrong way. "It's more than just a problem, Dan. He's being really weird and saying really cryptic things… I don't think this is Andries just being his normal level of dramatic." I run my hand through my hair, letting the strands fall through my fingers. "Look… if you want to tell him, go ahead, just do it when I'm not there. I certainly won't be the one to tell him myself, I can't compound his misery."

Dan curses, folding his hands behind his head and pacing the length of the room. "Fuck Elise, I don't know! It should be Roxanne telling him, not us."

"You know I agree with you."

"She's just being a fucking coward at this point, and doesn't even care that she's leaving us in such a difficult situation," he adds, sighing.

I approach Dan, taking his hands and holding them in mine, needing the comfort of his presence. "I know, I know. But he seems to know already, and he's just testing us at this point."

"You're probably right. We need to talk to her together and make sure she's going to tell him. This can't go on any longer."

"I hate to ruin their vacation…" I trail off, thinking about how it will ruin *everyone's* vacation, not just theirs.

"El, if your brother knows and is hiding it, then their vacation is already ruined." He must be able to see how frustrated I am because Dan lifts our joined hands and kisses my knuckles before letting me go. "Hey, let me go find our broody poet and try to talk to him man to man. Will you be okay on your own?"

"Yes. I'm just going to go walk a little more. I don't want to be in this creepy room anymore."

With that, Dan leaves, and I'm alone. Being by myself in the Opiarium is not an option, so I quickly follow the path Dan took down the hallway, but exit the villa in a different place than he does, that way he can have his alone time with my brother.

There is one area outside that I noticed when we arrived that I haven't gotten to visit yet, so I head that way, enjoying the sound of my sandals hitting the stone path. Of all the things on my mind, Andries's strange words and tone of voice when he talked about Fersen's suicide has me very worried about him. He's a giant pain, but the idea that he's hurting so badly is tearing me up inside. It doesn't matter how much he and I fight, I still love him. I want to say that I'd do anything to help him, but the fact that I'm still holding on to Roxanne's secret for her proves that would be a false statement.

I'm so annoyed with my future sister-in-law, and I know that Dan is right when he says this can't go on any longer.

We agreed to talk to her together, but I decide to get a head start on things and text Roxanne so she has some time to prepare for the inevitable when we arrive back at our villa.

Elise: You have to tell him! You are putting us in a horrible situation, and we can't keep pretending everything is fine.

She answers immediately, which makes me think she's scrolling through the news articles about her cabaret on her phone right this second.

Roxanne: I'll tell him once we are back home.

Elise: Not good enough.

Irritated, I shove the phone back into my purse, not even bothering to wait for whatever old and tired excuse Roxie is going to give me. It's absolutely ridiculous that she's made this go on as long as it has! Even if Andries doesn't know, there is no possible way he can stay in the dark for four more days.

Outside, I make my way around Villa Lysis until I reach the edge of the cliffside and the long, winding path that leads further out over the water. At the end of the pathway is a pale stone pergola, separate from everything else. The promise of solitude calls to me like a siren song. I see Dan and Andries sitting on a bench under one of the stone pines, their heads tilted toward each other as they talk quietly. I hesitate, wondering if I should go to make sure Dan isn't telling him about Roxanne's Bar Rouge news, but stop myself. If he wants to tell him, that's his business, not mine. I'm not getting involved.

Once I reach the pergola, I inhale deeply, letting my eyes flutter closed and the stress fades out of my bones. As I repeat this process over and over, I vaguely feel my phone vibrating in my bag. I choose to ignore it for some time, but finally, curiosity gets the best of me and I dig the device out. It isn't Roxanne like I expected, but my mother instead. I realize now that I miss her, even if she's being difficult by going along with whatever Dad says, and I'm happy to hear from her.

She's sent me a picture of the entire family, sans Andries and me, at Lake Como, looking happy and healthy. The text below reads, *I hope you're having a good time! Love, Mom.*

A smile comes over my face, and even though it's a bit of a lie, I respond, *Yes, Mom. Love you.*

It takes some time, but right before I consider the conversation over and tuck the phone back into my bag, my mother sends another message.

Mom: And your brother?

I wonder if this is the entire reason she messaged me in the first place, and consider ignoring her, since I believe if she wants to talk about Andries she should be messaging him directly, but it would be nice to get a second opinion on everything. I trust Mom a lot more than Dad right now, and since I've been planning on trying to get her to come to the wedding anyway, I figure that asking her for advice isn't out of line.

So, instead of the simple text just saying, 'Fine' that I was going to send, I erase it and call her instead.

"Hey, Mom," I say when she quickly picks up.

"Hello, dear. It's so good to hear your voice!"

I smile almost immediately at the compliment. "You too. Hey, so, weird question… is Dad around or are you alone?"

"No, I'm alone in our villa." Her voice becomes more serious. "Why are you asking exactly?"

"I just need someone to talk to, honestly, and Dad has been so difficult and laser-focused on messing with Andries that he's impossible," I inhale deeply, figuring out what I want to say. "As you know we're here for Andries's bachelor trip, but some information has come out about—"

"The scandal with the dancer and the drugs at Bat Rouge, yes," Mom interposes, finishing my sentence. "I already know all about it."

This doesn't exactly surprise me, since the information is everywhere, but it's unfortunate that she has probably already formed her own opinion on everything before I've had a chance to convince her that Roxanne can possibly be innocent. My mother has a more open mind than my father does, though, so maybe not all hope is lost.

"It's awful," I concede. "From the surface, it seems like Andries doesn't know what's going on yet, but I can't believe that's true with how prolific the news about it is. Dan and I think Roxanne should be the one to tell him, but she's panicking and won't do it, and now we're torn on whether to tell him ourselves or give her a little bit more time." In a moment of vulnerability, I let out a shuddering breath, wishing Mom was here with me. "I just don't know what to do."

Mom takes her time to answer, causing a short silence between the two of us. "Since you're being so kind to Roxanne and giving her time to tell Andries herself, does that mean you think she isn't involved?"

"Knowing Roxanne a little better now, I believe there is a chance she's been in the dark this whole time. I can't say for sure, but that's just the impression that I get."

Mom hums on the other end of the line thoughtfully. "You do know how serious this all is, right? This is a way more serious investigation than they're saying in the mainstream news. Roxanne may be taken to court for drug trafficking charges. If she's found guilty she can spend up to ten years in jail. Compared to all of that, I'm barely worried about the wedding at all anymore. Instead, all I can think of is that your brother is planning to commit himself to someone who may be in prison for a decade."

Shock ricochets through me. I can't even fathom what my mother is telling me right now. I expected Roxanne to be fined and be lambasted in the media, but a decade's worth of jail time? It just seems so over the top. Does Roxanne know how serious this all is? She hasn't given me any indication that all of this can possibly go so horribly, and if she doesn't know the gravity of the situation, then it's no wonder she doesn't want to tell Andries yet. Or maybe it's the other way around, and she does know how bad this might end up being, and she just can't face those facts and is terrified of how Andries will react. Would he wait for her for ten years? She'll be forty-six by the time she's released...

The answer that I know in my heart is sobering... if it was something he believed Roxie was innocent of, he would wait for her without a second thought. But for this? No; he wouldn't wait for her, at least I don't think so, and I'm terrified of what that might mean for his mental health.

"Are you there, Elise?" Mom asks, and I realize how long I've been silent, deep in thought.

"Yeah sorry. I-I just didn't know all that. The jail time and all." My mouth is dry, and I swallow, trying to relieve it. "Mom... do you think Dad or Karl, or even the two of them, could have something to do with this? We both know how focused Dad is on splitting up their engagement. It's just so odd that this dancer would do something so egregious while Roxanne is away when they've never had any trouble like that at the cabaret before."

I hear my mother take in a breath to speak, but then she doesn't, as if she's reconsidering her answer. "Your dad has been quite private about his mingling with Karl. I have no idea unfortunately..."

She sounds genuine, if unsettled by the idea of it. "Is there a way you can find out, though?"

Her sigh is long and full of discontent. "Elise, no... you know I can't do that. I'm trying to stay out of all of this as much as possible."

"Mom, this is your son's happiness we're talking about, for fuck's sake!" I complain, my exasperation with all of this tip-toeing around peaking. Mom gasps at my cursing, but I don't let that stop me from making my point. "You know Andries. He was already depressed and a huge mess after their breakup the first time. Do you want him to do something even worse if Roxanne goes to jail?" I almost want to tell her that he's been musing about a long-dead poet's suicide, but I think it might be too much on her all at once. "If we can prove Dad or Karl has got something to do with this, we can *help* her. For all her faults, it's the right thing to do. I don't think Roxanne has done anything wrong, honestly, and we all have our faults, you know."

"Well, I..." Mom starts, but then she trails off, making an incredulous noise before laughing slightly. "I don't really know what to say to all of that. I guess I didn't realize that you were rooting for your brother and his fiancée now."

"I am," I tell her firmly. "I'm trying to be my own person and not just a mirror of what Dad wants from me. I root for my brother's happiness now, Mom, and you should do the same."

When Mom speaks next, the disbelief in her voice is joined by something new—respect. "I will see what I can do."

A wave of relief comes over me, but my life has been so up and down that it's muted in a way. Like I'm too emotionally drained to feel anything fully anymore. Still, I'm glad that she's coming around. "Thanks Mom, that's all I can ask."

"I know. But it's still a lot, my love." She sighs again, soft and maybe even tired. "I will talk to you soon. I love you, and give your brother my love as well."

"I will, Mom. Love you too."

I pocket my phone and fold my arms on the railing, leaning forward and letting the view over the cliffside help to clear all my jumbled thoughts. It's so quiet out here, just the push and pull of the waves and the soft sounds of the city in the distance. Of course, my respite isn't long, and I hear the sounds of two people walking down the walkway to meet me. Andries and Dan's body language is more relaxed with each other than it has been in a while. Maybe this is a good sign?

When they make it to me, they both seem quiet, as if they don't know what to say. All I'm given is a quick greeting. I don't think Dan has spoken to him about Roxanne yet, because I think his reaction would be much more volatile. So what is making them act so odd, then?

"So... what were you guys up to?" I ask finally, unable to bear them being silent anymore.

"We were talking about your little affair, actually," Andries deadpans, and I feel my cheeks heat with embarrassment. What could Dan and my brother possibly be talking about when it comes to Dan and my relationship? I can only hope nothing too graphic. I shoot a look at Dan, but he smiles reassuringly, and it helps me relax a bit.

"And, um..." Andries continues, coughing into his hands when he can't find the right words. "Dan told me Johan left because he saw you two making out on the beach. Not that I like that explanation, but I appreciate his honesty, and well... as long as you two behave in front of me, I guess it's none of my business what you guys do behind my back."

It's clearly difficult for him to get those words out, which makes me appreciate it even more. At first, I'm unsure of how to respond, but I'm so over talking myself in circles that I opt for pulling my brother into a hug. He's stiff, which makes me laugh, but it also helps alleviate some of the worries I have for him. I want him to know that I love him and that I'm here for him, even if I don't know the correct phrases to get the message across right this second.

"Thanks," I say quietly, blowing out a breath.

"You're welcome, El."

It feels like the three of us are closing a chapter when Andries pulls away from my hug, looking between Dan and me without any hate in his eyes for the first time. He obviously doesn't like that we're together in a way, but his grudging acceptance is a step forward that I really didn't expect all of us to take today. I'm so happy about this forward momentum, but Andries's gradual acceptance also makes me feel a wave of remorse.

Remorse, because he's trying to make amends with Dan and me, and at the same time, we're still hiding things from him. The cocaine scandal that Roxanne is in the center of burns in my chest like hot coal, impossible to ignore. His bride-to-be is currently being investigated for criminal charges, and we're keeping it from him. We're guilty by omission.

It makes the olive branch that he is offering very, very bittersweet.

CHAPTER 14

Elise

I shouldn't be surprised, but as soon as we get home and walk out to the terrace, somewhat somber from our beautiful but melancholic trip, everyone that has remained at the villa wants to see us.

Lili and Robin are in the infinity pool, and while Lili is floating serenely on a raft, tanning, Robin looks thrilled to have all the men back.

"Finally!" he exclaims. "I've been so bored. You guys up for more volleyball? A rematch?"

He sounds like an excited kid, but it would take an act of God to make me play freaking volleyball again. Even thinking about it makes my nose ache, and I rub it absentmindedly.

The request for a game, though, makes Andries and Dan perk up like they've been given a shot of espresso straight into their veins.

"Hell yes!" Dan exclaims. "Let me go change. El...you want to join?"

"Absolutely not," I tell him straight away.

"I'm in," Andries declares, as if there was any doubt. "How about you, Roxie?"

Roxanne is sitting in one of the lounge chairs, her dark eyes hidden by a large pair of cat eye sunglasses. She's in a scarlet two-piece, her skin shimmering with tanning oil, and it's hilarious to me that Andries would even ask her if she wanted to play volleyball. She looks perfectly content right where she is.

"No thanks, love," she says, confirming my guess. "I'm good right here."

"Okay." Andries shrugs, giving her no emotion one way or the other. I'm desperately trying to get a read on how they're acting with each other, but my brother is making it nearly impossible.

The two men head back inside to change, and Roxanne lowers her sunglasses, watching them go. Now that I can see her entire face, she looks absolutely exhausted. The things she's dealing with mentally seem to be zapping her of all her energy and vibrance, and I feel for her. But, she's made her own bed, and she's lying in it because of her own choices.

Once Dan and Andries are out of sight, Roxanne stands, grabbing her black lace coverup, and pulls it on before fixing her gaze on me. "Elise, can we talk? In private?"

I raise my eyebrows, surprised. "Roxanne, no offense, but I'm not the one you need to be talking to in private right now. That's my brother."

She shakes her head emphatically. "Not yet. So, will you talk?"

I suppress a groan, but agree. "Alright, lead the way."

She slips her feet into her sandals and I follow her into the house. Roxanne skips both our suites and instead takes us to the dining room, checking the hallway and shutting the door behind her when she's sure we're alone. Instead of sitting in a chair, she paces the floor, nervous energy radiating off her. I have no such qualms, so I go ahead and pull a seat out and sink down into it, figuring that this conversation is going to be a long one. I wish I had a drink, something alcoholic preferably.

"I know I already apologized to you over text, but I need to do it in person, too," she starts as she rakes a hand through her short hair. "I shouldn't have said what I did, especially in front of everyone. We've both been making strides to be better to one another and I hope I didn't destroy that yesterday, but I understand if you feel like you need to reconsider the... understanding that we have with one another."

"It was low of you," I tell her, my eyes fixed on her hopeful expression. "But I've said things I regret, too. I'm not worried about what you said yesterday, if you're being honest, then I can let it go. What I can't move past, though, is that you *still* haven't been honest with Andries. Do you know exactly how serious this all is getting?"

"I'm the main person involved, El, so I think I know the gravity of the situation, yes," she huffs.

"You might have to go to court for drug trafficking, but I assume you know that already, too. This is swiftly getting out of control and you aren't doing anything to mitigate damage here."

"I know about the criminal investigation," Roxie confirms, sounding grim as she continues pacing the floor around the dining table. "I've been talking to my lawyer, so it isn't like I'm avoiding it altogether."

"Sit down," I push the chair next to me out with my foot. "You're stressing me out with all the pacing. So, what you're saying is that you're working to fix the damage legally but you're letting things fall apart with your fiancé in private because you're too scared to be honest with him?"

"You have no idea of how this is all affecting me, El, so I wish you'd just quit pretending like you do." Her tone is snappy, but she does as I ask and sinks into the chair next to me, letting her head fall into her hands with her elbows on the dining table.

"Have you considered how badly this could play out between the two of you if you don't own up to things before we get home?" I ask, folding my hands in my lap.

"Yeah, our engagement—"

"No," I interrupt. "That's not what I mean. What if once we are back in Amsterdam you get arrested? If you don't tell Andries what's going on he's just going to watch this happening under his nose and have no idea what for."

Roxanne blanches. "That's... fuck... I don't know, Elise..."

"You *have* to give him time to process it," I insist.

"I don't want him to know anything just yet." She sounds desperate, even lost. "He hasn't figured it out yet, what's so wrong with giving us a few more days of peace together before everything goes to hell."

There's no way she can be so blind to what is going on here. Roxanne's denial has me on the edge of being angry, but I tamp it down the best I can. I need to be reasonable if I'm going to get her to finally confess. I can feel her teetering on the edge of telling Andries everything, but if I push too hard she's going to balk. I have to be careful. All of the time in my life that I've spent manipulating people to do what I want for less-than-noble reasons can finally be used for something positive, and that's saving my brother from embarrassment and mental ruin.

"He likely already knows, Roxanne," I tell her, reaching over to touch her knee so she looks up at me. "It's destroying him. He's testing us all, I'm sure of it."

"I've had that thought too." She pauses, taking my hand that I laid on her knee and holding it between both of hers, trying to express her sincerity to me. "You know why I'm hesitating so much, don't you? I'm usually not scared of things like this, El. I'm not afraid of the media, or what this could do to my public reputation, which has already been dragged through the mud lately... but now I have something that I am frightened of, and that's losing your brother. I'm so scared that he will leave me just like he did when he found out about the escort agency, and as much as I loved him then, the amount of love I have for him now is unimaginable, and losing him would utterly destroy me."

There are tears both in her voice and glimmering in the corners of her eyes. My heart aches for her, and for my brother, and I wish so badly that there was an alternate path for us to take where everyone could walk away without being hurt. But it's too late, and Roxanne's single lie about being the owner of Bar Rouge has snowballed out of control, and now the revelation of that fact will harm us all. But it has to be done... there's no way around it. I just have to convince her of that.

"Roxie, you have to come to terms with the reality that you've been lying to him your entire relationship now. First about your job, and now about Bar Rogue. That's why he broke up with you then, and that's why you're afraid he's going to do the same thing now. Andries is going to come to this same conclusion—that the two of you have not had one day of your relationship that hasn't been shadowed by a lie of yours."

Roxanne swallows hard, and I think she might be sick, but I can't stop now. "It might have been okay if you told him immediately about owning Bar Rouge," I continue, "I'm not sure how much that would bother him, since it isn't outright sex work, but you kept that a secret. You should have just sold it along with your escort business, but that's neither here nor there. Now, the single lie about you owning the cabaret has become a firestorm of drama. You went from owning a slightly inappropriate business to being *investigated* for drug trafficking charges."

"Don't you think I know that?" She nearly sobs, her eyes holding back tears on the verge of falling. "Don't you think I've thought about that every second of every day since the scandal first broke?"

I take my hands from hers and sit back in my chair. It looks like she might crumble in on herself, and I figure that if there's ever a time she's going to be vulnerable enough to be influenced by me completely, it's now. Roxanne and I are wildly different women, but we both share a stubborn streak a mile wide, so this might be my only opportunity.

"Let me call Andries and the three of us can talk. I'll stay by your side if you need me to, but we can end this agony once and for all. I will help you talk to him, Roxie. You just have to let me."

My words roll over her like the ocean itself, they are so heavy, but with tears streaming down her lovely face, Roxanne Feng nods and puts her heart in my hands. "Okay," she utters, her voice barely audible. "I'll do it."

I'm on my feet before she can even process changing her mind, all but running down the hallway and out to the terrace. My pulse is racing faster even than my thoughts, and I can't even believe that I've finally gotten this chance to clear us all of the heavy guilt we've been carrying. If Roxanne does it with me there, then Andries can't hold anything against me for not telling him in the first place, because his fiancée and I will be doing it at the same time.

I slow myself down when I reach the terrace so I don't alarm anyone, but Dan sees me immediately and knows that something is different. He stops the game and swims to the edge of the pool, watching me like a hawk as I approach the water.

"Andries, Roxanne, and I need to talk to you in the dining room," I announce, causing everyone in the pool to look at me. My brother stiffens, and out of the corner of my eye, I can see Dan already climbing out of the pool. I don't need him with us, because I'm afraid he'll be too quick to back Andries and encourage his anger without even realizing he's doing so, just by being overly supportive. Their friendship has been on the rocks the past few days, and I can see Dan overcompensating to try and repair it at the worst possible time.

"Alright," Andries says simply, climbing out of the pool as well. He goes to dry himself off, where Dan has just finished doing the same thing before coming to me and speaking quietly.

"Can I join you?"

"I'd rather that you didn't," I tell him seriously, but Dan is already pulling his t-shirt on.

"El, I only asked as a courtesy. I'm coming no matter what."

I roll my eyes, resisting the urge to punch him in the arm. "Fine, but you aren't there to be a cheerleader for my brother. We're trying to salvage their relationship if we can, not make Andries feel righteous or whatever."

"Have a little faith in me," Dan says just as Andries comes to join us. His expression is stony, and I can't read him at all. He's been so impossible this entire trip that sometimes it feels like I'm talking to a stranger and not my brother that I've grown up with.

"I'm ready," Andries informs us, and we all make our way to the dining room in silence, where Roxanne is no doubt waiting in agony for us. I have the bitter thought that I should take as long as possible to bring Andries to her, just to give her a little taste of how Dan and I have felt this entire time she's been holding back from telling my brother the truth, but the longer I keep this discussion from happening the longer we all have to suffer.

When we enter the dining room, Roxanne has gotten herself under control and looks calm and collected, at least compared to the way I left her. The way Andries goes to sit across from her instead of next to her is telling, and I can see the hurt on her face when he does so. I decide to sit next to her instead, and Dan takes the seat next to my brother.

"I feel like this is an intervention," Andries drawls. "What did I do wrong now?"

"You didn't do anything wrong," Roxanne replies, keeping the look on her face soft and open. "I… well, I'm not sure if you already know what I'm here to talk about, because I feel like things have been off between us these last few days, and I promise that I never meant to do anything to hurt you. In fact, I only kept quiet so I *didn't* have to hurt you, and in the beginning, I thought I could get it all taken care of before we got back and then it wouldn't even be a big deal. I mean it's just one business, right? It's not like—"

I put my hand on her leg under the table and she jumps. "Roxie, you're rambling."

She lets out a shaky sigh, still trying to look calm even though I can feel the nervous energy rolling off her. "Sorry, you're right. Let me start over." She inhales deeply and looks her future husband in the eye as she speaks carefully. "Do you remember that cabaret Bar Rouge? You went there once."

Andries nods. "Yeah, what about it?"

"I own it," she says quickly to lessen the blow of it. "I have been the owner for a little less than a year, but I don't manage it. I have a team there that does everything for me, so I'm not involved in the day to day operations."

"I'm sorry… what did you just say?" Andries' eyes go wide, and his tone is disbelieving, but I'm not sure if he is just pretending or not. "Why didn't you tell me? I thought you wanted an honest relationship based on mutual trust."

"I know, and I do. That's why I'm telling you now," she explains. "I know it's not the right time, and that I should have told you in the beginning, but I never really lumped Bar Rouge and my escort business together. When you asked me to close the latter, I figured that Bar Rouge wouldn't be a problem. I was still afraid, and even though I meant to tell you, I kept putting it off over and over..."

"And I'm assuming there's a reason you're telling me this now instead of continuing to keep it to yourself?" Andries asks, his jaw clenched as he leans back on his chair.

"There is, yes," Roxanne looks desperately at me and Dan in turn, but only for moral support, not because she wants us to do her dirty work for her. She's already taken the first huge step, and I know that she'll tell him everything now. "One of the new dancers behaved very inappropriately on stage which led to an investigation of the cabaret. During the investigation, they found employees consuming and selling cocaine on-site, and that caused the investigation to ramp up and become much more serious." She nearly breathes a sigh of relief after getting it all out. "Andries, please listen to me. I swear that I knew nothing about it."

Instead of storming out of the dining room or screaming, my brother just crosses his arms and shakes his head, chuckling in disbelief. "Let me guess, you are telling me all this now because Elise and Dan knew already and have been pressuring you to do so?"

Roxanne looks down at her hands, which are clenched together on the table in front of her, and says nothing. Her silence speaks volumes, though. Now it's time to try and lessen the damage of the just-dropped bomb, for better or for worse.

"It was Dad who told me," I tell him before she can do so. "Not Roxanne, so it's not like she confided in us before you."

Dan nods and does the same. "I also found out because my Dad told me, coincidentally."

"That's no surprise," Andries replies casually, as he keeps his arms crossed over his chest. "Of course, she wouldn't tell a soul about it, not even her future husband. It's like she hasn't learned anything from her past mistakes."

He sounds coldly furious, but I press on anyway. "While it's not ideal that she lied about being the owner, I believe that Dad and Karl are responsible for the dancer and the cocaine. From what I've seen, Bar Rouge has a relatively clean record otherwise."

Roxanne jumps back into the conversation now, seeing a way out of Andries' bad graces. "Yes, Karl is most likely behind it for the sake of revenge. You know as well as I do that he's petty and conniving. The cabaret doesn't just have a relatively clean record; it had zero issues before I left for vacation. Everything was totally above board. I'm absolutely certain it was premeditated."

Andries huffs, still reeling from all the information being thrown at him. "And what happens now?"

"It's currently shut down, and what's next is still up to the prosecutor, but I suspect they'll want to put me on trial," Roxanne tells him. She's leaning across the table, drawn into Andries like a moth to a flame, hungry for his forgiveness and approval. It's so unlike the sharp, intelligent, unshakeable Roxanne that had been a thorn in my side before I began to consider her a friend of sorts. It makes me look at her in a different light; not because she seems weak right now, but because this vulnerability tells me just how much she values and loves my brother. She loves him enough to bare her soul, and I know that can't be easy for her.

"You? On trial for drug trafficking?" It takes Andries a second to put it all together, but when he does, he's in absolute shock, just like I had been earlier in the day when Mom filled me in. Roxanne goes silent again like she's hit a roadblock, and the laugh that Andries backs out is cruel. "Right before our wedding. Well done, Roxanne."

He pushes out of his chair so hard that it scrapes across the floor, but Dan rockets out of his own seat to stop him. "Oh, for fuck's sake, Andries, why are you pretending you had no idea about all of this?"

He narrows his eyes. "Because I didn't."

Dan has had enough, and I can feel the confrontation swiftly pivoting from Andries versus Roxanne to Andries versus Dan. I guess my fear that Dan would support my brother no matter what was misinformed, and it makes me respect Dan even more, knowing that he will do the right thing even if it's difficult.

"Oh, shut up," Dan snaps, causing my mouth to hang open at his reaction. "Of course you did. You even took us to that villa where the poet died of a cocaine overdose. The hints were all over the place, dude. You wanted *this*. You made absolutely certain that Elise and I would force your fiancée to speak up, and now that she did, don't you dare behave like some sort of victim." I don't notice that he's truly angry, not just annoyed until he points at Roxanne and then at Andries. "*She* is the one who might have to go to trial, so the least *you* can do is to support her."

It's deathly silent in the dining room. Roxanne's eyes are wide as she looks at Dan, her lips parted, while my brother is completely frozen in place. Dan himself is breathing heavily, his chest rising and falling, and I can't take my eyes off him. He makes me feel so many things, but seeing him stand up for Roxanne changes the way I see him permanently. Even if

I know that he is upset with her for putting us all in this position in the first place, he put all that aside when seeing how Roxie needed someone to support her unequivocally, and rose to the occasion brilliantly. Meanwhile, my brother is so focused on his perceived betrayal that he'd leave his obviously suffering fiancée alone to be miserable with no support from the man she loves.

I've never wanted to pounce on Dan and kiss him more than I do right now. If we were alone, I would crawl across the table just to get to him as fast as possible, but I manage to hold myself in my seat. Dan's loyalty is the most arousing thing I've ever experienced, and it lets me know that no matter how bad life can get, Dan will always stand up and support the ones he loves.

This is a good man. Maybe the best man I've ever known. And he loves me.

After the dust of Dan's vehement defense settles, Andries, who is rendered speechless, sits back in his seat and simply stares straight ahead.

"As Roxanne said," Dan continues, his voice more even now that he's calmed down. "The cabaret used to be run without any problems, so it's clear that this is Karl's doing. We just need to prove it and send his ass to jail once and for all."

"I agree, but don't forget that my dad might be involved as well," I add quickly. I'd love to see Karl go to jail. But my father... despite all his shortcomings... well, he's still my dad, and I love him. I'd rather not see him go to jail. "He didn't outright say that he was, but he was very happy about sharing the news with me."

Andries looks disturbed by this, but he is still mute, and I wonder what exactly he's thinking. He stands again, this time discreetly enough for Dan not to catch him, walks to the small bar cart, and pours himself a glass of whiskey. It's more than two fingers, and maybe it's because my nerves are so frayed by everything that has happened today, but I lose my cool about it.

"I can't believe you're drinking again!" I exclaim. "Did you not just recover from being black-out drunk the other night after your little sailing escapade?"

This snaps Andries out of his silence. "It's just one damn glass, Elise!" he blurts out, all but stomping to his seat and sitting back down. Through my annoyance with him, I notice that he doesn't once look Roxanne's way.

"Now that everything is out in the open, we need to come up with a plan of attack," Dan proceeds, bringing our focus back to him. "Karl, and whoever else is working with him, has managed to catch us unaware, but we can't let that happen again. Once we get back to Amsterdam, we've got to hit the ground running, and give him no chance to get one over us again."

Agreeing with his statement, Roxanne asks, "What do you suggest, then?"

Dan takes the reins of the conversation now, his control comforting my raw emotions and how out of control I feel. Putting my trust in him helps me focus, and by the way, Roxanne turns her entire body towards Dan as he speaks, I get the impression that she feels exactly the same. All of this feels like chaos, and his offering to bring it all into order is like a safe port in a storm.

"There's four—" he looks over at Andries, who is holding his whiskey glass and looking away from all of us, sulking. "Three or four of us, depending on Andries' mood, apparently, so we all need to be tackling the problem from different angles. Roxie, your job is the most obvious. I assume you already know what you need to do, considering that you're no stranger to being lambasted in the media."

She nods, confidence creeping back in. "I'll do an interview and showcase an unarguable statement about not being involved with any of the scandals that have happened. I can provide the completely clean history of Bar Rouge over the past years. If I can get even an inkling of proof that Karl is involved, I think I can turn the tide of public opinion, considering that Karl has so recently been in trouble because of everything that happened with Patricia."

"That's perfect. Elise?" He shifts his attention to me. "You're closer to Karl than the rest of us are since you work with him, so your goal will be to get as much information from him as possible. Play nice if you want, I trust you to handle it."

"I can do that, no problem." I almost glow under his praise, especially when he gives me a subtle wink after checking that my brother is still looking elsewhere.

"I'll write up a testimony as a previous patron of Bar Rouge, just in case Roxanne goes to trial. Maybe I can even get a few of my friends that have also attended regularly to do the same, as sort of a character witness."

"That's good." Roxie nods. "But what about submitting something written to the media as a former patron beforehand? I'd like to avoid a trial if at all possible."

"Possibly. I'll look into it. I have some contacts in the media here and there that might be helpful. Do you two know anyone in particular that you have in mind?"

With that, we all dive into the discussion of how to tackle the Bar Rouge scandal when we get home. I think it's best that Roxie talk to at least one reporter before we return, just so the pressure is lessened somewhat and there won't be as many journalists hounding her to get the very first interview from Roxanne Feng. Roxie herself isn't quite sold on the idea, and I get the feeling that she wants a break from the reality of this horrible situation. I can agree with the sentiment… I'd love to stop thinking about it all, too.

Even if it's tough to talk about, I feel like an enormous weight has been lifted now that everything's out in the open, and making these plans for the upcoming week makes all of it feel much more manageable. I keep glancing over at my brother, and then back to his fiancée, noticing that the two of them still seem pretty weighed down by their own things, though. For Roxanne, I suspect it's guilt and fear of the future, and for Andries, it's because of the break in Roxanne's loyalty and the fact that none of us are really on his side. My brother never seems to care if he's the only one with his specific opinion, no matter what the subject is, so instead of coming to the conclusion that he might just be wrong, he'll just pout and be pissed off instead. He has a really hard time admitting that his worldview isn't the perfect one.

I think about his friendship with Dan, and see it in a new light now. The dynamic between the two of them has always been a hedonistic, easy-going Dan and a buttoned-up, broody Andries, which has led people to believe that Andries was the more mature of the two. Seeing how both men handle this situation, though, makes it clear that Dan is not only the older friend in age, but he's also the more mature of the two by a mile. He might have a goofy streak, but Dan is sharply intelligent and capable. His petty issues with Johan have blinded me to that side of him as of late, but now I think it's only because the love he's feeling towards me is a totally new emotion for Dan, and he's still coming to terms with how strong it really is.

I feel pretty strongly for him, too, so when am I going to come to terms with that myself..?

Dan catches my eye and jerks his chin toward the door. I catch his drift right away and stand. "Dan and I are going to leave the two of you. I'm sure you have a lot to talk about."

Andries tries to stand, saying, "I've got nothing to say," which makes Roxanne flinch. Dan prevents him from getting up with a forceful hand on his shoulder, pushing Andries firmly back into his seat. Once my brother relents and falls back into his chair, Dan lets up and pats him on the shoulder instead, as if encouraging the resigned man.

He comes around the table to me, and we escape the room and all the tension there within, shutting the door behind us. I let out a massive breath once we are alone in the hall, happily allowing Dan to lace his fingers through mine as we depart in the direction of both of our suites. I don't even care where we are going, just that it's away from the troubled couple and the ocean of issues they have to work through.

We end up in Dan's suite, and once he shuts us inside, I kick off my sandals, not even caring where they end up. I throw myself on the bed, arms akimbo, and Dan lands beside me. I giggle, rolling over to face him, and it feels like a whole new day, even though the sun is bright outside.

"It's finally over," I marvel as my eyes lock in his. "I feel like I can breathe again."

"I know what you mean," he smiles, relaxed.

"I just have to say, I'm so proud of you for the way you stood up to my brother when he threatened to storm off. I was really into you at that moment, as inappropriate as the timing may have been."

His smile turns sharper as he grabs me by the hips and pulls me closer. "Into me how?"

"Like this," I purr, closing the distance between us until my lips touch his. It's so exciting, so electric every time we kiss that it's almost impossible not to get lost in him completely. But we're behind closed doors, and the hardest things that have been plaguing us are all over, so there's no better time than now to get a little lost.

I take my time, going slow before I touch the seam of his lips with my tongue. Right as Dan opens up for me and we deepen the kiss, we hear the sound of the dining room door opening down the hall. We both instinctually pause and then flinch when the door is slammed shut hard.

"See? This is why I kept saying they shouldn't get married. My brother is too immature. I'd just like to point out I've been saying this from the beginning and no one listened to me." I may sound a little bit smug, but deep down I do feel awful that Andries just ran out on Roxanne like that.

"Okay, first off, I might love you now, but your intentions for splitting them up in the beginning had little to do with Andries being immature and more to do with Roxie's career choice, so don't act like you're some all-knowing soothsayer," Dan replies back. I try to push away from him, but he holds on tight, kissing my neck until I'm laughing and limp against him once more, but apparently he isn't done with the point he's trying to make. "It's not easy for your brother. He fell in love with a woman who is full of secrets and hides a lot of stuff from him. I could write a book explaining why they're both responsible for the tough situation they are in right now, but it's best to let them work it out. I have to trust that your brother will make the right choice in the end."

It amazes me to hear Dan take up for Andries like this, after just doing the same for Roxanne. He isn't taking sides at all, just holding everyone accountable and trying to get them to work things out instead of pointing fingers at one another. He's not just loyal, he's also protective of the ones he cares about, and I find myself so happy to be considered one of those people.

"You've got a point, but don't expect me to admit to that often," I breathe, snuggling closer to him and resuming the kiss.

It's so nice to just languidly make out with him, unhurried, pressing my lips to all those places I adore about him throughout the day but have to resist touching. The line of the tendon in his neck, the curve of his jaw, and the dip in his throat are all areas I pay special attention to, loving the way he rumbles against me when I do so.

During a brief pause in our kissing, he says, "Tonight we have to celebrate."

"Celebrate what?" I ask, hands pushing up under his shirt.

"Mostly the fact that your ex is gone," he tells me, completely serious, and I can't help but giggle again at how sincere he is.

"You know, things have been so crazy with Andries and Roxie that I haven't really thought about him in hours. I sort of forgot he left," I admit, a flash of the manila envelope in my luggage passing through my mind before I brush it away. "How do you want to celebrate?"

Now it's Dan tracing kisses down my neck, making his way swiftly to my collarbone, where he swipes his tongue before replying, "You could spend the rest of the day in here with me."

I let out a shuddering breath when his mouth is on me once more, but I thread my fingers through his hair, pulling so he has to look up at me. "Are you sure about that?"

Dan's eyelids are heavy with lust as he nods, "Yes, I'm sure. Every other couple here is sleeping together, why not us?"

Well, because we aren't a couple, my paranoid mind supplies. After all, it's the truth, and as much as I want to spend time with Dan, I'm not ready to commit to a label right now. Especially when everyone is so on edge, and I don't want to make any rash decisions that I might regret later.

But pointing that out will only hurt Dan, and he's just been too amazing for me to do that to him right now. It's a split second decision, but one that I'm sure about because it doesn't go against any of the agreements I've made with myself about this relationship. It comes a little close, but I want this so badly, and I'm through denying myself all the time.

"I'd love to stay with you," I tell him, throwing a leg over his so our bodies are flush together. "But only if you promise to make it the best use of my time."

Dan grabs my chin between his thumb and forefinger, gazing deep into my eyes. "You won't regret it," he vows, and before I can respond, his lips are on mine and I'm floating away on the cloud of lust that always seems to follow the two of us around when we're alone together.

I let Dan roll us until I'm under him, and it gives me the perfect opportunity to drag his damp t-shirt over his head and discard it somewhere to the side. His skin is so warm, and his skin has tanned bronze from all our time swimming this past week. When I arch up to plant kisses along his chest, fingers trailing up his sides, I think that he tastes just as hot as he feels.

Since he's still in his swim shorts, it takes almost no effort to get them down his legs just enough that I can get my hands on his long, hard length. Dan hisses through his teeth, both in pleasure and frustration. I don't think he expected me to be so needy since he's got me underneath him, but I can't help it.

I throw my arms around his neck and pull him down to me so we can kiss deeply while my hand works his shaft at an achingly slow pace. Feeling him twitch and thrust against my palm is making me wetter than I would have thought, but his pleasure makes me feel good, too. I love that I can please Dan and that he's so helpless to my touch.

"I'm supposed to be ravishing you," he murmurs against my lips, biting my bottom lip before licking away the small sting of pain. "You're messing with my plan."

"If I'm spending my day in here, then I think we have all the time in the world for me to ravish you."

"Hmm. Fair point."

He lets me keep stroking him, but that doesn't mean Dan isn't doing his damndest to distract me, pulling the straps of my romper down my shoulders until my tits are bare. When he sees that I'm not wearing a bra, I feel his cock pulse in my hand, and he curses a string of filthy words, before telling me, "If I had known you were braless all day I wouldn't have waited this long to get you alone." His voice is deep with lust, and he plumps my breasts with his hands before dipping his head down to suck one taut peak into his mouth, and then the other, alternating like this with little nips and sucks until I feel like I'm going to scream. Each touch of his lips and tongue makes me ache between my legs, and I rub my legs together to try and get some relief.

Dan pulls himself out of my grasp, and I make a small noise of complaint before his mouth is on mine again and I can complain no more. He's thrusting against my still-clothed thigh, and I can feel the dampness of his precum through the thin fabric of the romper. He swipes his tongue against mine as if we're doing battle, before breaking the kiss and tracing a path back to my nipples. I'm so sensitive now that I arch off the bed when he licks a slow circle around one, and now I'm the one pushing myself into him, hands in his hair as he drives me absolutely wild before he even gets the rest of my clothes off.

I don't want to lose control just yet, but Dan's clever tongue is making it hard to concentrate. I don't know how it happens, but before I know it, he has both of my wrists pinned over my head with one of his hands while the other drags down my torso—only his fingertips touching me as he makes his way towards my aching pussy oh so slowly. Infuriatingly, he doesn't even undress me all the way, stroking me over the romper once he reaches my hips. When his fingers graze my swollen pussy, I whimper, and he chuckles.

"I can feel how hot and wet you are already," he tells me. "I can't wait until I get your panties off so I can touch your bare pussy."

An idea cuts through the haze of arousal, and suddenly I know how to take control of this situation once more. I smile wickedly, even though he's not even looking at my face, and drop a bomb on him. "I'm not wearing panties, Dan. I haven't been all day."

He sucks in a harsh breath through his nose, pressing his cock into the skin of my hip as he does so. "Fuck, you little witch. You did that on purpose didn't you?"

"Maybe," I admit, squirming until he releases my wrists. Blessedly, he's undressing me all the way, and the next time he stretches his body across mine, it's skin to skin everywhere. "Maybe I wanted you to get me off in those gardens," I gasp, eyes rolling back in my head when he finally touches me where I need him most, parting my folds and running a quick circle around my engorged clit.

"Next time just say the word," he tells me, his voice just above a whisper. "Anywhere, anytime baby."

"Now," I demand, the world turning into a cry when he sinks a single finger, and then two, into me. "Get me off *now.*"

His free hand cups my jaw, kissing me before speaking with his lips still against mine. "One question then, Elise. Did you take your pill this morning?"

"Yes," I tell him, " I swear."

"Good," he growls back, "Because I'm going to cum inside you. Is that what you want?"

"God, yes,"

"I want to hear you say it. I want to hear you call me by my name, so you know who's making you feel like this." He punctuates his words by curling his fingers inside me, making me see stars. "Say it, Elise."

"I want you to cum inside me Dan," I keen, and as soon as the last syllable is out, he's kissing me harder than ever, pulling his fingers out of me and replacing them with the head of his cock. He's so hot and hard that it feels like a burning brand, like he's about to mark me as his own forever.

He sinks into me with one long stroke, and we both moan as we join. Dan paces himself, making every stroke of his cock count, sucking my nipples until the pleasure of his manhood stretches me out and his teeth grazing my sensitive peaks coalesce into one enormous well of pleasure.

No matter how I push against him and whimper, he doesn't speed up, fucking me with even strokes that hit deep every single time. He worships my body with an onslaught that I can't escape, not that I would ever want to, and when he slips a hand between us to where we are joined, I think I might burst into flames on the spot. All of his energy is focused on licking and stroking and fucking me in every way possible, and it's *devastating*.

"I'm going to cum so hard," I confess, and he rewards me by sliding his thumb over my clit directly, a sharp spear of pleasure following the action.

"Good, because after you do, I'm going to turn you over and fuck you exactly how I want," he promises, voice dark and honeyed. "I'm going to fill you up just like I said I would."

DAN.

It starts as a shuddering at the base of my spine, before my orgasm blooms fully and pulls me under with long, soul-deep spasms. It doesn't hit like a strike of lightning like usual, but my climax builds and builds until my entire body is shaking with it. I don't even know what I say as I cum—all I hear is the wet sound of Dan thrusting into my swollen pussy as my inner muscles squeeze at his cock rhythmically, and the sound of my blood rushing in my ears.

I'm still coming when he pulls out and in one swift movement, flips me over and pushes inside of me once more. Dizzy from the force of my orgasm and the sudden change of positions, I can only grip the sheets in my fists as he fucks me—now at a faster and harder pace than before. Aftershocks wring out of me until I think that I can't feel an ounce more of pleasure without perishing. Dan's hands grip my hips so hard I hazily wonder if his fingers will leave bruises, but all other thoughts fly out the window when Dan's thrusts stutter. He makes a noise behind, feral and vulnerable at the same, only a portion of a second before I feel the hot rush of his seed filling my channel. Dan whispers my name falling forward and brushing the hair off the back of my neck so he can kiss me there.

I let go of any muscle control I still have, and we both fall to the mattress tangled up together—satisfied, tired, and covered in one another in every possible way.

CHAPTER 15

Dan

I didn't know how much the weight of a woman could put me at peace until Elise. Having her head on my chest as she traces small circles on my skin, her body pressed to mine, is the definition of heaven.

I move my fingers through her hair over and over again, amazed by how soft and silky it feels. Everything about her is like that—surprisingly soft and gentle—even though Elise herself can be so sharp and almost venomous when she's angry. I'm the only man that knows what she's like when she's well pleased and sleepy, and I plan on being the only one until the end of time.

I can't tell her that, though. Given her commitment issues and all that.

She smells sweet and floral, with just the slightest hint of sun kissed skin. I'm absolutely smitten with her, so much so that I have no problem sharing it with her every minute of every day, if it wouldn't make her uncomfortable. For now, this is perfect. She's mine, and I'm hers.

I can't believe how much she's grown as a person, and my pride for her is almost as strong as my love. I was secretly infatuated with Elise back when she was still just an ice queen to me, but it had been hard to feel that way toward her when she was still treating Roxanne so badly. Her transformation from a self-centered girl to a brave, compassionate young woman was hard won, but it's even sweeter for all the work she had to put into it. Now she's even ready to go against her own father, the man she has looked up to for her entire life, to defend Andries and Roxanne's relationship. No one has said it out loud yet, but everyone knows that if she really goes through with it and Sebastian finds out, he will no longer trust her or offer her the company when he retires, and that must be quite hard for Elise to come to terms with. I hold her a little closer, making a silent promise to her to do everything in my power to support her and help her succeed once he retires. We have years to convince him she's the right choice, but if not, we will fight for it. Even if she decides we won't be together, I'll still help her with this, no matter what. She deserves it, maybe more than anyone else on the planet.

And there's no doubt she'll be a better executive than Andries would ever be. The idea of my best friend running Van den Bosch industries is almost laughable, but the woman in my arms is a different story. She was born for something like that.

We don't talk much, just relax, and I'm just coming to terms with sleeping the afternoon away when I hear my phone vibrate on the charger. I look down, seeing that Elise is dozing, and slowly extricate myself from her grasp. I slide over to the bedside table and pick up the phone, finding that it's Andries who has texted me, which is sort of surprising considering that we had just finished arguing about Roxie's confession a little more than an hour ago.

Andries: Hey, man. Want to join me for a late lunch?

I check the time, confused, since it's almost 4 pm. It's definitely odd that he wants to eat at this time of the day, but I have a feeling this is more about getting away from everything than it is eating. I look back at the sleeping Elise, and since she's totally out, I go ahead and accept the invitation, telling him that I need to shower first.

Andries: You're fine, let's just go. I'm already ready.

I roll my eyes at my friend's typical behavior as I pull on some Bermudas and button my shirt up before going out of the room to meet him. As I make my way out, I close the door behind me as quietly as I can so I don't wake up my sleeping lover.

Andries is waiting for me by the front door, dressed the same as he was this afternoon, and looking restless. He is obviously relieved to see me, and I pat him on the back a few times as we walk out to meet the driver.

"Are you doing okay, buddy?"

"Hell no," Andries admits. "But some seafood and wine might help, we'll see."

He directs the driver to take us to a beach club restaurant, Ristorante Da Luigi.

Once we reach our destination, it's becoming quite clear that Andries's choice of an early lunch is solely because he wanted some privacy, since we're one of only three tables in the entire place. The lack of other guests means we get a prime table on the edge of the outdoor dining area, overlooking the turquoise Mediterranean Sea and views of the towering Faraglioni. Scents of buttery seafood and fresh bread waft over me, and my stomach growls. I guess I didn't even realize how hungry I was until right now.

The server is quick to greet us since the restaurant is so slow, and when Andries just gives a listless shrug when the young man reads off the list of wine, I go ahead and order for us. I choose something light and fresh, internally thinking that the last thing Andries needs is something else heavy and complicated in his life right now. My friend adds on a basket of fresh bread before the server leaves, and then he's back to staring out into the ocean, his chin balanced on his fist, elbow on the table.

I keep waiting for him to initiate conversation, but he's silent, even as the server pours our wine and delivers our bread—baked with fresh herbs and served with olive oil for dipping. The crunch of the knife cutting into the crust seems almost deafening compared to how quiet Andries is, and while he takes his own slice of bread and empties half his wine glass in one drink, he still doesn't have much to say to me. I've never seen him like this. Sure, Andries can be moody and melancholic, but there is always a lot of venting or ranting to accompany it. He's never silent like this, and the strange behavior he's showing makes me uneasy.

"Wine is good," he says finally, still not looking at me. "What are you ordering?"

"The prawns, probably…" I say, wondering how I'm supposed to stretch that one question into an entire conversation. "It says they are fire grilled."

"Nice," he comments, emotionless. "I'm getting scampi."

"Uh… great…" I take a long drink of my own wine glass, stopping myself from drinking the entire thing just to ease the awkwardness of this meal. I need a little liquid courage, and as the refreshing wine pools in my belly, I decide to do something about all of this. I'm not going to eat in utter silence, after all. "Are you okay, Andries?"

Now he looks at me, and his eyes look haunted. "Should I really get married, Dan?" He pauses, taking a deep breath. "I mean, what if she is found guilty and spends the next decade in jail? Am I supposed to just spend ten years without seeing my wife, knowing she's locked away in some prison?"

Ah, here it is. The real reason for this trip. "We don't even know if she's going to go on trial or not, man. She wasn't in the area when all of this happened, and, like she said, her cabaret had a squeaky clean reputation before all of this."

"I shouldn't have done it, but I couldn't help myself... I looked up some of the news about the whole scandal after I talked to her alone, and there is a new video where the prosecutor is saying on television that they believe she left the country on purpose."

"First off, don't do that to yourself. Don't go searching for things like that when you know it's just going to upset you. Plus, I'm sure this PR stunt is being financed by—"

"My dad?" Andries interrupts, his words sharp like the blade of a knife. "Yeah, maybe. Let's say he's funding it. That doesn't take away the fact she is the owner *and* that she lied to me, Dan. *Again.*"

Out of the corner of my eye, I can see the server hesitating to approach the table, so I wave him over. "Let's order, and then we can get into all of this."

He nods tightly, and we place our orders, the heat of the argument we were almost getting into fading away.

I chew on some oiled bread to keep myself busy while I try to figure out the best way to support Roxanne while still admitting that Andries has a point. "She didn't really lie. She just… didn't tell you about it," I say lamely

"That's called a lie of omission," he replies just as fast, pinching the bridge of his nose between his fingers. "It's the same shit. She knew I wanted her to quit that industry, and a cabaret in the red light district is not much different from that agency she owned."

I furrow my eyebrows, an argument forming in me. "It's not exactly the same, and you—"

He holds up a hand. "Don't. I'm not trying to convince myself that it's okay that she hid an entire fucking cabaret from me, okay?" My mouth snaps shut, and I pour us both a refill just to have something to do. As soon as we're done arguing, Andries starts to fade back into himself once more, looking pensive and far away. "I bet Dad is laughing all the way in Lake Como about what is happening."

"Don't let him win, Andries," I tell him. Thinking about Sebastian and all the shit he's pulling to make his own son miserable makes me feel heated, and my words reflect it. "We can get great lawyers, the best around, and go against Karl and your dad. Roxanne might have a lot of flaws, but she really does love you. I've been able to tell that from the very beginning, and it hasn't changed. In fact, I'd even argue she loves you more."

"Is love enough, though?" Andries asks, visibly broken. His words startle me… Andries is a true romantic.

"Um, what do you mean by that exactly?"

The server brings our food by, and my stomach rumbles again, louder this time at the scent of the prawns. Andries's shrimp scampi is swimming in clarified herb butter, and he has a side of roasted vegetables to go with it. Not that he's paying any attention to his food, that is.

"We are just so fucking different," he answers after a moment. "Her life choices are now biting us in the ass and they are taking her away from me."

"That's why you have to fight back," I answer, my tone overly excited, but Andries just scoffs. How can he be so dismissive about everything? It drives me insane! "I promise you that Roxanne never thought owning a cabaret would lead to so much trouble. She was, and still is, a savvy businesswoman, Andries. I bet that cabaret was the last little piece of the empire she built for herself. It was wrong of her to keep it from you, I agree, but I really don't think the intent was at all malicious."

"Yeah, right..." Andries says between bites, tearing off little pieces of the crusty bread to soak up the herb butter as he talks. "It's so hard to tell when she is doing something on purpose or not, so I have a hard time believing that she's so innocent when it comes to lying to me." He pushes the food around on his plate, the wind blowing his hair. "So... do you really think I should go ahead with the wedding for next month or what?"

"Which day was it, exactly?"

"Twenty-sixth of August," he says, sounding nostalgic, his gaze drifting up to meet mine. "The day I met her a year ago."

This is the longest year of my entire life thanks to you, Andries, I can't help but think. Out loud, I tell him what I genuinely feel, even if it might not be the wisest decision on paper. "I think you should, yeah. But at the end of the day, it's up to you. I can't make that decision for you. No one can."

There's a lull in our talk as we enjoy our food and let all the events of the last few days wash over us. It feels like a waste to be so down and sad in such a beautiful place, but I can't exactly tell my friend to cheer up. He has all the reason in the world to be gloomy, for once. My prawns are citrusy and bright tasting, paired with rice pilaf.

"Are you actually mad at Roxie?" I ask, curiosity getting the better of me. Scared for her I can understand, but I hope he isn't outright angry with her. They have enough to deal with, and that will just make it harder.

"I... I'm still processing, to be honest. She's hidden so much from me over the course of our relationship, and it's only been a year. It's hard to pretend that everything is fine when it's not. It's not like it should be between us now."

I level him with a serious stare. "Be real with me, Andries. Can you really not see that she kept this information from you because she knows how dramatic you can be?"

It was a risky thing to mention, and at first, I think he's going to get mad, but then Andries laughs. "I'm not as chill as you are, that's for sure. You and Elise will have a much more relaxed relationship than Roxanne and I." He stops, a bite of food halfway to his mouth. "If you two decide to get in one, that is."

It feels like whiplash to suddenly be talking with Andries about my relationship status with his sister after he spent so long being pissed off at us for getting together. Plus, Elise and I haven't spoken about being an official couple, even though I've told her that's what I want. Still, I can't exactly lie to him about this, so I don't even try. "I'd love to be her boyfriend, but your sister isn't exactly the hopeless romantic that you are."

He huffs, amused. "Ha, we are all aware that Elise is not any sort of romantic, and definitely not a hopeless one. I'm sure you know that it is going to take some time for her to move on from Johan, especially with all those old memories being close to the surface of her mind now."

I set my fork down and cross my arms, staring at him. "Yeah, thanks for that, by the way. I really loved you bringing in a third wheel to trip me up. Asshole."

Andries smirks, but it doesn't quite reach his eyes. "No problem, man. I know you like a challenge."

I let the subject drop after that, as I feel supremely uncomfortable discussing my relationship with Andries, considering that my lover is his little sister. Thankfully, he doesn't bring it up again, and it seems like being able to vent about his fears surrounding his upcoming marriage has at least made the day a little more bearable for him.

Our food is fresh and delicious, and the server is great at bringing a second bottle of wine quickly when I motion for one. We let our conversation trail off to more casual things, and before I know it, things feel more normal than they have this entire trip. This is what I wanted… this bonding time with Andries before his wedding. I just want him to be happy, and while he can't help the bad things that happen to him, like the Bar Rouge incident, he also has a major problem with getting in his own way and making things more difficult than they need to be.

"Dan…" Andries sighs. "Thank you for everything. I know I don't say it enough, but you've done so much for me and I really do appreciate it. Truly. I will never forget this amazing stay here in Capri, and I hope to be able to return the favor and plan your bachelor trip one day."

Emotion wells up in me, and I clear my throat so I can speak without sounding strained. "Of course. And I look forward to that day, too… and honestly fear it a little. I don't want a bachelor trip to a poetry retreat, I'll tell you that right now."

He chuckles, genuinely amused, and I consider it a win. At least he's speaking to me, if nothing else.

I don't pay it any mind when Andries gets a text, but when he sets down his utensils and his expression changes from calm to concerned, I sit up a little straighter. "What's going on?"

"It's Elise… It looks like the court of second instance believes a rapist doesn't need to do jail time."

His words ping around in my head for a second before they start to make sense. I swallow my bite and take a drink before I can speak past my shock. "Are you talking about *Karl?* The court already gave a verdict… in his favor!?"

"Yep," Andries says, resigned. "They kept the fine but removed his jail time. I guess the fact that everyone found out that Patricia was paid to go to court helped his appeal."

With his mouth a thin line, Andries puts his phone away before pushing his half-empty plate aside. I look down at my food and feel the exact same way: I've lost my appetite, thinking of Karl once more getting to go free. What a piece of human garbage.

I'm pissed, but I need to keep it under wraps because I can already see Andries start to spiral again. "Don't bother yourself with this. You've got enough going on. Even Patricia didn't care about the outcome, so just let it go."

"None of that changes the fact that we need to get this Karl behind bars for good. He's nothing but a scheming predator that has enough money to get himself out of trouble again and again. If he and Dad are behind this new drug trafficking scandal, we can prove it. I'm sure of it."

"How are we going to prove it though," I ask, leaning forward with my elbows on the table. There isn't anyone else around us, but I still feel like we need to speak quietly about things like this. Karl has proved himself untouchable again and again, and I'm sick of it. The thought of Elise working with him, and getting closer to him to try and get information, makes my stomach roll. I know she can take care of herself, but that doesn't mean I don't worry about her. I have to shelve that thought for the moment, though, because it's not like she's going back to work while we're still in Capri. That's an issue I have to work through when we're back home.

"So how do you plan on proving it?" I ask, genuinely curious.

Andries shrugs, but he is restless. Like he has an idea, but it isn't sitting easy with him. "Maybe Dad can throw Karl under the bus to save himself..?"

Wiping my hands off with the cloth napkin, I raise my eyebrows. "I don't understand what you mean by that."

"Once we get back to Amsterdam, I'll contact Kenneth, and Roxanne and I will do an interview saying Karl and my dad are behind this drug-trafficking scandal," Andries clarifies, but what he says is so foreign and unexpected that my brain refuses to absorb the words at first.

When I untangle it all, the revelation that I find is astounding. The truth of what Andries is saying—the absolute scorched earth plan that he's hatching—hits me like a bomb going off. This is the Van den Bosch family, after all, and what Andries is saying he'll do is tantamount to blasphemy of a sort.

"Wait... you want to drag your dad through the mud?" I blurt out, still not sure that I understand what he's saying. It can't be, can it? Is Andries really going to fight for Roxanne like this?

Maybe I judged him too harshly. Apparently, Andries's form of battling for his loved ones is just more subtle than my own.

"Yes," Andries says, his tone leaving no more room for questions. "If it's war that he wants, then it's war he will have."

Andries has rendered me speechless, so I busy my hands by pouring us the rest of the wine and draining half my glass in one gulp. My thoughts are all over the place right now, concerned with how Elise will react to this news and what kind of inter-family drama this will cause with Julia, who strongly prefers to fly under the radar when it comes to the media. Andries going public, accusing his own father of being a fraud, and creating a fake crime to implicate his bride in a public interview is anything but under the radar. Poor Julia.

Still...it's a good plan. A great plan, even, and I'm shocked that Andries is so willing to hit back now. "Man, this is... well, this is very bold."

"It is," he nods. "Can I count on your support?"

I hold up my wine glass, pride swelling up in my chest for one of the Van den Bosch heirs for the second time today. "Always."

Andries raises his own wine glass and taps it against mine. The clinking of our glasses sounds like a new era being born.

CHAPTER 16

Elise

Lying on the plush lounge chair, it's hard to concentrate on the book in my hands while the Mediterranean sea stretches out before me. The sun slowly descends beyond the horizon in a fiery display of orange and pink hues, painting the sky in a brilliant array of colors. The terracotta roofs of the nearby houses are bathed in the warm glow, creating a picturesque scene that takes my breath away. It's more captivating than any words on the page, and I find my thoughts drifting aimlessly until I see Dan arriving through the double doors.

In the fading evening, Dan looks like some sort of model, stalking toward me with that lazy confidence he always has. I pretend like my eyes are fixed on the pages of my book behind my large sunglasses, but he isn't fooled.

Once he reaches me, I feel my pulse quicken. Something about his presence always does this to me. Dan settles into the chair beside me and asks, "Has everyone already eaten?"

I look up at him and with a hint of disappointment in my voice, I reply "Yeah, they have." I can't help but wish we could have shared a meal together, just the two of us.

When he just shrugs, I can sense the weight of his meeting with my brother still heavy on his mind. We sit like that for some time, no doubt both thinking about the heaviness of the situation we find ourselves in. Chest filled with worry, I ask him about Andries, "How is he doing, Dan? Really?"

I can feel my heart heavy with concern as he replies, "He's had better days."

Dan then asks me if I had a chance to speak with Roxanne. I confirm that I did and that she had mentioned that Andries was being distant and cold with her, which was expected. Dan's expression turns serious as he expresses his concern and warns me that we need to keep a close eye on Andries, given his self-destructive tendencies.

"There's just something darker, almost sinister, about how deeply depressed he seems to be right now. I worry, especially with the impromptu visit to the suicidal poet's villa. We have to work together to keep watch over him."

The reality of the situation sinks in as I look at Dan with a worried expression on my face, and I ask him in a voice barely above a whisper, "Is the wedding still on?"

Dan's hesitation before replying fills me with dread, which surprises me somewhat, considering how much I thought I didn't want this wedding to happen only weeks ago. "I guess so," he tells me, and then pauses, as if he's weighing how much to share. "Your brother wants to go to war against your dad," he announces like it's nothing, picking at his fingernails as he speaks. "That was the big thing the two of us talked about at dinner."

The weight of his words hangs heavy in the air as I start to contemplate the implications of Andries's actions. My mind races with thoughts of the chaos that would ensue if this wedding falls apart. "What exactly does my brother have in mind?"

Dan watches me closely for a moment before asking, "Elise, is your loyalty still with your father?"

I look at him with a determined expression and declare, "Not anymore." I can see the resolve in his eyes as he proceeds to tell me about Andries's plan to reveal the dark secrets belonging to both my father and Karl during an exclusive interview with his wife-to-be by his side... depending on whether Roxanne will go for it or not. The gravity of the situation hits me like a ton of bricks, and I wonder what the consequences of this revelation will be.

As the reality of the situation sinks in, I can feel as my expression turns to one of shock and disbelief, my chest growing tight. "This is going to cause chaos," I tell him, voice barely above a whisper. "If Dad finds out I knew about this and did nothing, I might lose my job."

"You can lie and tell him you knew nothing about it, there's no way of him knowing otherwise." He tries to reassure me, but I still feel unconvinced. When his words don't help, he then says, "Think about it, El, this is the perfect time for you to advise your dad to fire Karl to save himself."

I've spent so much mental effort to convince myself that Dad is just going to have to be the enemy in my story that I didn't even ponder the possibilities and the potential consequences of trying to get him on our side, all of us facing off against Karl. Would he even humor that idea, or does his company mean that much more than his family?

The tension in the air is palpable as we both weigh the gravity of my brother's plan, knowing that the truth could finally be revealed but at a cost. The thought of the potential fallout is daunting, but the possibility of putting a stop to my father's and Karl's bad deeds is too tempting to ignore.

Finally, I meet Dan's gaze with determination, and say, "You're right. I'll play my part and get Karl fired once everything hits the fan. But, honestly, I think Mom might be our secret weapon here. She fears shame so much... she always freaks out when dad or the rest of us are involved in some sort of media scandal. If Mom starts pressuring Dad to oust Karl from the company and reconcile with Andries, she is one of the only people on earth that he'll listen to."

There is pride in Dan's voice when he responds. "You will succeed with your dad. I promise your efforts won't be in vain, and I'll be with you every step of the way."

I can feel a tiny seed of hope starting to bloom inside of me. "I hope you're right, I'll need all the help I can get."

The weight of the situation is heavy on both of us as we sit in silence, lost in our own thoughts. We know that what's to come will not be easy, but we are determined to see it through and make sure that justice is served.

As I lay next to Dan, longing washes over me as I'm once more taken aback by how loyal he is. I lean over and kiss him, expressing my gratitude for his unwavering support. He responds with a gentle kiss on my forehead before scooting our chairs completely together, and we continue cuddling while taking in the evening. I am drawn to the scent of his cologne mixed with the natural musk of his skin, calling me like a siren song. As I start to kiss and nibble his neck, Dan sighs and leans into me at first, before he pulls back, reminding me that we are out in public.

"My brother already knows about us, why hide?" I ask, trying to mask my frustration.

"Yes, but there's no point in flaunting it in front of him."

I feel a sense of disappointment at his answer. "Didn't you want us to be official?"

"Are we?" he replies, his voice uncertain.

I'm quiet for a moment, unsure of how to respond. Dan then says, "If you were my girlfriend, I wouldn't hide anything from your brother. But since that's not the case, let's behave in public."

I nod in agreement, but my heart aches with the knowledge that we have to keep our relationship a secret. I wish we could be open about it, but for now, I'll have to settle for stolen moments like these. Really, it's my fault for being such a coward about my intense feelings for the man beside me, and how much I want him in every way.

I am torn between my feelings for Dan and the fear of losing our close bond. I am uncertain whether to take the risk and tell him that I want us to be officially together. But I remind myself that being together means a potential heartbreak, and I am not ready to be vulnerable again. "Dan, I need time," I finally tell him, my voice trembling with emotion. "I know I'm being difficult, but I need time to process everything."

He looks at me with understanding and nods once. "I know. Take all the time you need." Dan then sighs, sitting up and stretching his arms above his head. "I'm going to go check on our favorite melodramatic poet and make sure he's feeling alright after dinner." I see his eyes drift down my body, over the pale gold bikini I'm wearing and the way my skin, covered in tanning, glimmers in the dying light of the day. "Well, um, see you later."

"See you later," I say, voice husky as I look up at him through my lashes.

I can tell he wants to say something more, but his eyes drift over to the pool, where Robin and Lili have arrived and are sitting on the edge, quietly talking to each other, and Dan shakes his head to dispel whatever dirty thoughts were starting to rise. He kisses me quickly on the corner of my mouth and leaves to find my brother, and I lay back down with a sigh.

Left alone again, I reflect on all the good moments I spent with Dan and wonder if loving him and being in a relationship with him would jeopardize our friendship. My mind races as I try to make sense of my feelings. Full of uncertainty and fear, as I am not sure if I am ready to take such a big step and open myself up to the possibility of heartbreak. I am afraid of losing him, but I am also afraid of losing myself in the process. The thought of it all is overwhelming and I am at a crossroads, unsure of which path to take.

I know I love Dan as more than just a friend, but the thought of potentially breaking up and never talking to him again fills me with dread. As the sun starts to set over the terrace of our villa, casting a warm glow on everything, I make up my mind to retire to my room for the night.

My nighttime routine gives my thoughts plenty of time to wander, and my shower seems almost lonely. I wish it were Dan's hands washing me, his fingernails scraping across my scalp as he washed my hair, but it isn't meant to be. The two of us have been with one another during any spare moment of time, and I sort of feel like I'm becoming addicted to his company… to his touch. I need to hit the brakes on everything or I'll be absolutely miserable back home when he's not around.

The memory of Dan's invitation to sleep with him tugs at my mind, unbidden, and the temptation is too powerful. Feeling his body against mine is a desire that I can't so easily brush away. I slip into my nightwear and make my way to his bedroom, my heart pounding with anticipation.

As I enter, I see him lying in bed, his chest rising and falling with each breath. I hesitate for a moment, not wanting to disturb him, but the pull of being close to him is too strong. I slip into the bed beside him, and as the mattress dips under my weight, he startles awake. Once when he sees it's me, he pulls me close, pinning me against his body. His breath is warm on my skin as he mumbles a small, "I love you," still half asleep.

Through the open curtains moonlight pours in, bathing our bodies in a silvery glow as I lay there in his arms, feeling safe and content. I smile as I let myself be lulled to sleep by the sound of his breathing and the gentle sway of the trees outside.

CHAPTER 17

Dan

I'm an early riser most mornings, wanting to take a quick run or enjoy my tea with the rising sun by myself, but this morning is a little different. There is a soft, warm, sweet-smelling woman in my arms, and she is precious to me beyond measure. Elise pressed up against me as I float to consciousness is a fantasy I have had many times, but today I actually get to bury my face in her hair and inhale as she wiggles against me.

It wasn't just a dream. She really did crawl into bed with me last night. Not for sex or any sort of physical release, but just because she wanted to be near me. The feeling is mutual, and I squeeze her tightly.

Elise sighs, but doesn't stir, content to sleep the morning away. I stare up at the ceiling, my mind racing with thoughts of her. Why can't she be mine? We have such a strong connection, the chemistry between us is undeniable. But every time I try to bring up the subject of taking our relationship to the next level, she avoids answering directly and changes the subject.

As I replay our recent interactions in my head, I feel a sense of frustration and longing. The more we spend time together, the more I realize how much I want her to be my girlfriend. The way her eyes light up when she laughs, the way she fits perfectly in my arms, it all feels like it's meant to be.

But then a wave of doubt washes over me. Maybe she doesn't feel the same way. Maybe I'm reading too much into things. Maybe she's just using me for physical pleasure. The thought makes my heart ache, even as my mind insists that it's impossible. She has proven, with her actions if not her words, that she *does* love me. There's just some disconnect between her heart and mind that is making it impossible for her to verbalize.

I crane my neck and glance at the clock. It's still early, and I know she's going to sleep for a while if I let her. When Elise sighs, pressing her backside into my hips, I can't help but wonder if she's dreaming of me, or if I'm just a temporary satisfaction. The thought of losing her is too much to bear, and I know I have to find a way to either make this thing between us completely official or let her go once and for all.

Unacceptable, I think. *She's mine, and nothing can change that. She just needs to admit the truth.*

Elise makes a sighing noise that I swear I've heard her make during sex before, and it snaps me out of my heavy thoughts, making me rock hard in an instant. I sleep in the nude, and I can feel the silk of her tiny nightgown against the head of my manhood, and all my thoughts flee. Carefully, I twirl her hair around my fist and move it to the side, kissing the back of her now-bare neck and shoulders until I feel her stirring. Elise hums in contentment, and when I can tell that she's truly awake, I grasp her chin and turn her head just enough to seal my mouth over hers.

With eyes still lidded and heavy from sleep, Elise looks rumpled and soft. Her lips are warm against mine, and despite her drowsiness, she returns my kisses with enthusiastic swipes of her tongue. We make out lazily, our bodies touching from head to toe. My hips unconsciously know the rhythm to thrust against her and make her begin to whimper with pleasure as my cock presses against her core in a mimicry of what's about to come.

I have no idea how much time passes, but when Elise starts to pant between kisses, pushing her ass back against me impatiently, I begin to push her nightgown up her body. My need is frantic, but I have enough self-control to take it slow, kissing and nipping at her full lips and stroking my tongue over hers until I can sense her trembling with need. Then I push the gown up the last few inches, and finally, the head of my cock can feel the smoothness of her skin, painting it with precum.

We don't exchange any words, which makes it that much hotter somehow, using only body language and the music of our labored breaths and sighs to signal to one another what we need. What is between Elise and I needs no words, our bodies and souls align perfectly without them.

I take her leg and pull it up and over my own, keeping us in the spooning position but opening her up to me just enough to slide my cock between the wet folds of her pussy. Elise is ready for me, and the hot tightness of her channel sheathes my cock—every inch taking effort with how snug the fit is—until I hit home deep within her. She throws her head back on my shoulder and moans, a shudder of pure pleasure running through her as I press my hand against her belly and hold her body tight to me, pushing in and out with controlled movements, never fully leaving the tight grip of her pussy. How did I ever live without this? Without her, and this connection?

The way her pussy tightens each time I push deep, or bite the sensitive skin of her neck, makes me feel almost feral, and the way she responds with her whole body when my mouth captures hers makes me even more so.

One of her hands lands on mine where it's still pressed into her belly, and she boldly pushes it downwards until it's between her legs. I know what she wants without having to ask, parting her nether lips and circling her clit, making her buck in my arms and speak the first word of the morning— my name, cried out like a prayer.

"*Dan!*"

"How good does it feel, El?" I growl into her ear. "Only I can make you feel this way, remember that."

She lets me hold her for a few moments more, shivering with how overwhelmed she is, but when I flick my thumb over her clit directly her excitement boils over, and before I can take my next breath, she's wresting control from me. I let her do so happily.

Elise straddles me, her silvery nightgown bunched around her hips to give me the perfect view of the way her pussy takes my cock inside as she lowers herself onto it without preamble. She throws her head back and cries out to the ceiling as she does so. Her neck and chest are flushed just as red as her face, and I want to see more. My eyes are hungry for her skin, just like my mouth.

While she rides me without hesitation, setting a devastating pace with the way she rolls her hips, I push her nightgown up her perfect body until I can see her tits, nipples picked hard with arousal. I lift up onto my elbows and suck one turgid peak into my mouth, swirling my tongue over it, and then kissing a heated path to her other nipple and doing the same.

Elise buries her hands in my hair, and when I look up at her she's watching me lick and suck at her with wide, lust-filled eyes. There's a sheen of sweat on her brow, but she shows no signs of tiring. Just like me, her appetite for the way we come together is endless.

It isn't until I add teeth to the mixture, nipping at her pebbled nipples, that the muscles of her stomach begin to quiver and her pussy spasms around my cock. I feel my balls drawing up against my body, my climax looming, so I release her nipple with a wet pop, falling back flat onto the bed.

She starts to complain, but I quickly slide a thumb over that bundle of nerves between her swollen pussy lips again and all complaints fade instantly. Her pace stutters, so I grab her hip with my free hand and guide her, thrusting up into her as she nears the precipice. I lose control of her body as the tension within her snaps and she comes on my cock hard.

My teeth are clenched so I don't spill inside of her too early, but the moment I can see that she's coming down from her high—a new rush of wetness covers my cock—I grab her by the hips with both hands, hard, and fuck up into her just the way I need. Elise takes it all perfectly, and when my orgasm explodes out like a thunderclap, seed coating the walls of her inner channel, she shivers with the echoes of her own pleasure before collapsing on top of me. It all feels so incredible that I screw my eyes shut, breathing through it, hearing my own heartbeat in my ears as pleasure threatens to drown me.

Somehow, we manage to separate just enough to make out way back into the spooning position, where I can kiss her neck and nibble her ear as we catch our breath. Elise sighs contentedly, turning her head and kissing me on the mouth before telling me, "Good morning."

Her voice brings me back to reality, but for once, it's just as sweet as whatever haze of arousal I was just in. Elise is still in my arms, well pleasured and utterly relaxed, and I wonder why we can't be like this always. Why can't she be my girlfriend when the sex is so undeniably good? I lock away those resentful feelings, wanting to savor this moment, but before I do, one traitorous thought slips through:

She's so close, and yet, so far away.

* * *

Only three days. Three measly days to bask in the beauty of this Italian paradise with my love, and only three more days before we have to return home to our real lives, as drama-filled and difficult as they are. The clock is ticking and it feels as though time is slipping through my fingers like sand.

On the first day, we set out to make the most of every moment, determined to see all the sights we haven't had the chance to experience yet. We don't even stay for breakfast, grabbing croissants and coffee from the breakfast table while Lili and Robin look at us strangely before disappearing out the front door, eating in the backseat of the private car as we discuss our plans. Neither Andries nor Roxanne had been up yet, so we managed to avoid any awkwardness from the two of them, and that's the way I like it.

As we cruise down the streets, guilty thoughts of Andries's engagement flood my mind, making me uneasy. It's not like I didn't want to spend this time with my best friend, but circumstances beyond my control have ruined this trip for him, and I don't think he would even want to spend much more time with me alone, anyway. Not with how messy his engagement is right now. So I'll take advantage of that and steal his sister away before he can protest. This may be my last chance to create memories with Elise on this trip.

We make our way to the Marina Piccola, a peaceful haven tucked away from the hustle and bustle of the island. It's still busy, but the urgency and flash over Marina Grande is lessened at the smaller boat dock. The sound of the waves crashing against the shore fills my ears as we stroll hand in hand, taking in the serene beauty of the place. We feel just like tourists and spend the morning chilling by the shores, before stopping at a quaint cafe for lunch and sharing a meal together, the taste of the local cuisine filling my senses, just like the woman across from me, who slides her foot over my calf flirtatiously as we dine. But all too soon, it's time to return to the villa and change into our hiking clothes so we can complete our main objective of the day—reaching the highest point on the island.

We take the chair lift up to Anacapri and the views take my breath away. The island stretches out before us, a tapestry of colors and textures. We explore the small town, taking in the sights and sounds, but our ultimate destination is Monte

Solaro. It's not the easiest hike, and there is the option to take another chair lift to the summit, but Elise and I are both in fantastic shape, and we savor the chance to make our muscles work—enjoying to burn and the exhilaration that comes with working up a sweat somewhere besides the bedroom.

The hike is challenging, but we push on, driven by the desire to reach the summit before sunset. The sky is painted in a spectrum of colors when we reach the top, and we sit on the edge of a cliff, watching the sun dip below the horizon. It's a moment that feels both fleeting and eternal, and a reminder of how precious time can be. I kiss the woman I love as the sun dips below the horizon, flashing red across the sky.

As we make our descent, my heart aches with the knowledge that this may be the last time I experience this with Elise. I know we have come to an unsteady agreement on wanting to be together, but things can change in an instant in Amsterdam. Only three days left in this place, and it's not nearly enough.

The second day, I have more of a plan in place, so we aren't quite as spontaneous. Days before, my heart had been heavy with the weight of disappointment as Elise recalled her Blue Grotto tour, and explained how she wished we could have experienced it together. Instead, I had been sailing with Andries and Johan, and while I had enjoyed it immensely, the memory of Johan sort of taints the whole thing for me. I knew I had to make it right, to create a memory that would rival the one she had experienced without me.

So, I take matters into my own hands. I rent a small, private boat, determined to explore the hidden gems of the island. We set off, the boat slicing through the water as we head towards the smaller grottos. The Red Grotto, White Grotto, and Green Grotto may not be as spectacular as the Blue Grotto, but they offer us something even more precious: privacy.

As we make our way through the grottos, Elise's face lights up with wonder and delight. I had packed the boat with fresh fruit, cheeses, sparkling water, and champagne, and we enjoy the feast at our leisure, sometimes sitting on the back of the boat with our feet hanging in the water, feeding each other from our fingers. The sun beats down on us, and the cool water provides a refreshing respite.

But as the day comes to a close, and we make our way back to the dock, I feel the rush of time passing by almost painfully once more. We had planned to go shopping in the evening, but we barely make it to two designer shops downtown before we're both desperate to head back to the villa, exhausted from the sun and sea. We enjoy dinner on the terrace with all the other villa guests, trying to make stilted conversation with Andries and Roxanne before Andries cuts out early and heads back to his suite without a word, making his fiancé flinch. I try to cheer up Roxie, but it doesn't work, and once she, too, excuses herself, El and I finish our meals and then retire to our room. We busy ourselves with showering off the sea salt and falling asleep in each other's arms.

But as I lay here, listening to Elise's soft breathing, I can't shake the feeling that it's not enough. Only one day remains, and feel a sense of dread at the thought of leaving. I know that these memories will have to last a lifetime since there is no guarantee we'll even be together to make more down the line. Holding her close, I whisper promises of love and the future we will share into the darkness, meaning every syllable. I don't know if she's awake to hear them or not, but either way, I mean them with all my heart.

* * *

Our last day of vacation has sadly arrived and I can sense finality pressing down on me like a heavy stone. As we sit on the terrace for maybe the last time, enjoying the most extravagant breakfast yet, taking in the stunning views of the island in the early morning, I try to focus on the here and now, and not what our lives will look like back home.

Elise and I managed to slip away from the group, but I feel Andries eyes boring into my back as we do so, and whisper to El that we can't stay away as long today without pissing him off too much. He may have ruined part of his own bachelor trip with his sullen attitude and weird move of inviting Johan, but it really is still supposed to be about celebrating his upcoming wedding, so we can't ditch the couple completely—even if they do seem to hate each other right now, considering the circumstances.

After breakfast comes to an end and everyone else goes back to their rooms to pack up, with plans to spend the day poolside, relaxing, I have something different in mind for Elise and me. I've rented a private boat for us, but this time with a driver, determined to make this last day one that will be burned into her memory forever. I want Elise to think of me every time she lays out on the sand at any beach, or slips into warm ocean water, for the rest of her life. Especially if she chooses not to spend it with me. I want this time we spend together to be the best she ever has, and for nothing else to ever live up to it. Selfish? Maybe… but I've never pretended to be a selfless man.

We set off to Piscina di Venere, also known as the Pools of Venus, a small cove and beach that is tucked away and the closest thing on the island to the way Capri must have looked before human habitation. It's hard to find, the location only known by locals, and the entire place is stunningly beautiful. Since it's only accessible by boat, we're one of the few couples at the Pools of Venus, and we take full advantage.

Our boat skims through the crystal clear waters, surrounded by lush greenery and dramatic, rocky cliff-sides. I've only just told her where we are going, and I can feel Elise's excitement and anticipation growing. This excursion will be one that none of her friends will have ever taken, and it will be something only she and I will ever share.

The Piscina di Venere is a place of seclusion and natural wonder, and we feel like we have the island to ourselves. We swim, snorkel, and sunbathe; we even manage to find a private corner behind a rock outcropping for a private interlude. I take Elise against a wave-smoothed wall of stone, both her legs wrapped around my waist, and my lips locked onto hers until we both shatter in ecstasy.

"I love you, El," I tell her, pressing my forehead against hers. "Fuck, I love you so much."

All she whispers back is, "Dan, please don't stop," and while she doesn't give me those three precious words that I desire so badly, the way she clings to me and kisses me like she's a drowning woman and I am air, tells me that the love is there. Soon she will say it, I just have to have faith in her. That might make me a fucking fool, but I'm beginning to believe that feeling foolish is just part of loving Elise Van den Bosch.

It's a moment that feels both fleeting and eternal, and I know that it will stay etched in both of our souls forever.

But, as the sun starts to dip below the horizon, I know it's time to go back to the villa and return to our roles as sister and best friend to Andries. We've managed to avoid him for almost two days during a difficult portion of his life, and to do so anymore is just cruel.

Still, looking at Elise in her tiny bathing suit, hair wet and slicked back, it's tempting to stay and just deal with Andries's anger later.

Staying longer isn't feasible anyway, though, because there are no amenities at Piscina di Venere. Even if we have to cut our visit short, the time we had here is unforgettable.

Back at the villa, Andries and Roxanne are once again nowhere to be found. I should be more bothered, but I have one last surprise for Elise—the romantic dinner date I promised—so I'm not too upset about my best friend being impossible to find.

I can sense that something is off, and it isn't hard to guess what it is. I know that Andries needs time to process everything that has happened with the Bar Rouge scandal. I feel a tad guilty that I'm enjoying Capri more as a romantic vacation than the couple that's supposed to get married next month. Maybe I should be doing more to help Andries and Roxanne, but I don't know what it's supposed to be.

As the days have passed, the tension between Roxanne and Andries has seemed to grow instead of dissipating, which leads me to believe that they haven't been working on it when we aren't around. can see the strain on their relationship, which means it's obvious to everyone else, too. I wonder if they will make it through this and if their upcoming wedding is even still on. I try to push the thoughts out of my mind and focus on enjoying the remaining time with Elise, but the cloud of uncertainty lingers.

Since today is our last day before returning to Amsterdam, I have meticulously planned the perfect evening for Elise. I have reserved a table at a fancy restaurant—one that is renowned for its romantic ambiance and delectable food—and eagerly anticipate seeing the look on her face when she realizes where we're going.

As we're getting ready to leave the villa, Andries appears for the first time in hours. I'm dressed in a light tan linen suit, with a white shirt beneath and the collar open, clearly dressed for a night out and not dinner on the terrace like usual. Trying to talk to him without showing my hand about my plans for the evening seems to be working until Elise shows up in a pale pink silk dress that reminds me all too much of the nightgown I had fucked her in the previous night, with her hair loose around her shoulders and her long legs bare. She's so hot that it makes my mouth go dry, but seeing the two of us together seems to tip off her brother that we are going out. He curiously asks why we're leaving all dressed up, so tell him that I wanted to take Elise out for a special dinner, hoping that he also has private plans with Roxanne, but before I can finish my sentence, Andries interjects with a suggestion of his own. "Let's have dinner with all of us. It's our last night here after all," he says.

Elise and I exchange a glance, both of us taken aback by Andries' sudden change of plans and almost rude interjection into our evening, but we shouldn't be surprised. Andries does what he wants, when he wants to.

My heart sinks as I realize that my carefully crafted evening has been thwarted by his impulsiveness. I can see the disappointment on Elise's face, and I know that she feels the same way. But we put on a brave front trying to make the best of the situation and agreeing to take the other couples with us.

"Let's just ditch them all," I whisper to Elise once Andries leaves to collect the rest of the group.

"We can't," she laments, rolling her eyes. "It's *his* wedding we're celebrating. Maybe he wants to patch things up with Roxie but doesn't want to have to do it alone."

"Or maybe he just wants to drag us all into his misery," I pinch the bridge of my nose and sigh. "Whatever. I can't imagine the sulky attitude he'll throw if we don't take him now."

"It's fine," Elise shrugs one bare shoulder. "It will be a nice way to close out the trip as long as everyone behaves."

I step in front of her and put one finger under her chin, tilting her face up so she's looking me directly in the eye. "When we get back to Amsterdam, I don't care if you try to end this thing between us or not. I'm getting my romantic date alone with you, if it's the last thing I do."

A small smile plays at the corner of her lips, and I can't resist kissing her briefly before she pushes me away with a giggle. "You know you'll be busy with your playboy life when we get home," she jokes, but her words make me frown.

"El, when I say I love you, I mean it. There is no one else for me."

"I know," she breathes, suddenly serious. "Trust me, Dan, I know."

This time when I kiss her, she doesn't pull away, even though we're standing in the middle of the villa.

It's not much, but it's a start.

* * *

The entire group of us arrives in two cars, and I have a bad feeling as soon as I see Andries climb out of the front seat of his, while Roxanne climbs out of the back with her sister and Robin. I look over at El, who has seen the same thing, a line of worry between her brows.

"That's not good," she muses.

"No joke," I shake my head. "Let's just make the best of this without getting too drunk."

"No promises."

Ziqù Restaurant is situated on a terrace overlooking the beautiful views of the island, and it has been beautifully decorated with lights that twinkle like fireflies as we enter. There is lush greenery and trees surrounding the place, giving it an intimate and welcoming feeling. Elise's eyes sparkle with anticipation as we walk inside together, and she's uncommonly affectionate, maybe emboldened by the fact that her brother now knows we're basically together, holding onto my arm as we enter the terrace. Even though the view of the sea draws my eye like it does everyone else's, I find myself looking at Elise more than anything, wanting to memorize this night and the way it feels for her to treat me like her partner out in public. Like she's proud of the fact that we're together.

It's almost a shame that Elise is taking up all my senses at the moment, I picked this location for our date for a good reason. Ziqù serves a variety of local and Mediterranean cuisine, which is prepared with fresh ingredients that are sourced from the island's local farms and fishermen. The menu is designed to showcase the rich culture and nature of Capri without being too pretentious, and the wine pairings are just as stellar. This was supposed to be something special for Elise and me, but at least I've still had the chance to bring her here, even if our date has been crashed by our friends.

I want to have a good time no matter what, but as we sit at the table, I can't shake off the feeling of unease. My gaze keeps drifting toward Roxanne and Andries, who seem to be behaving like two strangers. They don't touch, kiss, or even really look at one another. When they speak, they don't look into each other's eyes, just stare straight ahead like it's painful to see each other. The tension between them is palpable, and it's hard for me to enjoy my evening while they are clearly struggling.

We all toast to our last evening in Capri with champagne, but the conversation is stilted and forced. Andries, sitting on the other side of the table, is quiet and withdrawn, and Roxanne seems distant and preoccupied.

"Ready to go home?" I ask, trying to break the silence.

"I don't know," Andries responds, his voice heavy with uncertainty.

As the conversation continues to be awkward and disjointed, Elise starts to discreetly caress my inner thigh under the table. When I first feel her hand, I almost bite the inside of my mouth in surprise while I chew, and she chuckles softly. Having her here sitting so close to me is wonderful, but nothing can compare to the last few nights together. We've had sex on every surface in my suite, Elise never losing her hunger for me, and the more I've been able to have of her, the more addicted I become. Falling asleep and waking up together in a facsimile of domestic bliss is an adding cherry on top, and those moments have been some of the most satisfying of my life. I can't believe that commitment is the one that I crave right now, after spending so many years never seriously dating and chasing pleasure above all else. Each moment, each touch, each kiss, all of it feels like a dream.

Tonight will be our last night sharing my suite, and tomorrow I will be back in my empty bed while Elise catches up on everything she has to deal with back in the real world. The thought is so disappointing that I feel a pang in my heart. I'm not ready for this to be over.

I want to distract myself, so I take Elise's hand where it's still on my thigh, and slowly move it toward the white napkin I've placed on my lap. I meet her gaze and raise my eyebrows, which makes her smirk before picking up her champagne with her free hand and taking a heavy sip just as her fingers slide under the napkin and she palms my erection fully. Even just the touch of her hand through the fabric of my pants has me harder than I would have thought possible.

The antipasti course ends and entrees come up, along with a crisp white wine, which I all but chug as Elise's caresses become more direct and forceful. Lili and Robin are gushing about how incredible the holiday has been, while Roxanne smiles hollowly as she listens. When Elise starts stroking me fully through my pants, I clench my jaw to hold back a moan.

The ambiance at the restaurant is perfect, with the soft candlelight and the gentle sound of the Mediterranean Sea in the background. But even the stunning view of the sea from the terrace and the delicious food on my plate can't distract me from the storm brewing inside of me. And then, just as I'm about to take a bite of my risotto, Andries's voice pierces through my thoughts. "And you, Dan? Ready to go back to Amsterdam?"

The question catches me off guard, and I find myself staring at Elise, wondering if our summer fling will continue once we return to reality. Her hand stills on my rock hard cock, the mischievous look on her face fading. I open my mouth to speak, but I'm at a loss, my mind reeling with emotions. Andries and Roxanne look at me expectantly, waiting for a response.

"Not really, but we have a wedding to prepare for, don't we?" I manage to choke out. I realize it's the wrong answer immediately when my best friend sits his fork down with an audible clang and Roxanne blanches white, looking slightly ill.

It's Elise who eventually breaks the silence. "To the groom and bride," she says, raising her glass of wine, and we all join in for another toast. But even as we clink glasses and laugh, I can't shake the feeling that something has shifted forever.

CHAPTER 18

Elise

Breakfast is brief, with just a quick espresso and croissant, and before I know it, I find myself heading to the airport with the rest of the group to fly back home. I had this one last morning to wake up in Dan's arms, and now, our interlude in paradise is over. We had a lot of ups and downs, but more than anything my feelings for him have grown so large I can't write them off as a crush anymore. I think I'm in love with him, but I still don't know if there is room in my complicated life for a committed relationship. Losing Dan is also unthinkable... so I do just that. I don't think about it. At least not for now.

After boarding the private jet with the rest of the group and taking my seat beside Dan, I notice a sense of unease creeping over me. Andries and Roxanne, once so undeniably in love and committed to each other, now sit opposite each other, their bodies turned away and their eyes fixed firmly on the ground. Andries grips his whiskey glass tightly, his knuckles turning white as he takes sip after sip, while Roxanne absently swirls her gin and tonic, lost in her own thoughts. Alcohol before midday? Well, that's never a good sign. The atmosphere is tense, and it's a stark contrast to the lively chatter and laughter that fills the rest of the cabin.

I lean in close to Dan and whisper, "Have you noticed how my brother and Roxanne have been acting? They seem so distant." The weight of their silent suffering hangs heavy in the air, casting a shadow over the otherwise celebratory mood as we make our way back to Amsterdam.

Dan nods, his expression grim. "I've noticed it too. They've been like this for the past few days. I tried to talk to Andries about it, but he shut me down, saying everything's fine."

I bite my lip. "Something is off. I expected them to be distant after Andries found out about the cabaret scandal, but I never expected them to ice each other out like this. I thought it'd be passionate arguing or that they'd make up as soon as possible."

Dan shrugs. "I'm not sure, but it's not our place to ask. We've done enough. More than enough, really. We'll just have to wait and see."

As the plane takes off, sadness grips me, watching the turquoise blue water and the emerald green of Capri fade. Not only is my time with Dan coming but also the end of this carefree and magical holiday. I look over at Dan, and give him a small smile, feeling grateful for the memories we've created together. But as I glance over at Andries and Roxanne, I wonder what their future holds, and if their relationship will survive.

I lean over to Dan again, "Are you sure we shouldn't say something? Who knows how long it will be before we see either of them once we're home. Especially if Andries decides to isolate himself like he seems to love to do."

Dan shakes his head. "I still don't think it's a good idea. They'll talk to us if they want to. Let's just enjoy the flight back home."

I nod, understanding Dan's perspective, but I cannot shake off the feeling that the clock is ticking down too fast. Not just when it comes to Dan and me, but with everything.

I doze off, not even caring about everyone watching me as I rest my head on Dan's shoulder. The flight slips by me, and when he wakes me up while we circle the airport to land, I have to shake off my sleepiness. I'm oddly exhausted… maybe from how much my emotions have been through the past few days. I gaze at Dan, and think of how I may just love him, and then over at my brother and Roxanne, and consider how lost they must be feeling. I know I must not be the only one who is exhausted down to their very bones.

As we step off the plane onto the tarmac, my eyes widen in shock as I notice the cars parked nearby. They're not normal cars, but instead are blacked out—more discrete than marked cars but clearly armored. They're police cars.

I blindly reach beside me and find Dan's hand, never taking my eyes off my brother and Roxanne where they stand a few steps ahead of us.

"What's going on?" I ask, throat tight.

"The worst case scenario," Dan answers, his voice emotionless.

My heart races as we watch a group of police officers exit the vehicles where they were waiting for us. Their expressions are grave, and my eyes narrow at the stern-looking woman with short brown hair who follows them—the only one without a police uniform—as she holds a stack of papers and folders. My mind reels as I try to understand what is happening.

"Dan," I start again, but he squeezes my hand and shakes his head.

"I don't know anything, El. Let's just see how it plays out."

Just like we all expected, the group of law enforcement officers makes their way towards Roxanne and Roxanne only. They surround her, their expressions somber, and the stern-looking woman steps forward and reads out the charges. Her voice is firm as she does so, her group of officers making a ring around us so she doesn't try to escape. She gives no indication that that's her plan, though, just stands next to Andries with a stubborn—if nervous—look on her lovely face. She steps closer to Andries, and he takes her hand in his, linking their fingers together in the one loving exchange I've seen between the two of them in days. It's like he's offering her comfort in her time of need, but I don't think that a handhold would be nearly enough for me. Roxanne is stronger than me in some ways, I guess.

Then, before any of us can ask any questions, Roxanne is arrested and everyone else is in disbelief. The police take her into custody and escort her to a waiting police car, the sirens wailing as they take her away to be interrogated. The woman with short-brown hair exchanges a few words with my brother and nods once before she makes her way to her own car, and follows the rest of the caravan back to the station.

I'm in shock, my mind struggling to process what just happened. The image of Roxanne being taken away in handcuffs... the sound of the sirens fading into the distance...the feeling of shock that grips me is overwhelming.

Lili is inconsolable, Robin tries to comfort her with his hands on her shoulders. Oddly, though, Andries is still watching where the police cars disappeared, his arms crossed and his spine rigid.

I turn to Dan, heart in my throat. "What's going on? Should we call her lawyer?"

But before Dan can respond, my brother speaks up, cutting his hand through the air with finality. "Her lawyer is already on the way. We knew this would happen."

I stare at Andries, my mind racing with questions. "What do you mean you knew this would happen? Why didn't you tell us?"

But Andries doesn't respond, and I'm left feeling more confused and worried than ever before. My brother is so stoic, almost cold, even after seeing the woman he loves arrested in front of him. I think back to all the whiskey he drank on the plane, and then it hits me... he was drinking so he could keep his cool while his wife-to-be was put in cuffs.

Poor Andries. Poor Roxanne.

Dan looks at Andries with a mix of confusion and concern. "How can you remain so calm after seeing your fiancée be taken into custody? We should all go to the police station, meet her lawyer there, and make sure Roxanne is safe."

Everyone agrees with Dan—Lili especially, who locks onto this idea immediately. After everyone begins to insist, Andries finally agrees to put in a call to Roxanne's lawyer. He's clearly annoyed by everyone getting into his business, but what did he expect when we just watched her get taken away in cuffs?

Her lawyer doesn't sound thrilled, but he swears to send Andries the address, but only Andries himself can come. Lili starts to wail at this, but Robin shushes her so Andries can finish the call.

Once he hangs up he looks around at all of us, expression blank. "There. See? You guys can't come. Just go home."

The implication of Andries being the only one who is allowed to go to the police station and meet the lawyer adds to the sense of unease that has been building inside me since Roxanne's arrest. I can't shake off the feeling that something is not right and that there's more to this story than meets the eye. As we wait for Andries to receive the address, I wonder what the future holds for Roxanne and for all of us. The thought of leaving her alone in this situation makes me feel horrible, and it's impossible not to worry about her well-being. I try to push the thoughts away, but they linger in the back of my mind.

Once the address comes in, we all throw caution to the wind, even though it clearly annoys Andries, disregarding the need for proper protocol, and set off towards the police bureau in our respective cars. Three vehicles are waiting for us, one for Andries, another for Lili and Robin, and a third for Dan and me. The cars are sleek and black, uncomfortably similar to the one Roxanne was taken away in. With her gone, we offer Andries a ride with us so he doesn't have to be alone, but he ignores us, getting into his own vehicle without a word.

As soon as we enter the station, a middle-aged man—most likely Roxanne's lawyer—approaches Andries and greets him, looking at the rest of us with irritation. "I thought I made it clear that only my client's fiancé was to come," he says, looking at my brother first, then at us all, his voice laced with annoyance. "Ms. Feng will be fine, she's just going to be interrogated."

Ignoring the first part of his statement, my brother steps forward and asks what everyone is thinking. "Is she going to stay in jail until trial?"

The lawyer sighs and shakes his head. "There's no way Ms. Feng will stay in jail," he delivers the news, sounding quite sure of himself. "She's not part of the cabaret's management team and we have plenty of testimonials who confirmed she knew nothing about the drug trafficking. I don't even think she'd have been arrested today if she hadn't been in Capri this whole time. Law enforcement was afraid she was on the run or would never come in for an interrogation if they didn't arrest her I believe, so once they see that she's cooperative, she'll be let go."

But despite the lawyer's reassurances, I still worry about Roxanne. I can see the stress etched on her face as they put the handcuffs on her in my mind as clear as day, and it makes my stomach clench with stress. I can't even imagine how she's feeling.

After spending so many months all but hating her, it strikes me now how strange it is that I'm feeling so much empathy toward this woman. I'm not just worried about how my brother feels right now—even if that is a big concern of mine—I'm genuinely worried about Roxanne herself too, thinking back to eating sorbet and her holding my hand outside of the Blue Grotto. I think… I think we might be able to be friends in the future. I want her to be okay. I want her and my brother's relationship to be okay too.

As the lawyer insists that we should all go home and only Andries can stay, I feel a wave of emotions crashing over me out of nowhere. I start thinking about my own father, and the thought of him being in a similar position to Roxanne sends shivers down my spine. Sterile and foreboding, the police station is not a place I could imagine Dad being taken to, let alone poor Mom coming here to try and get him free. All the stress and turmoil that my mother would have to endure… the idea of it makes me feel ill. If Andries goes ahead and does that interview, the judgment of it will be inescapable for Dad. It feels like a heavy burden on my shoulders, and it's impossible to shake off the feeling of dread.

But as I ruminate on it, I remind myself that this is the right thing to do. My father could have chosen to love his son for who he is, but he didn't. He chose to be cruel and vindictive, and I won't let him and Karl get away with it. It's a difficult decision, but I know that it's the right one, even if it means facing the wrath of my father and his disapproval… maybe even losing my job and my place as the future CEO of Van den Bosch industries. But I guess it's time to stand up for what is right, even if it means standing alone.

Except, I'm not alone, am I? Glancing over at Dan, my nerves settle some. *No, not alone at all.*

As Lili and Robin leave to give moral support to Yao, who is no doubt beside herself at what is happening with her daughter, Dan turns to me and says, "I have to head to my parents' place. I promised them I'd be there for lunch. Do you want me to call you a cab since we came here in the same car?"

Thinking about being alone right now feels terrible, and, in truth, I'm not ready to be separated from Dan just yet. Capri is over, but now that we're back in Amsterdam, and sure that Roxanne is going to be okay, Dan and I can start fresh. What better way to do that than to have lunch at his side with his parents?

I try to hide the annoyance that he wouldn't automatically invite me and casually ask, "Maybe your mom would like some female company? She seemed very welcoming last time I saw her."

Dan is taken aback by my suggestion and a look of hesitation washes over his face. I see him trying to come up with an excuse, but before he can say anything, I quickly grab his hand and say, "Let's go, we are already running late."

He hesitates for a moment before nodding, and we ask Andries to keep us updated about Roxanne on the way out.

My brother looks haggard, washed out in a way, but he promises to keep us in the loop, not even seeming annoyed that Dan and I are leaving together. Dan glances at me a few times as we walk to the car together, eyes shining with curiosity, but I keep quiet, happy for the moment to let him ponder why I'm so insistent on going with him.

I might be falling in love with him, but that doesn't mean I can't still be a little mysterious when I get the chance.

CHAPTER 19

Dan

Despite Elise looking content during the drive to my parents' home, I can't help being a little bit suspicious of her. "We are not even a couple," I start, breaking the comfortable silence that settled between us since we departed. "Why do you want to join us for lunch?"

She shrugs one delicate shoulder. "You have had so many lunches and dinners with my parents, what's the problem with me joining in for one of yours? Your mother always says Andries and I are welcome."

I narrow my eyes at her, trying to figure out what game she is playing. The last time my parents and Elise ran into each other was when she was leaving my home after she and I slept together for the first time. I know it must have been mortifying, and I figure that she'd want to avoid them, not come to lunch at the next opportunity.

I refuse to entertain the all-too-tempting idea that she just wants to spend more time with me. If I'm wrong, it will hurt too much.

I feel a rush of warm happiness as we pull up to my family home, the emerald green grass and shrubbery are always a welcome sight. Even if Elise is complicated, at least spending time at home with my parents will be good. It always is, and I send up a silent thanks for the fact that my parents are so much different from hers.

Elise and I walk out onto the back terrace side by side where my parents sit at a round table in the shade, enjoying cucumber water and talking to one another before they see us both. Once they do, they both stand, embracing me while Mom kisses Elise on the cheek.

Both Mom and Pops look at the two of us with bright eyes, and I realize they think her being here is significant. I hate to disappoint them but Elise hasn't accepted that we should be together yet. "Thanks for lunch. Elise was starving, so I dragged her along," I tell them as some sort of rushed explanation for her presence.

"You're more than welcome here, dear Elise," Mom warmly interposes, her smile up to her ears causing me to roll my eyes at it.

My parents exchange a confused look before taking their seats again and gesturing for us to do the same.

Conversation is normal at first, but I can see the way my mother keeps looking at El with stars in her eyes, and the way she turns all conversations towards her, giving her more attention than Dad and I combined.

"Caroline," Pops says, amused. "Give our guest a minute to breathe."

She flutters her hands in the air. "Oh, stop. Elise, you are the first woman Dan has ever brought over, so excuse me if I'm over the moon about it."

"Mom…" I groan.

"What!? It's the truth, isn't it?"

It takes some effort, but I manage to steer the talk back to anything else besides Elise and me. It takes some time, but we finally broach the subject of the Bar Rogue scandal, and my mother asks worriedly how Andries is handling it all.

"As well as one might expect," Elise tells her, before taking a sip of her water. "He's still processing the shock of it all, and while he loves Roxanne beyond words, it's a big blow to discover that she owned a secret cabaret."

"Not to mention the fact that we think that Sebastian and Karl, the man that Roxanne had all the trouble with before, might be behind the entire ordeal," I blurt out, until I realize speaking of her dad might make Elise uncomfortable. *Shit.*

"I can see where that would be difficult," Mom comments and reaches over to pat Elise on the hand, in a sign of warm understanding. "Are you handling it all okay, dear?"

Elise seems taken aback by her concern, but her smile is warm and genuine as she answers. "Oh, yes, I'm fine. Handling scandals is almost like a sport in my family."

"I hope you still had a good time in Capri, though," my mother offers, and Elise nods.

"I definitely did," I tell them, trying to change the subject to our vacation time. "It was so much fun, and I discovered so many new things."

Dad chuckles next to me, and before I can kick him under the table, he says, "Oh, I don't doubt that one bit."

For all Elise has become loving and affectionate with me, she's still cold and aloof with others, so when I get to see her warm up to my parents—especially my mom—in real time, it's touching. I wonder how much different she would be if she had parents like mine growing up, who showed her love and support through thick and thin. She and Mom laugh and joke throughout lunch, my mom constantly reaching over to touch her hand or wrist as they speak, so Elise knows that she has her full attention. I don't want to be so affected by it, but watching the two of them makes my heart swell with love for them both.

After lunch, Elise and I both hug my parents goodbye before I offer to take her on a tour of the house. She saw the main parts during the engagement party, but she insists on seeing the rest. I don't pick up on what she means at first, but it quickly becomes clear that she has one destination in mind.

"I want to see your room."

I huff. "Absolutely not."

"Please Dan…" She grabs me by the shoulders and plants a soft kiss on my lips. "I want to know more about you. Come on, show me!"

I try to deny her, but when she's so sweet and soft it's impossible, so despite my better judgment, I find myself letting the woman I love into the bedroom I've had since childhood.

Of course, I've updated it, since I still stay here often, but it's not as presentable as the room I have at my own place. The shining wood floors and pale gray walls play well with the natural light coming in from the numerous windows. There are all the things I'm sure she's come to expect from me—books, vinyl records, and a luxurious king-sized bed with down bedding—but her eyes are drawn to the one thing I hoped she wouldn't see.

The fencing trophy case.

"Elise…" I sigh. "Don't look at all that."

"Hush," she tells me, and I exhale in annoyance, crossing my arms and silently letting her look her fill.

Her expression is one of awe at first, a soft smile on her lips as she peruses the trophy case, running her fingers over the bronze awards as she goes. She seems to be reading each nameplate, and after a few minutes, I start to feel a flush of embarrassment at how closely she's paying attention to it all.

"It's just stuff from when I was a kid and a teenager," I tell her, trying to prompt her to move on, but she doesn't listen, picking up one of my more recent awards.

"Oh, really? So why does this one say it's from last year?" she teases.

I roll my eyes to the ceiling. "Fine. You've caught me. Now can we move on?"

She lifts the trophy in her hand, looking at the figurine on the top with amusement. "I'm surprised you don't have all these displayed proudly at your own place, considering that you take every opportunity to show off how wonderful and talented you are."

I go to swipe the award from her hand but she pulls it out of the way with a giggle, placing it back on the shelf under the display lighting.

"If you must know," I start as I run a hand through my hair in slight embarrassment. "I didn't even take any of the trophies home after I turned fifteen until Mom found out I was leaving them behind. She was insistent after that, so I just give them all to her, and they turn up here," I sigh. "Even now."

"That's sweet, actually," Elise leaves my side again to examine the rest of the room, a dreamy look on her face as she does so. "It's so nice here, Dan. Why did you even bother moving out? Your parents live so close. Their home is so lovely."

I level her with a serious look, sliding my gaze over to the bed and back to her, and Elise laughs. "Do you really think I wanted to spend my young adult life under their roof? Forget it. I like to have my own space, throwing my own parties when I want..." I close the distance between us, bringing Elise against me and sliding my hand down her back to cup her ass. "Having girls over whenever I want..."

Elise moves as if she's going to shake me off at first, but her humor gives her away, and I just hold her closer and kiss her neck until her laugh fills the air again. Hearing her joy makes me feel warm inside. No other woman has ever made me feel quite like this. No other woman has made me fall so in love. Elise is simply singular.

"Oh, so you didn't bring all your other flings here?" she asks, and I shake my head.

"What Mom said at lunch is true; I've never brought anyone here, El."

She looks up at me, smirking but clearly pleased by my answer. "And yet, I'm here."

"So you are," I muse, backing the both of us until I have Elise's back pressed into the wall. Like this, there isn't even a breath of space between us, just like I like it.

Arching her body against mine, El lets out an exhale, her arms coming loosely around my neck. There is a languidness to the way she rises to her tiptoes to kiss me, the frantic pace that usually accompanies our kisses absent, replaced by unhurried, hot hunger.

She drags her lips over my jawline and neck before I take her chin in my fingers and tilt her head so I can do the same, not stopping until I reach the line of her collarbone. Her breezy sundress, comfortable for the plane ride, comes off her shoulders and down her chest, just like her white lace bralette is simple for me to roll down her torso so I can get my lips and tongue on her nipples.

Having her here, in the room I spent so much of my life in, is like something out of a fantasy. She hums in pleasure as I suck and nip at her breasts, her enjoyment quickly turning to moans as her fingers thread themselves through my hair restlessly. I'm so hard, thrusting against her core, and Elise is so hot for me that I can feel the heat of her through the thin fabric of her dress.

After some time, she pulls my hair to bring my mouth back to hers, tongue demanding as it slides against mine. I can hear my pulse in my ears, pounding hard as I push my hand under her dress, fingers slipping through her folds and pressing against her clit underneath her panties, swallowing the shocked gasp she gives with her mouth still pressed to mine.

When I pull her panties down some, she gets the picture quickly enough and removes them the rest of the way herself, wrapping one bare leg around my waist while I work myself out of my pants, pushing them down just enough so that they're around my hips and I can fist my cock in my hand.

Elise is quick to replace my hand with her own, pushing her hands under my shirt to feel the skin of my chest under her palms, almost purring with pleasure when I press my cock into her hand even more urgently.

"Should we move to the bed?" she pants when I drop my mouth to her chest again,

I look up at her, nibbling at her taut peaks once more before answering. "No. Right here," I stand straight again, gripping her legs in my hands. "Wrap your legs around my waist. I'll hold you."

Elise looks around, color high on her cheeks and her kiss-swollen lips parted. "Here? Are you sure?"

I steal her complaints with my mouth on hers, and she complies, letting me hold her with my hands on her ass, braced with her back on the wall. We come together so naturally that as soon as I move my hips forward, the head of my cock slides over her pussy until I find her entrance.

"You're so tight," I grit out between my teeth, pressing forward slowly as her body allows me inside inch by inch. Elise doesn't answer with words, but just wraps her arms around me again and buries her face in my neck as I fill her.

It feels like it takes an eternity, but finally, I'm completely sheathed within her. She lets out a load moan, her body shuddering in my grip.

"You're going to have to help me, El," I tell her breathlessly. "Move with me, baby,"

I feel her nod as I pull out and slam back home, going slowly until I can set the perfect pace. Elise's body matches my movements perfectly, meeting me thrust for thrust. I don't even notice her weight in my arms, all my focus pinned on where we are connected, entranced by the way my cock disappears into her pussy. The erotic sight makes arousal roar through me like a flash fire.

All of it combined—the setting, the way Elise is so eager to work herself on my cock, the sight of her coming apart—

coalesces into a surge of sensation that has my balls tightening and my jaw clenching.

I start to tell Elise, between claiming her mouth with mine and watching the way her expression changes as I fuck her, that I'm about to come, but just now I feel the flutter of her walls around me.

"You're close," I growl, "Come for me, El,"

She was already there, but my words make it inevitable, and her pussy spasms around the hard length of my manhood as she milks me dry, muffling her moans of pure bliss in my neck, her entire body shuddering with the force of it. When I follow her, the pleasure explodes out of me like a firebomb, and I have to concentrate hard not to drop her. I can only press my forehead against her when she raises her eyes to look at me, spilling my seed into her, so lost in everything that is Elise that it's hard to breathe.

I only start to lower her slowly to her feet when I know she's starting to relax, and while she sags against me as her feet hit the floor, Elise stands, letting out a breathy laugh.

"Was I really the first one you've been with in here?" she asks, pushing sweat-damp hair from her face.

"I never kiss and tell."

She gives me a scathing look, fixing her clothes while I do the same for mine, hissing as I touch my overly-sensitive member while tucking it back into my pants. Once we're decent again, I lead her over to the edge of my bed and we both nearly collapse into a sitting position, Elise laying her head on my shoulder as we give our shaking legs a respite.

"Dan," she starts out, sounding almost apprehensive.

"Hm?"

"What if we give it a try?"

Furrowing my brows, I look down at her. "What exactly do you mean by that?"

Raising her head off my shoulder, she sighs, fingers plucking at the duvet. "Like being a couple. What if we give it a try? I don't know if it's a good idea, but…."

Time seems to stop and then pick back up again at triple speed. I grab both of her hands in mine, elated. "It's a brilliant idea, El," I see her open her mouth to contradict me, so I do the only thing I can think of—I kiss her passionately, pouring my love into each press of lips and swipe of tongue until we're both breathing hard. "A very brilliant idea."

Elise looks happy, her smile bright. "I'm glad you're so enthusiastic, but are you sure about this? I don't want to force anything on you."

I can't help the laugh that slips out. "Elise, I'm more than sure, love."

"Okay." She nods, but it's clear the apprehension is still there. "Just promise me that if this doesn't work out we can continue to be friends. I can't lose our friendship. I can't…" Elise takes a deep breath and exhales slowly. "I can't lose you."

Thoughts swirl in my mind; I imagine Elise near me but untouchable, or spotting Elise with a different man at a party from across the room. It makes a headache bloom to life in my skull almost immediately. Being her friend after loving her would be almost impossible. I just know it. But… looking at her beautiful face, and feeling her hands in mine, I can't imagine my life without her, either. "I promise."

The tender moment is interrupted by the sound of Elise's phone going off. I try not to be annoyed at how fast she jumps up, but I realize it might be Andries calling, which would explain the reason for her rush. Taking out the phone, which has now stopped ringing, I see Elise frown.

"Is it your brother?"

She shakes her head. "Actually, it was Tatiana. She texted me, too. Looks like she wants me to come to her place later on."

As nonchalant as Elise sounds about it, the idea of sleeping without her tonight makes me frown. "Is Tatiana already stealing my girlfriend from me?"

Tossing the phone back in her purse, Elise sways over to me, putting her hands on my shoulders and leaning down to smile at me. "You know I've got to talk to her. Tatiana is the reason that Andries knew about the two of us in the first place."

I shrug. "Honestly, not sure if that was a bad thing."

She hums thoughtfully, letting me skin my hands up her body as she does so. "Hmm, true. It's better that he knows now."

Giving me a little finger wave, Elise goes to my ensuite bathroom to clean up while I fall backward onto the bed completely, my hands behind my head. It seems like a dream that Elise actually wants to be in a relationship with me and not continue to hide everything from everyone. Finally, *finally* I can call her my girlfriend. It feels almost immature, but I can't wait for everyone to know. I want to scream it from the rooftops.

Or, instead of yelling it out to everyone in Amsterdam, I could call Johan and deliver the news to him myself. The thought makes me grin, loving the idea of revenge, but ultimately I decide against it.

I take her hand and lead her out into the warm summer day, my heart full of anticipation for what the future holds for us. As we stand under the rolling, white clouds, I can't help but steal a kiss, whispering in her ear, "I'm already missing you and you haven't even left yet."

She giggles and wraps her arms around me, whispering back, "Thank you for everything you did for my brother and me. I really wonder if I deserve someone as wonderful as you."

Her words leave me speechless, and I hold her even tighter still. This woman is so precious to me, and now she's all mine officially.

As she gets into the car that will take her away, I can't resist stealing one last kiss. I watch as she leaves with a smile on my face, knowing that even if I have to sleep alone tonight, it won't be a common occurrence from here on out. I plan to have her in my bed as much as possible.

As I make my way back inside, a feeling of wanting to check in on my father arises, and I know exactly where he will be. Entering his studio, I'm greeted with the sight of him admiring his collection of watches, a twinkle in his eye as he examines each one. A sense of warmth and familiarity washes over me.

The walls are lined with shelves filled with various tools and parts, and a large work table sits in the center of the room, covered in watches in various states of disrepair. The smell of oil and metal fills the air, and the soft ticking of the watches is the only sound that can be heard.

"So," he begins without even turning around, "are we attending Andries's wedding or yours this August?"

"Ha-ha, how funny you are, Pops."

But then he turns to me and chuckles, his deep laughter filling the room, and responds, "You have no idea how smitten you look when Elise is around, son. It's as cute as watching puppies."

Pride wells up inside me and I grin, announcing, "We are officially together, actually, so that might explain your wedding confusion."

He looks surprised for a moment, but then his face breaks out into a smile. "Really? Well, I guess congratulations are in order." The happiness in his eyes is evident as first he reaches out his hand to shake mine before pulling me into a full on embrace, patting me on the back as he does so.

It doesn't take long for Pops to notice me being pensive. Once the hug ends, he asks me what's going on. I try to say nothing and change the subject, but he keeps insisting. My father isn't one to take no for an answer when it comes to things like this.

After considering my options, I lay it all out and say, "We might be officially together, but she never said that she loves me."

He nods understandingly and asks, "And you think she doesn't feel the same as you do?"

"I know she feels something for me, but is it love? Or is it just the fact she loves what we have going on and she doesn't want to give it up." I shrug, feeling unsure, but Dad lays his hand on my shoulder and squeezes reassuringly.

"Give her some time, Dan. I'm sure she will say it back, eventually. You want to make sure she feels comfortable telling you and isn't rushed."

I smile and nod, but in my head, I can't help but think, *I certainly hope you're right, Pops.*

CHAPTER 20

Elise

As I enter my apartment, I drop my luggage on the floor with a sigh. It's good to be home, but it's also sad to have to admit that our time in Capri is truly over. Now that I have made Dan and I's relationship official, though, there will be many more luxurious trips in our future if I get any say in it.

With that wonderful thought in my head, I make my way to the bedroom and begin to unpack my things. Going through my belongings, I come across the one thing I don't really want to think about right now—the letter from Johan.

Looking at it makes me feel a mix of emotions. I've finally decided to be with Dan and Dan only, so the last thing I want to think about is my ex right now. But there is the meetup at Tati's place coming up, so I won't be able to put him out of my mind for long. Still, I can have a few moments of peace, surely, so I put the envelope in the first drawer of my bedside table, not wanting to deal with it.

I head to the bathroom to take a shower, letting the hot water wash away the stress of the day while also looking back fondly on the last few hours. Hanging out with Dan's family, getting to know them a little better, and getting the full tour with a quick hookup included was a great way to spend an afternoon.

Once I'm done, I grab my purse and head out to Tati's apartment to meet her. She answers quickly enough, smiling, but she has to know that I'm here to talk to her seriously. I hug her quickly anyway and let her lead me to the living room of her apartment, offering me a drink before sitting down across from me.

"So, I want to know everything," she starts, the excitement in her tone palpable. "How was Capri?"

"Good, except for the fact that you told Andries about Dan and I being together."

My tone is neutral, and Tatianna's eyes go wide. She tries to explain, but I cut her off. "Tatianna, why would you do something like that? I thought that we kept each other's secrets! I didn't realize your loyalty lies with my brother."

"I'm sorry, El, but I didn't think it would have this much impact." She pauses for a moment, taking a sip of her drink, before saying, "He just asked if you went to Dan's party and if you slept at his house, and I said yes. I never thought it'd be such a big deal."

I take a deep breath and try to let it go, but the sting of Tatianna's betrayal still lingers. It doesn't really matter though, in the long run, because Tati didn't tell Andries to be malicious. Of course, she couldn't have known about the weird promise between my brother and Dan.

My silence must unsettle her because she continues when I say nothing. "Really, I didn't know it was an issue."

The urge to hold the grudge is strong, but Tati looks so innocent and worried that I just can't stay mad. "It's fine, Tatianna. Just don't give my brother any more information about me without at least asking me first, okay?"

She nibbles her lip, still obviously feeling guilty, but eventually launches onto another subject. "So much has been going on here since you left. Did you hear about Karl's new verdict? I'm sure that made you mad."

"It did," I assure her.

"And you won't even believe what's going on with that cabaret, Bar Rouge! Apparently Roxanne—"

"Owns the cabaret. Yes, I know," I interpose, rolling my eyes. "I was just in Capri, Tati, not on another planet."

She looks abashed, rocking her glass back and forth on the table. "Yeah, sorry. So… you never really said how Capri was. How are Roxanne and Andries now that all that Bar Rouge stuff has come to light?"

My friend tries to keep her tone casual, but there is a stiffness to her shoulders and an intense focus in her eyes that tells me this is what Tati wants to know most of all. I have a sinking feeling about what this realization means.

"Tati…" I sigh, leaning forward to touch her hand and, as my eyes meet hers, I say, "Andries really loves Roxanne, and even with all of this stuff going on with Bar Rouge, he's going to stand by his bride no matter what. You need to let go of this crush you have on him. It's only going to hurt you in the long run."

"I know you're right." Her voice is small and barely audible, and her face falls as she comes to terms with the truth of it. "It's just so hard for me to see what Andries could see in a former escort and now the current owner of a cabaret that is in shambles. Roxanne isn't the type of woman he was supposed to end up with. It was supposed to be someone like…someone like—"

"Someone like you?" I finish for her, and Tati nods, her gaze dropping to her lap. "Look, you know better than most that I did not approve of their relationship at all, but spending more time with the two of them has made me realize that sometimes love doesn't have a rational answer. They are in love, and that's the end of it for Andries, public perception be damned."

"I know it's silly to still feel so strongly for your brother, especially since it was only ever just a crush, but I can't help it. The closer the wedding gets, the sadder I become." Her gaze shifts behind me to the large window overlooking the city, and she exhales slowly. "I just wish things were different."

My annoyance with her tattling to my brother fades as I see the genuine regret on Tatianna's face, so I close the small space between us on the couch and take her hands in mine. When she looks back at me, I smile reassuringly. "There is going to be someone so much better suited for you out there Tati, I promise. Plus, Andries is a broody bore sometimes."

Tatianna blinks a few times and then laughs. Feeling lighter than before I visited, I join her, happy to have reached an equilibrium with my friend.

* * *

Tatianna has brought out some biscuits that we're enjoying with some tea when my phone rings. It's been a long day, and

I don't necessarily want to talk to anyone else, but the chance that it might be my brother with news is too significant.

To my dismay, it's my father's name on my phone screen, and as much as I'd like to ignore him, I can't. Either I face him now, or dread it for days until he finally forces me to talk to him. After a deep inhale to ground myself, I answer.

"Hey, Dad. How are you?"

"Good to hear your voice, dear. I assume the flight went well and that you made it home safely?" His voice is clipped; not necessarily unhappy, but distant.

"Yeah... sorry I didn't call sooner. There were some, uh, difficulties when we landed and I've just worked it out and now I'm at Tatianna's place. It's been a busy day."

"Difficulties, you say?" he chuckles, and it makes me frown, causing me to think he knows exactly what I'm referring to. "That doesn't surprise me at all. But that's not why I'm calling. We're all missing you at home, why don't you come over? We can have a casual dinner and catch up on our respective trips."

I wrinkle my nose at the idea, but even as much as I just want to go to my place here in Amsterdam, I know I should take the invitation. I need Dad to trust me if I have any hope of convincing him to turn on Karl and fire him, and this is the perfect chance to get started. He'll be in a good mood from the trip, and relaxed.

"Okay, sure. I just have to go back and get my car—"

"Nonsense. You must be tired from all this traveling, a driver will pick you up from Tatiana's and bring you here."

I hate when he does this, but I can't really complain about seeing my family again. "Great. I'll be waiting."

When the driver arrives, I bid Tatiana farewell after finishing my coffee, promising that we'll get together again soon, and head out as soon as the driver arrives. Inside the car, I slip off my sandals and run my hands through my hair, trying to relax since the ride is going to be a long one. I wish Dan was with me… I've gotten so used to having him by my side that it's exceedingly strange to be alone.

A few minutes pass, and then I receive a text. As if drawn in by my thoughts about him, he's texting me a picture of his bed with the caption, *You should be here.*

It makes me smile, so I snap a picture of the empty seat next to me and reply, *No, you should be here!*

I still prefer the bed, he texts back, *but what are you up to right now?*

I'm on my way back home to the estate, I type. *Dad already called me.*

It takes him a little longer to reply this time, but when he does, it just says, *Damn, good luck!*

Thanks. I'm definitely going to need it.

CHAPTER 21

Elise

Arriving at our grand family estate, I feel a sense of familiarity wash over me. The Van den Bosch estate, surrounded by lush gardens and pristine landscaping, holds a special place in my heart despite the tensions rising between my father, my brother, and even myself. It still feels nice to be back where I grew up.

Inside, the windows are large, and they allow the last rays of sunshine to flood into the interior, illuminating the elegant furnishings and decor in gold hues. Dad and Mom are waiting for me, and they both embrace me one after the other as I arrive. It feels almost awkward with how much my relationship with Dad has felt like a business relationship lately, but Mom's hug is warm and full of affection, and I sink into it happily.

Hannah, the third oldest of the family, comes over, all tall and willowy, with her arms crossed and one hip cocked out. I hug her, too, but she seems distracted by the desire to ask me something.

"Is it true that Johan was in Capri with you?" she blurts out as soon as there is a natural lull in the conversation.

I'm slightly taken aback by her unexpected question, but answer it nevertheless. "Yes, he was. Sort of a last minute addition, but he stayed with us a few days."

Hannah's eyes are bright, and I swear I see her vibrate with excitement, but only briefly. "That must have been nice," she says, trying to sound neutral, but I know her well enough to know when something is of interest to my sister. Her excitement about Johan strikes me as odd, but I tuck that thought away to go over later.

"Speaking of Johan, he told me that you have a box of random things that you find and collect and that you showed it to him a couple of years ago. Is that true?"

Her eyes go wide as saucers, but she nods. "Yes! I can't believe he remembered that." She presses her hands to her cheeks. "I found a lot of interesting things in Lake Como, do you want to see them?"

I almost say yes, genuinely interested in my sister's collection, but then Dad clears his throat, and I'm reminded of why I am really here for. "Later, Hannah. I've got a few things I need to talk to Dad about first."

"Okay," she chirps. "Just come and find me when you're done."

* * *

As my father and I walk around the garden of our family estate, we catch up about our recent holidays. The gardens are lush and filled with vibrant colors. Roses of different hues adorn the pathways, their sweet fragrance filling the air. With the sun setting, the change in the sunlight from bright to golden only adds to the tranquility of the place.

"So Lake Como was a success?"

Dad shrugs, his hands in his pockets as we walk. "Yes and no. The sightseeing was good, of course, but your mother is still clearly struggling with all the nonsense regarding your brother and this sham of an engagement, and Hannah... well, Hannah is always out there with her head in the clouds. You know, teenagers. It's hard to tell if she enjoyed herself or not. The other kiddos seemed to like their time there though." He pauses, looking down at me. "And Capri?"

"There was so much to see," I tell him honestly. "We were there for a while and I still feel like there were things I didn't get to experience or visit. It really is almost unbelievably beautiful, though." I smile softly, thinking back to the memories I made over the past week. "I get why people call it paradise."

"What about your brother?" he presses, and my smile falls just as fast. Of course, Dad is only worried about what Andries is doing.

"He had a great time," I lie. "Maybe a little distracted, but he spent a lot of time with Dan, so I didn't see him all that much."

"Hmm," he mumbles as he studies my gaze with narrowed eyes. "You didn't notice if he was bothered by all the things going on with Bar Rouge?"

I grit my teeth, annoyed. "Maybe a little."

"That surprises me. I thought it would ruin his vacation."

As we stroll through the gardens, taking in the sights and sounds of nature, I decide just to cut to the chase, since Dad is so determined to talk about Andries and Roxanne anyway.

"Dad, did you know that Roxanne got arrested upon arrival and was taken into custody?"

My father looks at me, his expression unreadable. "Yes, I did know," he finally admits. "I have been helping the prosecutor in her investigation against Bar Rouge."

I'm so taken aback by this revelation, and how easily he gave it to me that I stop in my tracks for a moment. Does Dad still see me as an ally? "Really? Why didn't you tell me earlier?" I ask, my voice filled with confusion.

"Why would I? It wasn't much, honestly. The manager for the cabaret wouldn't give up any information about the employee's previous employment, but I used my connections to discover that some of them used to be Roxanne's escorts, so they might still work directly under her command." He sounds so nonchalant about the whole thing that it's hard to wrap my head around.

Dad must notice my silence, because he suggests, "Let's have a seat, Elise. I'm still tired from the return flight."

We find one of the stone benches that ring the area of the garden around the centerpiece fountain, the sound of the tinkling water pleasant and relaxing. I'm too twisted up to relax, despite the ambiance, and I can't let the subject of Roxanne and Bar Rogue go. It's eating away at me like a disease.

"Don't you think it's strange that a dancer would do something so controversial onstage?" I ask. "It's almost like she was paid by someone that hates Roxanne to do it."

Dad slides a look at me, and then laughs sardonically, slapping his hands on his knees. "Elise, I didn't have anything to do with that. I already told you that. Must we rehash this?"

"Are you sure you're not involved?" I press. "It just all seems too convenient, and everyone knows you hate the idea of them getting married."

He exhales, annoyed. "I give you my word, I didn't pay that dancer. Is that good enough for you?"

"Well…" I know I have to approach this carefully, or Dad will figure out what I plan to do in the long run too quickly. "What about Karl? He isn't exactly Roxanne's biggest fan." Dad takes a breath but says nothing, and my stomach sinks. I shake my head in disgust and laugh in disbelief. "I can't believe you let him do that, Dad!"

"Don't act like this was completely unexpected, Elise. At least now the wedding doesn't stand a chance, especially if Roxanne goes to jail."

He sounds so aloof that it pisses me off immediately. "They are still together, Dad! Even after Andries found everything out, they never split up. They're closer than ever, actually. You need to let this go."

I know that stretching the truth isn't ideal, but it is true that the wedding is still on. My father's expression shutters and he moves like he's going to stand, but I put my hand on his shoulder to stop him. This is a pivotal moment if I want to try to get him on my side. "Why don't you just let this whole war or hate against your son and his future wife go? I want us to just be a family again, Dad." I hear emotion creeping into my voice, but I don't stop it. "Just embrace that they love each other and that you love your son. That's all you need to do."

"Ha," he huffs. "Good to know where your allegiance lies, El."

"It's because I love you both that I'm telling you all this. You are destroying your relationship with Andries and it's going to be beyond repair if you don't stop soon." I grab his wrist to make him look at me. "Just because he's choosing to live his own life with the woman he loves, you're willing to lose him forever?"

Dad shakes my grip off and rockets to his feet, brushing off his clothing as he does so as if my words are sticking to him. "It's not your place to lecture me," he snaps.

But I'm not done. As long as he's here to listen, I'm going to try. "Dad, I wish you would stop being so blind. Your pride is destroying you." My voice breaks. "Destroying all of us."

He clenches his fist and closes his eyes, breathing deeply before finally responding. "You're starting to sound like your mother, and that's not a compliment."

"Wait—" I try to say, but Dad pivots on his heel and stomps back towards the house before I can stop him.

His rejection burns in my chest, and I have to swallow tears before they spill down my cheeks. His last comment stings, but it also seems so out of place. Dad never speaks ill of Mom, and if he's comparing me to her when I'm berating him for how he treats Andries, that leads me to think that Mom *has* been talking to him about similar things. She must have been trying to coerce him during their stay at Lake Como. I hope they aren't fighting too much, because I know Mom is on the edge right now anyway because of Andries being excluded from the family at the moment.

I make a decision to go check on my mother, hoping that she can tell me if Dad is any closer to forgiving Andries, and to check and make sure their relationship isn't too strained because of all of this. Of course, I can't imagine Mom loves the fact that my father is ostracizing their son, but she usually doesn't argue with him all that much.

I retrace my steps through the garden, back to the house, and ascend the stairs to find my mother in her office. When things are tense I can always find her there, surrounded by all the things that are strictly hers and not anyone else's in the family.

Just as I suspect, she's there in her leather office chair, not facing her computer. Instead, she's staring out the window and into the gardens. She must have been able to see Dad and me the whole time, but she wouldn't have been able to hear us. Still, Dad's body language probably told her all she needed to know. She doesn't even turn when I come in, flopping into the plush chair tucked next to her bookshelf.

"I assume you are coming to tell me how badly the talk with your father went," she starts, not looking my way just yet.

"Good guess," I groan, rubbing my face with my hands. "Mom, it's so cruel what Dad and Karl are doing to Roxanne and Andries! All this scheming is just making things worse, and he refuses to see it."

Mom hums to herself before answering me. "Your father hates this fact, but I actually agree with you. Sebastian is my husband, and I'll stand by him as much as I can, but he is taking things too far."

"Did anything happen in Lake Como?" I ask, hoping that she'll tell me what exactly happened between her and my father. I want to know exactly what she's said to him, and him to her. "How was the trip exactly?"

Mom huffs a laugh. "Not as exciting as your trip to Capri, I suppose." She stands, walks over to the couch, and sits gracefully down next to me, crossing one long leg over the other. "Tell me all about it, Elise. I'd love to hear how it went."

Now I'm suspicious that she's trying to move the conversation to something else... something like my personal life, and I start to withdraw into myself. I fold my hands in my lap and let my expression go blank. "It was a beautiful island," I tell her simply, but she continues to prod.

"Oh, come now. I want to hear more than that!" She lowers her voice conspiratorially. "I hear that Dan and Johan had to coexist under one roof. I'm sure that was eventful."

"It might have been more exciting, except Johan is just a friend, and I made that very clear to him."

Mom's eyebrows shoot up. "Oh, is that so?"

"Yeah," I fidget in my seat, but there's no reason to lie. "Dan and I have decided to give it a shot."

"What do you mean by a shot?" Mom asks. She's trying to sound casual, but not really pulling it off.

"Well, you know..." I cross my arms and look at the ceiling. "A shot as in we're going to try to be in a real relationship."

"So... Dan is your boyfriend?"

"I guess so," I admit, feeling a weight come off my shoulders now that I've told her. It hadn't been on my agenda, but maybe it's a good thing that it's out in the open.

Mom laughs softly, and it sounds happy, which I didn't expect. "What an interesting turn of events! Does Johan know Dan is your boyfriend now?"

I think back to Johan, catching us on the beach, and I feel my cheeks go red. "We actually just became official today, but I think Johan could see the writing on the wall. Plus, he's coming to the wedding, so he'll find out soon enough, anyway."

Now Mom sobers a bit, sitting back on the couch. "If the wedding even happens."

"It will," I tell her firmly. "They really love each other. I saw it with my own eyes. Even after Andries learned about the cabaret and the whole Bar Rouge scandal, he stood by her side."

Mom hums to herself again, thoughtfully. I take her hand with mine and lean against her, my head on her shoulder. "Dad is making a big mistake," I breathe, "But that doesn't mean you have to do the same."

She stiffens but doesn't push me away. "I told you I would think about it."

I close my eyes and take in the feeling of closeness with my mother, breathing in her comforting, familiar scent, before giving up on the subject and deciding to stop before I push her too far. "Okay, Mom."

I move to leave, but she stops me with a hand on my knee. I look at her, and she searches my eyes with her own, cupping my cheek briefly with her eyes bright before she straightens again. "Darling girl, do you need an appointment with our family doctor?"

Her question throws me. "For what?"

"Well, like we talked about before, now that you have a boyfriend—"

Her meaning catches me off guard, and I groan, embarrassed. "*Mom*, I told you I've got it handled! I got the pill in Capri, I'm good."

She frowns delicately. "El, it's best we make sure it's the best choice for you. A pharmacist is not a substitute for a doctor."

"I'm good, Mom. I swear."

Mom pats my hands, looking as uncomfortable as I feel. "If you say so, darling, but just tell me if you change your mind, alright? There are lots of options to explore."

I give my Mom an awkward hug and escape into the hallway, letting out a breath when I'm out of earshot of her. Leave it to my mom to make me so uneasy that I forget what I wanted to talk about in the first place.

I consider leaving but remember that I told Hannah I'd go to see her collection before I left. I knock on her bedroom door a few times before I hear my sister's voice from within. Once I enter, I realize that the pastel colors that her room had been painted before are long gone, replaced by lavish scarlets and creamy ivory. It's immaculate in decor and cleanliness, and my sister is perched on a stool towards the back of the room, leaning over something.

She doesn't say anything to me, so I shut the door behind me and approach her. What I thought was a makeup vanity appears to actually be a work desk, and Hannah is above it, holding a small, figure-eight shaped magnifying glass to her eye as she examines a stunning, glimmering emerald ring.

"That's beautiful," I comment, coming to stand beside her. "Is it yours?"

"No." Hannah doesn't stop examining her prize. "I found it on the beach in Lake Como. It must have fallen out of someone's bag."

The way she answers so smoothly sets off some alarms in my head, but I ignore them. "Damn, such a lovely ring, too. I'd be bummed if I had lost it."

"People lose precious things all the time," she responds deadpan, still not looking up at me. Her behavior is odd.

"Yeah, I guess they do. But Johan told me you have an entire collection of random things like this. How come I've never gotten to see it?" I keep my voice light and teasing, suddenly extremely interested in seeing her stash.

My sister shrugs, finally removing the magnifying glass from her eye as she looks at me. The harsh light she's using to see the ring clearly makes her look pale. "You never asked. Johan was the only one who was polite enough to inquire about it."

"Uh, ok. Can I see it?"

"Sure."

Hannah stands, and I'm taken aback by how tall she has become. How did I not notice it before? She has at least 4 inches on me, and her dark brown hair falls down her back in a sleek sheet that she brushes over her shoulder and out of the way. She's treating me with a strange aloofness, and while my sister has always been introverted, it almost seems like she doesn't want to be around me.

I follow her to her dressing room, which is just as stark and tidy as the rest of the room and watch as she pulls open a large drawer. I gasp, moving next to her to get a closer look. The drawer is full of antique jewels, broaches, and buttons. Some bear family crests that I recognize, others are unmarked but clearly expensive and precious. There is no rhyme or reason to her collection, only that everything is worth money and is striking in its own way.

"Wow," I breathe. "This looks like a pirate treasure. How long have you been collecting these?"

Hannah takes a second to reluctantly answer. "Since I was twelve or so. It's grown... quite a bit since I showed Johan. How is he doing, by the way? Since you saw him in Capri and all."

"Fine. Actually, I invited him to dinner here in a few weeks, so you can ask him for yourself."

"Really?" She becomes more animated than I've seen her this entire visit. "That's amazing! So you guys are..?"

I shake my head emphatically. "We're not together, no. We are just friends."

"Oh, okay," Hannah bites her bottom lip, thinking. "I just thought since he was in Capri with you and Andries—"

"Dan and I are together, actually," I interrupt, not wanting to talk about Johan anymore. Why does everyone seem so fixated on him?

Hannah gasps in surprise. "I had no idea!"

"It just happened today, actually, so you can stop teasing me about Johan once and for all, thank you very much," I joke.

"Huh. So that means—"

I whip my head to look at her, and her eyes widen. "That means what, Hannah?"

"That I have a chance?" she says quietly, almost like a question.

I regret the laugh that comes out of me immediately, but I can't help myself. "What! You're a fucking baby, Hannah, what do you mean a chance?"

Her briefly open expression shutters. "A baby?" She rolls her eyes. "I'm not only taller than you, but I'm turning sixteen in September."

"Nope, nope, and nope, forget about it." I cut my hand through the air, pacing the length of the dressing room now. "Johan is out of the equation. He's a friend of the family. And that's it. Are we clear?"

"Fine," Hannah snaps, crossing her arms. "Well I've got things to do, so can you go away now?"

"Gladly," I reply with just as much vitriol.

Once I'm out in the hallway, Hannah slams the door behind me, causing the light fixtures above to tinkle. I walk back down to the main floor almost in a trance, lost in my thoughts. I just can't believe that she would be so selfish to be into Johan knowing how much pain our breakup caused me. There's no way she knows that he wasn't the one to send the breakup text all those years ago, and the way she just lit up when she found out that I was with Dan really makes me feel like my own sister couldn't care less about my feelings.

I catch my own reflection in a mirror as I pass, and pause to look at myself. I feel like I look so much older than Hannah, even though she is just two years younger than me, and I can't help but think about myself at her age. Was it possible that I was just as self-centered and dismissive of everyone else's feelings?

I hate to admit it but... more than likely, I was. I don't even like the person I was six months ago, let alone two years ago. If it wasn't for Dan and his gentle guidance... well, maybe I would still be that little brat—just like Hannah.

Thinking about Dan makes me miss him terribly, and long to get away from my family drama already. I take one more look at my reflection, sigh, and continue towards the front door, trying to discover who exactly I am now if I'm so much different from everyone else in this home.

All I can hope is that I'm better now than I ever was.

CHAPTER 22

Dan

I had hoped that the falling water, cranked up so high that it nearly burns my skin, would be enough to clear my mind of Elise, but it only makes me think about her more. Washing off the traces of our interlude at my parents' house only makes me miss her more. I've finally gotten a portion of what I wanted from her—a real relationship—but she still hasn't told me that she loves me. My need for her seems like it will never be satiated, but hearing her confirm it would go a long way towards putting my soul at some sort of peace.

Being home, a space where I have brought so many women over the years, makes me feel almost guilty for wasting my time when Elise has always been the one for me. Maybe I need to redecorate and fill the refreshed space only with memories of her.

I've just rinsed out my shampoo, getting lost in thoughts of breaking in a brand new bed with my brand new girlfriend when I hear my phone begin to ring. I ignore the first call, needing some alone time to process everything, but when it immediately starts ringing a second time, I sigh, giving myself one more second under the water before stepping out onto the heated tile to take the call.

In this short amount of time the second call ends, and whoever is on the other hand doesn't waste any time in initiating a third call. I quickly grab a towel and rush to answer it, not knowing what to expect. My heart races, wondering if something is wrong with Elise or my parents, but let out a breath when I see that it's just Andries.

"Hey Andries, what's going on?" I answer, trying to steady my voice and banish the nerves that had just taken me over for a second.

"Hey, man, sorry for the repeated calls." Andries sounds stressed beyond belief, and any annoyance I may have had for him calling over and over fades. Of course, what he's going through is stressful, how could I have forgotten?

"No, I'm sorry for not answering right away. I was in the shower, but I should have been quicker. How is everything going? Do you have any updates?"

"Yeah, but they aren't really good or bad. Sort of middling. Roxanne is back home safely, but she was interrogated by the police for hours. The prosecutor didn't confirm to us if she will lift the charges or not," Andries answers, frustrated.

"Wow, that's intense. How is Roxanne doing?" I ask, concerned for my friend's fiancé. "She must be exhausted."

"She's holding up, but it's been a tough day for her. But you know Roxie…" Andries chuckles, but it sounds hollow. "She won't rest until this is settled. I've already got a hold of Kenneth and we're going to do an interview tomorrow to give our side of the story, and I'm sure it's going to blow up bigger than anything we've been involved with before."

I think back to how Andries decided to go to war with Sebastian, and how I swore to be on his side. Leaning against the bathroom counter, towel around my waist, I consider how messy this is all going to be, but I'm not overly worried. I'm a background player at most, and while I will play support no matter what, I don't plan on being dragged fully into the drama of it all.

"You sure you want to set this bomb off so soon? You guys should take a day or two at home to recoup from the trip and the police interrogation," I suggest, but Andries makes a noise of dissent immediately.

"We can't do that, not when my dad might be behind this, paying people to tarnish Roxanne's reputation," Andries explains, his voice laced with anger. "All I wanted was for him to just leave us alone. I accepted that he was going to hate me and shut me out, but the constant attempts to ruin both myself and Roxanne are too much. This interview is his comeuppance."

I flinch at his harsh words, all the enjoyable memories with Andries, his dad, and I flashing across my mind. But this is Andries's struggle, not mine, and I can't even pretend to understand what he's going through. "I hear you, and I'm with you. Just tell me what you need."

He lets out a long breath. "Thanks, Dan. I appreciate it. Right now, I just want to make sure Roxanne's name is cleared. I won't let my father destroy her reputation or our wedding. He can try, but by now I'm wise to all his tricks."

"Don't hesitate to call if you need something. For now, take care of poor Roxie and have a quiet night together. You're going to need it for tomorrow."

His sigh is deep, and full of a thousand different feelings. "Indeed we are. Have a good evening, Dan."

Once I hang up, I stay with my weight leaning against the bathroom counter for a few more moments, contemplating everything that has happened in the last day. It has flown by for me, but I bet that it has crawled by so slowly for Andries and Roxanne. I feel somewhat guilty that I've had it so easy while they're going through hell. Then, I think about Andries bringing Johan to the villa and scoff to myself. Okay, maybe Andries deserves some of the strife after all the meddling he did with me and his sister's relationship, but Roxie certainly doesn't. Regardless of his thoughtless actions, though, I will be Andries's right hand man as long as he needs me to.

I go to my empty bed and lay down, not bothering with any clothes, missing the warmth of Elise by my side. Again, the events of the day play in my mind like a film reel. The way my stomach had dropped when the plane landed it became apparent that law enforcement was waiting for Roxanne, the pleased confusion about Elise demanding to go to lunch with me, how welcoming my parents had been of her, showing Elise my childhood room before fucking her in it, and, most importantly of all, making our relationship official. I have the brief inclination to tell Andries that his sister and I have decided to give a relationship a real try, but his reaction is more likely to be negative than positive, and he has enough going on right now anyway. I'll keep it to myself for a few more days.

When I picture Elise's flush face, gasping my name, and her warm weight in my arms as I pressed her up against the wall, I feel my cock start to swell beneath the light duvet. God, she gets me going like nothing else. Without thinking,

I grasp myself and pump it a few times, but the action feels hollow somehow. I want her here. If I can't have the real thing, at least I can hear her voice before I go to sleep in this cold bed.

She picks up quickly enough, her voice deep and sleepy. "Hello, Dan."

"You sound so sexy right now," I tell her as a way of greeting, and I hear her snort.

"Thanks, I think. Do you need something?"

"Just to hear your voice," I say honestly, "When am I gonna see you again?"

Elise makes a thoughtful, humming noise before responding. "Is it you or your cock that misses me?"

The accused member jolts at the sound of the word in her mouth, and I grin. "You know me so well. Both of us."

"I figured," she says, amused. "It can't be tonight, I'm sorry to say. I was getting ready to head back to my apartment when Mom insisted I stay at the family estate for the night since I have to work in the morning and can just ride with my dad." Elise's tone sours when Sebastian comes up. "So yeah, I'm still here, but I'll be back in Amsterdam tomorrow."

"Huh. I guess I forgot how busy you are in reality." It makes me feel down to think about how little time we'll have for each other until an idea pops into my head. "Hey, how about next weekend we go somewhere, just the two of us?"

She seems surprised by the suggestion. "So soon? After everything my family is going through? I can't, there's too much going on." I hear the tension in her voice and I feel for her. I know that her family is going through a tough time and I don't want to add to her stress, but on the other hand, I'm a selfish man, and I want her all to myself.

"Did you speak to your brother yet?" I ask, trying to get a bigger picture of how involved Elise is going to be in the upcoming days.

"Yeah, he told me about how he and Roxie are doing the interview tomorrow." She blows out a long breath. "Dan, I've got such a bad feeling about this one. Dad is gonna lose his shit," her voice is filled with anxiety.

"Hey, don't worry too much. If Sebastian gets too angry, you can always come here and hide from him," I joke, but from her small noise of doubt, I'm not sure it landed.

"I'll keep that in mind," she offers before her voice softens. "Thanks for calling to check on me, Dan. Really. I appreciate it."

My heart goes soft at her words. "Anytime, sweetheart."

When we wish each other good night, a compulsion rushes over me to tell her that I love her. I've known for a while now that I do, and I've told her as much, but the certainty that she won't say the words back to me gives me pause. Every time she doesn't reciprocate, it hurts.

The need to tell her so fills me to the point that I begin, "El?"

In her sleepy, sultry voice, she responds, "Yes?"

Talking to her has been so calming and nice that I don't want to end it on the note of her not returning my affection, so the words die on my tongue. Instead I just tell her, "Take care, okay?"

She seems confused, but says, "You too, Dan."

When the line goes dead, I sit the phone on my bedside table, any inkling of arousal having fled my body completely.

It's still early, all things considered, but the only thing I want in the world is at her family estate, unreachable for now.

So, with nothing better to do, and an odd, empty feeling in my chest, I roll over and try my best to find sleep.

CHAPTER 23

Elise

The backseat of my father's private car feels like a prison. Sitting next to him as we make our way to the headquarters, I can't shake off the nervous feeling, knowing that the interview with Andries and Roxanne will be aired on TV in a few hours. Dan had messaged me before I even woke up, telling me that the interview has been recorded and what time it will air. I appreciate that he's keeping me in the loop, but I really wish that I had just been able to stay in the dark and be just as surprised by it as everyone else. No such luck, though, so now I'm trapped in this small space with the man who has raised me, my father, who I'm about to betray, just to help my brother.

What a mess...

My heart races as I think about the consequences this interview will have on my family and the reputation of my father. Andries and Roxanne have already done a number on Dad's ego, and even though they hadn't been in the news cycle for a while before the Bar Rouge scandal, Dad has never been able to forget that his son was getting ready to marry a former escort. I'm utterly unbothered by the way their engagement reflects back on me, being Andries's sister and all, but it's not so easy for Mom and Dad. For them, seeing as they are both old-fashioned children from old money, reputation is everything. Andries has irreparably tarnished theirs. Mom might be coming around, but Dad... not so much. He will torch his relationship with his oldest child to the ground to avoid being embarrassed, apparently.

I try to stay calm, but I can feel my palms sweating and my stomach in knots.

My dad has no idea that in just 90 mins the bombshell of the year will be aired on TV and that his secret plan to split Andries and Roxanne will be exposed to the general public. Any empathy he might have gained from being the patient father of a son gone rogue in the eye of the public will be destroyed with this interview. He doesn't want to admit it, but the idea of sex work is not nearly as scandalous as it once was, and if he and Karl had just left well enough alone, the drama behind Andries marrying Roxanne would have fizzled out. Now, though, his dark side is about to be laid bare to anyone and everyone. No one will side with a man who would try to destroy not just the business of an innocent woman, Roxanne, but his own son's marriage. Other old money families might understand, but the general public will not be nearly as kind.

My dad sits next to me quietly, staring out the window, completely unaware of the storm that's about to hit. I feel a mix of emotions... I'm angry with him for his actions but I also have this unmatched sense of loyalty towards him as his daughter. The dichotomy is dizzying. I've spent so much of my life planning to be the one to take over Van den Bosch industries that it feels surreal to be part of something that will hurt Dad and the company so much. But I have to do what's right, even if it's awful.

"Are you okay, Elise?" my dad asks, noticing my anxiety. "Nervous about going back to work?"

"Uh... yeah, I am, sort of," I tell him lamely, stumbling over my words before I get my bearings again. "I guess I just need to shake myself out of the vacation mindset." I pull my water bottle out of my bag and take a shaky sip of water, trying to tame my nerves, but it does little to help.

My dad notices how anxious I am and asks me again, "Are you sure you're alright? I don't think you were even this nervous on your first day."

"I didn't eat breakfast," I lie, hoping that it will explain my shaking hands.

"I'm sure it'll be fine. Just shake it off," my father says, patting my shoulder. I smile stiffly, and turn my attention back out the window, ending the conversation before I can dig myself into an even deeper hole.

As we arrive at the office, my dad hugs me and wishes me a good day, and my immediate reaction is to hug him back and take comfort in his embrace. How many times have hugs like this calmed me after getting skinned knees falling from my pony as a girl, or when I had trouble making friends at camp? I feel like a fraud and guilty as he releases me for hiding so much from him, especially when he behaves like the affectionate father I grew up with, not the petty man that he has proven he can be.

Once we split off and go our separate ways, him to his top floor office and me to the open concept intern floor, I can't help but wonder how he'll react when he hears the interview. Will he be angry or will he try to deny it? I hope that he can learn from it and change his ways, but I know that it's not going to be easy. Still, this is the first step in making him see the error of his ways, and while I know he's going to be undeniably pissed off at first, maybe he'll come to realize how much he's hurt all of us with his actions.

Throwing myself into work is easier said than done, but I manage to sink into it all, considering how many days I've been out of the office, and push the upcoming interview from my mind. I am sitting at my desk, fingernails clicking on the keyboard, when my phone dings with a text message from Dan.

My heart sinks as I read his message. *Have you seen the interview? Lol, your dad is gonna have a meltdown.* He includes a link to it. I feel a knot form in my stomach as I click it, unsure of what I'm about to see.

I look around the open layout of my office and notice that my colleagues are all whispering and standing up to watch a computer screen of a colleague who's playing the interview. Suddenly, they all turn and stare at me, given that I'm Sebastian's daughter. Blood drains from my face, and I shakily lower myself back into my chair, realizing that the chaos is about to start, whether I am ready for it or not.

It's only been minutes, but that means I'm running out of time before Dad sees the interview and calls me into his office. Having the sudden urge to be the one to break the news to him, I pick up the office phone and dial his office. No one answers, which tells me that I'm too late. I feel guilty for not warning him about it, but at the same time, I know that there's nothing I could have done to stop it.

As the minutes tick by, the tension in the office becomes palpable. It's barely any time before Dad's assistant shows up and tells me that he wants to see me in his office. As I leave, every person in the room follows me with their eyes. It's almost obscene how heavy their gazes are.

The walk isn't long, but it feels like it takes forever, almost like I'm walking to my execution. Breaking out in a cold sweat, I consider bolting and leaving the office altogether, dealing with Dad's disappointment later over the phone. But we are only steps from his office, and it's too late now.

Inside, Karl, the PR director, and my father are all waiting for me. Dad is seated while the other two stand, but all eyes are on me. My heart is pounding in my chest as my dad glares at me, his eyes filled with an angry, unreadable look.

"Did you know?" he grits out, tapping his pen on his desk.

"I-well…" I stutter, wishing I had prepared better for this inevitable moment.

"You don't have to bluff, I already know the answer," he scoffs, throwing the pen down and crossing his arms. "I take it that this means you're no longer on our side and are working with your brother and his little whore now?"

My mouth goes dry at his words, a fizzle of indignation in my stomach. "I'm not siding with anyone. I'm just doing what's right."

"Stop lying to me, El. Did you know about this interview, yes or no?" he demands, his voice low and menacing.

I glance nervously at Karl and the PR director, both of whom are standing nearby, and my dad notices. "Don't look at them. No one is going to save you from what you've done to yourself," Dad says before he dismisses them from the room, and once we are alone, I try to explain.

"I tried to talk to you about it, but you wouldn't listen," I begin, my voice trembling.

"You never told me they were about to expose me on TV!" he explodes, his face turning red, features twisting. "That trip to Capri messed with your head. And here I thought you were my smarter child. Turns out you're just as naive and impulsive as your brother."

My face burns with shame as I counter, "I told you to let it go, I told you to choose peace over war."

Now Dad stands, and my heart races as he towers over me. "I trusted you to report to me anything going on, but what did you do? Nothing!" he continues to shout, his voice echoing through the room. "You're such a disappointment, Elise."

Fury whips through me like cleansing fire, and I feel my fists clenching, chin tilting up stubbornly. "Oh, am I? Well, you too Dad."

The last thing I register as I storm out of the room is the disgust on my father's face, and it makes my insides feel like they're twisting. There's nothing else to do right now. I can't change what's been done.

As I walk through the hallway, the PR director—who had clearly been waiting on me—steps into my path and says, "Elise, we need to talk. We need to come up with a solution to fix this mess."

I push past him and keep walking, but he moves ahead of me swiftly and opens the door to an empty office, jerking his head to indicate that I should follow him inside. Against my better judgment, I do so, not wanting to deal with this confrontation in front of my coworkers.

I blow out a breath, stirring the little pieces of hair that hang in front my face. "You are aware that I'm not any of the guilty parties in this situation, right? I'm not the one marrying a former escort, and I'm certainly not the one paying Karl to bribe a dancer. So what exactly is it that you want from me?"

The PR director sighs, rubbing his temples. "All of that is the exact reason why I'm asking you what to do. It's clear that you hold sway over your father and your brother, so you might be the only one that can help. You have to."

I take a deep breath and reply, "The only solution is for Dad to make an official statement saying he conducted an internal investigation within the company and discovered Karl was behind all of it and then fire him. That would clean up his image once and for all and would leave Karl to take the fall for it all. Like he deserves."

The PR director looks at me with a shocked expression and asks, "You want your dad to throw Karl under the bus?"

I nod my head and say, "Absolutely I do. He's the one who bribed the dancer. Dad told me so."

The director opens his mouth to say something, but before he can a tall silhouette darkens the doorway. Suddenly, Karl appears out of nowhere and says, "And what are you going to do with that information, Elise? Are you going to surprise us with a lovely admission on TV, just like your brother did?" He chuckles, shaking his head. "I guess being a snake runs in the family."

I hold his gaze, unafraid and crossing my arms. "Depends on what my dad intends to do. If he decides to be reasonable, then it doesn't have to come to that."

Karl sneers. "Don't play games with me. You know as well as I do that your father will do whatever it takes to protect his image and his company. He'll do anything if it means saving his own skin."

I shrug, unphased. Nothing he is saying is news to me. "Maybe. But I also know that he's not stupid. He'll see that this is the only way to salvage his reputation and the reputation of the company, and I promise you that he doesn't care enough about you to put his own neck out for your sake."

Karl laughs, but I can tell that last line got to him some. "And what makes you think he'll listen to you? What could you possibly know about PR and damage control?"

I stand up straighter. "I know him better than anyone." I raise my eyebrows, looking Karl over. "I know what he's capable of and I know what he's willing to do to protect what's important to him, and guess what? *I'm* important to him, *this company* is important to him, and no matter what he says, *Andries* is important to him, too. Not you, Karl."

Karl's expression turns serious. "You're playing a dangerous game, and you're losing points with daddy dearest by the minute. You're not just risking your job, you're risking everything. Are you really willing to lose all of that just to take me down?"

I look him in the eye, my voice steady and firm. "I'm not just doing this to take you down. I'm doing this to protect my father, the company that will one day be mine, and my brother. If that means going up against you and anyone else who tries to stand in my way, then so be it."

Karl nods slowly, a hint of grudging respect in his eyes. "Alright then. It's your funeral." He shakes his head and laughs sardonically. "So young and so naive." With that, he turns and walks away, leaving me standing there, feeling a mix of fear and determination, pulse pounding.

The poor PR director has been silent this whole time, looking between the two of us as we argued. When I turn to him now he just shrugs. "I'll be in contact, but this is clearly more complex than I thought. I need some time to gather information and look things over."

I give him a single nod and leave the empty room, keeping my eyes straight ahead as I head for my desk, grabbing my bag while avoiding the eyes of everyone else who is currently working. I know they are all staring, but at this point my popularity among my coworkers is the least of my worries. Let them look, it doesn't bother me in the slightest right now.

I breathe a sigh of relief when my feet hit the sidewalk as I walk out of the building. I need to talk to someone, and the obvious choice would be Andries—since he has the biggest stake in what is going on with my father—but considering how strenuous the interview must have been for him and Roxanne, I decide that talking to Dan will be the better choice. Plus... I miss him, and this is a good excuse to hear his voice.

I pull out my phone and select Dan's contact. He picks up on the second ring. "Elise? What's going on? I thought you'd still be at work."

"Yeah, well… I just left. Dad understandably freaked out about the interview, but he really took it out on me more than I expected," I tell him, my voice still shaking slightly from the confrontation.

"Was he rude to you?" Dan asks, sounding surprised.

"Somewhat, yeah," I answer, swallowing hard when I remember how he called me a disappointment. "He had Karl and the company's PR director there too, and they are all pissed at me. I guess because I'm the only one around that they can be mad at, besides themselves."

"Well, what about Karl? How did he react?"

"He didn't take it well. He tried to intimidate me… cornered me in an empty office like the creep he is, but luckily, the PR director was in there with us." I frown, thinking back to all of it, and how nerve-wracking it had been. "He told me over and over again that I was risking everything, but I stood my ground. I know this isn't going to be easy, but I'm in this fight whole-heartedly."

"I'm proud of you, Elise. You're doing so well," Dan says, his voice filled with support.

His words, the first kind ones I've received since the interview aired, warm me from the inside. "Thanks. I just hope it all works out in the end," I tell him, unable to shake the uncertainty that is riding me.

"It will. I have faith in you," Dan reassures me. "Your Dad loves you, even if he is being a dick right now. He'll come around, eventually." He pauses, then asks, "What are you doing right now?"

"I'm heading to my apartment. I don't want to see anyone who might recognize me. I just need some time to myself."

"By yourself, do you mean..?" he queries, sounding almost mischievous, and I smile despite myself.

"I guess it'd be okay to have some company," I offer.

"I'll meet you there, then," Dan says, needing no other encouragement. "We can close out this day on a good note, I think."

As I hang up the phone, I can feel the tears prickling at the corners of my eyes. I'm not sure if they're tears of anger or relief. I just know that I need to get out of here before I break down. At least here soon I can be in Dan's arms, away from everyone who thinks of me as the enemy.

The driver comes quickly when I call him, and I scroll social media on the ride back to my place, wanting to shut my brain off and think of simple things.

When I finally make it to my apartment, I kick off my shoes immediately, all but running to my room to change into comfortable leggings and a sweatshirt. Out of my work clothing, it's easier to forget about the awful beginning of my day, but it's not enough.

Heading to the kitchen, I pour myself a glass of wine, despite the early hour. I go for a sweet riesling, wanting something a little decadent, and when I spot the menu neatly folded along with my mail, I decide to order a pizza and just chill out completely. Wine and pizza… not the best combination in the world, but the one I need right now.

Sinking into my couch, I exhale slowly and sip my drink, letting the alcohol hit my empty belly and help to loosen my limbs and ease my mind. The sun is warm coming in through the windows, and I wiggle my toes in the light, living in the moment while I wait for Dan to show up and fix this hellish day.

It doesn't take him long, and he only knocks once before letting himself in. When I hear his voice, it's like a knot inside of me begins to loosen. Tossing back the rest of the glass of wine, I pad out to the foyer to find my boyfriend, but I'm surprised when I see that he's brought company: Andries.

Seeing my brother makes all the emotions I've been trying to avoid come rushing back, and before I know it I'm blinking back frustrated tears that had wanted to spill earlier. I swallow, realizing I'm going to have to tell the events of earlier to Andries, but before I can say anything he comes forward and pulls me into a warm embrace. All of a sudden I feel like a little girl again, hugging her brother after he's been gone for a week at fencing camp. It feels like coming home.

I made the right choice. Right here, right now, I'm sure of it.

"Dan already told me everything," he tells me quietly. "You don't need to rehash it if you don't want to. I know it wasn't easy, but you did the right thing,"

I know that he's right. Hell, I've come to the same conclusion myself, but the acceptance of my brother doesn't heal the wound of my father's rejection.

I've done so much, and gone so far, to make up for the horrible things I did in the past to sabotage Roxanne and Andries, but now that I've come out the other side of it all I feel sort of hollow. I'm happy that I've done what I could to assist my brother and regain his trust, and I'm glad he's getting to move forward with the life he wants to live his dreams, but now... what about my dreams?

You're a disappointment, my dad's voice rings in my head and I pull out of the hug, dashing tears out of my eyes. I try to smile, but I must look crestfallen, because both Dan and Andries frown.

"What's wrong?" Andries asks. "Are you having second thoughts?"

I shake my head. "It's a little late for that, even if I was. Dad is beyond angry."

"Then what is it?" he presses.

I twist the hem of my sweatshirt in my fingers as I answer. "I don't know… This might sound petty, but I'm just thinking about how you're going to get married and move away to start your own life and now… I feel like I've sabotaged mine, even if it was for a good cause. You know my dream has always been to work with Dad and eventually take over the company."

My brother looks stricken. "El, Roxie, and I aren't going to just abandon you after all this."

"I know that. You just didn't see how mad Dad was. He was absolutely furious, and I don't know if he'll ever forgive me. Taking over Van den Bosch industries has been my life goal for so long that I don't know what I'll do if I lose the opportunity."

"El, he'll definitely forgive you," Andries reassures me. "It isn't like you did the interview yourself or even pressured me into doing so. Dad will come around."

"I don't know about that…" I look at Dan, who waves his hand for me to continue encouragingly. "You guys didn't see how pissed off he was today. At *me*, not just the whole situation. He might be too furious to want to throw Karl under the bus, just to spite us all. And we all know that if Dad wants to save Karl, the company will just throw a shit ton of money to lawyers and get him out of everything." My brother and Dan look at each other like they know something I don't, and I grasp onto it right away. "Hey… what's going on? Why are you two looking at each other like that?"

"His ass can't be saved this time," Dan admits, shoving his hands in his pockets. "Bianca, the dancer Karl paid, was interrogated by the prosecutor, and she admitted that he paid her."

"What!" I gasp, hands flying to my chest in surprise. Shock ripples through me at this bombshell revelation. "Are you serious? How do you guys know this!?"

"Roxanne's lawyer told us," Andries supplies. "The prosecutor is still on the fence about whether they want to send Roxanne to trial or not, but even if they choose to, her defense is stronger than Karl's. There's no way she could lose."

I have a million more questions, but before I can ask them, the door buzzes behind me, causing me to jump.

"It's just the pizza," I laugh nervously. "Why don't you guys get plates and napkins and we'll eat in the living room and chill out? I really need it after everything that has gone down."

Just like when we were younger, we circle around the coffee table in the living room, sitting on the plush carpet and enjoying the greasy food while talking about less serious things. Here with Andries and Dan, sharing a pizza, a sense of contentment washes over me. The warm and comforting aroma of the pizza fills the room, and for a moment, everything feels right in the world. But suddenly, Andries's phone rings as he receives a call from Roxanne. The expression on his face changes instantly, and I know he has to leave. As Andries excuses himself, I can't help but feel a sense of guilt wash over me. With everything going on, we still haven't told him that we're together. He isn't going to take the lie of omission very well, even if we were just trying to lessen his stress.

Now that Dan and I are left alone, I find myself staring at him, wondering if my brother knows about us somehow. Could he have guessed, or did Dan tell him when the two of them were alone?

The question that had been weighing on my mind for so long finally spills out of my mouth, "Dan, does my brother know?"

I can see the confusion etched on Dan's face as he replies, "Know what?"

I wave my hands in the air as I elaborate, trying to get the point across. "That we are like *together* together."

Dan's expression turns pensive, and he responds, "I didn't tell him yet, with everything he's going through…."

"Yeah, I get what you're saying." I set my slice of pizza on the plate in front of me and nibble my lip. "But you and I both know how Andries is when it comes to secrets."

Dan must sense my inner turmoil because he reaches out and takes my hand, "Elise, you don't have to worry. I've thought this through, and I believe it's best to wait until your brother and Roxanne are in a better place to tell him about us."

I look into his eyes, and I know he's right. I nod in agreement and say, "You're right. You did well not telling him. I'm not sure if I would have been able to hold it all in."

A smile plays at the corner of his lips. "Why? Because you're so excited to be with me that you just can't contain it?"

I slap him on the arm and he laughs. It's contagious, and before I know it, I'm laughing too, moving around the table until I can crawl into his lap and loop my arms around his neck. I finally get to kiss him, and it's playful at first, but I know it all has the potential to turn heated.

I keep everything light until we clean up our lunch, but when I see Dan go to grab his keys, I find that I'm not ready for him to get yet. After all, what's the point of leaving work early if I can't have a little fun?

Grabbing his wrist, I pull him away from the keys hanging on the hook by the door, and pull him towards me instead. I run my hands up his chest while gazing deeply into his eyes, and his amusement slowly shifts into something hot and electrifying.

"El…" he rumbles, leaning closer to me. "Is there something I can do for you?"

Tracing the bare skin at the collar of his shirt, I tilt my head to the side as if lost in thought. I can feel the warmth of his body, and smell his clean, woodsy cologne, and it shifts my need for him into overdrive.

"Oh, I was just thinking…" I start, pressing a kiss to his chiseled jawline, rubbing my lips over the slight stubble there.

"Thinking about what?" he coaxes, hands sliding from the small of my back down to cup my ass cheeks.

When I look into his eyes, I make sure to fill the look with all the fire I feel burning inside me all of the sudden. "I was just thinking about how we haven't done it in my bed yet."

Dan's gaze sharpens, and he inhales. "You're right. Should we rectify the situation?"

I take his hand, leading him down the hall to the bedroom. "Absolutely," I purr, pushing the center of his chest so he sits on the edge of the bed before I swing my legs over his and settle into his lap, feeling the hard line of his erection already pressing into me.

Dan kisses me fully, his tongue delving deep into my mouth, and finally, all thoughts flee from my head. All thoughts but those of him and me and what we're about to do in this bed.

CHAPTER 24

Dan

Late evening sunlight casts the woman in my arms in hues of gold. Her skin is as warm under my hands as if she and I had been lying under the sky for the past few hours instead of in her bed, enjoying each other unhurriedly. Now, she stretches, arms above her head and toes curling.

"Finally satisfied?" I tease, kissing the tip of her nose.

"Never," she replies, dragging an inquisitive finger down the planes of my chest to my abs before stopping. "But I think I'm good for right now. Maybe even a little tired."

"I'm not sorry," I tell her, holding her closer. The feeling of her pressed up against me like this is addictive, and each time we come together in this way it's harder to let her go. Even the idea of going home alone tonight makes my stomach flip flop, so I push the thought away for now. I'll cross that bridge when I get to it.

Elise casts a seductive glance in my direction as she speaks, her voice low, "We should get dinner, don't you think?" I hadn't thought about food for hours, the only hunger that has been plaguing me is my hunger for her, but now that she mentions it my stomach rumbles audibly. Elise laughs. "Glad to know you agree."

She rises from the bed, her lithe form moving towards the shower as she tosses over her shoulder, "I want Thai food."

"Yes, your majesty," I answer after her. She's already decided our plans for the evening and I haven't even been able to get a word in edgewise. Not that I'm complaining.

In order to do her bidding, I need my phone, but it's nowhere to be found in the bed or on the end tables by the bed. I wasn't thinking about where my things were getting tossed as we got undressed earlier, so now I have to fumble through my discarded pants for my phone. I curse when I realize the battery is almost dead, searching in all the obvious places for a charger so I can make the Thai order, but I can't find one anywhere. I call out to Elise, "Hey babe, do you know where your charger is?" but she doesn't hear me, lost in the sound of the shower.

I open the drawer of her bedside table, searching for a charger. But instead, I find an envelope with Elise's name written in a looping scrawl on the front. I have no idea what's inside, but for some reason, it feels like a stone weight settles in my gut at the sight of it. I have a really bad feeling about this.

My hands are strangely unsteady as I reach out and open it, hoping that my instincts are wrong, but those hopes are dashed as soon as I turn the glossy photograph over. It's a copy of the photo of Johan and Elise—the same photo she has in her study—along with a VIP ticket to attend the "Horse of the Year Show" in England this October. I spy a small note as well which says, in that same handwriting as the envelope, *"Let's meet in England this fall."*

At first, all I feel is grief, heavy and dark as it settles over me, but in a flash, I'm livid, betrayal searing through my veins as I realize the truth. Johan's words echo in my mind, *"You're just a summer fling,"* and I can now see why he left without caring much—he's been playing the long game. He thinks by the fall, Elise will tire of me, and he will be able to come into the picture and sweep her off her feet. I am left speechless, my mind a jumbled mess as I try to process this revelation. *Why didn't she throw the invitation away? Why did she keep it tucked inside her bedside drawer?* My head is spinning with so many questions, and my heart feels tight in my chest.

Without even me noticing, Elise comes back into the room, clad only in a silk robe that would have gotten all of my attention had I not been reeling, her voice light and carefree as she asks, "Did you already order? I'm starving." But her smile falters as she sees the envelope in my hand. Without missing a beat, she explains, "He gave it to me before leaving, but that doesn't mean I intend to go."

I stand up, my movements stiff and robotic as I start getting dressed. Elise tries to stop me, but I shrug her off. "Of course…" I mutter, my voice cold and distant.

Elise is talking, but it all sounds like static to my ears. She's pulling at my arm, and then my sleeves, but all her begging falls on deaf ears, and I shrug her hands off me as I go to leave the apartment. I'm desperate for fresh air and a second to think. But as I reach for the door handle, she steps in front of me and locks it, trapping me in the room with her.

"You can't leave until we talk," she says firmly.

I spin around to face her, frustration reaching its boiling point. "I'm tired of your bullshit, El. It's clear you only see me as some summer fling. If you had no interest in him, you'd have thrown that envelope in the trash. But no..." I laugh darkly. "You kept it in your nightstand like it's something precious. Something that you can't bear to lose."

"I just threw it in there when I unpacked my luggage! I didn't know what else to do with it," Elise sputters. "You're looking way too far into something that really is nothing. You have to believe me!"

I shake my head, my heart heavy with disappointment. "I want to, El. I really do. As much as you're fine sharing my bed, you still keep your heart closed off, and that makes it impossible to truly believe you. You still never told me you love me. *Never.*" I can hear my voice raising in volume so I close my eyes and tilt my head back, taking a few bracing breaths. "If you want me to believe you, look me in the eye and say you love me."

As I stare into her eyes, the intensity of the moment takes over. I can see the irritation growing in Elise's expression, a sign that she is still unable to tell me the words that I long to hear. She breaks eye contact, and I know then that she won't, which tears at my heartstrings. I love her so much, more than I would think possible, and although I've tried to convince myself that I'm fine waiting for her to get on the same page as me, the glacial pace at which she's moving is killing me slowly. I scoff, trying to brush past her and out the door, but Elise blocks me once more, fists clenched and fire in her eyes.

"You know what? Fuck you, Dan!" she snarls, her voice filled with anger. "I'm not going to be forced to say whatever you want to hear. We haven't even been official for a full week yet, for fuck's sake."

But instead of succumbing to her rage, I remain calm, my voice steady as I speak. It takes everything inside of me to remain level, but I don't want to fight with the woman I love, albeit one-sidedly. "Then let me go. If I cannot force you to love me, you cannot force me to stay."

The weight of my words hangs heavily in the air as I wait for her response, but the silence that follows is deafening. I let myself go numb when the reality of the situation sinks in. Her silence is all the answer I need, and it feels like a knife to the heart.

Johan was right. She really doesn't love me, I think almost frantically, the world slowly crumbling around me. My chest feels tight and my stomach is in knots as I try to hold back the emotions that are desperate to spill forth, but it's no use. The feeling is unbearable.

Elise is clearly still mad, but she freezes for a moment upon hearing my request, knowing that there is no way she can answer that will make me stay unless it's an actual confession of love—which she is still so reluctant to give me. I take the key from her hand while she's still in shock, unlock the door of the room we had just spent hours sharing passion in, and then I leave, my heart heavy with pain.

As I reach the hallway, I pray that she will come running after me, begging for forgiveness, or finally admitting that she loves me but that doesn't happen. Maybe Elise really is an ice queen down to her core, and she just can't break out of that role. Everyone has been telling me that I'm a fool for caring for her, and I've defended our relationship over and over again. Now what do I have to show for it?

With a rueful sense of irony, I am relieved that Andries doesn't know anything about our relationship, given how brief it was. How many days did it even last? 2 days? I was a love-struck idiot to believe we could make it work. Me, hot-blooded and head over heels in love, and Elise as icy as a winter storm. Johan will always be in her mind and heart, and I cannot seem to shake him off. Maybe he's the one that will thaw her out, but she's made it crystal clear that I'm not the one. My heart is shattered, my soul in tatters, as I walk out of her apartment and maybe... gosh, maybe her life, for good.

As I walk out onto the sidewalk, keys in my hand, I spot none other than Sebastian himself getting out of his car. I have to do a double take, remembering how cruel Elise had said he was to her earlier. Why is he here now?

Despite how awful Elise has made me feel, I still bristle at the idea that he's come to lecture her or tear her down more. I need to try and feel him out to see what his intentions are.

"Mr. Van den Bosch?" I call out to him, and he turns, eyebrows raising as he sees me and begins to cross the street to head over.

Once he reaches me, he holds out his hand for me to shake, and I oblige out of habit. "Oh, Dan, how are you?" Sebastian greets me, a hint of curiosity in his tone. "Is Elise upstairs?"

"She is, yes," I respond, my heart heavy in my chest thinking about how I had just left her. "She didn't mention that you were coming by, though."

Sebastian looks abashed, rubbing the back of his head. It's an odd look on such a self-assured man. "Ah... well. She doesn't know that I'm coming, but I need to talk to her about some things. I might have been a little harsh with her earlier today, and I need to make amends."

Surprise ripples through me. Has he really come here to apologize? I can barely believe it, but I'm also definitely not going to stay here to mediate. This is between father and daughter.

"I see. Well… she's up there. I'm sure she'll be happy to see you."

"Great," he seems to brighten. "How was Capri? Did you enjoy it?"

All the memories I made with his daughter flicker across my thoughts. "Yeah, it was wonderful."

Sebastian continues the small talk, despite my efforts to cut it short. All I can think about is the pain Elise has caused me, and how we will never have moments like we did in Capri ever again. I force a smile and give him non-committal answers, waiting impatiently for the conversation to wind down.

Finally, Sebastian shakes my hand again and heads towards his daughter's apartment, an uncharacteristic air of nervousness about him. As I get into my car, I'm grateful that Sebastian is polite enough not to bring up the cabaret scandal or my conflict with Andries. He must know that I'm tangentially involved at the least, but it's really the last thing I want to get into right now. With my chest aching, I drive home, a silent tear falling down my cheek as I realize the relationship I had with Elise was all for nothing. My heart is broken, and I can't shake the feeling that Johan will always have a hold on her. I should have never believed that we could make this work.

CHAPTER 25

Elise

I stand in front of my front door, staring at it in disbelief as the reality of what just happened sinks in. Dan, the man I have finally admitted I want to be with seriously, just stormed out of my apartment after accusing me of betraying him. I can't believe it. Just hours ago we were lying in bed together, making love and speaking sweet nothings to one another between rounds. But now, it's all over.

It's not as if I blame him for being suspicious when he found the letter from Johan, but his reaction was so over the top and combined with his refusal to hear my explanation, I'm reeling. Yeah, the photo, ticket, and note looked bad, but Dan and I have become almost inseparable, the feelings between us burning bright and true. How can he still think that I'd want Johan? I haven't even thought about Johan since Hannah and I's conversation.

I try to process what went wrong. Dan is so fixated on me saying those three little words that they just feel like ash in my mouth every time I try to. Why is the affection between us—physically and emotionally—not enough for him? I've given him so much of myself that it makes me feel empty to think that it's so easy for him to give me up.

I pace the foyer, vacillating between anger and devastation. I had wanted to explain, but the words had fallen short. He's gone and he might not be coming back. I'm left standing here in shock, feeling like my heart has been ripped out of my chest. I just can't believe this is happening. How could everything fall apart so quickly? I try to hold back the tears but they come anyway, streaming down my face as I realize that things might never be the same. I have to make this right somehow, but I just feel broken.

Then, the door buzzes, indicating that someone is waiting outside. My heart jumps into my throat as I open the door, pulse racing with anticipation, believing it to be Dan returning to apologize and make things right. I jerk open the door, and my hopes are quickly dashed as I come face to face with my father. Dad is the last person I want to see right now, and having him right in front of me all of the sudden makes me rear back slightly.

I don't say anything, but out of old habits, step aside and let him into my apartment. He walks in with a concerned look on his face, his eyes following me. "Hello, El. I'm glad to see you made it home okay."

I shrug, crossing my arms and looking away from him. While he shuts the door behind him, I desperately wish he would just reopen it and leave.

In the wake of my silence, Dad scuffs his feet on the floor before speaking again. "I, uh, saw Dan leaving as I came in.

It was good to catch up, except he looked quite serious and sad, though."

I can feel hurt rising within me as I struggle to keep my emotions in check. "Yeah, he was just visiting."

Frowning, my father tries to initiate a conversation about my relationship with Dan, but I shut him down, my voice cold and distant. "What are you doing here, Dad?" I snap, unable to hide my frustration.

Dad flinches. "I just think we needed to talk, is all. Not about Dan, though. About you and I."

When I huff and move to walk away, he tries to reach out to me. I'm in no mood to hear Dad blame me for not telling him about the interview sooner, so I brush him off. I don't need his words of wisdom or his attempts at understanding.

As I stand there, staring blankly at my father, I can't keep my focus on him. Dan is still taking up all of my thoughts. I can't help but think about all the missed opportunities and the what-ifs. Like if I had done something differently, if I had said something more if I had given him more of myself, would things have turned out differently? All Dan had wanted was some assurance of my love, but it just so happens that it's the one thing I can't easily give him.

I'm snapped out of my thoughts when my Dad clears his throat to get my attention. With a glare, I whip around. "Fine. If you're going to stand here and force me to listen, go ahead."

He starts, but my father, usually clear and concise with his words, seems flustered. He stops and starts, trying to bring up the fight we had earlier before fizzling out and starting back over at the beginning. His behavior is so out of the ordinary that I feel some of my anger bleed away and curiosity take its place.

"Dad, what's going on?" I ask, as he starts rambling.

He takes a deep breath and finally centers himself enough to make a coherent sentence. "Look. I'm sorry for my behavior, I know it's hard for you to be stuck between your brother and the company's interest. But I want you to know that I love you. I always have."

I am taken aback, my Dad hasn't said those words to me in years. I can't even remember the last time he uttered that phrase. "Really?" I ask past the lump in my throat.

"Yes, really," he says and opens his arms. "Can I give you a hug?"

I step into his embrace and hug him tightly, overwhelmed with emotions. It's been such a strange day, full of every possible feeling, that the peace from this hug is so needed. "I love you too, Dad," I say, feeling grateful that he was so humbled by the meeting this morning. I could have never expected this outcome, let alone so quickly.

My father squeezes me once more before letting go. Now he looks at me seriously. "Can I ask you something?" When I accept, he then asks, "Are you and Dan together? Like... a couple?"

It's not like I don't expect this question, but it's still my first instinct just to lie so we don't have to talk about it anymore. But this isn't something I can hide forever, and if Dan forgives me and we continue dating, my parents will know that I lied to them about it. I am very emotional from the hug and everything else that has happened to me in the last few hours, so I dry my tears, saying, "We were. But I think I messed everything up."

"Why is that?" he asks gently.

I find it hard to open up, especially to my father, but since he has driven all the way down here not just to see me, but to do something as difficult as apologizing and admitting his wrongdoing. So as uncomfortable as it makes me, I decide to tell him the truth.

"Dan is so sure that he loves me and is quite vocal about it, but I can't tell him I love him. It's messed up, I know, but every time I feel like I want to, I lose my courage and retract. It's like my tongue gets tied up in knots," I confess, my voice barely above a whisper.

My father looks at me with a mixture of understanding and concern. "And you're sure he loves you?"

I nod, tears streaming down my face faster than I am able to wipe them away. "He does. He's told me so many times, but I can't bring myself to do the same. He deserves to know how I feel, but I just can't seem to say the words."

Dad hums in thought. "Let's go sit down, shall we? This is a lot of big revelations for us to still be standing in front of the door."

So we do just that. I haven't had him over in some time, and I resist the urge to tidy up as I lead him to the living room, leaving him there so I can go make us some tea. Dan has gotten me in the habit of drinking it every time I need to relax or think deep thoughts, and while I don't have the fancy blooming tea that he is so fond of, my father is plenty pleased with the small basket of tea bag choices and the water from the electric kettle when I return.

I sit down on the opposite side of the couch, tucking my feet underneath me and letting the warm ceramic tea mug center me. I chose chamomile, and Dad is having Earl Grey.

"Now," he starts, giving me an easy smile. "You were telling me how you care for our friend Daniel, but are still running into trouble?"

I huff a sad laugh. "That's putting it lightly. Dan is such an amazing person," I continue, my voice cracking with emotion. "I don't know what's wrong with me."

I expect Dad to placate me with soothing words, considering how our interaction has gone so far, so what he says next takes me off guard. "Is it because of that Englishman? That Johan you met at summer camp?" Dad asks, his voice gentle.

I am shocked that he knows about my previously deep feelings for Johan. Sure, Mom and Dad both knew that he and I had dated years ago, but my father has never been overly interested in Johan before this. I figured he still thought of him as a summer crush I had long ago, and nothing more. "How do you know that?"

He gives me a sly look. "I will give you one guess, and one guess only."

"Ha, of course," I smile despite myself. "Mom told you, didn't she?"

"Indeed she did." He chuckles. "Your mom told me he was in Capri and that he'd be coming to have dinner with us," he explains. "Also that your sister was oddly excited about it. Not many things interest Hannah, so it's got your mother thinking."

"Yeah," I reply, my mind racing. I'm definitely not going to let him in on the hunch that I have about Hannah having a silly childhood crush on the much-too-old for her Johan. Especially when Johan and I still haven't resolved our own relationship issues fully. "He invited me to England this fall… to an equestrian show. If Dan wasn't in the picture, I'd go—at least as Johan's friend—but I think that he expects more from me than just friendship."

"And this decision is more difficult for you since Dan is around?"

"Yes. He definitely would cut things off permanently if I went with Johan, I don't know what to do. Dan is very important to me, and I love our relationship, but at the same time, I can't help but think about what could be with Johan." I feel the storm of sadness brewing in me again, so I take a sip of the calming tea and hope that it subsides. "It's tearing me apart."

Now Dad does something else that surprises me greatly. He sets his teacup down and motions for me to do the same before he reaches out and takes my hand in his, "I know it's hard, but you have to listen to your heart and do what feels right for you. It's funny… you remind me so much of myself," Dad says with a hint of nostalgia in his voice.

Tonight he's like a completely different person, as if he's dropped the persona of the cold, hard businessman that is unshakeable, and donned the mantle of a caring, loving father. I've seen hints of it before, but never like this. "Of yourself?" I ask, surprised by his words. "What do you mean?"

I can't help but be curious about his change in demeanor, and he humors me by proceeding to tell me a story about how he fell in love with my mother. She was unafraid of expressing her feelings, unlike him who came from a very emotionally repressed family.

"Your mother was fearless when she told me her feelings. I had always thought of myself as the strong one, but when she looked at me, so sure of herself and her words, it humbled me."

My mother is more emotionally open than my father, but I don't exactly see her as a wellspring of feelings, so this surprises me. "I guess she got a little more reserved with age."

"I don't think so... she just expresses herself more quietly now, but she feels just as deeply." He sighs, but there is a fond smile on his face. "You know, it's funny in a way. I might be the oldest, but Julia was always the unafraid one," he says, with a hint of sadness. "I nearly lost her for being so... well, emotionally repressed. Don't make the same mistake."

My mind races as I process his words. Even though Sebastian van den Bosch is the last person I expected to hear this from, he's right, I've been so afraid of expressing my feelings to Dan because of the fear of rejection or heartbreak. But what if I don't tell him how I feel and end up losing him?

"What if he doesn't work out, though? I don't want to break his heart," I say, looking down at my hands, unable to look him in the eye.

"Telling someone you love them is an act of maturity and responsibility," Sebastian reminds me in a stern but loving tone. "It takes courage to do so, but be honest with what you feel for Dan. Just... don't play with his feelings, alright?" He smirks, trying to lighten the mood. "We all really like Dan, and I'd hate for my daughter to be the one to break his heart."

It's time for me to take responsibility for my feelings and be honest with Dan, even if it means risking my heart. The thought of losing him is too much to bear, and I know deep down that I must take this chance if I want to right my wrongs.

"I understand, Dad," I say, looking up at him with determination in my eyes. "I'll talk to Dan and tell him how I feel. I just hope he can be patient with me."

My father nods, a proud smile on his face, and reaches out to squeeze my shoulder. I close my eyes, feeling a sense of peace wash over me. I know it won't be easy, but I'm ready. The thought of it is both terrifying and exhilarating.

We finish our tea, and the conversation drifts from the heavy subject of my dating life to more mundane things—like the Lake Como trip and the way that things have been at home. I feel settled now, and more hopeful that Dad can open up to me like this and be vulnerable. Maybe he can do the same for Andries, and accept that his son's love story is not something he's able to control.

Dad leaves eventually, and I have a little bit of bread and cheese to settle my hunger before going through my usual nighttime routine, playing music over the built-in surround sound in the apartment to keep my mind busy while I do so.

As I lay in bed, I think about what my dad said to me earlier. His words weigh heavily on my mind as I replay our conversation over and over again. I can't shake the feeling of regret as I glance at my phone and see that there's no new message from Dan. I know I should have been more honest with him about my feelings, but the thought of losing him terrifies me. I toss and turn, the emptiness surrounding me feels suffocating. The sheets that were once warm with the presence of my boyfriend are now cold and foreign. The darkness of the room only amplifies the ache in my heart as I lay here alone. In the deafening silence, each passing moment feels like an eternity as I replay the events that led to this moment. Our last conversation, the hurt in his eyes, the finality of his words… it all plays on a loop in my mind. The weight of my regret and longing for him to be here with me is overwhelming. I close my eyes to escape the reality of this empty bed and the reality of my broken heart. There is hope, if I play my cards right, and if I can be brave, but it's difficult for me to see a bright future right now.

Lonely and drained, I finally drift off to sleep.

CHAPTER 26

Dan

Morning comes too soon, and I roll over, still half asleep and content. My hand reaches out to touch the warm body next to me, memories of Elise's soft skin and the sounds of the ocean in my ears so powerful that it's almost reality, but my reaching hand is met with cold emptiness. Everything from the night before comes flooding back to me—the luxuriant afternoon in bed, the envelope and invitation from Johan, and then leaving Elise behind—and my heart sinks all over again.

"Fuck this," I mutter, pulling the blanket over my head, hoping to shut it all out. The stuffiness of the blanket doesn't help, and I throw it off, laying her and staring at the ceiling, feeling a mix of sadness and regret. Was I too hard on Elise? I can't help but wonder if I made the right decision and if there's any chance of going back. But deep down, I know it's too late. I close my eyes, trying to push the thoughts out of my mind and go back to sleep, but the emptiness next to me is a constant reminder of what I've lost.

I've just managed to doze into a fitful sleep when I hear tentative rapping on my bedroom door. When I call out to see what the issue is, my maid informs me that Elise is downstairs and I immediately feel a knot form in my stomach. I don't want to speak to her, so I ask the maid to send her away. Knowing that she is so close has my stomach churning and my pulse racing, and the urge to run downstairs and sweep her into my arms is almost irresistible, but I'm well aware that doing so is just a way to prolong my heartache.

I don't know why I even thought for a second that Elise would listen and leave without issue. When the door slams open and the cause of all my anguish stomps into my room, dressed in a powder pink matching yoga set that leaves nothing to the imagination and her hair cascading around her shoulders like a river of gold, I feel like kicking myself.

Of course, she was going to storm in here, you idiot. This is Elise we're talking about. How many times did she invite herself in and interrupt you when you were with Jessica? You know she doesn't take no for an answer, I think ruefully, considering covering myself with the blanket once more.

There is a fire in Elise's eyes, and determination is sizzling in the air around her as she plants her hands on her hips and looks straight at me.

"Dan," she says simply, and the sound of my name on her lips goes directly to my heart... and my cock. To make matters worse, I slept naked last night—as always.

My maid, Felicity, is hovering behind Elise, wringing her hands nervously. "I'm sorry sir, she just—"

I hold up my hand. "It's fine. Just go, and close the door behind you."

She does as she's told, leaving Elise and me alone. I rub my temples while she stalks to the edge of the bed, and lowers herself to sit on the edge. "Dan, look at me." When I oblige, I find her eyes pleading with mine. "Please just listen to me. Then I'll leave and you'll never have to see me again."

I sigh. "Don't be dramatic. Break up or not, you know we're going to be in each other's lives."

"Are you going to hear me out or not?" she asks, ignoring me. I wave at her to go on, and Elise takes a deep breath before speaking.

"Dan, I know you're angry and hurt, but I need you to know that I never betrayed you. I'm giving Johan's invitation to Hannah for her sixteenth birthday. I have no interest in going to England to be with him, even if it is at an equestrian show. He gave me that envelope before he left Capri, and I didn't know what to do with it."

"That's a convenient excuse," I scoff, but I have to admit I'm curious about her choice to give the invite to Hannah. What better way to show Johan she's not interested than to shackle him to her little sister instead? It's almost funny, but I'm in no mood to laugh.

She pauses and looks at me with a mix of sadness and hopefulness in her eyes. "You know that we agreed that you would give me time and not force me to say those three words back until I was ready. But yesterday, you broke that agreement, and in doing so, broke my trust, too."

I feel a pang of guilt, but I can't shake off the feeling of betrayal. "As if you're one to talk about trust. You were hiding what equates to a love letter from your ex in your bedside table while fucking me in the bed right next to it! I thought you loved me, Elise," I say, my voice cracking.

"Dan, I…" she replies, her voice barely above a whisper. "I just need more time."

I don't know what to say, so I remain silent, and Elise takes it as her cue to leave. She turns to go, but before she reaches the door, she adds, "Like I said, I'm giving Hannah the invitation, and I won't be going to England, even if you don't forgive me. I want to be with you, Dan."

"Wait," I say, and she freezes with her hand on the knob. "Sit back down, El."

She seems surprised, but does as I say, this time sitting closer to me, so she's almost touching my outstretched legs beneath the blanket. I suck in a bracing breath and speak.

"Look… I was admittedly furious when I found that envelope, and that anger definitely clouded my judgment, but even now, with the air cleared between us for the most part, I still don't know if you're actually serious about me." I exhale slowly, looking her in the eye. "Am I just a game to you, El?"

She looks at me with a pained expression, "You aren't. But it's not that easy for me to be so open about my feelings. Just yesterday my dad told me he loved me after years of not hearing it from him." Conflicted emotion plays across her features, and I see her plucking at the fabric of my duvet with her fingers. This subject is making her supremely uncomfortable, but she soldiers on. "It's not something my family says very often and it's… well, It's mostly seen as a sign of weakness."

I can feel my anger dissipating as I realize the struggles she must have faced growing up in a family that doesn't express their emotions. I think of my loving parents—all of their hugs and emotional support throughout the years—and feel immense sorrow for this woman in front of me. Slowly, things start to make a lot more sense.

"They aren't like your family," El continues. "When Dad told me he loved me yesterday I thought for a brief moment that he had some hidden agenda when doing so, but I don't think he could be *that* cruel. I think his heart is starting to soften, but that doesn't mean I can just change the way he raised me with a snap of my fingers. It will take longer than either of us want, but I can't help it."

"So, you're telling me that you can't even bring yourself to say you love me because of your emotionally repressed family?" I ask, trying to keep my voice steady. She wanted to please Sebastian so much that she went so far as to be just as emotionally suppressed as he is. Poor El.

Elise nods, her eyes downcast. "It's not that I don't care about you, Dan. I just have a hard time expressing it with words. Especially after my dad said it to me for the first time in years, it's all so new and overwhelming," she explains.

I let out a sigh, running a hand through my sleep-mussed hair. "I understand where you're coming from, but it still hurts. I want to be with someone who can be open and honest with me about their feelings."

Elise looks up at me, her eyes big and full of understanding. "I know, and I'm sorry. I'll work on it, I promise. But please, just give me that chance."

I hesitate for a moment but ultimately nod. She's being so open and vulnerable, and my love for her is just as strong as ever. This is just another painful moment of metamorphosis for Elise, and sending her away just because she's stumbling with it isn't something that I can do. "Okay, I'll give you some time. But know that I'm not going to wait around forever,"

Elise nods, understanding the gravity of my words. "I know, and I wouldn't expect you to," she says softly. "I really like our relationship and I need you in my life."

I take a deep breath, pulling in the sweet smell of her perfume, and I ache to hold her. "Come here, El," I rasp, my voice low, and she crawls across the bed into my waiting arms. My body responds to having her so close, but fucking her right now will just complicate things more. Still... I have to admit that the idea of make up sex doesn't sound terrible right now.

"Elise, I love you too much to just send you away," I tell her. "But I need to know, do you really want to give this a shot? I can't keep going through this back and forth."

"Yes, Dan, I want to give us a shot," she says firmly, leaning in to kiss me. But as our lips meet, a small voice in the back of my mind whispers, *Sooner or later, this woman is gonna break my heart. I just know it. At the same time, I'm too helpless to stop it.*

CHAPTER 27

Dan

It's been a week since Andries and Roxanne's interview aired, and it's all that anyone has been talking about. Something about the two of them—the tall, good looking heir to the Van den Bosch fortune and the stunning former escort—just captures the attention of the masses like nothing else. Finally, though, things have calmed down enough that Andries is comfortable appearing in public without being harangued, and he called me this morning, desperate for an outlet for all the nervous energy that he had been holding inside for the past few days.

"I love Roxie," he told me over the phone. "But I need to get out of this penthouse. Can you help me out?"

"Of course. I'll pick you up in a few hours, okay? Bring your foil."

The fencing gym isn't crowded when we arrive, and the people that are there are polite enough not to invade our privacy, no matter how many screens they might have seen Andries's face on lately. That, or two men armed with foils aren't the best targets to be bothered. Whichever it is, I'm fine taking advantage of it. Not only do I want Andries to be able to unwind, I'm looking forward to doing the same.

It feels great to be back after some time away, stiff muscles giving way to the easy, loose yet precise movements that are so familiar I can probably do them in my sleep. Things between my best friend and I have been tense in the past few weeks, but now that we've worked through it all, it feels like nothing has changed between us. Stepping onto the fencing strip, it feels like we've never been away from the sport.

The familiar weight of the foil in my hand, the sound of blades clashing, and the adrenaline rush of competition all come flooding back to me. We both know each other's moves so well and it's like we're reading each other's mind. It's a friendly competition, but we're both very accomplished fencers, so the intensity level is high. I've always been a few steps ahead of Andries, due to my age, I suppose, but I've noticed that he's been closing in on me skill-wise. Either I need to step it up or just accept that he might eclipse me in the future, but I'm not ready to admit defeat yet.

Crossing blades, I can't see my longtime friend's face past the mask, but his frame has gotten tense and his movements jerky, and I can sense something is amiss.

"Let's take a break," I call to him, stepping off the strip and pulling the mask off my head. "I need a drink."

Andries just grunts in response, but he follows suit, removing his helmet and sitting on the wooden observation bench next to me, pushing his sweat-soaked hair off his forehead before grabbing his water bottle and drinking deeply.

"What's weighing on you?" I ask when we are both done drinking.

"Oh, you know. Everything," he grumbles. "I thought this would make me feel better, and it does, but I also feel guilty because I'm out here enjoying myself and not focusing on the potential trial and all the fallout of the interview."

I frown. "Hey, you need to relax sometimes or you'll snap. There's no need to feel guilty." I can tell he's about to argue, so I ask, "How's Roxanne? Any new information about the case?"

He replies with a heavy sigh, "We are waiting for the lawyer's update, but nothing yet."

"That's rough."

"Yeah. I wish I just knew either way what we need to prepare for. It sounds wrong, but I'd rather be preparing for a trial than sitting around doing nothing and waiting for someone else to make a decision."

"I get it," I say, patting him on the shoulder. "The helplessness is the worst part, I'm sure." I search his face from the profile, since he isn't looking at me, and make a decision. "Let's go one more time and call it a day. I'm rusty, and I can already tell I'm going to be sore as hell."

Neither of us hold back for the last match, and once it's over, we're both panting. Andries claps me on the back as we walk to the locker room, desperate for a shower and a clean change of clothes.

Out of my fencing clothes and rifling through my locker, I pull out my fresh clothing before turning to look at my suspiciously quiet friend. Andries has stripped from the waist up, but is frozen, holding his cell phone in his hand. As he reads whatever is on the screen, the color drains from his face, and I know something is wrong. "Andries, what's wrong? What happened?"

He looks at me with a mix of disbelief, and anger and replies in a low, ominous tone, "The prosecutor has decided to go ahead with the charges against Roxanne as the main suspect of the drug scandal."

His words cause ripples of shock to hit me as well. We had all been under the impression that Roxanne had enough supporting evidence in her favor that it would be pointless to charge her.

I can see the weight of the world on his shoulders and I know this is the beginning of a long and difficult journey for him and Roxie. I vow to stand by him and help in any way I can, but deep inside I know, this is going to be a fight that no one is going to come out of unscathed.

"What? That doesn't make fucking sense!" I exclaim in disbelief as Andries relays news of the prosecutor's decision. "We know the dancer was bribed by Karl and your dad. That's fucking nonsense," I continue, my voice growing louder with each word.

Andries begins to pace the length of the locker room, his face etched with frustration. "Maybe he's got the prosecutor in his hand. God... I can't believe it."

"Who is she?" I ask.

"You mean the prosecutor?" Andries replies, momentarily taken off guard.

I nod, my mind already racing with thoughts of how to uncover the truth. "Yeah. I'm gonna do a background check. I'm sure we can find something."

Andries shares her name with me, and I immediately note it, shooting off a few text messages to contacts of mine that are professionals in the art of finding out everything there is to know about a person. I ask them to do some research and see if the prosecutor has any link with the Van den Bosch family, and almost all of them agree to start digging.

"I got things started," I inform my friend, "but I can do more once I get home."

Andries, still wan, thins his lips and nods. "Thank you, Dan. I hope it does some good, but at this point, there have been so many roadblocks that I am starting to lose hope." He sits on one of the benches and pinches the bridge of his nose. "It's almost like the universe wants us to suffer and go through all this. Like my love story with Roxanne is cursed somehow."

"Don't go all broody poet on me now, man," I try to joke, but the humor doesn't come off quite the way I want it. "You have to have faith that this is all going to work out, or you're going to drown in the stress of it all. We can see the finish line, and we just have to get there. Top priority right now is to stop Roxanne from having to go to trial."

"It just feels impossible," Andries sighs. "Like we're never going to make it to the wedding."

"You will," I insist, putting as much conviction into my voice as I can. "I'm going to do everything in my power to make sure that we get you both to the altar. Just hang in there right now, okay?"

He looks up at me, strained, but finally nods. "Okay. I hope your contacts come through."

I can see the weight of the world on his shoulders and I know this is the beginning of a long and difficult journey for him and Roxanne, but I swear to myself that I will stand by him, and help in any way I can, knowing that this is going to be a fight for justice and truth against all odds. The stakes are high, and the consequences are severe, but I am ready for the battle.

CHAPTER 28

Elise

Mixing my personal and work life is something I've tried to avoid since the first day I started at Van den Bosch industries, but everything always seems to come back around to who I'm related to and not how good of a job I'm doing.

Not that I'm doing a very good job right now. In fact, I'm finding it difficult to work at all, but at least things have improved some since the interview dropped a week ago. No one ever says anything to me directly, but there are certainly plenty of gossip-ridden conversations happening all around me during the day.

I try to bury myself in my work, but the constant chatter and bustle of the open office cubicle make it nearly impossible. Everywhere I turn, I hear snippets about me and my family. My coworkers whisper behind their hands, shooting furtive glances in my direction, and it's hard to shake the feeling that they're all talking about me and my father, who owns the company. The weight of their judgment is suffocating, and it's hard to shake the feeling that they're all judging me for my family's actions.

For once, I'm not involved in the drama at all, as far as the public is concerned, but it's still all blowing back to affect me here. I'm sick of it, and I don't know how much more I can take.

I try to push the thoughts away and focus on my work, but my mind keeps drifting back to Roxanne and the charges she may be facing. The thought of her potential upcoming trial consumes me, and I find myself checking my phone for updates every few minutes. It's improper, but I can't help it. I need to know what's happening with her case. The constant distraction makes it hard to do anything else.

Every choice I make from here on out has to be made extra carefully, because my entire family is under the microscope of public scrutiny. Not only that, but even though Dad came to my apartment to apologize to me the other night, I'm certain that he will still be angry beyond words with me if he discovers how much I really have been supporting my brother and his soon-to-be wife. He's coming around slowly, but I know if I push too hard then he's likely to balk and go back to the cold, hard-headed man he was before.

I know now how unlikely it was, but after the night Dad came to my apartment, I had thought for a moment that he would embrace Andries and his upcoming marriage. I felt like it was a breakthrough, but things have since gone back to normal for the most part. Sure, he treated me more kindly—affectionately, even—but we never spoke about my brother or the interview scandal again. At work, Dad appears to be happy, if a bit distant, and while there has been a simmering energy around the office ever since the interview aired, no one dares to talk to Dad face to face about it.

I've barely seen Karl, except in passing, but whenever I do he either sneers at me or pretends that I don't exist. No matter how things play out with Andries, I refuse to work with someone who is so hostile towards me, so Dad will have to figure out what to do about that—whether he's fighting with Andries or not.

It's still so hard to comprehend the kind man that hugged me and talked me through my relationship problems and one that would pay off a dancer to do outrageous things just to sink his future daughter-in-law's reputation. The dichotomy of it makes me vaguely nauseous, and I can't think about it for too long without feeling overly emotional, as if my brain just can't compute that those actions can come from the same person.

I try to remind myself that I am not responsible for my father's actions, but the guilt still gnaws at me. The fact that I am powerless in stopping this train wreck of a situation only adds to my helplessness. The thought that my brother's future happiness and Roxanne's freedom are at stake fills me with dread, not only because I want them to be happy—as unconventional as their relationship is—but also because I don't know how I'm supposed to continue on with my life knowing that my father is responsible for such heinous acts and feels no remorse for them.

As I try to focus on my work, the din of my coworkers—both their chatter and the normal sound of printers going, fingers tapping on keyboards, and low-voiced phone calls—becomes a background hum to my own internal turmoil. It might sound dramatic, but it feels like the weight of the world is on my shoulders, and I can feel the pressure building with each passing moment. All of this has been going on for so long and just doesn't seem to ever let up. I need a break, which sounds silly considering I've just returned from vacation, but there was plenty of drama to drive me crazy in Capri, too.

I am trapped in this cubicle, surrounded by people who are judging me and my family, while the fate of those that I care about hangs in the balance. The reality of it all is almost too much to bear.

The news that Roxanne is going to trial has sent shockwaves throughout the city; I guess Dan and I weren't the only ones that had gotten comfortable thinking that she would never actually have to go in front of a judge. Now everything is calm enough, but I know it's only because Amsterdam is waiting as a whole with bated breath to see if she really will have to enter the courtroom.

Feeling suffocated by my cubicle walls, I scroll aimlessly through my email inbox for what must be the tenth time today, looking for anything to keep my mind busy until the day is over. Just as I decide to do some actual work, my cell phone rings. Despite everything, I smile a little when I see that it's Dan.

"Hey," I say as I pick up. "Don't you know I'm at work?"

"If you were that busy then you shouldn't have answered," he jokes, but there's a serious note to his voice. "I do have important news, though, if you can spare a moment for me in your terribly busy day."

I lean back in my chair, feeling more content just hearing his voice. "I suppose so. What's up?"

"As you know, I put out some leads to try and get information about the prosecutor that has decided to press charges on Roxanne. Since I'd never heard of her before I wasn't sure I would be able to get any useful information, but I think I've actually solved the mystery of why she's so eager to send your future sister-in-law to jail."

Interest piqued, I sit up straighter. "Oh? Already?"

"Yeah. It's actually way more simple than I would have guessed," Dan pauses, maybe for dramatic effect. "Do you happen to know who she went to law school with?"

"No. I have no idea who she is, even."

"Well, our favorite prosecutor was a classmate of none other than Julia Van Dieren," he says smugly, dropping the bomb so casually that it takes my mind a second to make sense of what he's telling me.

"Mom?" I whisper, my heart sinking. "Oh, no. I really thought she wasn't involved in all of this on anything more than the surface level."

"Yep, I knew she was doing a favor to your family," Dan says. "I'm not positive that your mom requested this of her, though. Maybe your father did, telling the prosecutor that the request was coming from Julia. Or maybe one of them knows something about the prosecutor that could get her in trouble. It strikes me odd that she would do something as huge as prosecute Roxanne just as a favor, but I have no idea how close she and your mother were, so there's no way to know for sure what her motives are."

I swallow hard, pulling my water bottle out of my backpack and taking a sip to ease the dryness that is suddenly in my mouth. "Wow. I can't believe this!" I laugh, but it verges on hysterical. "It seems like every single day I'm finding something out about one of my family members that I wish I had never learned."

Dan sounds sympathetic, but firm. "I know it must be hard, but we've got to see this through. Look, El, you need to convince your mom to talk to her and make her drop the charges."

"That's impossible," I respond, my voice filled with despair. "I'm already on such thin ice with Dad, that if he finds out I did that, he's gonna get me fired. All the progress we've made fixing our relationship will go out the window, and with it, any sway I have over him when it comes to forgiving Andries and firing Karl. I can't do it all, Dan. It's too much."

"You have to tell your mom the truth," Dan urges, his voice filled with urgency. "Tell her it's her husband and one of his minions that are behind the Bar Rouge scandal. If my suspicions are correct—and she wasn't the one to contact the prosecutor—then I don't see why she would have to tell your father anything. The prosecutor's name is all over the papers too, so it'd be easy to just assume Julia saw it herself and took action all on her own."

"Maybe she already knows and doesn't care," I say, my voice filled with despair. "Maybe she's just as bad as Dad, just better at hiding it from me."

"It's worth trying," Dan insists, his voice filled with conviction. "You told me in Capri that your mom is close to going to the wedding and breaking ranks with Sebastian. This might be the final straw to her putting her foot down and make him take Andries back into the family fold whether he likes it or not."

Holding the phone against my ear with my shoulder, I lower my head into my hands. "You're not going to let me get out of this, are you?"

"Don't you want this to be over, El?" Dan asks, sounding tired out of nowhere. I feel similarly exhausted. "If we just sit around and do nothing it's going to last so much longer."

"I know you're right, I just hate the idea of taking on more responsibilities... what choice do I have?" Sighing, I lean back again, letting my shoulders fall with defeat. "Fine. I'll talk to her, but I think I need to do it in person, so give me a few days."

"Of course, sweetheart," he says softly. "I know it's tough, but you're one of the most capable people I know. I believe in you." My stomach somersaults from his sweet words.

I wish I felt the same way about myself, I think, telling Dan bye and hanging up.

What he's just told me is totally unexpected, and changes the course of how I need to handle both my father and my mother until I know for sure how connected they both are with the prosecutor. The thought of confronting Mom and finding out that she's somehow more involved than I imagined, or having her reject the idea of coming to the wedding once and for all, makes my stomach churn. I wish I didn't have to do it by myself, but Dan is busy helping Andries, and this is my part to play in the machine of defeating this scandal.

I wrack my brain to try and come up with an ally to help me break my mother down and make her sympathetic to our plight. Hannah is the first person to come to mind—especially if I bribe her with the tickets to the equestrian show with Johan—but there is some underlying tension between her and Mom that may actually be detrimental to what I'm trying to accomplish.

Tatianna is another option, but it would be cruel to try and drag her into the process of getting my mother to accept Andries' marriage, knowing that Tati still holds a candle for my brother. Andries wouldn't look towards anyone but Roxie even if his life depended on it, but that doesn't mean I'd feel okay shoving his upcoming wedding in Tati's face, either.

I circle back to the thought of buttering Hannah up with the tickets from Johan when I run out of options, but then something strikes me. At first, the idea seems strange and unlikely to work, but the more I consider it, the more it makes sense.

I'll ask Johan to help me. My mother and father both hold him in high esteem, which means they'll listen to him—maybe even more than me. I think it's in all parents' nature to tune out their children's opinions at times, but Mom won't do that with Johan. Plus, I already told her that I invited him over for dinner, so she won't be suspicious about it. She'll have no idea that it will be a low key ambush.

So, for the first time since arriving back in Amsterdam, I call Johan. Just making the call causes guilt to settle over me, and I wonder if I should have disclosed my plan to Dan before enacting it, just so he wouldn't have reason to be suspicious. But I think he's still guarded enough over finding the envelope that he'd shoot down the idea immediately, and I know in my heart that this has a better chance of working than if I just approach my mom to talk about this all on my own.

He answers quickly and seems surprised to hear from me. "Elise, what a surprise," he says, his deep, accented voice making me smile.

"Hopefully not a bad one?"

"Never," he chuckles. "To what do I owe the pleasure of hearing from you again so soon?"

"I know we talked about you visiting the family estate, and I was just wondering when you plan on returning to the Netherlands next?" I try to keep my tone light so he doesn't suspect that I'm using him for my own means.

"I'm thinking of flying back just a few days before the wedding," he replies.

"Well, what about coming sooner? Like... this weekend, maybe?"

"Elise," his tone sharpens with interest. "Surely you haven't tired of Dan so soon and want me by your side instead?"

"It's not like that..." I tell him reluctantly, wishing that he hadn't just jumped to conclusions. "I was actually hoping that you could help me *save* the wedding... we're dealing with some heavy stuff over here."

"Like what?" he asks, curious.

"So, when we got back from Capri, Roxanne was immediately arrested. I'm sure you've seen in the news that she's going to be prosecuted for criminal drug charges, which we all know is bogus. What isn't common knowledge..." I pause, knowing that if I tell Johan everything, then there is no going back. It will change the way he views my family forever, but there is no help for it. I need his assistance, even if it damages my mother and father's reputation in his eyes. "Is that the dancer who confessed to everything told the prosecutor that Karl—the man that works at our company and recently had the scandal with the 18-year-old escort— paid her off, and all signs lead back to Dad being the one to provide Karl with the idea and the funds to do so."

"Woah…" Johan sounds thunderstruck. "So your dad..?"

"Is going to some extreme lengths to make this wedding not happen, yes," I exhale slowly, keeping my voice low to avoid any kind of eavesdropping. "And that's why I need your help. I just found out that the prosecutor went to law school with my mom, and considering that it makes no sense to charge Roxie now that the dancer confessed to being paid off, we're all thinking that the prosecutor is doing it as some weird favor for someone in my family."

"Do you think your mother asked her old friend to do this? If so, I don't think even the Pope himself could help you convince her to call everything off," Johan points out.

"I agree, but I don't think Mom has it in her to cause her own son that kind of pain, even if she doesn't approve of his decision to marry Roxie. Plus, when we were in Capri, I talked to her and she seemed closer than ever to come to the wedding with or without Dad, so I really think she's on the edge enough that the two of us could change her mind." I let my words settle for a moment, and when Johan doesn't say anything for a minute, I add, "Please, Johan. Spend the weekend at my family estate. Not for me, but for Andries and Roxanne."

"Why do you think that my presence will make such a difference?" he asks.

"Because my mother really respects you and likes you quite a lot. She doesn't hold many people in high esteem, but you are one of the rare few that she does. Plus, it's a simple fact that the chances of me convincing her are higher if there are two of us, and not just one. The more people we have putting pressure on her, the better. It will show her that her dirty secret isn't as secret as she thinks."

Johan thinks it over, humming in thought, before he finally agrees. "What I wouldn't do for you... Ah, alright, Elise. Confirm the details and send them to me when you can, and I will make room in my schedule to be there this weekend." He takes a deep breath before saying, "But don't think explaining all of this means that I'm not still going to focus on the chemistry between us when I am at your family home. There is so much left unsaid between us two."

I roll my eyes, wondering if I should tell him that Dan and I are officially together now, but decide to refrain, on the off chance that he changes his mind if he has that information. A cloud of worry hovers over me, knowing that I am now lying by omission to both Dan *and* Johan, but it's a very small necessary evil. Dan made it seem like I needed to convince my mother by any means necessary, and well... this is one of my means, and in my opinion, the best choice I have at hand right now.

"Johan, this is a friendly visit, just with the added task of smoothing the way for your new best friend Andries' wedding," I try to tease him a little at the end, and get a reluctant chuckle for it. "Plus, there is someone else who I know is going to be over the moon to see you."

I can hear the frown in his voice as he responds. "Huh? Who do you mean?"

The image of Hannah, willowy and lovely, standing in front of her drawers of treasures and asking me if she has a chance with Johan flashes in my mind's eye, but I don't dare tell him all of that—not when he still believes that he's interested in me. Plus, Hannah is much too young for Johan, and her interest might make him uncomfortable, so I need to make sure to make it sound totally platonic.

"Hannah. Her collection of bits and baubles has grown quite a bit since you were last over. At least I assume so, since I didn't even know about it before you told me, but she certainly has a lot of things."

"Oh! Well, I will look forward to perusing Ms. Hannah's collection when I arrive," Johan says politely. "But not nearly as much as I look forward to our time together, El."

"Uh-huh, sure," I tell him noncommittally, feeling more uncomfortable about keeping secrets from him and Dan. "I will send you all the information after I talk to my mother, okay?" Then, I lick my lips, deciding carefully what to say next without making him think anything romantic is possible between us. "I really do appreciate you being there for me in my brother and I's time of need. This is going to be a big help, Johan. Thank you."

"Like I said," he rumbles, "Anything for you, Elise. I'll see you soon."

"See you," I respond weakly before hanging up the phone. As soon as the line is dead, I have a bad feeling about this plan, but it's too late now. The wheels are set into motion, and there's no stopping them. Once the uneasiness passes, relief washes over me at how easy it was to convince Johan to help. With Johan's help, maybe I can make this right and we can clear Roxanne's name.

Now, for the next step in my plan. I pick up the phone once more and dial my mother's number.

"Hey Mom," I say when she answers. "I was wondering if Johan could come over this weekend."

"Well hello to you too, daughter!" she huffs, taken off guard. "This is all a little last minute, don't you think? I was under the impression that it would be in a few weeks, before Johan had time to come and visit, and now you're saying he wants to stay for the whole weekend in just a few days?"

"I invited him," I confess slyly. "It was spur of the moment, but he and I were talking, and it came up that he had no plans this weekend, so I just extended the invitation without thinking to ask you first. But I'm sure it's fine... right?"

"You two were just talking?" she says in disbelief. "I thought you and Dan–"

"Mom!" I hiss, cutting her off while still trying to remain quiet enough that no one else in the office overhears me. "Johan and I are just friends, and friends talk! That's all."

"Hmm," she hums. "It's all very sudden, but I suppose we have plenty of room for Johan if he truly wants to visit us this soon." Then, her tone changes to weary. "Goodness knows that we could use a distraction from all the doom and gloom around here."

I consider asking Mom about coming to the wedding, or even her prosecutor friend, right here and now, but resist the urge, biting my lip to keep the words from spilling out. I don't want to show my hand just yet and have her become suspicious of Johan's visit.

"I know, Mom," I say simply, instead. "It will be fun to have him over. I'll let him know that you approve. So, I'll see you soon! Love you!"

"Love you too, El. It will be good to have you home for a few days, too." She sighs. "The house has felt very empty and loveless lately, so I'm ready for something different. Have a good evening, my love."

She sounds so down that it makes me sad, and wish that I had spent more time at home since returning from Capri, but things between Dad and I aren't exactly normal, and my schemes to bring Mom around to Andries' side would be much easier to figure out if I was under the same roof as her and my father. Still… I hate knowing that she's so lonely. Hannah needs to step up and spend more time with her and not be so weird and antisocial.

I send Johan the information about this weekend, promising that we will hammer out flight details and everything else after I get off work. With that completed, I have a hard decision to make—do I tell Dan what I've done or do I keep quiet and just hope that the weekend will pass without him realizing Johan is involved at all? Finding the envelope is still fresh in his mind, I'm sure of it, and I don't want him to sabotage this over jealousy.

So, feeling terrible about it, I quickly message Dan: *I'm gonna go home this weekend to see if I can convince Mom to speak to the prosecutor so she can drop the charges*, I type, hitting send, conveniently leaving out the fact that there would be a guest at the estate for those few days, too.

I feel even worse when Dan replies back almost immediately. *You are the best. Love you! X*, he says, and it makes my stomach sink. He's so happy with me, and I'm positive he has no idea what I'm up to. After the confusion he caused just a few days ago when he found the invitation on my bedside table, I decide it's best to keep it to myself for now, even when there is the possibility it will come back to bite me in the ass.

Oh well, there's nothing to be done about it now, and if I succeed, then he'll certainly forgive me quickly.

If I *don't* pull this off, though… I don't want to think about it.

I must push through. I must do everything in my power to persuade Mom to call the prosecutor so she can drop the charges, and for that, I need Johan by my side. I can feel the tension building in my chest as I type out another text to Dan, trying to put on an innocent front for him, but deep down, I'm filled with doubt. I try to push those thoughts aside and focus on the task at hand. I will have to tread carefully when it comes to Dan, making sure not to reveal too much, at least not until the time is right. I'll have to be strong and courageous, not just for myself, but for my family and for Roxanne and Andries. This is not just about me, it's about all of us and the future that lies ahead.

When I sit the phone back on my desk and look at my now-dark computer screen, the other big worry of my life begins to surface once more, too.

If I do all this to improve everyone else's lives and bring our family back together, then where do I stand once the dust settles? What about my dreams? If everything goes according to plan, do I still have a future at Van den Bosch industries as the future CEO?

I just don't know, but for now, it's one selfless step at a time. During this turmoil, there is no room for me to worry about myself. No time.

But… will there ever be?

CHAPTER 29

Elise

After heading over to my parents' house a few hours earlier, I've been running through what feels like a hundred emotions while waiting on Johan to arrive. After the stunt Dan and I pulled on Capri, there is obviously going to be some awkwardness, especially with the equestrian show situation, but I think he will be the perfect person to help me out tonight, so I have to set all of that aside.

Not to mention the fact that I need to firmly make Johan understand that nothing is going to happen between us— ever. I hope I can keep him as a friend, but that possibility will be up to him completely.

As the clock rolls around to 5 pm, I head to the foyer to greet Johan at the entrance of my family's estate. Everything has been cleaned and polished to a mirror-like sheen, no doubt on the command of my mother, but despite the lavishness of it all it just feels like home to me. Johan is punctual as usual, handing the keys to the pearlescent white Bentley to the valet and walking up the stone stairs to meet me.

I'm not the only one waiting on Johan, of course. Mom is with me, ever the perfect hostess, and Hannah is on my other side, almost vibrating with excitement. I give her the side eye, but she doesn't notice, only having eyes for Johan. Whatever, let her have her little teenage crush. It's not like anything can come of it.

Tonight, something feels different. Johan is an old friend, one who has always had feelings for me, feelings that I once reciprocated, but no more. And yet, here he is, standing before me, ready to spend the weekend at my family's home, and it's all too easy to imagine how things could have been different if someone hadn't sent him that message and blocked him on my phone years ago. If that had never happened, then Johan might be coming here tonight to have dinner with my family as a way of announcing our courtship. Maybe even an engagement. But that possibility is long gone, and it's a little bittersweet even now.

He certainly looks handsome tonight, in charcoal dress pants and an ivory oxford with the sleeves rolled up to his elbows and his dark-blonde hair perfectly styled. Casual but sophisticated—which is very on-brand for Johan.

Once he reaches us, he greets my mother first with a kiss on the cheek that leaves her flustered and laughing and does the same with Hannah, except pressing his lips to her knuckles instead. She turns so red that it's almost as if he kissed her on the mouth instead, which makes me roll my eyes right before Johan makes it to me. He kisses my cheek, lingering much longer than he did with my mother, but doesn't press the issue when I turn away to break the connection with a smile.

"Johan," I say simply. "Welcome back to the Van den Bosch estate."

"It's always a pleasure," he replies, the corner of his mouth tilting up.

We enter the home, and a warm breeze blows in from the gardens outside behind us. The summer evening is a beautiful one, with a clear sky overhead and the sun just beginning to dip below the horizon.

We make our way to the library where my father is waiting, enjoying a glass of port. His eyes are distant as he stands to shake Johan's hand, and I can't help but wonder if he's been talking to Karl, plotting more revenge. I want more of the version of my dad that came to my apartment the other night to comfort me, but he always seems to fall back into the familiar role of the stoic businessman we all grew up with when at home. Our relationship is better than it was, truthfully, but I've been waiting on pins and needles for the same thing to happen with him and Andries. I can't help but be disappointed that it hasn't.

Dad seems glad enough to see Johan, though, and even gives me a sly look when Johan turns to say something to Hannah, speaking quietly enough so only I can hear, "I think you invited the wrong one."

I shoot my eyes at Johan to make sure he didn't hear before saying, just as quietly, "Hush, Dad. It's just dinner."

"Dinner and the weekend," he points out, but I know he's joking, so I just wave my hand dismissively at my father and let the night move along.

Mom goes to the kitchen to talk to the staff about when everything will be ready, and when she sees Hannah hovering around Johan and me with doe eyes, she grabs my sister by the elbow and drags her along behind her. Dad makes his exit shortly after, going to his home office, and Johan and I are left alone.

"Thank you for coming," I tell him immediately. "I know we parted ways… oddly… but this is going to mean so much to Andries. It already means a lot to me."

"It means a lot that I've come to see you, huh?" he teases, shoving his hands in his pockets, and I scoff.

"Well, yes, but I mean helping me talk to Mom after dinner about the prosecutor and Roxanne's charges."

"Yes, I didn't forget we are here on a mission," he chuckles. "I hope I will get good compensation, though."

I ignore the quip and its obvious double meaning, inviting him to walk through the library with me as we go over what exactly our plan with my mother is. Johan doesn't take his eyes off me, but he listens and doesn't try to flirt with me like I've been afraid of, and it makes me hopeful that this might really work. The library is quiet and still, the air smelling of paper and ink. It's the perfect place to hatch a scheme like this one, but our discussion is cut short when I hear someone clearing their throat from the other end of the stacks.

Johan and I both turn at the same time to see Hannah, who must have just escaped our mother, her hands behind her back. I didn't notice before, but she's over dressed for a semi-casual family dinner in a black sheath dress with short sleeves, her long hair hanging straight down her back.

"Sorry to interrupt," she starts. "But I was wondering if you wanted to come and see how much my collection has grown, Johan? We have about thirty minutes before dinner."

"Hannah, leave Johan al—" I try to say, but Johan is stepping in front of me and offering my younger sister his arm before I can finish.

"I'd love to."

It happens so fast that I can barely process what is happening before I'm following behind the two of them, feeling like the third wheel. Hannah, usually stoic and quiet, talks to Johan like he's an old friend that she has missed terribly, and it doesn't surprise me as much as it should. Mom told me earlier that she had been counting down the days until Johan's arrival, but I guess I hadn't taken it seriously. It's bizarre, especially for Hannah.

Reluctantly, I stay a few steps behind as we reach her bedroom, and they start exploring Hannah's collection. As I watch from a distance, I can see how smitten Hannah is with Johan, her eyes lighting up as she shows him her prized possessions. After only seeing Hannah's collection a single time myself, I crane my head to try and look at everything she's showing him, fascinated by the part of my sister that she kept secret from me for so long. There are bits and baubles everywhere, ranging from trinkets that I would have walked right past had I seen them on the ground, to jewelry that I can't believe would be so easily found on beaches and other such places. To Johan's credit, he seems genuinely interested in what she has to show him, which makes my heart feel soft. Johan is a good man, and I'm reminded of that fact over and over again.

Then I hear Hannah say something that catches my attention. "Here Johan... I want you to have this. I've been collecting sea glass in some of the little jars I find and this is my favorite. The red glass is rarer than the others."

She hands him a tiny jar, which looks like it might have held buttons in the past, but is now full of smooth, colored glass shards in shades of red, green, and blue. Johan takes it from her hands, holding it up to the light, but shakes his head, giving it back to her.

"It's beautiful, Hannah, but I can't accept this. You already gave me a gift last time, remember? I haven't given you anything."

"I still want you to have it," she insists, pushing it back into his palms. "Just give me two gifts next time."

Those words hit me like a bolt of lightning. Suddenly, everything starts to make sense in my head and I realize that there is more going on here than I initially thought. I need to pay closer attention to what's happening around me. I'm filled with a mixture of emotions as I watch my sister and Johan together. On the one hand, I'm definitely not interested in Johan romantically. But on the other hand, I'm filled with a sense of unease, wondering what the future holds for all of us.

Hesitantly, Johan accepts the gift once more, pocketing in with a soft smile. "Thank you, Hannah. I'll cherish it."

"Johan," I pull him aside, which makes Hannah frown, but I don't care. "Why don't you go down and see if Mom is ready for us? I'll catch up. I need a moment with my sister."

He looks between the two of us, seems to sense the tenseness of the situation, and shrugs. "Alright. I'll see you ladies downstairs, then."

"Why did you make him leave?" Hannah grumps once we're alone, crossing her arms. "I wasn't finished showing him everything."

"Since when do you have a crush on him?" I ask bluntly.

Taken aback, Hannah's eyes go wide. "What do you mean?"

I stand my ground, not letting her pretend to be ignorant about what I can clearly see with my own two eyes. "I need to know the truth, Hannah," I demand, my voice rising in intensity. "Did it start the day he came here the first time and you gave him one of your precious random treasures?"

"You're being ridiculous. We just get along, that's all."

I can't help the bark of laughter that bursts out of me. "Cut the bullshit. You look at him like you want to eat him alive."

"Like I said," Hannah moves about her room, turning off the lights on the displays of her treasures and speaking to me dismissively, "you're being ridiculous."

I can feel my frustration growing, and it's never been so obvious how young Hannah really is. "Why did you go into my phone and block Johan's number?"

Hannah's demeanor changes, her body tense and her eyes narrows. "I already told you, I don't know what you're talking about."

I won't be deterred so easily. I take a step closer to her, my own eyes burning with a mix of anger and determination. "You're a very bad liar. It's obvious it was you, and I want to know why. So tell me, Hannah, why are you trying to keep Johan and me apart?"

My sister tries to push past me, but I don't let her. She stops, hands fisted at her sides. "Let me go or I'll hurt you."

It's true that she's taller than me, but I'm not scared... instead, I'm hurt, the reality of it all becoming clearer and clearer by the minute. "Just tell me the truth, Hannah."

"I did," she snaps, shouldering me aside and not even looking back in my direction. "Now, drop it."

Watching my sister stomp down the hallway, lithe and beautiful, a shiver rolls over me. This conversation isn't done, and I know there is a lot more to come regarding her and Johan. I start to second guess having him take her to the equestrian show in my place, but it's the best way to keep the peace with my old friend and my boyfriend all at the same time. I just hope Hannah has enough sense to stay out of trouble.

* * *

Walking down the grand staircase to the dining room, I see that everyone is already seated at the table, waiting for me to join them. Hannah is missing at first, but just when I think she's gone to take her meal elsewhere, she appears in a huff from the other side of the room and immediately moves to take a seat next to Johan. Clenching my teeth in annoyance, I take the empty chair on the other side of him, ignoring her obvious eye roll. She doesn't speak to me, but Johan does, leaning closer to me and whispering,

"Is something going on with you two?"

"Just normal sister bickering," I tell him, not totally dishonest. "Don't worry about it."

Johan looks amused, but he nods, and with that, dinner can finally begin.

My father engages Johan first, asking him about his time at Oxford. Johan raves about the school and how it was the perfect place for him to get his education. He talks about the beautiful grounds and the quality of all of his classes, and while everyone listens politely, no one is as fixated on his words as Hannah, of course. She ignores her meal for the most part, pushing it around her plate with her chin resting in her hands as she hangs onto his every word with shining eyes. It's almost comical how lively she is around him when all of us think of Hannah sort of like a tall, silent shadow most days. Something about him really brings out the latent personality she apparently has, and I think about the tiny bottle of sea glass in his pocket right this second, and how different it is from the other treasures she collects. Unlike things that other people have lost, the sea glass is something Hannah picked up piece by individual piece all on her own, and the little jar she gave Johan is a collection of her personal choices. It's meaningful and sort of touching, even if Hannah is being a bit of a jerk.

"I dream of going to Oxford someday too," Hannah muses, eyelids low. "I know everyone thinks I should go to Amsterdam with Andries and Elise but Oxford is where I really want to be."

Dad and Mom look at each other, confused, and then back at my sister, but stay quiet. Johan raises his eyebrows in interest. "Is that so? Well, I definitely have some pull with the staff and admissions with how much my family donates to the school, so when you're ready I'm more than happy to help make your dream a reality."

"Really?" Hannah sighs blissfully. "That would be wonderful."

I try to mask my expression by taking a long drink of wine, but her tone makes me snort in amusement, and she shoots me a black look.

DAN.

As dinner progresses, I realize that my sister is monopolizing the conversation, constantly talking to Johan. Even though she told me she didn't block his number, it's crystal clear that she is the culprit. My sister is always so mysterious and secretive, it's no surprise that she would have done something like that. She would have been only thirteen at the time, which makes it seem crazy that she would have that sort of forethought and cruelty towards me, but the last few months have taught me that people are much more complicated than they appear on the outside. To think that Hannah's infatuation could have been intense enough to make her block Johan and ruin my budding relationship makes me feel a little ill, but that's a problem for another time. Specifically, after Andries's wedding.

I watch in silence as my sister flirts with Johan; it's clear that she has a crush on him. I can't help but feel a twinge of jealousy, but at the same time, I know that I don't have any romantic feelings for him. I can only hope that Hannah will come to her senses and see that her crush on Johan will only lead to heartache if he's still as fixated on me as I think he is. Even if Johan *has* moved on from me, though, Hannah is much too young for him, which is just another reason pursuing him will simply shatter her instead of leading to something meaningful.

Hannah might be unnecessarily standoffish toward me right now, but that doesn't mean that I want to see her hurt, either. I know what it's like to lose a first love, and it just so happens that mine was the same man that she's so hung up on right now.

***

After dinner, Dad and Johan retire back to the library for cigars and more port, much to Hannah's disappointment. I send Johan a quick text telling him not to forget that we have to talk to my mother and to keep the chat with my Dad short, but it turns out that I don't have to worry about it for long.

Johan: *Your Dad just excused himself to go take a call in his office if you want to talk to your Mom now. He seemed like he was in a hurry so I bet it's going to take him some time anyway.*

Gathering my courage, I head out to the terrace where Mom is reading in the cooler night air, the wind stirring her hair. She looks young in the moonlight and peaceful. I hate to disturb her, but it's necessary.

I clear my throat to get her attention. "Mom, can Johan and I speak to you in private, please?"

She looks at me with surprise, sitting her book on the loveseat beside her, but quickly recovers and nods. "Of course," she says, her tone soft, as she stands up, smoothing her dress. "Would you like to speak out here or inside?"

"Your office would be best, I think. Johan is already there."

She gives me a quizzical look but shrugs one delicate shoulder. "Okay. Lead the way then, dear."

Johan is indeed waiting outside the dark office, his hands in his pockets as he leans against the wall patiently. Mom must think he and I are here to talk about our relationship or something like that, but she's going to be in for a rude awakening once she learns what it really is we intend to say.

Once we are alone, I take a deep breath and begin to speak. "Mom, there's something I need to tell you," I say. "It's about Dad and that snake, Karl. They're in this together, and what Andries said on TV wasn't a lie. It was all the absolute truth, and I think you deserve to know that."

Mom's eyes widen in shock, and she leans in closer to hear more. "How do you know that?" she asks.

"We put all the pieces together in Capri," I tell her, looking to Johan, who nods in agreement. "Roxanne is innocent, Mom. You know it. She found out about the scandal at the same time as we all did. Johan was there, too."

As I explain to my mother the truth about Roxanne and what really happened, I can see the shock and disbelief in her eyes. She struggles to comprehend what I'm saying and I can sense her unease and anxiety rising.

Mom sits back in her chair slowly, her expression thoughtful. "I see," she says, and I can tell she's trying to process the information I've just given her. "Even if she is innocent, I have nothing to do with all of it. You have to know that."

I can only imagine what's going through her mind right now, and I feel a pang of guilt for bringing this dark secret to light. But I know it's the right thing to do, for our family and for the truth. "Mom, we looked into it and we know that you're friends with the prosecutor charging Roxanne. You guys went to school together. Can't you just call her and have a word with her?" I plead. "I'm sure if it's coming from you, she'll drop the charges."

My mother hesitates for a moment before she speaks, "These things aren't that simple, Elise."

I can see the guilt and frustration in her eyes, and I know how difficult this must be for her. She has always tried to not get involved in Dad's schemings, but sometimes circumstances force us to make difficult decisions.

"I know it's not easy, Mom," I say, trying to offer her some comfort. "But you have to do what's right. Roxanne deserves a chance to clear her name, and you have the power to help her."

My mother exhales, still deep in thought, and I know that I have planted a seed of hope within her. I can only pray that she will be able to find the courage to do what is right, even if it means facing difficult consequences with Dad and how he's going to react to all of this.

"I will do my best," she says after a long moment, looking tired.

I jump up from my chair and hug my mother, the weight falling off my shoulders knowing that she will help. "Thank you, Mom. That's all I can ask."

Then, just like we planned, Johan says, "It'd mean the world to us all if you could be present at Andries's wedding." Mom looks up at him in surprise when I release her from my embrace. "Elise and I would love to see you there."

Her eyes shutter, and she shakes her head. "Oh, I can't do that to Sebastian."

"Mom, everyone will be there," I point out. "I know you well enough to know that you want to go. We won't push you anymore tonight, but just think about it. Think about how it will look to all of our family if you aren't there for your oldest son's wedding. Please, do the right thing."

Mom waves her hands at the two of us before massaging her temples, eyes fluttering closed. "I have a lot to think about. Leave me, you two, and we'll talk later."

Johan and I look at each other, and without another word, leave the office. But not before I lean down to kiss my mother's cheek, and thank her once more, this time quiet enough that only the two of us can hear.

* * *

As I escort Johan to his guest bedroom, I can sense that the atmosphere between us has shifted slightly. We engage in some small talk about the evening and the events that have taken place, but I can sense that he's trying to be overly affectionate with me. He's trying to read into the signals I'm sending, but I'm not interested. I want to be clear about my intentions and make sure that he knows where I stand.

So, as we reach the door to his bedroom, I take a deep breath and turn to him. "Johan, I want you to know that we're just friends." His eyes go wide at my announcement. "I know that there might be some confusion lingering, but Dan and I are officially together."

He looks at me with a mix of shock and disappointment, and I can see that my words have caught him totally off guard. "I understand," he says, a hint of sadness in his voice.

I then hand him the tickets to the Horse Show which I have been holding in my pocket and tell him to invite Hannah, knowing that she would love to go. "Hannah?" he repeats with a raised eyebrow.

"Yes, Hannah, she's always been a big fan of horse riding and I think she would really enjoy the show. This would be a great way to repay her generosity towards you," I explain, despite knowing all too well that Hannah couldn't care less about horses. But she'd attend any event on the planet if it meant spending some time with Johan on her own. "It's just a friendly gesture, Johan. Nothing more."

He nods, but I can tell that my words have left him a little bewildered. Despite that, I can see that he's trying to be a good sport about it and I'm grateful for his understanding. I say goodnight and leave him to his thoughts, but I can't help but wonder what he's thinking. Is he disappointed? Confused? I hope that he understands where I'm coming from and that he doesn't take my words the wrong way.

As I lay in bed, my mind races with thoughts of the events of the day and the challenges that still lie ahead. I think back to my conversation with Johan, and how I managed to delicately navigate the situation while still securing an opportunity for my friend to experience the joy of the Horse Show.

I feel a sense of accomplishment wash over me, but at the same time, a pang of guilt for not having told Dan about Johan. I know that Dan is incredibly supportive and understanding, but I can't shake the feeling that keeping this from him is wrong. I make a mental note to talk to him about it in the morning and clear the air, but wonder if I'll chicken out tomorrow. Dan will be pissed knowing that Johan is here, but I hope seeing Johan helping as much as he is will temper Dan's anger some.

As I close my eyes and let out a deep sigh, I remind myself that despite the challenges, I have a strong support system made up of my loved ones, and I have faith that with their help, I can overcome any obstacle. I'm doing the right thing for my brother and his fiancée to atone for the trouble I've caused in the past. I think of Dan's comforting embrace and the love he brings into my life, and I feel a warm sense of peace.

And with that thought, I finally succumb to the embrace of slumber, dreaming of a brighter future filled with love, hope, and happiness.

CHAPTER 30

Dan

Dinner with Andries, Roxanne, and her family seems somehow subdued without Elise by my side, but I have a feeling that I'm the only one fixated on her absence. There is a sense of emptiness without her, and I miss her contagious laughter and her sparkling smile. I had asked her to come, but she said she needed to stay at the estate this weekend to try to persuade her mother to go to Andries's wedding.

It almost feels stupid how much her presence, or lack thereof, affects me. Before, spending an evening with my best friend would be a good time, but now the only thing on my mind is his sister—which I know doesn't make me the ideal friend right now... not with everything Andries is going through. But there's nothing to be done about my emotions right now, except to look forward to El coming home sooner rather than later, and the time we will spend together when she does.

We eat takeout from a local Chinese restaurant, and once the meal is through, the women excuse themselves to go over some last minute wedding details. Robin, Andries, and I make our way out to the terrace, but Robin gets a work-related call that he goes out front to take in private, which leaves me with a rare opportunity. Andries and I are finally alone, and not arguing for once, meaning it's the best moment I can ask for to tell him that Elise and I are officially a couple. I'm sure that, on some level, he already knows, but it's time to put it all out in the open.

I suck the fresh air deep into my lungs, accepting the glass of amber brown whiskey that Andries hands me before we sit down on the wrought iron antique patio furniture of Roxanne's. The moon is high in the sky and the stars twinkle like diamonds, and there is a pang in my heart thinking about El struggling with her mother at this very moment while I relax and unwind. Andries starts talking about relationships and commitment, and I can't help but think of Elise.

"It's getting so close," Andries muses out loud, breaking my reverie. "I'm going to be married before I know it, and things will never be the same. It's crazy to think about."

"I have to admit, I never guessed you'd be getting hitched so young, or that you'd be the one in such a serious relationship, but I guess I should've known better." I elbow him good-naturedly, shaking the alcohol in his glass. "You never do anything by half measures, as we all know."

"I always wanted commitment," he tells me, rubbing the spot where my elbow hit his arm. "I hated the idea of meaningless casual relationships, so I guess this was always in the cards for me. Roxie... well, she changed the way I view the world, you know?" He exhales, and then annoyance flashes over his face. "Plus, you're sort of in a relationship with my *sister*."

I laugh. "We're just one big happy family now, Andries. You know you love it." He scowls, but I can see the corner of his mouth twitching in amusement, which tells me he's relaxed enough to hear the news I'm about to break. "But hey, I, um, I have to tell you something, man. El and I have decided to take this to the next level. We're um… officially a couple. Publicly and everything."

I expect the normal reaction when a friend tells another friend that he's found a partner, a congratulation, maybe a quick hug and slap on the back—tempered, of course, since Elise is his sister and he obviously didn't want us dating in the first place—but instead Andries's face falls into shadow. My heart sinks at his expression.

"What?" I demand, the nervous joy disappearing from my tone. "What's that look about?"

Andries tips his entire whiskey back in one drink and sits the glass down on the side table. "Finish yours too. You might need it."

I sit the glass aside, stomach churning now, unable to take another sip. "No. Just get on with it."

He pinches the bridge of his nose before speaking. "Dan, I love my sister, but I don't think she has your best interests in mind. Elise can't help but manipulate people, it's what she's always done, and I think she's manipulating you right now. Has she told you that she loves you?"

I swallow hard. "No, but—"

"She hasn't, and I don't think that she does, Dan. Look."

Pulling out his phone, Andries scrolls for a second before handing it to me. As soon as I look at the screen my heart falls to my feet. All I can mutter is, "What the hell..?"

"You didn't even know Johan was staying the weekend at my family's estate, did you?" he asks, laying his hand on my shoulder. "I'm sorry, Dan."

"Who sent you these pictures?" I ask, throat tight as my gaze continues fixed on Johan and Elise's selfie. I'm not sure I've ever felt so betrayed.

"Johan himself, of course," Andries says. "I thought it was a weird thing to do, but it makes sense now. He must still be trying to get her back or something, and I bet he was sure I'd tell you what was going on."

I'm not angry at Andries, but I can't sit in this chair and be still any longer. I take my friend's advice from earlier, down the abrasive whiskey in one gulp, and storm off the terrace, even as the straight hit of alcohol makes my head start to spin and my stomach burn. I hear Andries calling after me, and as I reach the front door and burst into the hallway, I run directly into Robin returning from his phone call, who looks shocked to see me moving with such purpose.

"Hey, you okay?" I hear the other man ask, but I just hold up a hand in acknowledgment as I rush past him, jamming the elevator button with my finger as if that will make it arrive faster.

I feel as though I've been punched in the gut and all the air has been knocked out of me. It's hard to breathe, and I barely see the street in front of me as I burst back out into the night air. All I see is Elise and Johan, laughing in the gardens of her family estate in the picture Andries just showed me.

Of course, I drove here myself, and I palm the keys out of my pocket, annoyed that I'm too emotional right now to feel comfortable driving my vintage Ferrari home. The last thing I need is a broken heart and a crashed car.

Before I can call an Uber, I hear the door open behind me, and then Andries is there at my side, looking stricken and slightly out of breath from chasing me down.

"I'm so sorry," he utters as he wraps an arm around me. "I know that wasn't what you wanted to hear, but I thought you should know."

Andries, after all the difficulties he put between El and me in the beginning, is an easy target to take my anger out on, but I stop myself before I can rage at him. We are all trying to be better, and that includes me, too. I take a deep breath before speaking. "I appreciate your honesty," I tell him sincerely. "That's what best friends do. They tell each other the truth, no matter how painful it is."

"Doesn't mean it feels good," he points out. "It isn't fair to either of us that Elise put us in this position. Making me be the one to hurt you instead of doing it herself."

I lean against the wall of the building and take a deep breath, trying to steady myself. "You knew beforehand that she's never told me she loves me, huh?" I ask Andries, my eyes searching the answer on his face. "She's shown me that she cares about me, but it's like she's incapable of saying those three little words. And yet she so easily said them to Johan. You're probably right... it's not love, it's just manipulation."

Andries exhales slowly, leaning on the wall next to me. "You know I've always been against this relationship you two have. I can't speak for my sister, but we both know she's terrible about being honest with herself and others, and that kind of dishonestly would have made you miserable. Maybe she loves you, maybe she doesn't, but one thing is for certain. I'd much rather her ruin Johan's life than yours."

I laugh, but it's hollow. "Really? I was beginning to think you liked Johan more than me. You sure were obsessed with him in Capri."

Andries winces. "We were all drinking a lot, okay? And emotions were running high. Give me a break."

I know he's trying to make light of things, but I can't bring myself to do the same. We stay in silence for a few long minutes, before Andries tells me he'll call me a car if I want to go home, and that he'll have his family valet bring my car back to my place later. I agree, shaking my best friend's hand and thanking him again for his honesty, however brutal it may be, and I climb into the Uber when it arrives, desperate to be home and alone with my thoughts.

I feel heartbroken, betrayed, and naive all at once. The thought of Elise inviting Johan to stay with her family and spending the entire weekend with him is like a knife twisting in my chest.

Would she really be so dishonest with me, or did I just miss it when she mentioned her ex would be staying over? There had been mention of him visiting her home estate for dinner while we were all in Capri, but I never expected it to happen so fast and so secretly. I can't shake the feeling that something isn't right, so I start scrolling through my messages with Elise, rereading every single one, searching for any indication that she had intended to have Johan spend the weekend at her parents' estate. But there's nothing, not a single mention.

Once home, I hand my jacket to my maid and go immediately to bed, not even bothering to shower before I strip my clothes off and climb beneath the sheets. I start to question everything about our relationship and whether I ever really knew Elise at all. The memories of the past start to flood my mind and I can't help but think about the invitation to England that she had hidden from me. It all feels too familiar like history is repeating itself.

I know I need to talk to Elise about this, but I also don't want to jump to conclusions. So I make the decision to wait until Monday to see if she will openly tell me about Johan's weekend at her parents' estate. I can only hope that she will be honest with me and that we can work through this together. But as I lie in bed, sleep evades me as my mind races with uncertainty and doubt. I roll towards the large windows, the light of the city visible through even the closed curtains, and war with myself. I want to call her right now, but I can't. I have to give her the chance to be truthful with me on her own, even if it's killing me to sit here knowing she's with him.

If she does tell me, will it make any difference? It will just be her asking for forgiveness instead of being honest with me in the beginning, and no matter what, that fact has damaged what we have together. All I can really hope for is that my love for her, and the love I think she has for me, will be enough to fix this mistake of hers.

CHAPTER 31

Dan

I've surprised myself by not contacting Elise for three entire days now, waiting for her to be the first one to reach out, but to my dismay she never does. Each hour that passes makes me more frustrated and feel even more betrayed, but I hold my ground. I'm not going to be the one to contact her first, no matter how much it's bugging me. If I mean anything to her, she'll call eventually.

So why has it taken so damn long?

I try to put her out of my mind, getting ready for a meeting with Dad and Mark, the art collector. He's far from my favorite person after he hit on both Elise and Tatiana last time we were at the bar, but his pockets are deep and business is business. I'm getting ready to shave, running the razor under the tap, when I hear my phone ring from my bedroom where it's connected to the charger. Some sixth sense tells me that it's Elise—or maybe it's just misguided hope—and this time my suspicion is correct.

"It's been a while," I tell her as a greeting, trying to keep my cool, and Elise stutters on whatever she is trying to say.

"Um, hello to you too," she gripes, annoyed. "You know the phone works both ways, right? You could have called me."

"Maybe I didn't have anything to say."

I hear her inhale sharply. "Why are you being an asshole? Look, I just called to tell you that Dad confirmed that the open season for hunting begins on Monday the 15th, so we're walking down to the lake to see if there are some mallards to hunt that day. Is that okay with you? Since you've got so much of a problem with—"

I feel my anger and frustration boil over as I interrupt Elise mid-sentence. "You really think I'm that dumb, huh?" I ask, unable to contain myself any longer. "First you make up some lame excuse about that invitation to England, and then Johan goes and stays at your parents' for the weekend, and I know nothing about it? Do everyone a favor and go with him."

Elise is taken aback by the harshness in my voice, and by being caught, I assume, and she stammers. "W-what? I don't understand—"

I cut her off again. "You understand perfectly well. You're playing games with me, Elise. You're playing games with my heart, and I'm done with it. You promised me honesty and transparency, but instead, you've been lying to me and hiding things from me. That's not the kind of relationship I want to be in."

"Wait, Dan," she rushes to say. "I know this looks bad, really I do, but I only invited Johan here to help me persuade Mom to talk to her prosecutor friend and have her drop the charges against Roxanne. I figured that Johan is respected enough and that his presence would be novel enough to throw her off guard some, and it worked! Mom is even thinking about coming to the wedding."

I scoff. "Whatever you need to tell yourself to sleep at night, El. Your mom barely knows him, and now I'm supposed to believe that it's his presence that is going to make all the difference when it comes to her choices? Yeah, right."

"You don't get it," she insists. "Mom is comfortable telling us no about coming to the wedding since we all know how Dad will react, but when Johan asked her, it's not like she could tell him no without looking like the worst parent ever. She hasn't confirmed it for sure but I know she spoke to her friend, and I really think she'll surprise Andries and come to the wedding!"

"This is all very convenient."

"I even had him give Hannah the tickets," she continues, blurting her words out quickly, as if she's afraid that I'm going to hang up mid-sentence. The idea is tempting. "Nothing happened between Johan and me, I promise you, Dan. I know I'm not the easiest person in the world to trust, but—"

"That's an understatement," I laugh harshly. "I'm getting off the phone now, El."

"Wait!" she exclaims. "Just… please come hunting, okay? It's really important to me and my father and he's excited for you to join us."

Not wanting to drag this painful argument out anymore, I acquiesce just enough to satisfy her. "I'll see what I can do."

"What does that even mean? Are you coming or not?" she asks, but I hang up before I can hear anything else that she has to say. Elise has already told me everything I need to know about her little secret weekend with Johan, and nothing else that she has to tell me will make any difference. She's a liar, and she managed to fool me *again*.

I spend the next few hours going over everything in my head. I think about all the moments Elise and I shared and all the promises we made to each other. I feel like a fool for believing in our relationship, and I wonder if I'll ever be able to trust anyone again.

But as the hours pass, I realize that I still love Elise and I'm not sure I want to throw everything away so quickly. Maybe it makes me an idiot, but I think there is still more to be said between us before things end completely. We're going to have to speak face to face, but the idea of doing so makes my chest hurt to the point I ball my fist up and press it against my sternum to ease my aching heart. I need to see her and speak to her, but not now. Maybe not anytime soon....

Still feeling raw and hurt from Elise's deception, I finish getting ready to go to my parents' home, not wanting to be late for the meeting with Mark. Elise occupies my every thought. I believed we had a chance to make things work, but now I realize that it was all just a facade. I can't believe that she would invite Johan to stay overnight and not tell me! If I had done the same with one of my ex-girlfriends Elise would have lost her mind, but apparently, she expects me to just be fine with her and Johan having little sleepovers whenever they feel like it. The thought of them being together, just the two of them, makes me physically ill.

I go back to the bathroom sink and run the tap as cold as it will go, splashing the water on my face to clear my head and any residual nausea from my own awful thoughts, trying to center myself. As I meet my reflection's gaze in the mirror, water dripping down the bridge of my nose, I can't help but to cringe.

"You look like shit," I tell myself. "Get it together. We've got work to do."

* * *

Dad and I sit in his atelier, surrounded by the tools of his trade. Unlike the messier, more chaotic basement workroom, this part of Pop's business is cleaner and much more organized and acts as a public face when he deals with clients. The walls are lined with shelves covered in brushes, jars of polish, and watch parts, but most of them are simply for display. There is ample overhead lighting and a view of the family gardens through the windows.

My dad runs his fingers over the watch we're looking to sell today thoughtfully. "You said you know this guy?"

"Yeah, I've had drinks with him a few times," I confirm. "He's not my favorite guy on the planet, but he's a well-respected buyer, so I guess we could do worse."

Dad nods, rubbing his chin. "Alright, that will do, then. Anything is easier than going to an auction."

"You seem hesitant," I point out, walking across the room to stand beside him and look down at the piece. "Getting sentimental in your old age, Pops?"

He chuckles. "Maybe. It's just always bittersweet when I put hours of my work into these things and then it's time for them to go. I can't be greedy, even if I want to be."

It isn't long before the butler arrives, escorting Mark to us. He's dressed smartly in a casual dark blue suit, and his eyes sparkle as he walks into the atelier—probably recognizing my father's talent as a restoration artist, and looking forward to the business we're about to dive into.

"Good afternoon, gentlemen," Mark greets us as he enters the atelier. He shakes both of our hands. "Good to see you again, Dan. Is this the watch I've been hearing so much about?"

"It is," my father says proudly, moving aside so Mark can get a better look at the piece. "I restored it to its original condition. It's a rare piece, a 1950s Rolex Datejust."

Mark approaches the workbench and inspects the watch closely. "What a beauty," he says, with admiration in his voice. "May I see it in action?"

My father hands him the watch, and Mark puts it on. He tilts his wrist back and forth, admiring the way the light catches the dial. He whistles low, taking it off carefully and handing it back to my father. "It certainly has been well taken care of. Something tells me I'm about to leave here with significantly lighter pockets, but I believe Dan mentioned lunch? Would you two like to discuss the sale over the meal?"

I can tell by the look on my father's face that he's pleased. He's always been meticulous in his work, and it's gratifying to see it appreciated. "Yes, that will do. The table is being set as we speak. Would you like to follow me?"

I watch as my father wraps the watch in soft cloth and carefully places it in a small box before waving us after him. It's once again a sunny, warm day, the shade from the pergola is a welcome sanctuary from the heat. I sit down at the table on the terrace with my dad and Mark, and we order drinks from one of the house servers. It's tempting to start drinking already, with El hovering at the back of my mind, but I resist. This is a business matter, not time to mope, so I end up settling for sparkling lemon water. Fat white clouds pass in front of the sun and a light breeze is blowing in floral scents from the garden, which is full of vibrant colors, with lush green bushes and cheery flowers in every hue of the rainbow.

It's the total antithesis of how terrible I'm feeling, but at this point in my life, I'm plenty familiar with faking happiness for appearance's sake.

We start digging into the Mediterranean food that's been placed in front of us. There's a plate of fresh, juicy tomatoes and mozzarella, drizzled with a balsamic reduction. Another plate holds a variety of cured meats, olives, and pickled vegetables. The food is light and flavorful, the perfect accompaniment to our discussion.

"So, let's talk about the watch," Mark says, taking a sip of his own sparkling water.

"Of course," my dad replies. "It's a vintage Rolex that I've restored to its original condition. It's a beautiful piece, with a silver-tone stainless steel case and bracelet. The blue dial is simply stunning, with hour markers in silver-tone, and the classic Rolex logo sitting at the 12 o'clock position."

"Wonderful." Mark nods. "It's a rare beauty of a piece. I'm very interested in acquiring it."

We continue our discussion over lunch, talking about the details of the watch and how my dad restored it. Mark is impressed with the work that's gone into the restoration, and I can tell he's genuinely interested in making a deal.

The art collector leans back in his seat, tapping his fingers on the arm of the chair. "So, how much are you thinking?"

"$70,000," Pops says immediately. "Otherwise I plan on sending it to auction. It's my usual way of doing things, but the auctions are becoming tedious for my liking, so I'm giving you a preview. So, what do you think, Mark?"

He pops an olive in his mouth and chews thoughtfully, and after he swallows he answers, "I can do $67,000."

They continue to haggle, even though I know Dad is fine with Mark's price. It must be a thrill getting the price up, though, because my father only agrees to the sale once Mark comes up with a few hundred dollars before the two men shake on it. Afterward, Dad escorts him back upstairs to give Mark his new prize, leaving me outside while the staff cleans up. I discreetly wave one of the maids over and have her bring me two fingers of scotch, on the rocks to combat the heat, and I'm just beginning to sip the smoky, dark liquid when my father returns to find me once more.

He looks down at the glass in my hand and frowns, but doesn't say anything about it. Instead, he tells me, "Let's take a walk, son. I think we have some things to talk about."

I consider arguing, but this is my father, one of my favorite people in the world, and I don't want to deny him. Plus, the company sounds nice, even if I'm also craving absolute solitude. I stand and join him at his side, letting the older man lead our stroll across the grounds.

"I wanted to talk to you without your mother around," he admits. "Because something tells me that there is a man to man conversation that we need to have, hm?"

"We don't have to have any conversation" I counter, but he shakes his head.

"I think I know my own son well enough to see that you've got a lot on your mind. You've been quiet and melancholic—two words I wouldn't usually equate with you. So, what's going on?"

"It's nothing, Dad. I–"

"Cut the crap," he says, and I snap my mouth shut. "It's Elise, isn't it?"

I groan, closing my eyes. "Yes, fine. You guessed it. It's not like she's been the bane of my existence for months now."

"Well, what is it about now?"

I plan on giving him the abbreviated version, but as soon as the seal is broken and I open my mouth, the words begin to flow out faster than I could have anticipated. I tell Dad everything—about Johan sleeping over, the envelope in the side table, the equestrian show tickets, and even the way she told Johan that she loved him a few years ago but has never been able to do the same for me. He listens intently, nodding along but letting me say my piece, until I run out of steam. It feels good to have it all out in the open, but I have no illusions. I know soon enough I'll be full to bursting with these feelings all over again.

"So her exact reason for having Johan over was..?" Dad asks when I'm finished.

"Some bullshit excuse that she needed him to pressure her mom to make a phone call to the prosecutor and drop the charges." Saying it out loud has me angry all over again. "I can't believe she honestly thought I would believe that."

"Maybe that was really the case?" Dad suggests, surprising me.

"No way. If that was the case she would have told me the truth instead of hiding it."

"Well, maybe she knew you'd be pissed," he points out, and I look at him incredulously.

"Are you seriously taking her side right now?" I ask, stopping dead in my tracks.

"No, I'm just giving you the perspective that you refuse to see, son," he tells me, voice comforting and familiar. "There is a chance she's telling you the honest truth, and it's just that her timing was terrible."

"Maybe," I mutter with a sigh. "But the fact that she didn't tell me just makes me feel like she doesn't trust me enough. And if she doesn't trust me, then how can she truly love me?"

"I know it's tough, Dan," he says sympathetically, squeezing my shoulder. "But try to put yourself in her shoes. She might have thought that you would react the way you did, and didn't want to put that stress on your relationship. Sometimes it's hard to know the right thing to do, especially in matters of the heart."

My thoughts are a jumbled mess, feeling like a dark tangled forest even in the light of day. I know my father is trying to help, but it still doesn't change the fact that I feel hurt and betrayed. I'm not sure if I can forgive Elise for keeping this from me, but I'm also not sure if I'm ready to let go of her completely.

"I just need some time to think," I tell him, walking forward once more, unable to keep still.

"And you're completely justified in taking it," he assures me, catching up. Dad runs his hands over the bushes as we walk, disturbing small butterflies resting on the blooms. "If Elise cares for you, she will happily give you that space and time. Elise is a good girl, I'm sure she will come around, but she's also very young."

So now he's defending Elise? I can't believe it, throwing my hands in the air and saying, "How can you defend her, Dad? After everything that's happened? After all the lies and the secrets?"

Dad remains calm and tries to reason with me. "Dan, I understand that you're upset, but let's not be too hasty. Maybe there's more to the story than you know."

"More to the story? What more could there be? She was hiding the fact that her ex was staying at her parents' estate, and now you're trying to make excuses for her? That's just ridiculous!"

I can feel my blood boiling. I've been a fool to believe that Elise could ever love me the way she loved Johan. I thought that after everything we went through together, she would finally tell me that she loved me. But of course, it never came.

"And what about the fact that she hasn't said those three words? We've been hooking up for like two months now, and she still hasn't said she loves me. After everything we've been through, you still think it's okay?"

Dad looks at me with sympathy in his eyes. "Son, I know it's hard, but maybe she's just not ready yet. Or maybe she's afraid of losing you. Who knows?"

But I'm not listening. I've had enough. I need to get out of here, to clear my head and think. I stand up and say, "Forget it, Dad. I know you mean well, but it's all too obvious. My relationship with Elise was bound to fail."

He lets me leave, sitting on a concrete bench along the walkway, but calls out to my back. "Where are you going, Dan?"

I turn to face my father. "I don't know. I just... need to get my head straight."

"Okay, text me if you need anything," Dad says, clearly concerned. "I love you, son."

"Love you too, Pops," I sigh and with a heavy heart, I walk out of the family gardens. I'm not sure where I'm going or what I'm going to do, but one thing is certain: my relationship with Elise is on incredibly thin ice, and it will only take the smallest shiver to make it all break into pieces.

CHAPTER 32

Elise

It's Friday, and still I haven't heard a single word from the man that is supposedly so in love with me. The office is rowdy as everyone prepares for the upcoming weekend, and work is… well, work—boring and monotonous—but at least it's something to do and to keep my mind occupied while my family melts down and my boyfriend is having his fun pretending that I don't exist.

Dan hasn't spoken to me since we had that argument about Johan's visit to my parents' estate, which is frankly stupid in my opinion. I knew we would argue somewhat about Johan's visit, but I never thought he would shut me out so completely. I have given him space and time to cool off, hoping that once he was calmer, he would be more willing to listen to me, but clearly, that is a fallacy I have convinced myself to believe. I thought that maybe if I just waited a little bit, everything would go back to normal, and I'm pissed at myself for being so naive.

As I try to call him again, I realize that my contact number is still blocked. He hasn't even tried to reach out to me, and there is no way for me to get a hold of him. What if there was an emergency and I really needed him? It almost feels like Dan doesn't care about me at all, and it is breaking my heart into a million pieces. Since I was fifteen, Dan was always available for me if I needed him, and now it's like he's fallen off the face of the earth.

The fear and uncertainty inside me are growing with every passing moment. I thought we had something special, that our relationship was strong enough to weather any storm. But now, as I face the reality of our situation, I'm starting to wonder if I'm just foolishly clinging to something that was never meant to be.

The thought of losing Dan is almost unbearable. He's been my rock, my support, my everything. But now, I fear that all of that might be slipping away. I don't know what to do or how to fix things between us. All I know is that I have to try. I can't just let everything we had together fade away without a fight.

I check my watch and sigh. In five minutes, I'm supposed to meet Dad and the PR team for a meeting, and something tells me I'm not going to like what it entails. Dad gave me no information about what we'd be talking about, but knowing that I'm the only intern who is supposed to attend makes it pretty clear that it will have something to do with the family drama and not just work things.

I am *not* looking forward to it.

The walk to the meeting is lonely, and as soon as I enter the room I can feel the pressure building. I know that my father called me here for a reason, and I can sense that it's not going to be a good one. The room is filled with tension and everyone is on edge.

Once we are all sitting, Dad clears his throat and begins speaking. "I'm sure you've all heard the news by now, but, regarding the case against my son's fiancée, the prosecutor has dropped the charges against Roxanne and is now targeting Karl and myself." The room falls silent as the weight of my dad's words sink in. "I want to know if any of you had anything to do with this," he continues, his tone serious and accusing, and while he doesn't look only at me, I know that I'm the only true suspect in the room.

My heart begins to race as silence falls over everyone else. I know he suspects me of having something to do with the situation, but I can't tell him the truth. I won't throw my mom under the bus like that, not after she stuck her neck out to help us. I take a deep breath to steady myself, but don't add anything to the conversation.

"I have no idea how this happened, Sebastian. I was as shocked as everyone else when I heard the news," the PR director says, and everyone else at the table murmurs in agreement.

Now Dad looks in my direction, and his piercing gaze doesn't leave me for a moment. It won't be long now. He's going to keep pressing me for answers, and I know that I need to stay strong.

Finally, after what feels like an eternity, Dad dismisses everyone from the room, leaving me alone with him. I feel my knees start to shake as I realize that this could be the moment that my secret is exposed. I'm not sure how I'm going to get through this, but I know that I need to hold my ground. I wish more than anything that Dan was here beside me to hold my hand, or, at the very least, available to be reached on the phone once this is all over.

"Elise…" he sighs, putting both his hands on the long wooden table. "Did you have anything to do with all of this?"

I don't even hesitate, and just tell him simply, "No," while folding my hands in my lap.

Unexpectedly, Dad explodes in anger, slapping his hands on the surface of the table loudly, making me jump. "Dammit, Elise! How can you be such a failure?"

Wounded, I rear back in my seat, putting my hands on my chest in shock. "Dad…"

"Don't 'Dad' me right now, this is your boss speaking to you," he growls, face twisted in anger. "You couldn't even break Andries up with that whore, and now I find out that you're going as far as getting Karl and I in legal trouble? Not to mention lying to my face."

Already committed to my plan of action, I continue to lie, telling him I have no idea how the charges against Roxanne got dropped and he and Karl became targets. But I can feel my father's piercing gaze on me and I know he doesn't believe me. He continues to press me for answers. I try to keep my voice steady, but my heart is racing with fear that my secret will be exposed.

"I don't believe you, El. How did the charges against Roxanne get dropped and Karl and I became the targets?"

"I swear I don't know, Dad. I really don't."

He crosses his arms and paces the room. "Don't lie to me, El. You were supposed to take care of this. And now, here we are stuck with the fallout."

"I know, and I'm sorry." I stand and try to walk next to him and put a hand on his arm, but he jerks away from me, and it makes me want to cry. But I press on. "You have to see now that even the cabaret incident didn't make Andries leave Roxanne. They're in love and there is no way they're going to leave each other. You have to face reality! All of our energies are so much better spent somewhere else."

He whips around, and before I can take another breath his face is just inches away from mine. "I don't lose, El. Do you get that? Never."

I back away, swallowing my fear. "Accepting what you can't change isn't losing, it's adapting. And it's a much smarter strategy than being petty."

"Since when did you decide to side with your brother and his whore of a fiancée?"

"I'm not siding with anyone… I'm just tired of these stupid games. You should stop wasting your energy." I can feel tears building in the corner of my eyes, so I take a few deep breaths to steady myself. "I love all of you, and this is so, so hard on me."

"Cut the bullshit, El. You're not making any sense."

"I'm done playing this game." I sink back into one of the boardroom chairs, suddenly exhausted on top of the anger and sadness. "I'm done being a pawn in your schemes. In *anyone's* schemes. I'm done lying and pretending. I just want to live my life and be happy."

Dad is quiet for a moment, taking his own seat, steepling his fingers, and resting his chin on top of them while he contemplates the situation. I'm not so much of a fool to think that he's going to drop the subject, but some of the sharp edged tension starts to bleed away, and for that I'm at least a little thankful.

"Fine," he says after a few long minutes. "Let's forget about Andries, since he's a lost cause. Let's change course—how are we going to help Karl?"

"Help Karl?" I ask, confused and surprised.

"Yes, the fact that he's going to trial again is unfair," he explains, as if it makes all the sense in the world. "We have to do something. We can set up an interview for you, like last time, and you could speak on Karl's behalf."

I immediately reject the idea of going on TV to openly support Karl. "If you're so keen on helping him, then *you* do the interview. I literally just told you that I'm done playing the pawn for everyone else's agenda."

"This isn't about an agenda, darling daughter," he points out, "It's about your job."

I shake my head firmly. "I don't care. I refuse to do it, Dad. Actually, let me offer a different path... if *you* testify against Karl, you can save yourself and the company," I say.

But Dad looks at me, horrified. "Are you really suggesting I throw my best employee under the bus?"

"I am," I reply seriously. "It will solve everything. Karl is a cancer to everything that he touches—women, friends, this company... everything. He just wants to screw over Andries and Roxanne for the sake of personal revenge, his helping has nothing to do with his loyalty to you or the company. It's all selfish reasons that help him get his revenge. So turn the tables and let him take the fall. Saving yourself and your family seems like a no-brainer to me."

The room falls silent, and I can feel the weight of his gaze upon me. I know that this decision is going to have serious consequences, but I also know that it's the only way to protect ourselves and our family. I stand my ground, waiting for my father's response, bracing myself for what's to come.

For one brilliant second, I think that he is going to agree with me. Dad searches my face slowly, and he doesn't look angry when he does, just thoughtful. But then, his expression shutters and he shakes his head once. "Get out, Elise," he tells me, voice like cold iron. "Get out and don't say another word."

So that's how it's going to be. My stomach drops to the ground, devastated. This is my dad, the man who raised me, who I love so much, and he's going to take Karl's side over mine. I can't believe it… but at the same time, it seems so obvious that this is the way things were always going to go.

Wordless, I stand, gathering my things as I walk out of the room with my head held high. I'm not going to let Dad see me cry, even if I really, really want to. Not when he's broken my heart so callously like this.

If I thought the walk to the boardroom earlier was long and lonely, it feels like I'm on another planet now. All the voices around me sound muffled, and if anyone calls my name or tries to speak to me, I don't hear them.

I go back to my desk, trying to call Dan but his number is still blocked. Angry and desperate, I call it again and again, but of course, the result is the same. In a moment of embarrassing weakness, I pick up the office phone and call his number, hope surging in me when it rings a few times, but Dan sends the call to voicemail, and when I try from the work phone a second time, it too is blocked.

"Fuck you, Dan," I whisper, dashing tears away. "I really need you right now, you asshole."

With nothing else to do, I settle back into my computer chair and turn the desktop back on. It seems asinine to try and finish the day out, but there's nothing else to be done about it. So without a single ounce of motivation, I work at a snail's pace for a few hours until it's time to go home.

The minutes finally drag by enough that it's time for me to leave, and I rush out of the building, wanting to avoid my father at all costs. I had the foresight to call my driver a few minutes before I was actually outside, so I'm able to go straight from the front door to the backseat of the car without having to speak a word to anyone. After I'm safely tucked inside, I pull out my phone to call Andries so I can ask if Dan is with him. If anyone knows where my missing boyfriend is, it will be my brother.

Much to my dismay, Andries hasn't seen him today, either. "I don't know, El," he tells me. "We had dinner the other night but I haven't seen him since. Is something wrong?"

"Nothing except the fact I haven't heard from him for an entire week. Was that dinner when you showed him those pictures of me and Johan?" I huff, annoyed. "Thanks for playing into Johan's plan to piss Dan off, by the way. That's going really great for me."

He's speechless for a moment, as if he can't believe that I caught him so easily, but my brother collects himself quickly enough. "Yeah, alright, Johan sent me a picture of the two of you and that's what I showed him. You should have told him yourself," Andries replies, nonplussed. "Until I showed him, I figured that he at least knew that Johan was having dinner with you and the rest of the family. Imagine my surprise when not only was he unaware of that, but I was also the first person to tell him that Johan was spending the entire weekend at the family estate. That was really enjoyable, thanks El."

"Why would you do that, Andries?" I ask, my voice rising with frustration. "You know how private I am about my personal life. And now, because of your actions, my relationship with Dan is on the line! I would have told him—"

"Again, I thought he already knew," Andries interrupts, sounding annoyed. "He's my best friend and I'm not going to hide shit like that from him. You should know that by now."

I can feel my pulse in my ears when I respond, spoken in anger. "Congratulations, then! Now thanks to you Dan won't even speak to me. But that seems to be exactly what you wanted, huh?"

Even more frustratingly, Andries is still unbothered, as if what he did was completely justified and unproblematic.

"Again, I didn't think I was causing any sort of harm, so get over yourself. But, honestly, it's not very nice of you to have your ex sleeping at our parents' without your current boyfriend knowing, don't you think?"

There's a tense silence between us, as we both try to process the situation. I take a deep breath, trying to calm myself, but then what Andries just said finally registers. "You said 'my boyfriend'... how long have you known he and I are officially a couple?"

Now Andries seems slightly uncomfortable. "Ah...well. Dan told me like right before I showed him the picture of you and Johan."

I pinch the bridge of my nose and exhale slowly, seeing stars behind my eyelids. "You have really messed this up for me, you giant asshole."

"You can't possibly think that I'm the one that messed up in this situation, El. You made this mess trying to be sneaky, and now you don't like how difficult it is to clean up. You continue to hurt Dan, and I'm going to continue to expose you. He's like a brother to me, you know that." There is a beat of silence before Andries adds. "If it was the other way around, with Dan messing around, I would do the same thing for you. It's not exactly easy being in the middle of you two."

"I know… I know." I sigh, seeing the silhouette of my apartment complex in the distance. "I'm not thrilled with how you handled this. I'd have done the right thing if anyone had given me a minute to work through all my thoughts, you know."

"I guess I'm sorry for being so quick to throw your business out there, but I'm still not sure that you two are good together. Especially with all of this. But…take care of yourself, El."

"Can you at least give him a word for me?" I plead with Andries. "Since I'm sure he's much more likely to speak to you than he is to me. Tell him that Johan is just a friend and belongs to the past and that he's the one in my future."

"Ugh… sure. I'll tell him. Just give him a few more days to relax." My brother reluctantly agrees, and I hang up the phone feeling torn apart. I can only hope that he'll be able to smooth things over with Dan and that our relationship can be repaired. But for now, all I can do is wait and pray that time truly does heal all wounds.

CHAPTER 33

Elise

I'm sitting in my bed, surrounded by the familiar and comfortable mess of my room. The rain is coming down in sheets outside my window, tapping against the glass and drowning out the sounds of the city. The gray light coming in through the open curtains casts a dull glow on everything in the room, making it feel as if the world outside has slowed down to a crawl.

I'm picking at a bowl of fresh fruit and yogurt, trying to distract myself from my thoughts. My mind keeps drifting back to Dan and his silence. I gave him the whole weekend to cool down and think, as per Andries's advice, but it's already Wednesday and I haven't heard a word from him. I feel like a weight is pressing down on my chest, making it hard to breathe.

Everyone back at the office is still in a state of shock over the news that Karl Townsend and Sebastian van den Bosch might have to go to court, and of course, as his daughter, the other employees have been hovering around me hoping to get an ounce of new knowledge about the charges.

Dad, on the other hand, has been holed up with his lawyers and PR team, trying to figure out how to handle the situation.

Today I've taken the day off, thinking that a little self-care would do me good, but I'm too jittery to relax. I considered going to the spa for the day or maybe even calling Tati to join me, but the nerves about Dan not answering are too much for me to handle right now. Not even a deep tissue massage or a soak in the mineral springs will help all the uncertainty hanging over me like a dark cloud.

So, I sit here in my pajamas, watching the usual rain on a summer day come down and feeling like my world is collapsing in on itself.

With nothing else to keep me occupied, my thoughts wander back to all the wonderful times I shared with Dan. Every memory seems so vivid and real, like it happened just yesterday. I can still feel the warmth of the sun on my skin and the sand between my toes as we lay on the beach in Capri, completely carefree and blissful. We were so caught up in each other, nothing could come between us. Now, back home, it feels like literally everything is trying to keep us apart...no small part of that separation caused by my less than stellar decision making. Was it even worth getting Johan's help if it means not having Dan anymore? Sure, he was integral in persuading Mom to talk to her prosecutor friend, and without him, we wouldn't be on the path we are now, but for me... well, I'm more miserable than ever.

Dan feels a million miles away, even when I know his home is only down the road a few miles. Mentally and physically, it seems like he's so far from me. The thought of it breaks my heart and tears at my soul. The idea that something could break us so easily after all we've been through is devastating.

I close my eyes and try to hold onto the memories, trying to remember the way he looked on that beach, covered in sand and sunshine. I try to remember the way his eyes lit up when he laughed, and the way he whispered sweet nothings in my ear. I cling to these memories, hoping that they can somehow bridge the distance between us. But no matter how hard I try, the memories seem to slip through my fingers like sand, leaving me feeling lost and alone.

I open my eyes and look out the window, watching as the rain beats against the glass. It's a fitting reflection of my mood, gray and gloomy. I don't know what to do or where to turn. All I know is that I miss Dan terribly, and I'll do anything to get him back.

Then, I hear a text alert.

My heart races with excitement, thinking it's finally Dan. I rush to grab my phone, feeling hopeful and nervous at the same time. My mind races with all the possibilities of what he might say—maybe he's finally realized how much he misses me, or maybe he's planning a surprise visit. It's been an awful two weeks without him, and I've been constantly checking my phone, hoping to see his name pop up.

As I unlock my phone and glance at the notification, I can feel my heart sinking. It's just a text from my dad. While also unexpected, considering how mean he had been to me after the prosecutor dropped the charges, I can't help but feel disappointed and frustrated. I've been waiting for days to hear from Dan, and now I have to deal with the reality that he still hasn't reached out to me. The silence has been weighing heavily on me, and now it feels like the pain of it is only getting worse.

I take a deep breath, reminding myself that I can't force anyone to talk to me. Once I'm grounded, I read Dad's message.

Dad: *Are you and Dan still up for the hunting trip next Monday?*

I read the message a second time, anxiety spiking. Normally, the thought of the hunt would fill me with excitement, but not today. The hunting trip has been something I've been looking forward to for days now, ever since my dad first mentioned it, but at this point, it just means I'm going to have to admit to myself that Dan really isn't going to join us.

With Dan not speaking to me, I'm not sure how I will even confirm his attendance or absence. I recall all the details of the quick day trip and the memories I had looked forward to making. The early mornings spent in the blind, waiting for the mallards to take flight, the smell of the damp earth and the sound of the birds overhead, the thrill of the hunt, and most of all, the time spent with my dad and Dan, talking, laughing, and enjoying each other's company. Now... what is there? An awkward morning and afternoon with my Dad who basically hates me at this point? No thanks.

But... I still don't want to disappoint my dad, no matter how bad he has made me feel lately. He has been looking forward to this trip too, but the thought of attending without Dan is unbearable. So, feeling trapped in this hunt one way or the other, I type out a quick response, hoping that my voice sounds steady and confident: *Yes, count me in.*

Dad must be having the same thoughts I am, because he responds almost instantly: *And Dan?*

I hesitate, the cursor blinking on the screen as I think about it. I type up an honest answer, telling my father that Dan and I are arguing, and erase it three different times before giving up. I simply don't want to face the reality that Dan might not be attending, so I take a deep breath and type, *Yes, we will be both there.*

But even as I send the message, I know that I'm only putting off the inevitable. The truth is, I don't know if Dan will join us on the trip or not. All I can do is hope and pray that he'll come around, that way we can work through this issue and be a couple again.

My father seems happy, at least, texting me all the details about the trip. It's the most he's spoken to me in almost a week now, and that makes me feel a little bitter. Knowing Dad as I do, it's a way for him to let me know we are on good terms, despite our last argument.

I'm tired of waiting for Dan, though. I've tried to call him countless times, but every time I dial his number, it just goes straight to voicemail. I have even tried calling my brother daily, hoping he could give me some kind of update, but he just told me that Dan didn't want to talk about me, and there was nothing else he could do. I feel like I'm hitting a wall with every attempt to reach Dan, and my patience is starting to wear thin. I have to go to his townhouse, even if uninvited.

Decision made, I don't spend a ton of time on my appearance, just braiding my hair back and putting on some tinted gloss and mascara in the back of the car as the driver takes me there, my pulse racing. It's time to be a woman of action and not just wait on Dan to decide that he wants something to do with me.

When I arrive, I ring the doorbell, hoping to see him standing there with a smile on his face, ready to listen to what I have to say. But instead, the maid answers the door, telling me that Dan isn't there. She even invites me in to check for myself, but I decline, knowing that it would be pointless.

"Well," I say, more to myself than the maid who is still standing in the open door, looking bewildered. "Hell, what do I do now?"

"Mr. O'Brian does spend a lot of time at his parent's estate," the maid points out. Considering all the times I've stormed into Dan's home, demanding to see him, I guess it's not surprising that she'd be so quick to tell me where he might be. It's not like I've taken no for an answer before.

Feeling defeated, I go back to my car and instruct the driver to go to the O'Brian family home. I've always felt comfortable there, surrounded by all the memories of my time spent with Dan and his family, but going there on my own to chase Dan down like some sort of fugitive is different. What if he's told his parents about the things going on between us and they hate me now? The idea of it makes me queasy. His family is so loving and accepting... how is this the first time I've considered their feelings?

I make a promise to myself to be respectful, no matter what their reaction to my arrival is, but when I arrive, I'm met with the same response that I received back at his townhouse. The butler tells me that Dan isn't here either, and I feel like I'm getting nowhere.

Desperate, and hoping to make this trip all the way to his parents' not be in vain, I quickly parse through my thoughts for a way to make some progress even without Dan here. Then, an idea hits me.

I ask to speak to Jack, Dan's father. I know that he's always been a strong advocate for our relationship, even when Dan wasn't so sure himself, and I'm hoping he can shed some light on what's going on with his son's disappearance from my life. The butler acquiesces with a nod of his head before leaving me to pace back and forth in the foyer, trying to calm my nerves as I wait for Jack.

When he finally appears, wiping oil off his hands with a white cloth, I can tell from the look on his face that he knows exactly why I'm here. He greets me warmly and leads me to one of the comfortable living rooms, where we sit down to talk.

"You look rattled, dear," he tells me, pushing his glasses up onto the top of his head as he observes me. "And a little pale. When's the last time you've eaten?"

I think back to the bowl of fruit and yogurt from this morning, and my stomach growls audibly. I'm embarrassed, but Jack just chuckles, speaking to the butler, who soon returns with tea and a plate of biscuits, which I happily partake in. It isn't the aromatic floral tea that his son prefers, but a rich black tea, already sweetened.

"Now, tell me why you're here," he says comfortingly. "Although, I think I may already have an idea."

"I'm looking for Dan," I admit, steadying myself. "He hasn't spoken to me in over a week, and I even went to his townhouse today and he wasn't there. I'm just so worried and… and I miss him."

Jack nods knowingly. "Yes, he hasn't been easy for us to get a hold of, either. Last time we spoke he was very down, and when we spoke it was clearly related to your, ah... well, let's call it your emotional unavailability."

I wince, but he's not wrong. "That's fair. But I want to make it up to him, and it's impossible when he's been radio silent like this for so long."

"Why don't you start at the beginning of whatever started this little tiff between the two of you, and then I can better guide you on how to deal with my son."

With nothing left to lose at this point, I pour out my heart to Jack, telling him how concerned I am about Dan and our relationship. I tell him about all the times I've tried to reach out to him, and how I feel like I'm being pushed away again and again. Jack listens patiently, his eyes never leaving mine. When I'm finished, he takes a deep breath and speaks.

"Elise, I know how much you care about Dan, and I know how much he cares about you. But right now, he needs some space. He's going through a lot, and he needs time to process everything. But I promise you, he still loves you. He's just trying to figure out how to handle everything that's going on."

Jack's words bring me some comfort, but I still can't shake the feeling that something is wrong. I know that I just have to be patient, give Dan the space he needs, and trust that everything will work out in the end. But I have already waited a lot and patience is running thin.

"Jack," I say, my voice shaking slightly. "I need to know where Dan is. I need to talk to him. It's really important and I have waited over a week already."

Jack looks up from his tea cup, his eyes meeting mine. I can see the kindness in his face, and how much Dan resembles him, but also the firmness in his expression, and I know that he's not going to sugarcoat anything for me. "Elise," he starts firmly. "I don't know where Dan is, but I can find him. Before I do, though, I have to ask what your intentions are when you find him."

"What do you mean?" I ask, trying to keep my voice steady.

"I mean, it seems like you're playing with his feelings, even if you don't realize it. You're not fully committed to this relationship, and it's hurting him. If you care for my son, truly, then you need to be all in. 200% in. Otherwise, you need to leave him alone."

I feel tears starting to prick at the corners of my eyes, and I know that Jack is right. I do love Dan. More than anything. And I need to tell him that. "I love your son," I say, finally fessing up. "And I need to tell him that."

At first, he seems taken aback, but after a moment, Jack nods and I see the softness in his gaze. "I know that you do," he says. "I think everyone around you two knows you are both crazy for each other, but it's just taken you longer to come around and admit it. I also know that he loves you as well. But you need to show him how you feel in no uncertain terms. You hurt him, so now you need to be there for him."

"I need him to unblock my number," I say, my voice trembling. "I need to talk to him. I have to. We're supposed to have this hunting trip with my Dad this coming Monday and if he doesn't come then everyone is going to know how badly I messed this all up…"

"I'll see what I can do," Jack assures me. "And I'll also let him know about the hunting trip next Monday. I know that's important to him since he mentioned it to me, and I think it would be good for both of you to spend some time together."

I nod, sniffling my tears back. "Thank you, Jack. Thank you for everything."

And with that, I turn and leave the living room, feeling like I have a glimmer of hope for the first time in what feels like forever. Walking out to the waiting car, the sun is just beginning to set, and I think the O'Brian's home might be the most beautiful place I've ever seen, at least for now. Maybe I feel that way because this is the closest I've been to Dan in what feels like forever.

CHAPTER 34

Dan

Booking time at Fort Beemster was a way for me to try to escape from the chaos of my life and leave my problems back in Amsterdam. But while my muscles are relaxing and my body is beginning to unwind, my mind is no less stressed than before.

Fort Beemster is a luxurious wellness spa resort, nestled in the rolling hills of the picturesque Dutch countryside. The spa is renowned for its thermal waters, rich in minerals, and known for their therapeutic properties. Surrounded by lush gardens and tall trees, the resort exudes a sense of tranquility and serenity, and I would do basically anything at this point to be able to absorb said serenity. Instead, I'm a loose-limbed, tight-minded ball of anxiety floating in the hot springs, getting nothing that I need out of this stupid getaway.

I should just go home, I think, closing my eyes and dipping my head beneath the water.

With my luck, it figures I would find myself at a wellness spa, more torn up than ever. I came here hoping to relieve some stress and find some solace, but it seems that my treacherous brain has other plans.

I can feel the tension leave my body as I try to sink deeper into the water, but I am plagued by thoughts of my Elise and the fight that we had, Elise and Johan, and Elise lying to me about everything that weekend he stayed at her family home. I keep replaying the days before in my head, trying to figure out where things went wrong, and what I could have done differently. I feel like I'm in a constant state of turmoil, and I just can't seem to shake it.

I know that I should be taking advantage of this opportunity to relax, let go of my worries, and be fully present in the moment. But no matter how hard I try, I can't seem to escape the endless stream of thoughts that are consuming me.

I feel frustrated and helpless, as I struggle to find a way out of this spiral of stress and anxiety. I long to have a resolution with my girlfriend, to figure out what's going on with our relationship, and to find a way to move forward. More than anything, I want to be holding her, smelling her sweet scent, and tasting her smooth skin, but every time I imagine such things, I see Johan's damned face.

I am acutely aware of the gap between where I am and where I want to be, and it only adds to my sense of frustration and disappointment.

I guess I shouldn't be surprised… not when Elise is always on my mind. I've tried everything at this point—drinking, exercising till I was too sore to move, and smoking myself into a cloud of oblivion, but nothing ever fixes my long-term issues.

All of this makes me undeniably bitter. I love Fort Beemster, and the indulgence of it all, and having it tainted, makes me annoyed. This is supposed to be a gift to myself, so why do I keep getting in my own way? Maybe I just need to bite the bullet and just talk to Elise... it's not like anything else has worked thus far.

I've been doing a circuit in the thermal waters, trying to find some serenity, when I see my dad wearing nothing but swim trunks walking towards me. The sight is so out of place that I do a double take, but when I look again, it really is my father. He's accompanied by one of the spa staff who leads him directly to me, and he grins as if joining me has been the plan all along. Like I'm the one out of the loop, not him.

"What are you doing here, Pops?" I ask, more confused than ever. "I've never seen you here before."

"You're not as sneaky as you think you are," he teases as I watch him enter the pool and swim over to me. "But I'm here to offer you some much needed fatherly advice."

Alarm skitters over my nerves. *Please don't let this be more talk about my relationship.* "And that is..?"

"Avoiding problems won't make them disappear, Dan," he says sagely.

I can feel a knot forming in my stomach as I ask, "Why did you come all the way here just to tell me that?"

Dad floats on his back for a moment, clearly enjoying the water much more than I am. "Elise came to speak to me," he blurts out, trying to gauge my reaction. "She wants to talk to you."

Her name hits me like a knife in the gut, but I don't let my face show how much it hurts. "She just wants to talk because she wants me to join her and her dad on that hunting trip," I tell him, feeling a mix of anger and disappointment. "It's only to save face."

But my dad just shakes his head, putting his feet down on the pool floor again and standing. "She loves you, Dan."

All I hear for a second is static, and I breathe deeply to get my racing thoughts under control. I can hardly believe what I'm hearing. "No, that's not true. She just loves herself," I say, trying to push down the feelings that are welling up inside of me. God, I have craved hearing her say those words to me... I've dreamed of hearing them fall from her lips so many times that it's almost impossible to believe that it might actually be true.

"She told me that herself," my dad replies, lowering himself into the water before rising again. "I think she was being honest."

I don't know what to think. I've been so focused on my hurt and anger, I haven't stopped to consider that Elise might actually love me. The thought is both comforting and terrifying, and I can feel the walls I've built around my heart starting to crumble.

Steam curls into the air around my father and me, the murmuring chatter of the other guests in the public part of the spa muffling the sounds of nature like the sounds of so many insects. The world is still turning, life goes on, and... Elise loves me.

"Fine, I'll talk to her," I say, finally, keeping my voice as steady as I can, not wanting to show him how much of a mess I am inside. "I need to see if she really means it."

Inevitably, the shadow of doubt tries to creep in. Could Elise *really* love me, or is she shallow enough to lie to my dad about it just to get my attention once more? I've always thought she only cared about herself, but what if there's more to it than that? I suddenly feel torn between wanting to believe in her feelings and my own fears of getting hurt.

"Are these mineral springs turning you into a statue?" Dad asks, breaking the silence with a chuckle. "I know your dad telling you that your girlfriend loves you isn't the normal order of things, but you could still look a bit more excited, no?"

"You could have just texted me…" I grumble, pushing my dripping hair out of my face.

"As if you would have answered," Dad shoots back with a smirk. "You've fallen off the face of the planet. We were all starting to worry that you joined a cult or something."

Despite myself, I grin, and then, the heavy weight misery slowly abating, I laugh. "Fine. You're persistent, old man, I'll give you that."

"Where do you think you get it from?"

I ask Pops to tell me about Elise's visit, and we swim over to the edge of the mineral pool, resting our elbows on the concrete lip as he fills me in on everything that happened. Hearing that Elise showed up to my family home looking for me, and then pleaded her case to Dad makes my chest ache. It's such a powerful gesture, a move so out of character for stubborn, ice queen Elise that I can barely breathe.

She really does love me. Holy shit.

"You look like you've seen a ghost, kid," he says, amused.

"Just thinking about something equally unlikely…" I slide a glance over at Pops as I think something through. "I suppose you won't leave without me?"

"I booked a room for the night, actually. But tomorrow I'm taking you back to Amsterdam, yes," my dad replies, a small smile forming on his lips. "She needs you, Dan. You and I both know her family is a real piece of work."

I nod, already knowing all too well the kind of pressure Elise is under from her family. "That I know."

"So be the boyfriend she needs you to be," he says firmly, his words ringing in my ears.

As we both sit in the warmth of the thermal waters, I can't help but reflect on my dad's words. I know deep down that I need to be there for Elise, no matter what her family may say or do. And I can only hope that in doing so, we can find our way back to each other.

Dad and I continue to chat, and eventually move away from the more dramatic topics, but Elise is still on my mind. I struggle to focus on the conversation, my thoughts constantly drifting back to her. I wonder what kind of boyfriend she really needs. Is it someone like me? My Dad seems so sure, but I still doubt my own capabilities.

Despite my doubts, it's impossible to deny the love I feel for Elise. I long for her to love me too, but I've been hurt by her before and it's hard for me to fully trust in our relationship. But at the same time, I can't imagine letting her go. I want to be the best possible partner for her and to make our relationship work. I just have to speak to her, there's nothing else to be done.

Now that I've made up my mind to have a heart to heart with Elise, I finally feel a sense of peace. My thoughts are no longer so completely consumed by her and I'm able to enjoy my spa day for once.

My Dad and I sit by the edge of the thermal pool once the heat becomes too much, discussing what services we should book to close out the day. "I think I might get a massage," he says.

"A massage sounds great," I agree. "But I was thinking of trying the hot stone therapy. I heard it's amazing."

"Hot stone therapy? I don't know, son. That sounds a bit too fancy for me."

I playfully punch his arm. "Come on, Pops. Live a little. It's our self-care day after all."

He chuckles. "Alright, alright. You've convinced me. Let's do the hot stone therapy."

We spend the rest of the afternoon indulging in different spa services, joking and relaxing. For once, I'm able to let go of my worries and just enjoy the moment. But as the day draws to a close, I know I have to face reality. I have to have that talk with Elise. But for now, I'll just enjoy this time with my dad and the peace that comes with it.

CHAPTER 35

Elise

I step out into the cool and misty morning, surrounded by the rolling hills and lush greenery of the countryside outside of the family estate. The air is fresh and crisp, and I take a deep breath, savoring the scent of the earth and the trees.

The sun is just starting to rise, casting a warm and golden glow over the landscape, and I can see tendrils of mist beginning to lift from the fields and distant lakes and ponds where we will be hunting. Despite the uncertainty that still hangs over the oncoming day, I am struck by the serenity of the scene. The only sounds are the soft rustling of the leaves in the trees and the occasional bird call in the distance. The world feels hushed and still, as if it's waiting for something to happen.

The mist continues to lift, revealing more and more of the landscape, and I can see the fields stretching out before me, dotted with trees. The sun is shining brighter now, and I feel a sense of anticipation.

Then, it's all broken when my father steps out of the house behind me, his rifle slung over his shoulder and his mouth pulled down in annoyance.

"He's still not here?"

"I'm sure Dan will be here any minute," I assure him. "Let's just wait a little longer."

Dad checks his watch and shakes his head. "A few more minutes, El, and then we have to go. I'm not going to waste prime hunting time on your late boyfriend."

I scowl, but turn my head so he doesn't see. During mornings like these I feel a sense of connection to this place, to the earth and the sky, and to all the life that surrounds me, but Dad is really ruining it with his grumpy attitude.

Well, his attitude, and Dan's lack of appearance.

As time passes, Dad is growing more and more impatient, urging me to go without Dan, but I can't bear the thought of hunting without him. And just as we were about to give up hope, Dan's car appears, parking in the roundabout.

As I watch Dan's car pull up at the gates, my heart beats faster with anticipation. He's finally here, after what feels like an eternity of texting him nonstop over the weekend. Just the thought of seeing him makes me feel emotional. I've missed him so, *so much*.

I keep my cool as Dan gets out of his car and my dad greets him with enthusiastic joy, displaying no sign of how annoyed he had been about the younger man's late arrival. Dan apologizes for the traffic jam that held him up, and all is forgiven between the two men. Apparently having a buffer between himself and his daughter, who he has been borderline cruel to lately is cause for celebration, but whatever… there's no way he's as excited to see Dan as I am.

While they speak, Dan unloads his things. I can't help but be impressed by the amount of gear he's brought, but I keep my observations to myself. Inside, I'm almost beside myself with the desire to throw myself into his arms and kiss him, but I'm not going to humiliate myself in front of both Dan and my father. I need to get my boyfriend alone so he and I can break this much too long silence between us.

When Dan pulls out a long, clean rifle, and checks it over, my father nods approvingly. "Glad to see you've got some quality tools, Dan. I had put aside some gear for you, but it's nice to see you've got your own," he says with a smile.

Normally, this sort of interaction between the two of them would thrill me, but today… it's different. When I look at Dan, I can't help but feel a twinge of sadness. He seems to be focusing all his attention on my father, completely ignoring me. I can't help but feel hurt and left out, but at least he's here now, and it isn't like him ignoring me is a surprise. He's been doing it for two weeks.

With everyone ready, Dad has the kennel-master bring out his two favorite dogs—a pair of German Shorthair Pointers named Bram and Toby. The dogs take the lead through the dense foliage of the woods, I can feel the early morning mist settle on my skin, the air cool and damp. The dogs trot ahead of us, their noses to the ground, their tails wagging with excitement.

"We've got a lake on the property where Elise and I always have luck hunting mallards," Dad explains to Dan. "It's a bit of a walk, but worth it in my opinion."

The woods are quiet, except for the occasional chirp of a bird or rustle of leaves underfoot. The trees are tall and thick, their branches forming a canopy above that blocks out most of the sunlight. But even in the dimness, I can see Dan clearly, his fit body outlined so well by his hunting attire that it makes me feel flushed. It really has been too long since we've been alone, and now that I know what his body can do, it's difficult to keep the steamy thoughts of what I want to do to him at bay. I swallow to relieve my dry mouth, and try to shake off the cloak of mixed emotions that almost drown me. Love, lust, excitement, and a burning need to fix things between Dan and I are all making it complicated to concentrate on the hunt at all.

When the dogs start to quiver excitedly, their noses picking up the scent of the ducks in the distance, my father picks up the pace to walk beside them. I can hear the distant quack of the mallards, and I know we're getting close, but I don't rush forward. Instead, I hang back, finally having Dan alone, even if it is just for a few minutes.

I've already resolved to have a heart to heart with Dan, and there is no better time than now to begin.

Walking through the forest, I manage to fall in step beside Dan. My dad is now quite a bit ahead, so I take the opportunity to lean in towards Dan and thank him for coming.

"I'm glad you're here," I tell him, keeping my voice not too loud. "For a minute I was really afraid you weren't going to show."

To my surprise, Dan replies with a flippant comment, "You should thank my dad, he's the one who literally dragged me here."

I know his words are meant to be hurtful, but despite his lack of enthusiasm, I want to show him how much I appreciate him, but I have to find the right time.

As we continue our walk towards the lake, my father calls Dan over to join him. The two men talk quietly, heads tilted toward one another while Bram and Toby circle the area. When I see my two companions talking and checking their rifles, I can't help but feel my heart warm, even though they are both pretty annoying to me at the moment. I am so thankful that my boyfriend and my father have such a good relationship, especially compared to the relationship that Andries and Roxanne have with him.

I take a moment to reflect on the situation and can't help but think about how lucky I am to have Dan in my life. Despite his initial resistance to the hunting trip, he still made the effort to come and be with me today. I know that we have had our challenges in the past, but seeing them work together and have a good time, gives me hope for our future. I vow to cherish every moment we have together and to make the most of our time during the hunt. And, whether Dan wants to or not, we're going to have that heart-to-heart.

CHAPTER 36

Dan

Trudging through the underbrush with Elise and Sebastian, I can't help but feel a bit out of place. Hunting has never been my thing, even if I am a decent hand at it, but here I am, trying to make a good impression on Elise's father, like he's a stranger I've never met before rather than my best friend's father. It's so complicated dating Elise, but in other ways, it's so much easier than dating someone from a family dynamic I'm not familiar with. At least I know that, on some basic level at least, Sebastian likes me.

Although, I'm getting the feeling that Sebastian and Elise don't like each other too much right now, making me a sort of extra awkward third wheel.

Sebastian begins to fill me in on the details of the day's trip after I peel away from Elise, not ready to talk with her about everything. I need a long period of time to set the record straight, not little minute long snippets of conversation here and there. Her father tells me about the beautiful lake we've just arrived at, as well as how often they see mallards here. The two sleek, muscular dogs are obviously excited about something, which bodes well for a successful hunt.

We circle the lake, and I'm thankful when we stick to the topic of hunting, but just as that thought crosses my mind, Sebastian takes the conversation in a totally different direction. His expression becomes serious and I can tell he has something important to say to me. If it has to do with his daughter, who is hanging about a dozen feet behind us, I know it's not going to be easy to hear, but there is nothing I can do but grin and bear it. At least it's a nice day out, if nothing else.

"Dan," he starts, checking over his shoulder to make sure his daughter is far enough away that she won't hear us. "I want you to know that Elise truly cares for you. She's been through a lot lately, and she needs someone like you in her life." I nod, unsure of where this is going, considering the fact that Sebastian himself is the catalyst for a lot of her problems. "And I also want to let you know that Johan is just a friend of hers. You don't have to worry about him," he continues.

I play dumb, hoping to get as many pieces to the puzzle of what went on the weekend Johan stayed at the family estate as possible. "How can you be so sure?" I inquire.

Sebastian hesitates for a moment, eyebrows drawing together as if he doesn't quite believe that I'm so in the dark, before continuing, "Hannah is quite excited about going to England for the Horse Show this fall, is all I mean. She's a handful, so trust me, Johan won't be thinking about Elise for long."

I'm taken aback. It almost sounds like he's inferring that Hannah and Johan… but no, certainly not. She's much too young for Johan to be showing any sort of interest in her. "But isn't Hannah a bit young to be going to a foreign country on her own?" I ask, genuinely concerned.

Sebastian shakes his head, shouldering his rifle. "She's turning sixteen and she's perfectly capable of going on her own. I just wanted to make sure you knew where things stand."

I thank Sebastian for his honesty and try to process everything he's told me. I knew Elise was giving her equestrian show tickets to Hannah, but now that I have time to think about it, I don't know how I feel about Hannah and Johan going alone. Still... I guess it's none of my business. At least I know El didn't lie to me about having no interest in attending the show with him. It makes me feel slightly better about whatever went on that weekend, but I'm still not convinced it was as innocent as Elise is making it out to be.

The morning is growing later, the smell of the pine-heavy forest mixing with the dark, earthy smell of decay coming from the edge of the lake. The water ripples and bubbles as the fish rise with the day to eat the insects that hover over the surface, but we aren't interested in that sort of animal today. This is so much different from being stuck in the dark woods hunting large game, and I think that maybe I might enjoy hunting more if it was always like this.

Things grow quiet, and I turn slowly to see Elise aiming her rifle, one of the dogs standing at her side at a perfect point. El moves with a silent grace, her head tilting to the side and her long braid falling over her shoulder as she moves her eye to the sight and with perfect precision, takes the shot towards the gathering of ducks that I hadn't even seen. The rest of them explode into the air as the sun-shot cracks the air, and the dog rushes forward into the brambles, returning with the limp bird, neck shining emerald green, between its teeth.

Elise beams at the dog, ruffling its fur before taking the mallard gingerly from its mouth. "Good boy, Toby," I hear her praise, and the dog runs circles around her legs, tongue lolling happily.

Sebastian, clearly impressed, walks over and praises her on her successful shot. Elise is tense as her father approaches, but melts under his approval like she always does. Even if Sebastian is angry at her, there's no denying that she had taken a beautiful shot, and her natural ability shined through. Hell, I want to congratulate her too, even if we've only spoken two sentences to each other in weeks.

As I reflect on this moment, I feel grateful to be somewhat a part of this family. They have accepted me with open arms, and I feel lucky to have them in my life, even if they can be out of control and at each other's throats at times. Andries is who brought me into the fold, but every member has been kind to me. I hope that once the dust settles, the family will be a united front again, and who knows, maybe one day I will be the one being praised for my hunting skills.

All of that depends, though, on how Sebastian and Julia react to Andries and Roxanne's wedding. Sebastian especially has done so much damage to his son that I have a difficult time imagining that they will make up with one another easily. Still, there is hope, as long as Sebastian makes the right choice.

Lost in thought, I wait while the ducks settle once more, and prepare to take my own shot. My head is in the clouds as

I decide what angle to take and when Elise appears next to me, I nearly jump out of my skin.

"Do you need help?" she asks quietly, a mischievous look on her face.

I scowl, my gaze focused on the mallards. "I'm good, thanks." But despite my confidence, I can feel her watching me closely as I take aim. Suddenly, she steps forward and her hands reach out to me. "Your shoulder should be a bit higher."

When Elise puts her hands on me, static shock fizzles over my entire body. God, I have missed this fucking woman, but she is not helping me right now by any means. Despite her well-meaning help, I miss my shot and let out a frustrated sigh as the birds take to the air in a flurry. Fortunately, Elise has got the decency to keep whatever snarky remark to herself.

With a question forming in the back of my mind, I glance over at Sebastian, who is a bit further away, and then back at his daughter, and ask, "Did you tell your dad we are together?"

She nods, looking slightly smug. "I did, yes."

I shoulder my rifle and scrub my hands over my face. Leave it to me to fall in love with the most unpredictable creature on the face of the planet. "Fuck! Why on earth would you do that?"

"Because I—" Before she can answer, we hear a sharp crack and turn to see Sebastian, who has just brought down a mallard. We watch as the dog, Bram this time, rushes over to retrieve it, and Sebastian follows with a triumphant smile, pumping his fist in the air.

But as the excitement of the successful shot dies down, Elise and I are left alone once again. She looks me in the eye and says, "Because I love you."

Her words hit me harder than the crack of the gun echoing across the lake just did, but I shake my head, still not sure of her sincerity. "Oh, stop it. You are just saying that because you are afraid of losing me."

But she firmly states, "No, I'm saying that because I genuinely do. Johan is just a friend. That's it. You need to understand that."

I examine her for a moment—back straight, small fists clenched, and chin tilted up stubbornly. I shake my head, a smile pulling at the corner of my lips.

What an infuriating little thing…

Lost in her gaze, I realize that I have been foolish to doubt her, and I know that I need to trust in our love and our future together.

Then, she drops another bomb. "Mom is really coming to the wedding, and she even called the prosecutor and managed to convince her to drop the charges against Roxanne. That's what I needed Johan's help for, just like I told you, and look… it worked, exactly like I knew it would." She blows out a breath, rolling her eyes to the sky. "Dan, I should have told you sooner, I know, but I haven't lied to you about anything that happened with Johan that weekend. Mom coming to the wedding should be proof enough that I told you the truth, and that my tactics worked."

Standing here, ankle deep in the soft earth, I can't believe what I've just heard. Elise's words are ringing in my ears like a loud clanging bell, and my mind is spinning as I try to process the information. Julia is coming to the wedding and she's even taken steps to have the charges against Roxanne dropped. I've heard rumblings about the dropped charges, but this is the first confirmation I'm getting that Julia is responsible for it happening. It's all too much to take in and I struggle to form coherent words as I stammer out, "She is? Are you sure?"

Elise nods, the weight of the situation evident on her face. "Yes, I'm sure. Mom is going to stay overnight at my grandmother's estate since it's obviously going to cause an issue at home once Dad realizes what's happening."

I can feel the shock and disbelief coursing through my veins. "He's going to lose his mind knowing that his wife is attending," I say, following the statement up with a string of curses. I can't imagine how Sebastian is going to react to the news, and it's unbelievable he's right over there through the reeds retrieving his duck while his daughter and I talk about his wife betraying him.

Elise just shrugs. "Yeah, well… I don't think they are doing okay, anyway."

In that moment, I see the pain and sadness in her eyes, and I realize the toll that the issues between her parents are taking on her. I can see how the once seemingly perfect relationship between Julia and Sebastian is now flawed and causing harm. It's a heavy weight on Elise's shoulders, and I want nothing more than to reach out and offer her my support and comfort. But I don't know if that's what she wants. I hesitate, not wanting to do anything that may make her feel worse, or that tips off her father, who could come upon the two of us at any second. I take a step closer to her and say, "Elise, if you ever need to talk or need someone to lean on, I'm here for you. I'll always be here for you."

She looks up at me under her lashes, eyes wide and innocent. "Do you promise?"

I cup her face in my hands. "Promise."

She nods, rising on her tiptoes just enough to press her lips to mine for a quick peck while her dad isn't around. "Good."

As I stand here, holding her face between my hands, I feel a thrill of nervousness as I ask her the question that has been weighing on my mind for so long. "So, um, do you really love me?"

She smiles, brilliant and shining, and I can see the affection shining in her eyes. "Yes, you fool, of course I do," she teases me, and I smile at her playful tone. And then, she turns the tables on me, "And you? Do you still love me?"

I pretend to consider the thought, and Elise huffs, slapping my hands away while I laugh. I can feel my heart swell with emotion as I say, "Of course, silly." I lean in and kiss her on the forehead, feeling the love and tenderness that I have for her radiating through every fiber of my being.

Pulling away slowly, I reflect on my own feelings, the torment they have put me through... and how Elise is worth that and so much more. I think about how much I have grown to love her over the months, and how grateful I am to have her in my life. And then, I turn my thoughts to the future and what the next chapter of our lives might hold.

I can feel my resolve strengthening as I take her hand and say, "Alright, let's find some mallard for me to shoot. I can't bear the idea of coming back home empty-handed." I lace our gloved fingers together and lead her out into the wild.

***

That night, we all sit down for dinner, and it's impossible not to notice the palpable tension between Julia and Sebastian. They're barely speaking to each other and it feels like they're just going through the motions for the sake of keeping up appearances, their movements stiff and lacking that shimmer of affection that typically fills the air between them.

The table is set for a celebration, with one of the ducks we hunted being the main course, but the atmosphere is subdued. The entire family is seated with us, the younger kids chattering animatedly, Hannah looking bored to tears, and, next to all of them, an empty chair where Andries should be. Seeing it makes my stomach twist with a sharp pang of sadness, even as Sebastian stands and holds his glass in the air for a toast.

"I want to raise a toast to Elise and Dan, who not only contributed to our successful hunt this morning and our dinner tonight, but who have also finally let the cat out of the bag and announced that they are officially a couple. Congratulations, kids."

Julia holds her glass up, a plastic smile on her face, and all the children raise their water glasses chaotically, water sloshing over rims and onto the tablecloth. I grin back at Sebastian and stand to shake his hand when he offers it, but my gaze is fixed on Elise. She doesn't look happy, and while the odd energy at the table might go over the heads of other people, I know this family well enough to pick up on it. Elise is sad, hollowed out from the bubbly girl she was this morning, and I hate it.

I look around the table and my eyes land on the empty chair that once belonged to Andries again. It's a painful reminder of strife we've all suffered and it makes me realize just how strained Julia and Sebastian's relationship truly is. I can only imagine what they must be going through, fighting over the wedding of their first son, but I know one thing for sure: I never want to end up like them.

Wanting to comfort the woman I love, I reach for Elise's hand under the table, giving it a reassuring squeeze. I promise myself that I will never let our love die like theirs has. I will always make sure to communicate with her and never let our relationship fall into such a state of disrepair. I'm more and more sure as the dinner goes on that Sebastian is already aware that Julia is planning to attend the nuptials despite his objection, and his coldness towards his wife makes me even more sure that if I marry Elise one day, I never want to be the same kind of man he is—aloof and empty, all for the sake of his reputation.

CHAPTER 37

Elise

The days are rushing together like mad and I can't quite believe that we're just days away from the wedding. That is until I step inside the posh dress store in downtown Amsterdam, inhaling the scent of fresh fabric and delicate perfume. The store is quiet and sophisticated, with soft lighting casting a warm glow on the racks of designer dresses lining the walls. I walk up to the counter, and a young associate with a tight bun hands me the two dresses that I was fitted for only a few days earlier.

"Do you want to try them on before you leave?" the associate asks, and I confirm that I do, letting her lead me back to the fitting rooms.

Inside the stall, my gaze settles on the stunning light blue dress that shimmers in the light. It's a perfect match for the pre-wedding party with a fitted bodice that accentuates my curves, and a short, flowing skirt that adds a touch of elegance. As I twirl in front of the mirror, I feel sexy and confident, excited to see what Dan thinks of the dress. The sales assistant walks up to me and compliments my choice, checking the seams and alternations with quick hands, and I can't help but smile in agreement.

Next, I unzip the heavier bag that contains the formal gown for the wedding ceremony. It's more regal, deep red, and perfectly fitted to my body. I wasn't sure about it at first, but now I'm positive that the dress is perfectly stunning. It also has a fitted bodice, this time with a deep v neckline, and a full, flowing skirt that trails behind me as I walk. The fabric is luxurious and soft to the touch, and the intricate beading along the neckline and sleeves adds a touch of glamor. I slip the dress on and admire myself in the full-length mirror. The dress fits me like a dream, and I can't wait to wear it on my brother's special day.

An errant thought creeps in, my eyes wandering over to the rows and rows of white and ivory dresses. I wonder what kind of dress I will have for my own wedding?

I get lost in the idea, letting the associate check the fit of my second dress, but I'm brought back to reality when I hear my iPhone buzzing. I pick it up, still wearing the heavy red dress, and see that it's Andries.

Jokingly, I answer by saying, "Don't tell me you're canceling the wedding."

Andries chuckles on the other end and says, "No, but I've got to tell you something almost as scandalous. You'll never guess who just moved into Oma's house."

"Who?" I ask, feeling intrigued.

"Mom," he replies, his voice filled with excited surprise. "She just move back into her old bedroom. Are she and dad going through a rough time?"

"Um, yes, that's the understatement of the century. I think the whole scandal exposing Dad's involvement isn't doing their relationship any good."

My brother takes a deep breath, no doubt trying to process the information. "So she's attending the wedding, I suppose?" Andries says carefully, as if he barely dares to hope.

I soften my voice. "Mom loves you a lot, Andries. It's not easy for her to do what she's doing. She's proven to you how much she cares about you, even to the detriment of her own marriage."

There's a short silence on the other side of the line. "I suppose we can find an empty chair for her at the wedding…" he says, trying to sound lighthearted, but I can hear the emotion in his voice, but I'll never point that out. I'm just so relieved that my brother and mother are going to make up that almost nothing else matters to me right now.

Just as I'm about to hang up, Andries adds, "El, thank you for everything you've done. You're the best sister I could have ever dreamed of."

His compliment catches me so off guard that I've got to steady myself. "Oh," I blurt out, still processing his words. Now I'm the one with tears in my voice. "And you're the best brother. I'll see you soon."

***

After being unzipped from the dress and having them packed back up and sent to my apartment for me, I head back to work, hoping that my extra-long lunch break won't be noticed. But, as soon as I sit back down and go to boot up the desktop, my office phone sounds off with the sharp three-buzz ring that indicates the call is coming from inside the building. With a sense of foreboding, I pick up the call and hear my father on the other end of the line.

"Elise, come to my office right away."

Before I can even respond he's hung up, and I'm left looking at the receiver, bewildered. He sounds serious, so I quickly knock at the door to announce myself, before entering his office. I find him standing by the window, staring outside with a deep, pensive expression. He has his hands clasped behind his back, and his posture is stiff.

I knock on the doorframe a second time to let him know I'm here, and he simply jerks his head towards the chair on the other side of his desk. After closing the door behind me, I sink down into the expensive leather piece of furniture, never taking my eyes off of him, but my father doesn't even give me time to speak before he begins his interrogation.

"Did you know your mom left this morning for your grandmother's place with three pieces of luggage?" he asks without even looking at me.

I bite my lip, feeling my stomach sink as I reply, "Yes, Andries told me, actually. He called me earlier today."

My father turns to me, his eyes searching my face as if he's trying to gauge my reaction. "Remind me again where your brother's wedding is being held?"

Oh, I know where this is going now. "Um… at Oma's estate."

He laughs darkly, leaning back on his chair. "So, your mother is attending the wedding then."

"Dad—"

"I never thought Julia would betray me like that, but here we are." There are eons of unsaid emotions behind his tone, but his expression doesn't change. "Tell me, Elise, how did you manage to convince her?"

"Me? What are you talking about?" I ask, confusion clear in my voice. Sure, I might have pushed Mom in the right direction, but I had no idea she had left home until Andries told me earlier.

"You think I'm stupid enough not to know that you and Johan are the ones behind it?" he asks, his volume rising as he bounces forward. "Why else would you invite your ex over to our home, if not to poison your mother's mind?"

"Johan has nothing to do with it! That's not why he came!" I protest.

"So, with or without Johan, you forced your mom to call the prosecutor to drop the charges against Roxanne and go after me, huh?" he asks, his eyes piercing into mine. When I don't answer, he scoffs. "Don't bother to come back to the office. I don't need traitors around here."

"I did it because Roxanne is innocent!" I explode, jumping up from my seat, unable to hold back any longer. "You and Karl are behind everything, and you lied to me saying you weren't!"

"Karl maybe, but not me!" he insists, but I don't believe a word of it.

"So tell the judge that, and choose your family for once!" I shout, before starting to pace around his office to calm myself down.

My father's face goes blood red before he turns his back on me, facing the window once more. "Get out of here."

I feel a crack start to form in my heart, but try my best to ignore it. "You are such a disappointment, Dad. I used to look up to you, but now all I see is a fool." My voice is shaking with emotion.

"I said get out!" he thunders, his temper flaring out of control. I wince, but do as he says, turning and rushing towards the door, desperate to escape the crucible this office is becoming.

Before I exit, I stop in the door frame and offer him one last heartbroken thought. "I hope one day you'll realize this could have ended differently," I say, my voice softening. "Goodbye, Dad."

With that, I turn and walk out of the office, closing the door behind me, my soul heavy with the weight of the situation. I can only hope that in time my father will see the truth and make amends. Until then, I must stay strong and keep fighting for what I believe in. Even if sometimes it feels like it might be the end of me.

* * *

I don't even bother calling Dan, just telling the driver to take me straight to his townhouse. By the time I'm at his door, tears are streaming down my face unbidden. For once, Dan answers the door himself, like he somehow knew I was coming, and as soon as he gets a clear look at me, he rushes forward, pulling me into a tight embrace.

"It's over," I tell him as I sniffle the tears back. "I lost my entire career, all of my future plans. He fired me, Dan! His own daughter!"

"Shh," he comforts, stroking my back as he walks me inside and shuts the door behind us. "You did the right thing. Sebastian is just a pathetic excuse for a human being."

I feel like I'm in shock now, the tips of my fingers and toes going cold. "How could he do this to me?" I ask, my voice shaking. "How could he do this to me *and* Andries? I thought he loved us!"

"Don't worry," Dan says, pulling away to look at me. "We'll make sure you get your job back after the wedding. I promise. Sebastian will realize what an ass he's being before you know it." Dan takes my hand and leads me over to the couch, sitting down next to me. "In the meantime, you're more than welcome to stay at my place if you don't want to be alone."

I nod, the idea of being able to sleep in his arms at night is a balm to my wounded soul. "Thank you so much, Dan." I lean forward, giving him a quick peck on the cheek. "I don't know what I would do without you."

"You don't have to thank me," he says with a smile. "I love you, and this is what you do for people that you love. We'll get through this together."

We remain sitting on the couch together, Dan turning on some mindless television show while I tuck my feet up underneath his legs, snuggling close while he continues to stroke my back and reassure me that everything will be alright. There's so much to be done in the next few days that losing my job almost seems like a minuscule problem in the big picture. But still, I can't help but mourn.

When my phone starts to buzz again, I'm surprised to see that it's Tatiana. I show the screen to Dan, who shrugs, so I go ahead and answer.

"Elise, it's so good to hear your voice," Tatiana gushes. "I feel like we've barely talked since you got back from Capri. How are things?"

Still a bit confused, I try to keep up as she starts chatting about this and that. But eventually, I have to cut to the chase, since nothing that she's talking about is really making much sense.

"Tatiana, what's going on?" I ask, trying to keep the suspicion from my voice. "Do you need something?"

There is a pause, and then she finally lets out a sigh. "Maybe, yes, I, um… I was wondering if I could come to Andries's wedding."

I'm immediately taken aback. Tatiana might not be Roxanne's favorite person in the entire world, and for good reason, but I've been under the impression that she and Andries were still good friends. "What do you mean? You didn't receive an invitation?"

"No, I didn't," she answers, her voice tinged with sadness.

Even if it's weird that she didn't receive an invite, I can't help but find the request a bit odd. I tell her I will text her the address regardless. Tati is thrilled, so much so that I immediately wonder if I've made some sort of mistake by inviting her, but it's too late now.

After hanging up, Dan asks what the call was about. I fill him in on Tatiana's request to attend the wedding and he's equally bewildered by the request but doesn't seem overly worried.

"Why would Tati want to see her crush get married?" Dan asks, as if he's trying to sort through to find the answer himself.

I shrug. "Maybe she just has FOMO. Who knows?"

"Whatever." Dan sighs, repositioning us so he can lift me onto his lap, straddling him. I giggle at the sudden change in position. "I'm so tired of talking about everyone else being weird. Can we instead talk about..." he begins to trail his fingers up my sides under my shirt, "you and I?"

I run my fingers through his hair, lowering my face to his as his pupils go wide. "What exactly did you want to talk about?"

"This," Dan answers, his voice deep, just as he brushes his lips with mine.

CHAPTER 38

Elise

If our home estate is grand, then Oma's estate is opulent, but the relief of arriving here and knowing that we are almost at the finish line of all of this eclipses any wonder I have of how gorgeously decorated everything is.

Dan hands the keys of his vintage convertible over to the valet, talking animatedly to some of the other guests, but I just can't seem to focus on anything. Knowing that Mom is here, and has been for the last few days, is simply unbelievable to me. She and Dad were supposed to be this inseparable force, and I always thought that if we were able to persuade her to come to the wedding that Dad would eventually follow suit. Instead, he's standing his ground, and our family continues to fracture further.

At least Andries will have his mother at his wedding. Small victories are better than none, I guess.

I loop my arm through Dan's, admiring his tailored, casual navy blue suit and the ivory shirt beneath it that he's left unbuttoned to display inches of bronze skin. "Have I told you that you look handsome tonight?"

He looks down at me and raises an eyebrow. "Only about six times. If you count the time you stripped the suit off me, then seven."

I slap his arm as we ascend the curving stone stairs up to the tall wooden French doors, where two doormen pull them open for us. Directly inside is an older woman, her dark emerald green dress brushing the floor as she approaches us with arms outstretched, her silver-white hair pinned into a perfect chignon.

"Darling Elise," Oma says, and I'm greeted by the warm smile of the woman who raised my mother and has always been a constant source of comfort and love in my life. She takes my hands and looks me over adoringly before pulling me into an embrace, smelling a sophisticated fragrance and whatever expensive champagne she's been drinking. Margaret might seem like a cutthroat, fearless, woman to a lot of people, but to Andries, myself, and the rest of my siblings, she's just Oma, and after all the turmoil of the last few days, I'm so glad to see her face and the acceptance that she radiates.

"And Daniel," she croons, moving on from me to take Dan in an equally warm hug. He looks over her shoulder at me, amused if slightly confused before Oma pulls away and pats him on both cheeks. "What a lovely couple the two of you make. Come, come, I've had the staff prepare a room for you, and they'll be bringing your luggage up shortly."

Dan and I are both a little taken aback when she gives us a shared guest bedroom, looking at each other as we follow her down the marble floor hallway. Oma doesn't say it out loud, but I'm sure that Dan and I both understand her message—she knows we are together, and she's perfectly fine with it. We've run into surprisingly little pushback from family besides Andries, but knowing that Oma approves is the highest form of acceptance we've received yet. A smile plays over my face at that thought.

She leads us to the cozy room, which is tastefully decorated and has a comfortable bed that seems to be calling out to us, inviting us to take a rest. We both thank her but before she leaves us, Oma pauses. "Dan, would you mind going to make sure that the staff is bringing your things up?"

He looks like he's about to question her request, but once he sees the way she's standing next to me with her hand resting lightly on my shoulder, he understands that she wants to talk to me alone, and nods his head in acknowledgment. "Absolutely. I'll be right back."

Once he's gone, Oma turns to me and starts to tell me that my mother is in her own bedroom and that I should go see her. She sits on the edge of the bed, smoothing her dress and patting the spot next to her for me to join her.

"Your mother is having a hard time, my dear. You and I both know that she did the right thing for all you children by coming here, but I believe she's having some trouble seeing it that way." She sighs, patting my knee. "That Sebastian has been a piece of work since day one, but Julia loves him, so we have to make do. For today, though, she could use some moral support before the welcoming reception starts."

I fight the urge to pick at the hem of my skirt, folding my hands in my lap instead. "Do you think there's still a chance that Dad might come around?"

"I can't say, Elise. That will be between Sebastian, Julia, and Andries. All you can do right now is let your mother know that she's not alone. Why don't you go and see her?"

"I will," I promise. "I'll head to her room as soon as Dan gets back."

"Good. Thank you." She leans over and gives me another quick hug and peck on the cheek before standing. "I will see you outside, alright? Don't get too distracted with your date," she teases.

"Yes, Oma." I laugh, watching her walk out of the room. It's so nice to be here, and I just hope that I can make sure my mom feels the same way.

* * *

About thirty minutes later, I find myself outside of my mother's room, knocking on the frame of the closed door, announcing myself through the barrier so she knows it's just me.

"Come in," she calls from within, and I turn the knob on the unlocked door and enter.

I find my mother sitting on the edge of her bed, the fluffy duvet and pillows a mess, as if she had just been laying down even though she's dressed for the party. My mother is looking tenser than I've seen her in a while, even more so than when Johan and I confronted her about talking to the prosecutor, and it worries me. Logically I know that walking away from Dad must be traumatizing for her, but seeing the weight of it on my mother's shoulders is much different from imagining it.

I can immediately tell that something is wrong. My mother, who is normally so poised and put together, is looking a little disheveled and her eyes are red and puffy like she has been crying. I sit down next to her on the bed, heart hurting for this woman that I love so much. She's been so brave, going against Dad like this, and all she's gotten in return thus far is hurt.

I reach over and hug her tightly, feeling her body relax just a little bit in my arms. "How are you holding up, Mom?" I ask her, hoping to ease her nerves.

"I'm fine," she says, but I can tell she's not telling me the whole truth. "It's just a bit overwhelming, with so many people staying here at your Oma's estate."

I frown, knowing that the amount of guests probably has very little to do with her downtrodden mood. "Is that really all, Mom?"

She lets out a heavy sigh, standing and running her hands over her powder blue silk dress as she paces. "You know it isn't, Elise, but what else is there to say? Your father is determined to ruin everything, and there is little that I can do about it at this point."

"Are you sure that he won't just forgive and forget once the wedding is over?" I ask hopefully, but she shuts me down almost immediately.

"I don't think so, my love. He's bound and determined to side with Karl for the sake of his company and tear down everything he and I have ever built together, so I'm not feeling very hopeful that there will be anything left of our marriage to come back to after all of this." She discreetly taps the tears from the corners of her eyes with a tissue before crumpling it in her hand. "I... I'm considering a divorce, Elise."

Shock ripples through me. "W-what? Really?"

Mom swallows hard. "Yes, unfortunately. I'm not going to take second place behind his company or have to fight for his loyalty. His own dad once chose his company over his family and now Sebastian is repeating his mistakes." She gives a sad shake of her head. "I can't keep living like this. He doesn't understand how much he's hurting us all... or he does, and he doesn't care."

"I..." I inhale slowly, trying to slow my pounding pulse. "I don't know what to say, Mom, but just know I'm on your side, okay?"

"Thank you, dear," she says, leaning into me. "It means so much to have you here for me."

We sit in silence for a few minutes, both lost in our own thoughts, before she finally stands up, straightens her dress, and turns to me with a small smile. "Enough with the sad things. How are you and Dan? I saw you two arrive together outside the window. In the same car, too, I noticed."

I blush, but realize there is no reason to lie to my mother at this point. She knows we are together after all. "Yes... Dad and I got into a huge fight at work, so I've been staying with Dan for the last few days. It's just been easier since we've both been helping so much with the wedding preparation."

"I hate knowing that your father's foolishness extends to you, too, but I'm glad Dan gave you a sanctuary when you needed it." Mom sighs, but this time it sounds wistful. Almost happy. "I must confess, I wasn't sure about the two of you at first, but now I'm over the moon about it. Dan is such a breath of fresh air compared to all these stuffy, prideful old money men. Plus he seems totally smitten with you. Someone like Dan is exactly who you need in your life."

I offer her a small smile. "I think so, too. He's amazing, Mom, seriously. I can't believe it's taken me this long to get myself together and realize that all on my own."

"Speaking of getting things together... I guess it's time for me to make my appearance, hm? Let's go enjoy the party, shall we?" she says, trying to put on a brave face. Despite her ring-rimmed eyes, she looks beautiful and regal in her mauve dress with her hair loose. My dad is such an idiot if he lets Mom walk away from him after all they've been through!

"I'll meet you out there, Mom," I tell her, kissing her on the cheek quickly. "I need to make a phone call beforehand. Will you be okay on your own?"

She waves her hands dismissively, even though I know she isn't as strong as she usually is. "Yes, of course. I'm a grown woman, El, I'll be just fine."

I nod, but once I'm out of the room, I grab one of the passing staff members and tell them to send Oma to Mom's room to escort her down since I won't be able to. I just know that she will be more comfortable with someone by her side, and who better to offer comfort than her own mother?

The problem Mom is running into is that everyone here was also at the engagement party and therefore noticed her absence. I hope everyone will have enough tact not to mention it, and just be happy that she changed her mind and went against her husband to be here for her son, but there are always vipers dressed like humans at social events like this. I'll try my best to make sure Mom makes it out unscathed since she did us all an enormous favor talking to the prosecutor, not to mention her attending the party tonight.

As I make my way back to Dan and I's bedroom, I pull my phone out of my clutch so I can make the call I mentioned to Mom. I'm not sure how well it will work, considering the fact that Hannah and I are sort of at odds right now, but I dial my sister's number anyway and leave a voicemail. "Hannah, Dad won't talk to me. Please, try to convince him to put aside his pride and join us tomorrow. The wedding starts at 2 pm. Please make it happen. Mom is seriously considering a divorce." I pause, collecting my thoughts. "I know that you're annoyed with me or whatever, but this is beyond important. Since Dad basically hates me you're my best shot at shaking him out of this horrible mindset he's forced himself into. Good luck."

I hang up the phone and take a deep breath, feeling a sense of foreboding. I know that the road ahead won't be easy, but I'm determined to do whatever it takes to heal our family and help them find their way back to each other.

Once I'm back in the bedroom, I sit at the vanity to touch up my makeup before we head down to the party that I can already hear outside. Dan enters the room shortly after I do, leaning down to kiss the top of my head, but when he catches a look at my reflection in the mirror, he pauses. I can immediately see the concern etched on his face, as if he can sense that something is up.

"What's wrong?"

I take a deep breath, gathering the courage to share my fears. It's one thing to be strong and try to fix my family's issues, but another thing altogether to be vulnerable and speak my fears out loud. "It's Mom," I blurt out, my voice quivering. "She's considering getting a divorce. I never thought this would happen. They've been married for so long and have six children together, for God's sake! I always thought they were the epitome of true love or something cliché like that. I can't even imagine one without the other."

Dan pulls me to my feet and into his warm embrace, holding me close as I struggle with my emotions. I can feel his muscular arms wrapped around me, providing the support I so desperately need. I lean back, looking into his eyes, and I can see the love and compassion shining through. He tucks a strand of hair behind my ear, his gaze always fixed on me. "I'm sorry. El, I'll never be like your dad. I'll always choose you over and over again. I'll always put you first."

I look up at him, feeling so much of the anxiety building inside me melting away. Dan just makes me believe that I'm safe above all else, and that's something I cherish. "Thank you for being my best friend and my boyfriend all at once." I wrap my arms around his neck, my eyes locked on his. "I love you, Dan."

"I love you too, El," Dan says, kissing me gently on the forehead, humming in pleasure. "Fuck, I will never get tired of hearing you say that. Can I hear it one more time?"

I giggle. "Fine. I love you, Dan."

He gives me a quick peck on my mouth, nipping at my bottom lip playfully. "Perfect. Now, let's go to the dinner party. Your family is waiting for us."

DAN.

* * *

We walk out of the room and into the beautiful garden where the dining party is being held, arm in arm. As soon as we're entrenched in the event itself, it's almost impossible to still feel so downtrodden. It's absolutely exquisite out here, but I shouldn't be surprised—Oma Margaret has impeccable taste, and there was never any doubt that she would pull out all the stops for her first grandchild's wedding. Family members are gathered around, chatting and laughing, and I can feel the love and joy in the air. My worries are falling away with each step we take. Dan takes his arm from mine and instead laces our fingers together as we stroll, taking in the sights and sounds of the celebration.

The party is held in the lush gardens of Oma's grand mansion, causing the air to be filled with the sweet fragrance of flowers and the sounds of live music from the saxophonist in the band. String lights are strung through the trees, along with torches around the perimeter.

The atmosphere is lively and festive, with guests mingling as they enjoy the delicious food and drinks. Everything edible has a distinct Eastern flair to honor Roxanne's heritage, just another marker of how much Andries adores his bride.

Finally, I see the small cluster of family members, but my mother is suspiciously missing. "I guess it's time to go and make appearances," I tell Dan, who squeezes my hand in response.

"I don't think you have much to worry about tonight. No one is going to ruin the mood by asking about Sebastian."

I squeeze Dan's hand back, taking a deep breath and putting on a happy face as we join my family where they are gathered under one of the fruit trees.

As Dan and I arrive, we are greeted by everyone all at once. Oma steps aside to let us into the gathering circle, and it becomes readily apparent that Dan is the most interesting person that they've encountered all night. It hits me that almost no one knows he and I are a couple, and while most of them have met Dan at family events, since he and Andries were basically inseparable as we were growing up, seeing him as my partner must be quite the shock.

"I'm sure you all know our darling Elise's boyfriend, but if not, this is Dan O'Brian," my grandmother says smoothly, gesturing towards Dan, who separates from me to shake everyone's hands. I take the opportunity to look over the faces in front of me, wondering who I will be spending most of my time with over the next two days. Seeing Yara, my favorite aunt and famous equestrian, I exhale a relieved breath. Once Dan takes off to be with Andries, she's who I'm going to gravitate towards.

Before I can go speak to Yara personally, though, my Uncle Alex's wife, Petra, approaches me first, giving me hesitant air cheek kisses in greeting. I always seem to forget that she's American, and how young she is. Young and stunning, I think, as the naturally beautiful woman steps back and smiles at me cautiously. She doesn't have the best history with everyone in the family, but there is nothing negative between the two of us, for which I'm thankful. I don't think I can deal with a single ounce more drama.

"You look lovely, Elise," Petra compliments with a bright, white smile. "Are you excited about your brother's wedding?"

"Excited and relieved," I admit, letting out a sigh. "How are the twins?"

I see Yara scowl at Petra out of the corner of my eye, but Dan and Uncle Alex are engaged in conversation now, so I keep his wife occupied nonetheless, asking to see pictures of her adorable children and talking about their trip over from New York. I know when my Aunt Yara has had enough and is ready to talk to me herself because I see a flash of anxiety on Petra's face right before Yara appears beside me and takes my arm in hers to lead me away—but not before she flashes a predatory smile towards Petra.

"I still don't really know why you hate her," I comment as Yara and I walk along the perimeter of the garden, away from everyone else.

"She's a little brat, and that annoys me," Yara says offhandedly, and I roll my eyes, laughing.

"If you say so. So what did you need me for?"

"I see you're dating your brother's best friend. I'm assuming your parents approve of that match?" she asks, raising her eyebrows.

"Everyone loves Dan," I assure her. "But I'm also my own person, so I'm not looking for a parental approved love match, or whatever they want to call arranged marriages these days. It just so happens that my parents adore Dan too, so it's a win-win."

"Hmm," she hums, her dark brown eyes scanning my face attentively. "Love, huh? You're so young, El. Just don't shackle yourself down until you're sure."

"I know that. Don't worry." I brush her arm affectionately, knowing that she means well.

The conversation migrates to horses and the tournaments Yara has been in recently, and once we've completed our circuit of the party to talk privately, we're back with the rest of the family. I speak briefly with my Aunt Maud before finding Dan once more, and we excuse ourselves to talk to Roxanne's family next.

Further into the gardens, we come across Yao, Lili, and Robin. Dan and Robin greet each other with a lively embrace, patting each other on the back while Lili and I laugh at their antics.

"You'd think they hadn't seen each other in years," Lili comments. "As if we weren't together for over a week just a little bit ago."

"I think Dan is just desperate for male companionship," I tell her with a chuckle, plucking two glasses of champagne from the tray of a passing server and handing one to Lili. "I haven't seen Roxie or Andries yet, have you?"

She shakes her head. "From what I understand Roxie is taking some time to collect herself. Everything is happening so fast, with the charges being pressed and then just as quickly dropped, and now the wedding... her head is spinning, I think."

I wince in sympathy. For as difficult as everything is for me right now, Roxanne has it ten times worst. "Poor thing. I hope she knows that everyone here accepts her openly. We have plenty of drama in the family organically, so there is zero judgment from this group."

Lili blows out a breath before taking a sip of her champagne. "I don't know how all of you do it. I'd be a nervous wreck all the time."

"We are nervous wrecks," I admit, amused. "We're just really, really good at hiding it."

Next to Robin, I see Dan still, looking to the left of us with a hardened expression. I follow his gaze and feel like sinking into the ground when I see that it's Johan who has caught Dan's eye. He's heading in our direction with a determined look in his eye, and I can feel Dan tense up beside me as he gets closer.

"Of course, this fucking guy had to show up," Dan mutters, but when Johan reaches us, he pastes on a stiff, fake smile and shakes his hand nonetheless.

"Well, if it isn't my favorite sailing student," Johan tries to joke, but Dan isn't having it, and Johan's face falls before he turns to me instead. "Elise, is Hannah going to be at the wedding tomorrow?"

I take a deep breath and try to keep my cool. Talking about Hannah means talking about Dad, and I've managed to avoid that subject thus far, but I guess I have to answer him honestly. Maybe Johan can be convinced to help me with my family one more time.

"I don't know," I say, shrugging my shoulders. "As of right now, she's with Dad, who is still being an asshole and refusing to show up. Maybe you should call Hannah and try to persuade her to come to the wedding. You and I both know she'll listen to you before she will listen to me."

Dan looks at the other man strangely but doesn't say anything. Manipulating Hannah by using her crush on Johan might not be the most responsible course of action, but time is swiftly running out, and I need to use whatever advantages I have.

Johan, to his credit, also looks a bit uncomfortable. "I, ah, I guess I could—"

"Cut it out, Johan, I'm sure you have her number. I don't care about all of that, just please try to get her to come. It would be great to have the whole family together for my brother's special day."

"Okay, yeah. I can do that." Johan looks between Dan and me, his shoulders falling in defeat. "I guess I'll go and make that call, then."

I can see the tension between Dan and Johan as they exchange a look before Johan turns on his foot and leaves. There's a palpable animosity between them, and I can't help but feel a little nervous about what might happen. But I try to keep a smile on my face and hope for the best, at least until my ex is out of sight.

As soon as he's gone, I turn to Dan and ask him to behave. "Ignore Johan, okay?" I say, trying to keep my voice steady. "You two are acting like two angry dogs. Knock it off."

Dan smirks. "Oh, don't worry. I already made sure that jerk knows you're my girlfriend."

I feel a knot form in my stomach. "Seriously, Dan… what did you do to Johan?" I ask, my voice filled with concern. Surely he hasn't already started trouble while I was off talking to Yara..?

Dan just grins in return. "Nothing, I swear. I just told him the truth. I made sure to send him a quick message before we all arrived so there wouldn't be any misunderstanding when we all saw each other in person."

I don't know what that means, but I can sense that there's more to the story. "You have to know I don't totally believe you."

Dan, to my annoyance, just laughs. I trust him and know that he has my best interests at heart, but I can't help but feel a little uneasy about the situation. I just hope that everything will go smoothly tomorrow at the wedding and that our family can come together and put aside any tensions or conflicts for one day to celebrate the happy couple. Using Johan to get Hannah firmly on our side is a good idea, and I don't want Dan to ruin that for me.

Before I can question him further, I feel a sense of excitement wash over everyone. I turn to look at what everyone else is seeing, and a smile blooms on my face when I see that it's Roxanne and Andries, finally descending the terrace stairs to join everyone in the garden. After months of planning, drama, heartbreak, and anticipation, my brother Andries and his bride-to-be Roxanne are finally here for their celebration dinner, and then tomorrow is the wedding itself.

I can see Andries holding Roxie's hand as Oma rushes over to their sides, but my brother looks past our grandmother to another female figure standing off to the side. It's my mother, a hesitant, sweet smile on her face as she watches her oldest son, and if I'm not mistaken, her eyes are misty, too.

The couple is dressed semi-formally but still make for a stunning duo. Andries wears a pale gray suit with no tie, while Roxanne looks as if she's been poured into a gorgeous gold silk dress that shimmers in the soft glow of the torches that illuminate the garden.

As they make their way towards the party, I watch as they are greeted by friends and family, each person exclaiming how beautiful they both look. It's clear that everyone is elated to see the happy couple arrive, and knowing that Roxie has gotten over her worries reassures me that everything is going to go smoothly from here on out. Hopefully.

My heart swells with pride as I watch my brother and his soon-to-be wife move through the crowd, their love for each other radiating in every step they take. I feel a little choked up, thinking back to how I almost ruined my chances of sharing this special moment with them and everyone else. I was such a fool to want to split them up. Their devotion to one another is just so clear.

Dan and I move to intercept them, and Dan shakes the hand of his best friend before pulling him into a tight hug, while I embrace Roxie softly, emotion welling in me. "You look so beautiful."

"So do you," she tells me, her voice slightly shaking. "Thank you for coming, El. And for… well, everything you've done. Knowing that Julia is here has made Andries so happy. I just… thank you."

Then I'm hugging my brother, just like when we were kids, and the laugh I let out as he pretends to muss my hair is shivery with tears. "I can't believe it's almost time!"

"*You* can't believe it?" Andries barks a laugh. "Imagine how I feel."

I open my mouth to answer but then hear someone delicately clearing their throat behind us. I turn, seeing my mother looking up at her son with a mix of pride and love in her eyes, and quickly step aside, taking Dan with me so they can have their moment together.

Mom approaches Andries, and I can feel the energy shift around us. Andries's face lights up as our mother kisses him, and the two embrace tightly. I can see tears welling up in both of their eyes as they hold each other, their love for one another still as strong as ever, despite the separation that they have experienced.

I watch as they talk quietly, Mom holding Andries's hands in her own. I strain to listen, but I can't hear what they're saying. Whatever it is, it must be important, as they both look so emotional.

Next, she turns her attention to Roxanne, and my heart skips a beat. I know that they've had their differences in the past, and I'm hoping that they've managed to put them aside for this special day. Roxanne looks stiff, but not upset, which is a good sign.

To my surprise, Mom leans forward and kisses Roxanne as well, before she hugs her. Whatever issues they may have had are now gone and off to the wayside, and it's almost like the entire crowd here releases a sigh of relief. The tension that was once between them seems to have dissipated totally, and they both look genuinely happy to be in each other's company. They must have had a heart-to-heart before I arrived.

Watching this emotional moment unfold, I feel a sense of catharsis. It's heartwarming to see two women come together and reconcile their differences in the name of love.

After a few more minutes, we are all invited to take our assigned seats at the table. Once we are all seated and Oma has circled the table to make sure everyone is content and has everything they need, Mom stands up and clears her throat to make a toast before the meal even arrives, as if she's so excited that she can't wait a moment longer.

She raises her glass and begins. "To the happy couple, my handsome son Andries and his beautiful bride, Roxanne. May your love continue to grow and flourish for many years to come." Her eyes are filled with love as she turns in my direction, "I also want to thank my daughter, Elise, for everything she has done for us. She always stood by her loved ones and without her, I never would have been brave enough to be here at the side of two of my beloved children—my real family." She looks at me with a proud smile and then looking at Oma, she adds, "And a special thank you to my wonderful mother, Margaret, for hosting this beautiful evening and bringing us all together."

The table cheers while Dan gives me a small squeeze and a kiss on the head. I sniffle and blink away tears, my cheeks flushing red. I did not expect Mom's toast to include me at all. I can see the real connections everyone around us share as we raise our glasses and toast to the newlyweds, united.

Everyone is having the time of their life, laughing, eating, and drinking, but there's a noticeable absence. Even after everything, I miss my father, and I think Andries must feel the same way. If only he could be here to celebrate with us, to put aside his differences, and enjoy this special night. But even in his absence, I'm grateful Mom chose to show up. With any luck, Johan will tempt Hannah into arriving tomorrow, too.

As the evening progresses and the meal finishes, we all reconnect with one another under the stars, eager for the marriage of Andries and Roxanne that we all have to look forward to tomorrow.

CHAPTER 39

Sebastian

I pace back and forth in my home office, staring at my phone with frustration. It's been three days since I last saw my wife or even heard her voice, and every time I call her, she doesn't pick up. I can't help but feel the hot rush of anger as I'm forced to leave yet another voicemail for her.

Of course, the call doesn't even ring. Instead, it goes straight to her inbox, and I curse under my breath.

"Julia," I start once the tone alerts me to start speaking. "You haven't been home for the past three days. This is beyond ridiculous. Just because of what? A fucking wedding?" I pause, trying to calm myself down. "Please, pick up your goddamn phone so we can talk."

I hang up and let out a sigh. Julia has been living at her mother's place since we had the blow up argument once I discovered she manipulated the prosecutor—her old friend from college—into dropping all the charges against our son's whore of a fiancée, Roxanne. I also uncovered the information that it was Elise, my own daughter for fuck's sake, and that idiot Johan who convinced her to do so. My entire family is turning against me one by one, but Julia... I can't believe she would side with them against me and the rest of our children.

I thought she was on my side no matter what. Oh, how very wrong I was, because even now, I have a glimmer of hope that she will still come back to me and drop all this nonsense.

Choosing to stick with Elise and Andries means my wife has left not only myself, but Hannah, Joris, Aleida, and little Arthur at the Van den Bosch estate without her. As mad as I am right now, I still miss her every minute that she's absent. It's as if my world is turned upside down, and I don't know how to fix it. All I know is that I need to talk to Julia and try to find a way to make things right between us. But first, I need her to pick up the phone and talk to me.

I'm interrupted from my thoughts by a single knock on the door before Hannah lets herself in.

"Dad..." she starts as she walks slowly in my direction. "Are we not going to the wedding? I thought you'd have come around by now."

Despite her soft tone, the simple thought of that wedding makes me frown and I wave my hand dismissively. "If you want to go, by all means, it's tomorrow at 2 pm and I can arrange a way for you to get there. The entire stupid affair is at your grandmother Margaret's estate."

"I didn't say 'me', I said 'we'. What about you?" she presses, now standing tall in front of me, her arms crossed over her chest.

"I'm staying here," I answer firmly, leaning back in my chair. "I thought you knew."

My daughter is clearly upset, throwing her hands in the air and groaning. "Dad, come on, this is ridiculous," she tells me, her voice rising.

"What is ridiculous is what your mom has been doing to us. She left out of the blue. And for what? To watch your brother screw up his life?" I retort, bitterness in my voice.

Hannah isn't done, though, and putting her hands on her hips she glares at me, before saying, "Wasn't Oma Margaret the one who thought Mom was also screwing her life by marrying you?" she reminds me just as fast. "Doesn't that make you a hypocrite if you protest what Andries is doing?"

Now I sit up straight, shocked. "How do you even know that?"

"I've got my ways." Hannah raises her eyebrows, challenging me to refute her statement, but what's the point? What she's saying is the truth. Margaret has never been a fan of me, and after this debacle, it's doubtful she ever will be.

Instead I tell her, "It's very different, Hannah. Your grandmother was just worried because your mom was fairly young and I was much older."

"Doesn't seem much different to me," she says, shrugging. "Dad, if you still love Mom, please, put your pride aside and let's go to the wedding tomorrow."

"I refuse to go to that sham of a wedding. Your mom must understand where I'm coming from. She'll forgive me once it's all said and done."

Hannah huffs, and before I can ask her to leave, my daughter drops a bombshell on me. "According to what Elise told me, Mom's considering a divorce."

"A divorce?" I repeat, incredulous. "What the hell do you mean a divorce?"

"If you don't know what it means, look it up," she snaps before disappearing out the door in a cloud of long hair and attitude.

I'm left alone in my study, reeling from this new information, feeling like my stomach has dropped out of me.

A divorce? After more than twenty years of marriage? The thought of losing Julia fills me with dread. She's been my rock... my everything. And now she's considering leaving me.

I pour myself a drink, trying to make sense of it all. How did we get here? It feels like just yesterday that we were madly in love, building a life and a family together. And now, here we are, on the brink of losing it all.

I can't go to that wedding, though, that's non-negotiable.

I take a sip of my whiskey and try to calm myself. I need to think rationally and figure out what my next move should be. How do I save my marriage and keep my pride and company intact, all at the same time?

I'm overcome by a sense of emptiness. I know I need to make a choice, but I'm not sure I'm ready for the consequences of whichever path I choose. All I know is that I need to talk to Julia, to try and understand what's going on with her and if there's anything I can do to fix this without going against everything I believe in.

Knowing I really need to consider every variable, I settle into my deep red leather armchair, nursing my whiskey, my beautiful, frustrating wife on my mind.

Ah, Julia, sweet Julia... She came into my life and turned it upside down. I have never been the type to be pushed around. On the contrary, I'm known for sticking to my word, to my gut feeling, until the very end.

I know that going to that wedding tomorrow will be the ultimate humiliation. I can't bear the thought of facing everyone, especially Margaret, and having them see me as a defeated man. They will all know I stood my ground for so long, risked so much, and still folded in the end. At the same time, I can't bear the thought of losing Julia.

I take a sip of my whiskey and let out a deep sigh. This is going to be a long night.

THE STORY CONTINUES IN JULIA.

Don't have the next bundle yet?

Get the next bundle of the series at 10% off